RIP VAN WINKLE

AND

THE LEGEND
OF SLEEPY HOLLOW

WASHINGTON IRVING

RIP VAN WINKLE

AND

THE LEGEND
OF SLEEPY HOLLOW

penguin books

PENGUIN BOOKS

Published by the Penguin Group

Penguin Books USA Inc., 375 Hudson Street,
New York, New York 10014, U.S.A.
Penguin Books Ltd, 27 Wrights Lane,
London W8 5TZ, England
Penguin Books Australia Ltd, Ringwood,
Victoria, Australia
Penguin Books Canada Ltd, 10 Alcorn Avenue,
Toronto, Ontario, Canada M4V 3B2
Penguin Books (N.Z.) Ltd, 182–190 Wairau Road,
Auckland 10, New Zealand

Penguin Books Ltd, Registered Offices:
Harmondsworth, Middlesex, England

Published in Penguin Books 1995

ISBN 0 14 60.0071 4

Printed in the United States of America

CONTENTS

Preface

[The following Tale was found among the papers of the late Diedrich Knickerbocker, an old gentleman of New-York, who was very curious in the Dutch history of the province, and the manners of the descendants from its primitive settlers. His historical researches, however, did not lie so much among books, as among men; for the former are lamentably scanty on his favourite topics; whereas he found the old burghers, and still more, their wives, rich in that legendary lore, so invaluable to true history. Whenever, therefore, he happened upon a genuine Dutch family, snugly shut up in its low-roofed farm house, under a spreading sycamore, he looked upon it as a little clasped volume of black-letter, and studied it with the zeal of a book-worm.

The result of all these researches was a history of the province, during the reign of the Dutch governors, which he published some years since. There have been various opinions as to the literary character of his work, and, to tell the truth, it is not a whit better than it should be. Its chief merit is its scrupulous accuracy, which, indeed, was a little questioned, on its first appearance, but has since been completely established; and it is now admitted into all historical collections, as a book of unquestionable authority.

The old gentleman died shortly after the publication of his work, and now, that he is dead and gone, it cannot do much harm to his memory, to say, that his time might have been much better employed in weightier labours. He, however, was apt to ride his hobby his own way; and though it did now and then kick up the dust a little in the eyes of his neighbours, and grieve the spirit of some friends, for whom he felt the truest deference and affection; yet his errors and follies are remembered "more in sorrow than in anger," and it begins to be suspected, that he never intended to injure or offend. But however his memory may be appreciated by critics, it is still held dear among many folk, whose good opinion is well worth having; particularly certain biscuit bakers, who have gone so far as to imprint his likeness on their new year cakes, and have thus given him a chance for immortality, almost equal to being stamped on a Waterloo medal, or a Queen Anne's farthing.]

Rip Van Winkle

A POSTHUMOUS WRITING
OF DIEDRICH KNICKERBOCKER

By Woden, God of Saxons,
From whence comes Wensday, that is Wodensday,
Truth is a thing that ever I will keep
Unto thylke day in which I creep into
My sepulchre—

CARTWRIGHT

Whoever has made a voyage up the Hudson, must remember the Kaatskill mountains They are a dismembered branch of the great Appalachian family, and are seen away to the west of the river, swelling up to a noble height, and lording it over the surrounding country. Every change of season, every change of weather, indeed, every hour of the day, produces some change in the magical hues and shapes of these mountains, and they are regarded by all the good wives, far and near, as perfect barometers. When the weather is fair and settled, they are clothed in blue and purple, and print their bold outlines on the clear evening sky; but some times, when the rest of the landscape is cloudless, they will gather a hood of gray vapours about their summits, which, in the last rays of the setting sun, will glow and light up like a crown of glory.

At the foot of these fairy mountains, the voyager may have descried the light smoke curling up from a village, whose shingle roofs gleam among the trees, just where the blue tints of the upland melt away into the fresh green of the nearer landscape. It is a little village of great antiquity, having been founded by some of the Dutch colonists, in the early times of the province, just about the beginning of the government of the good Peter Stuyvesant, (may he rest in peace!) and there were some of the houses of the original settlers standing within a few years, with lattice windows, gable fronts surmounted with weathercocks, and built of small yellow bricks brought from Holland.

In that same village, and in one of these very houses, (which, to tell the precise truth, was sadly time worn and weather beaten,) there lived many years since, while the country was yet a province of Great Britain, a simple good natured fellow, of the name of Rip Van Winkle. He was a descendant of the Van Winkles who figured so gallantly in the chivalrous days of Peter Stuyvesant, and accompanied him to the siege of Fort Christina. He inherited, however, but little of the martial character of his ancestors. I have observed that he was a simple good natured man; he was moreover a kind neighbour, and an obedient, henpecked husband. Indeed, to the latter circumstance might be owing that meekness of spirit which gained him such universal popularity; for those men are most apt to be obsequious and conciliating abroad, who are under the discipline of shrews at home. Their tempers, doubtless, are rendered pliant and malleable in the fiery furnace of domestic tribulation, and a curtain lecture is worth all the sermons in the world for teaching the virtues of patience and long suffering. A termagant wife may, therefore, in some respects, be considered a tolerable blessing; and if so, Rip Van Winkle was thrice blessed.

Certain it is, that he was a great favourite among all the good wives of the village, who, as usual with the amiable sex, took his part in all family squabbles, and never failed, whenever they talked those matters over in their evening gossippings, to lay all the blame on Dame Van Winkle. The children of the village, too, would shout with joy whenever he approached. He assisted at their sports, made their playthings, taught them to fly kites and shoot marbles, and told them long stories of ghosts, witches, and Indians. Whenever he went dodging about the village, he was surrounded by a troop of them, hanging on his skirts, clambering on his back, and playing a thousand tricks on him with impunity; and not a dog would bark at him throughout the neighbourhood.

The great error in Rip's composition was an insuperable aversion to all kinds of profitable labour. It could not be for the want of assiduity or perseverance; for he would sit on a wet rock, with a rod as long and heavy as a Tartar's lance, and fish all day without a murmur, even though he should not be encouraged by a single nibble. He would carry a fowling piece on his shoulder, for hours together, trudging through woods and swamps, and up hill and down dale, to shoot a few squirrels or wild pigeons. He would never even refuse to assist a neighbour in the roughest toil, and was a foremost man at all country frolicks for husking Indian corn, or building stone fences. The women of the village, too, used to employ him to run their errands, and to do such little odd jobs as their less obliging husbands would not do for them;—in a word, Rip was ready to attend to any body's business but his own; but as to doing family duty, and keeping his farm in order, it was impossible.

In fact, he declared it was no use to work on his farm; it was the most pestilent little piece of ground in the whole country; every thing about it went wrong, and would go wrong, in spite of him. His fences were continually falling to pieces; his cow would either go astray, or get among the cabbages; weeds were sure to grow quicker in his fields than any where else; the rain always made a point of setting in just as he had some out-door work to do; so that though his patrimonial estate had dwindled away under his management, acre by acre, until there was little more left than a mere patch of Indian corn and potatoes, yet it was the worst conditioned farm in the neighbourhood.

His children, too, were as ragged and wild as if they belonged to nobody. His son Rip, an urchin begotten in his own likeness, promised to inherit the habits, with the old clothes of his father. He was generally seen trooping like a colt at his mother's heels, equipped in a pair of his father's cast-off galligaskins, which he had much ado to hold up with one hand, as a fine lady does her train in bad weather.

Rip Van Winkle, however, was one of those happy mortals, of foolish, well-oiled dispositions, who take the world easy, eat white bread or brown, whichever can be got with least thought or trouble, and would rather starve on a penny than work for a pound. If left to himself, he would have whistled life away, in perfect contentment; but his wife kept continually dinning in his ears about his idleness, his carelessness, and the ruin he was bringing on his family. Morning, noon, and night, her tongue was inces-

7

santly going, and every thing he said or did was sure to produce a torrent of household eloquence. Rip had but one way of replying to all lectures of the kind, and that, by frequent use, had grown into a habit. He shrugged his shoulders, shook his head, cast up his eyes, but said nothing. This, however, always provoked a fresh volley from his wife, so that he was fain to draw off his forces, and take to the outside of the house—the only side which, in truth, belongs to a henpecked husband.

Rip's sole domestic adherent was his dog Wolf, who was as much henpecked as his master; for Dame Van Winkle regarded them as companions in idleness, and even looked upon Wolf with an evil eye, as the cause of his master's so often going astray. True it is, in all points of spirit befitting an honourable dog, he was as courageous an animal as ever scoured the woods—but what courage can withstand the ever-during and all-besetting terrors of a woman's tongue? The moment Wolf entered the house, his crest fell, his tail drooped to the ground, or curled between his legs, he sneaked about with a gallows air, casting many a sidelong glance at Dame Van Winkle, and at the least flourish of a broomstick or ladle, would fly to the door with yelping precipitation.

Times grew worse and worse with Rip Van Winkle as years of matrimony rolled on; a tart temper never mellows with age, and a sharp tongue is the only edge tool that grows keener by constant use. For a long while he used to console himself, when driven from home, by frequenting a kind of perpetual club of the sages, philosophers, and other idle personages of the village, which held its sessions on a bench before a small inn, designated by a rubicund portrait of his majesty George the Third. Here they used to sit in the shade, of a long lazy summer's day, talk listlessly over village gossip, or tell endless sleepy stories about nothing. But it would have been worth any statesman's money to have heard the profound discussions that sometimes took place, when by chance an old newspaper fell into their hands, from some passing traveller. How solemnly they would listen to the contents, as drawled out by Derrick Van Bummel, the schoolmaster, a dapper learned little man, who was not to be daunted by the most gigantic word in the dictionary; and how sagely they would deliberate upon public events some months after they had taken place.

The opinions of this junto were completely controlled by Nicholas Vedder, a patriarch of the village, and landlord of the inn, at the door of which he took his seat from morning till night, just moving sufficiently to avoid the sun, and keep in the shade of a large tree; so that the neighbours could tell the hour by his movements as accurately as by a sun dial. It is true, he was rarely heard to speak, but smoked his pipe incessantly. His adherents, however, (for every great man has his adherents,) perfectly understood him, and knew how to gather his opinions. When any thing that was read or related displeased him, he was observed to smoke his pipe vehemently, and send forth short, frequent, and angry puffs; but when pleased, he would inhale the smoke slowly and tranquilly, and emit it in light and placid clouds, and sometimes taking the pipe from his mouth, and letting the fragrant vapour curl about his nose, would gravely nod his head in token of perfect approbation.

From even this strong hold the unlucky Rip was at length routed by his termagant wife, who would suddenly break in upon the tranquility of the assemblage, call the members all to nought; nor was that august personage, Nicholas Vedder himself, sacred from the daring tongue of this terrible virago, who charged him outright with encouraging her husband in habits of idleness.

Poor Rip was at last reduced almost to despair; and his only alternative to escape from the labour of the farm and the clamour of his wife, was to take gun in hand, and stroll away into the woods. Here he would sometimes seat himself at the foot of a tree, and share the contents of his wallet with Wolf, with whom he sympathised as a fellow sufferer in persecution. "Poor Wolf," he would say, "thy mistress leads thee a dog's life of it; but never mind, my lad, while I live thou shalt never want a friend to stand by thee!" Wolf would wag his tail, look wistfully in his master's face, and if dogs can feel pity, I verily believe he reciprocated the sentiment with all his heart.

In a long ramble of the kind on a fine autumnal day, Rip had unconsciously scrambled to one of the highest parts of the Kaatskill mountains. He was after his favourite sport of squirrel shooting, and the still solitudes had echoed and re-echoed with the reports of his gun. Panting and fatigued, he threw himself, late in the afternoon, on a green knoll, covered with mountain herbage, that crowned the brow of a precipice. From an opening between the trees, he could overlook all the lower country for many a mile of rich woodland. He saw at a distance the lordly Hudson, far, far below him, moving on its silent but majestic course, the reflection of a purple cloud, or the sail of a lagging bark, here and there sleeping on its glassy bosom, and at last losing itself in the blue highlands.

On the other side he looked down into a deep mountain glen, wild, lonely, and shagged, the bottom filled with fragments from the impending cliffs, and scarcely lighted by the reflected rays of the setting sun. For some time

Rip lay musing on this scene; evening was gradually advancing, the mountains began to throw their long blue shadows over the valleys, he saw that it would be dark long before he could reach the village, and he heaved a heavy sigh when he thought of encountering the terrors of Dame Van Winkle.

As he was about to descend, he heard a voice from a distance, hallooing, "Rip Van Winkle! Rip Van Winkle!" He looked around, but could see nothing but a crow winging its solitary flight across the mountain. He thought his fancy must have deceived him, and turned again to descend, when he heard the same cry ring through the still evening air; "Rip Van Winkle! Rip Van Winkle!"—at the same time Wolf bristled up his back, and giving a low growl, skulked to his master's side, looking fearfully down into the glen. Rip now felt a vague apprehension stealing over him; he looked anxiously in the same direction, and perceived a strange figure slowly toiling up the rocks, and bending under the weight of something he carried on his back. He was surprised to see any human being in this lonely and unfrequented place, but supposing it to be some one of the neighbourhood in need of his assistance, he hastened down to yield it.

On nearer approach, he was still more surprised at the singularity of the stranger's appearance. He was a short square built old fellow, with thick bushy hair, and a grizzled beard. His dress was of the antique Dutch fashion—a cloth jerkin strapped round the waist—several pair of breeches, the outer one of ample volume, decorated with rows of buttons down the sides, and bunches at the knees. He bore on his shoulder a stout keg, that seemed full of liquor, and made signs for Rip to approach and assist him with the load. Though rather shy and distrustful of this new acquaintance, Rip complied with his usual alacrity, and mutually relieving each other, they clambered up a narrow gully, apparently the dry bed of a mountain torrent. As they ascended, Rip every now and then heard long rolling peals, like distant thunder, that seemed to issue out of a deep ravine, or rather cleft between lofty rocks, toward which their rugged path conducted. He paused for an instant, but supposing it to be the muttering of one of those transient thunder showers which often take place in mountain heights, he proceeded. Passing through the ravine, they came to a hollow, like a small amphitheatre, surrounded by perpendicular precipices, over the brinks of which impending trees shot their branches, so that you only caught glimpses of the azure sky, and the bright evening cloud. During the whole time, Rip and his companion had laboured on in silence; for though the former marvelled greatly what could be the

13

object of carrying a keg of liquor up this wild mountain, yet there was something strange and incomprehensible about the unknown, that inspired awe, and checked familiarity.

On entering the amphitheatre, new objects of wonder presented themselves. On a level spot in the centre was a company of odd-looking personages playing at nine-pins. They were dressed in a quaint, outlandish fashion: some wore short doublets, others jerkins, with long knives in their belts, and most had enormous breeches, of similar style with that of the guide's. Their visages, too, were peculiar: one had a large head, broad face, and small piggish eyes; the face of another seemed to consist entirely of nose, and was surmounted by a white sugar-loaf hat, set off with a little red cockstail. They all had beards, of various shapes and colours. There was one who seemed to be the commander. He was a stout old gentleman, with a weather-beaten countenance: he wore a laced doublet, broad belt and hanger, high crowned hat and feather, red stockings, and high heeled shoes, with roses in them. The whole group reminded Rip of the figures in an old Flemish painting, in the parlour of Dominie Van Schaick, the village parson, and which had been brought over from Holland at the time of the settlement.

What seemed particularly odd to Rip, was, that though

these folks were evidently amusing themselves, yet they maintained the gravest faces, the most mysterious silence, and were, withal, the most melancholy party of pleasure he had ever witnessed. Nothing interrupted the stillness of the scene, but the noise of the balls, which, whenever they were rolled, echoed along the mountains like rumbling peals of thunder.

As Rip and his companion approached them, they suddenly desisted from their play, and stared at him with such fixed statue-like gaze, and such strange, uncouth, lack lustre countenances, that his heart turned within him, and his knees smote together. His companion now emptied the contents of the keg into large flagons, and made signs to him to wait upon the company. He obeyed with fear and trembling; they quaffed the liquor in profound silence, and then returned to their game.

By degrees, Rip's awe and apprehension subsided. He even ventured, when no eye was fixed upon him, to taste the beverage, which he found had much of the flavour of excellent Hollands. He was naturally a thirsty soul, and was soon tempted to repeat the draught. One taste provoked another, and he reiterated his visits to the flagon so often, that at length his senses were overpowered, his eyes swam in his head, his head gradually declined, and he fell into a deep sleep.

On awaking, he found himself on the green knoll from whence he had first seen the old man of the glen. He rubbed his eyes—it was a bright sunny morning. The birds were hopping and twittering among the bushes, and the eagle was wheeling aloft, and breasting the pure mountain breeze. "Surely," thought Rip, "I have not slept here all night." He recalled the occurrences before he fell asleep. The strange man with the keg of liquor—the mountain ravine—the wild retreat among the rocks—the wo-begone party at nine-pins—the flagon—"Oh! that flagon! that wicked flagon!" thought Rip—"what excuse shall I make to Dame Van Winkle?"

He looked round for his gun, but in place of the clean well-oiled fowling-piece, he found an old firelock lying by him, the barrel encrusted with rust, the lock falling off, and the stock worm-eaten. He now suspected that the grave roysters of the mountain had put a trick upon him, and having dosed him with liquor, had robbed him of his gun. Wolf, too, had disappeared, but he might have strayed away after a squirrel or partridge. He whistled after him, shouted his name, but all in vain; the echoes repeated his whistle and shout, but no dog was to be seen.

He determined to revisit the scene of the last evening's gambol, and if he met with any of the party, to demand his dog and gun. As he arose to walk, he found himself stiff in the joints, and wanting in his usual activity. "These mountain beds do not agree with me," thought Rip, "and if this frolick should lay me up with a fit of the rheumatism, I shall have a blessed time with Dame Van Winkle." With some difficulty he got down into the glen; he found the gully up which he and his companion had ascended the preceding evening; but to his astonishment a mountain stream was now foaming down it, leaping from rock to rock, and filling the glen with babbling murmurs. He, however, made shift to scramble up its sides, working his toilsome way through thickets of birch, sassafras, and witch hazel, and sometimes tripped up or entangled by the wild grape vines that twisted their coils and tendrils from tree to tree, and spread a kind of network in his path.

At length he reached to where the ravine had opened through the cliffs, to the amphitheatre; but no traces of such opening remained. The rocks presented a high impenetrable wall, over which the torrent came tumbling in a sheet of feathery foam, and fell into a broad deep basin, black from the shadows of the surrounding forest. Here, then, poor Rip was brought to a stand. He again called and whistled after his dog; he was only answered by the cawing of a flock of idle crows, sporting high in air about a dry tree that overhung a sunny precipice; and who, secure in their elevation, seemed to look down and scoff at the poor man's perplexities. What was to be done? the morning was passing away, and Rip felt famished for his breakfast. He grieved to give up his dog and gun; he dreaded to meet his wife; but it would not do to starve among the mountains. He shook his head, shouldered the rusty firelock, and, with a heart full of trouble and anxiety, turned his steps homeward.

As he approached the village, he met a number of people, but none whom he knew, which somewhat surprised him, for he had thought himself acquainted with every one in the country round. Their dress, too, was of a different fashion from that to which he was accustomed. They all stared at him with equal marks of surprise, and whenever they cast eyes upon him, invariably stroked their chins. The constant recurrence of this gesture induced Rip, involuntarily, to do the same, when, to his astonishment, he found his beard had grown a foot long!

He had now entered the skirts of the village. A troop of strange children ran at his heels, hooting after him, and pointing at his gray beard. The dogs, too, not one of which he recognized for his old acquaintances, barked at him as he passed. The very village seemed altered: it was larger and more populous. There were rows of houses which he had never seen before, and those which had been his familiar haunts had disappeared. Strange names were over the doors—strange faces at the windows— every thing was strange. His mind now began to misgive him, that both he and the world around him were bewitched. Surely this was his native village, which he had left but the day before. There stood the Kaatskill mountains—there ran the silver Hudson at a distance—there was every hill and dale precisely as it had always been—Rip was sorely perplexed— "That flagon last night," thought he, "has addled my poor head sadly!"

It was with some difficulty he found the way to his own house, which he approached with silent awe, expecting every moment to hear the shrill voice of Dame Van Winkle. He found the house gone to decay—the roof fallen in, the windows shattered, and the doors off the hinges. A half starved dog, that looked like Wolf, was skulking about it. Rip called him by name, but the cur snarled, showed his teeth, and passed on. This was an unkind cut indeed—"My very dog," sighed poor Rip, "has forgotten me!"

He entered the house, which, to tell the truth, Dame Van Winkle had always kept in neat order. It was empty, forlorn, and apparently abandoned. This desolateness overcame all his connubial fears—he called loudly for his wife and children—the lonely chambers rung for a moment with his voice, and then all again was silence.

He now hurried forth, and hastened to his old resort, the little village inn—but it too was gone. A large ricketty wooden building stood in its place, with great gaping windows, some of them broken, and mended with old hats and petticoats, and over the door was painted, "The Union Hotel, by Jonathan Doolittle." Instead of the great tree that used to shelter the quiet little Dutch inn of yore, there now was reared a tall naked pole, with something on top that looked like a red night cap, and from it was fluttering a flag, on which was a singular assemblage of stars and stripes—all this was strange and incomprehensible. He recognised on the sign, however, the ruby face of King George, under which he had smoked so many a peaceful pipe, but even this was singularly metamorphosed. The red coat was changed for one of blue and buff, a sword was stuck in the hand instead of a sceptre, the head was decorated with a cocked hat, and underneath was painted in large characters, GENERAL WASHINGTON.

There was, as usual, a crowd of folk about the door, but none whom Rip recollected. The very character of the people seemed changed. There was a busy, bustling, disputatious tone about it, instead of the accustomed phlegm and drowsy tranquillity. He looked in vain for the sage

Nicholas Vedder, with his broad face, double chin, and fair long pipe, uttering clouds of tobacco smoke instead of idle speeches; or Van Bummel, the schoolmaster, doling forth the contents of an ancient newspaper. In place of these, a lean bilious looking fellow, with his pockets full of handbills, was haranguing vehemently about rights of citizens—election—members of congress—liberty—Bunker's hill—heroes of seventy-six—and other words, that were a perfect Babylonish jargon to the bewildered Van Winkle.

The appearance of Rip, with his long grizzled beard, his rusty fowling piece, his uncouth dress, and the army of women and children that had gathered at his heels, soon attracted the attention of the tavern politicians. They crowded around him, eyeing him from head to foot, with great curiosity. The orator bustled up to him, and drawing him partly aside, inquired "which side he voted?" Rip stared in vacant stupidity. Another short but busy little fellow pulled him by the arm, and raising on tiptoe, inquired in his ear, "whether he was Federal or Democrat." Rip was equally at a loss to comprehend the question; when a knowing, self-important old gentleman, in a sharp cocked hat, made his way through the crowd, putting them to the right and left with his elbows as he passed, and planting himself before Van Winkle, with one arm akimbo, the other resting on his cane, his keen eyes and sharp hat penetrating, as it were, into his very soul, demanded, in an austere tone, "what brought him to the election with a gun on his shoulder, and a mob at his heels, and whether he meant to breed a riot in the village?" "Alas! gentlemen," cried Rip, somewhat dismayed, "I am a poor quiet man, a native of the place, and a loyal subject of the King, God bless him!"

Here a general shout burst from the bystanders—"A tory! a tory! a spy! a refugee! hustle him! away with him!" It was with great difficulty that the self-important man in the cocked hat restored order; and having assumed a tenfold austerity of brow, demanded again of the unknown culprit, what he came there for, and whom he was seeking. The poor man humbly assured him that he meant no harm; but merely came there in search of some of his neighbours, who used to keep about the tavern.

"Well—who are they?—name them."

Rip bethought himself a moment, and inquired, "where's Nicholas Vedder?"

There was a silence for a little while, when an old man replied, in a thin piping voice, "Nicholas Vedder? why he is dead and gone these eighteen years! There was a wooden tombstone in the church yard that used to tell all about him, but that's rotted and gone too."

"Where's Brom Dutcher?"

"Oh, he went off to the army in the beginning of the war; some say he was killed at the battle of Stoney-Point—others say he was drowned in a squall, at the foot of Antony's Nose. I don't know—he never came back again."

"Where's Van Bummel, the schoolmaster?"

"He went off to the wars too, was a great militia general, and is now in Congress."

Rip's heart died away, at hearing of these sad changes in his home and friends, and finding himself thus alone in the world. Every answer puzzled him, too, by treating of such enormous lapses of time, and of matters which he could not understand: war—Congress—Stoney Point!— he had no courage to ask after any more friends, but cried out in despair, "does nobody here know Rip Van Winkle?"

"Oh, Rip Van Winkle!" exclaimed two or three, "Oh, to be sure! that's Rip Van Winkle yonder, leaning against the tree."

Rip looked, and beheld a precise counterpart of himself, as he went up the mountain: apparently as lazy, and certainly as ragged. The poor fellow was now completely confounded. He doubted his own identity, and whether he was himself or another man. In the midst of his bewilderment, the man in the cocked hat demanded who he was, and what was his name?

"God knows," exclaimed he, at his wit's end; "I'm not myself—I'm somebody else—that's me yonder—no—that's somebody else, got into my shoes—I was myself last night, but I fell asleep on the mountain, and they've changed my gun, and every thing's changed, and I'm changed, and I can't tell what's my name, or who I am!"

The bystanders began now to look at each other, nod, wink significantly, and tap their fingers against their foreheads. There was a whisper, also, about securing the gun, and keeping the old fellow from doing mischief; at the very suggestion of which, the self-important man in the cocked hat retired with some precipitation. At this critical moment a fresh likely woman pressed through the throng to get a peep at the graybearded man. She had a chubby child in her arms, which, frightened at his looks, began to cry. "Hush, Rip," cried she, "hush, you little fool, the old man wont hurt you." The name of the child, the air of the mother, the tone of her voice, all awakened a train of recollections in his mind.

"What is your name, my good woman?" asked he.

"Judith Gardenier."

"And your father's name?"

"Ah, poor man, his name was Rip Van Winkle; it's

twenty years since he went away from home with his gun, and never has been heard of since—his dog came home without him; but whether he shot himself, or was carried away by the Indians, nobody can tell. I was then but a little girl."

Rip had but one question more to ask; but he put it with a faltering voice:

"Where's your mother?"

Oh, she too had died but a short time since; she broke a blood vessel in a fit of passion at a New-England peddler.

There was a drop of comfort, at least, in this intelligence. The honest man could contain himself no longer. —He caught his daughter and her child in his arms.— "I am your father!" cried he—"Young Rip Van Winkle once—old Rip Van Winkle now!—Does nobody know poor Rip Van Winkle!"

All stood amazed, until an old woman, tottering out from among the crowd, put her hand to her brow, and peering under it in his face for a moment, exclaimed, "Sure enough! it is Rip Van Winkle—it is himself. Welcome home again, old neighbour—Why, where have you been these twenty long years?"

Rip's story was soon told, for the whole twenty years had been to him but as one night. The neighbours stared when they heard it; some were seen to wink at each other, and put their tongues in their cheeks; and the self-important man in the cocked hat, who, when the alarm was over, had returned to the field, screwed down the corners of his mouth, and shook his head—upon which there was a general shaking of the head throughout the assemblage.

It was determined, however, to take the opinion of old Peter Vanderdonk, who was seen slowly advancing up the road. He was a descendant of the historian of that name, who wrote one of the earliest accounts of the province. Peter was the most ancient inhabitant of the village, and well versed in all the wonderful events and traditions of the neighbourhood. He recollected Rip at once, and corroborated his story in the most satisfactory manner. He assured the company that it was a fact, handed down from his ancestor the historian, that the Kaatskill mountains had always been haunted by strange beings. That it was affirmed that the great Hendrick Hudson, the first discoverer of the river and country, kept a kind of vigil there every twenty years, with his crew of the Half-moon, being permitted in this way to revisit the scenes of his enterprize, and keep a guardian eye upon the river, and the great city called by his name. That his father had once seen them in their old Dutch dresses playing at nine pins in a hollow of the mountain; and that he himself had heard, one summer afternoon, the sound of their balls, like long peals of thunder.

To make a long story short, the company broke up, and returned to the more important concerns of the election. Rip's daughter took him home to live with her; she had a snug, well-furnished house, and a stout cheery farmer for a husband, whom Rip recollected for one of the urchins that used to climb upon his back. As to Rip's son and heir, who was the ditto of himself, seen leaning against the tree, he was employed to work on the farm; but evinced an hereditary disposition to attend to any thing else but his business.

Rip now resumed his old walks and habits; he soon found many of his former cronies, though all rather the worse for the wear and tear of time; and preferred making friends among the rising generation, with whom he soon grew into great favour.

Having nothing to do at home, and being arrived at that happy age when a man can do nothing with impunity, he took his place once more on he bench, at the inn door, and was reverenced as one of the patriarchs of the village, and a chronicle of the old times "before the war." It was some time before he could get into the regular track of gossip, or could be made to comprehend the strange events that had taken place during his torpor; how that there had been a revolutionary war—that the country had thrown off the yoke of old England—and that, instead of being a subject of his Majesty George the Third, he was now a free citizen of the United States. Rip, in fact, was no politician; the changes of states and empires made but little impression on him. But there was one species of despotism under which he had long groaned, and that was—petticoat government: happily, that was at an end; he had got his neck out of the yoke of matrimony, and could go in and out whenever he pleased, without dreading the tyranny of Dame Van Winkle. Whenever her name was mentioned, however, he shook his head, shrugged his shoulders, and cast up his eyes; which might pass either for an expression of resignation to his fate, or joy at his deliverance.

He used to tell his story to every stranger that arrived at Mr. Doolittle's hotel. He was observed, at first, to vary on some points every time he told it, which was, doubtless, owing to his having so recently awaked. It at last settled down precisely to the tale I have related, and not a man, woman, or child in the neighbourhood, but knew it by heart. Some always pretended to doubt the reality of it, and insisted that Rip had been out of his head, and that this was one point on which he always remained flighty. The old Dutch inhabitants, however, almost universally gave it full credit. Even to this day they never hear a thunder storm of a summer afternoon, about the Kaatskill, but they say Hendrick Hudson and his crew are at their game of nine pins; and it is a common wish of all henpecked husbands in the neighbourhood, when life hangs heavy on their hands, that they might have a quieting draught out of Rip Van Winkle's flagon.

Note

The foregoing tale, one would suspect, had been suggested to Mr. Knickerbocker by a little German superstition about Charles V. and the Kypphauser mountain; the subjoined note, however, which he had appended to the tale, shows that it is an absolute fact, narrated with his usual fidelity.

"The story of Rip Van Winkle may seem incredible to many, but nevertheless I give it my full belief, for I know the vicinity of our old Dutch settlements to have been very subject to marvellous events and appearances. Indeed, I have heard many stranger stories than this, in the villages along the Hudson; all of which were too well authenticated to admit of a doubt. I have even talked with Rip Van Winkle myself, who, when last I saw him, was a very venerable old man, and so perfectly rational and consistent on every other point, that I think no conscientious person could refuse to take this into the bargain; nay, I have seen a certificate on the subject taken before a country justice and signed with a cross, in the justice's own hand writing. The story, therefore, is beyond the possibility of doubt.

D.K.

The Legend of Sleepy Hollow

(FOUND AMONG THE PAPERS
OF THE LATE DIEDRICH KNICKERBOCKER)

> A pleasing land of drowsy head it was,
> Of dreams that wave before the half-shut eye;
> And of gay castles in the clouds that pass,
> Forever flushing round a summer sky.
>
> CASTLE OF INDOLENCE

In the bosom of one of the spacious coves which indent the eastern shore of the Hudson, at the broad expansion of the river denominated by the ancient Dutch navigators the Tappaan Zee, and where they always prudently shortened sail, and implored the protection of St. Nicholas when they crossed, there lies a small market town or rural port, which by some is called Greensburgh, but which is more universally and properly known by the name of Tarry Town. This name was given it, we are told, in former days, by the good housewives of the adjacent country, from the inveterate propensity of their husbands to linger about the village tavern on market days. Be that as it may, I do not vouch for the fact, but merely advert

33

to it, for the sake of being precise and authentic. Not far from this village, perhaps about three miles, there is a little valley, or rather lap of land among high hills, which is one of the quietest places in the whole world. A small brook glides through it, with just murmur enough to lull you to repose, and the occasional whistle of a quail, or tapping of a woodpecker, is almost the only sound that ever breaks in upon the uniform tranquillity.

I recollect that when a stripling, my first exploit in squirrel shooting was in a grove of tall walnut trees that shades one side of the valley. I had wandered into it at noon time, when all nature is peculiarly quiet, and was startled by the roar of my own gun, as it broke the sabbath stillness around, and was prolonged and reverberated by the angry echoes. If ever I should wish for a retreat, whither I might steal from the world and its distractions, and dream quietly away the remnants of a troubled life, I know of none more promising than this little valley.

From the listless repose of the place, and the peculiar character of its inhabitants, who are descendants from the original Dutch settlers, this sequestered glen has long been known by the name of SLEEPY HOLLOW, and its rustic lads are called the Sleepy Hollow Boys throughout all the neighbouring country. A drowsy, dreamy influence seems to hang over the land, and pervade the very atmosphere. Some say that the place was bewitched by a high German doctor during the early days of the settlement; others, that an old Indian chief, the prophet or wizard of his tribe, held his powwows there before the country was discovered by Master Hendrick Hudson. Certain it is, the place still continues under the sway of some witching power, that holds a spell over the minds of the good people, causing them to walk in a continual reverie. They are given to all kinds of marvellous beliefs; have trances and visions, and see strange sights, and hear music and voices in the air. The whole neighbourhood abounds with local tales, haunted sports, and twilight superstitions; stars shoot and meteors glare oftener across the valley than in any other part of the country, and the night-mare, with her whole nine fold, seems to make it the favourite scene of her gambols.

The dominant spirit, however, that haunts this enchanted region, and seems to be commander of all the powers of the air, is the apparition of a figure on horseback without a head. It is said by some to be the ghost of a Hessian trooper, whose head had been carried away by a cannon-ball, in some nameless battle during the revolutionary war, and who is ever and anon seen by various of the country people, hurrying along in the gloom of night, as if on the wings of the wind. His haunts are not confined to the valley, but extend at times to the adjacent roads, and especially to the vicinity of a church that is at no great distance. Indeed, certain of the most authentic historians of those parts, who have been careful in collecting and collating the floating facts concerning this spectre, allege, that the body of the trooper having been buried in the church-yard, the ghost rides forth to the scene of battle in nightly quest of his head, and the rushing speed with which he sometimes passes along the hollow, like a midnight blast, is owing to his being belated, and in a hurry to get back to the church-yard before daybreak.

Such is the general purport of this legendary superstition, which has furnished materials for many a wild story in that region of shadows; and the spectre is known at all the country firesides, by the name of The Headless Horseman of Sleepy Hollow.

It is remarkable, that the visionary turn I have mentioned is not confined to the native inhabitants of the valley, but is imperceptibly acquired by every one who resides there for a time. However wide awake they may have been before they entered that sleepy region, they are sure, in a little time, to imbibe the witching influence of the air, and begin to grow imaginative—to dream dreams, and see apparitions.

I mention this peaceful spot with all possible laud; for it is in such little retired Dutch valleys, found here and there embosomed in the great state of New-York, that populations, manners, and customs, remained fixed, while the great torrent of emigration and improvement, which is making such incessant changes in other parts of this restless country, sweeps by them unobserved. They are like those little nooks of still water, which border a rapid stream, where we may see the straw and bubble riding quietly at anchor, or slowly revolving in their mimic harbour, undisturbed by the rushing of the passing current. Though many years have elapsed since I trod the drowsy shades of Sleepy Hollow, yet I question whether I should not still find the same trees and the same families vegetating in it sheltered bosom.

In this by-place of nature there abode, in a remote period of American history, that is to say, some thirty years since, a worthy wight of the name of Ichabod Crane, who sojourned, or, as he expressed it, "tarried," in Sleepy Hollow, for the purpose of instructing the children of the vicinity. He was a native of Connecticut, a state which supplies the Union with pioneers for the mind as well as the forest, and sends forth yearly its legions of frontier woodmen and country schoolmasters. The cognomen of Crane was not inapplicable to his person. He was tall, but exceedingly lank, with narrow shoulders, long arms and legs, hands that dangled a mile out of his sleeves, feet that might have served for shovels, and his whole frame most loosely hung together. His head was small, and flat at top, with huge ears, large green glassy eyes, and a long snipe nose, so that it might have been mistaken for a weather-cock perched upon his spindle neck, to tell which way the wind blew. To see him striding along the profile of a hill on a windy day, with his clothes bagging and fluttering about him, one might have mistaken him for the genius of famine descending upon the earth, or some scarecrow eloped from a cornfield.

His school-house was a low building of one large room, rudely constructed of logs; the windows partly glazed, and partly patched with leaves of old copy books. It was most ingeniously secured at vacant hours, by a withe twisted in the handle of the door, and stakes set against the window shutters; so that though a thief might get in with perfect ease, he would find some embarrassment in getting out; an idea most probably borrowed by the architect, Yost Van Houten, from the mystery of an eelpot. The school-house stood in rather a lonely but a pleasant situation, just at the foot of a woody hill, with a brook running close by, and a formidable birch tree growing at one end of it. From hence the low murmur of his pupil's voices, conning over their lessons, might be heard of a drowsy summer's day, like the hum of a bee-hive; interrupted now and then by the authoritative voice of the master, giving menace or command, or, peradventure, the appalling sound of the birch, as he urged some tardy loiterer along the flowery path of knowledge. Truth to say, he was a conscientious man, that ever bore in mind the golden maxim, "spare the rod and spoil the child."— Ichabod Crane's scholars certainly were not spoiled.

I would not have it imagined, however, that he was one of those cruel potentates of the school, who joy in the smart of their subjects; on the contrary, he administered justice with discrimination rather than severity; taking the burthen off the backs of the weak, and laying it on those of the strong. Your mere puny stripling, that winced at the least flourish of the rod, was passed by with indulgence; but the claims of justice were satisfied, by giving a double portion to some little, tough, wrong-headed, broad-skirted Dutch urchin, who sulked and swelled and grew dogged and sullen beneath the birch. All this he called "doing his duty by their parents;" and he never inflicted a chastisement without following it by the assurance, so consolatory to the smarting urchin, that he would remember it and thank him for it the longest day he had to live.

When school hours were over, he was even the companion and playmate of his larger boys; and would convoy some of the smaller ones home of a holyday, who happened to have pretty sisters, or good housewives for mothers, noted for the comforts of the cupboard. Indeed, it behooved him to keep on good terms with his pupils. The revenue arising from his school was small, and would have been scarcely sufficient to furnish him with daily bread, for he was a huge feeder, and though lank, had the dilating powers of an Anaconda; but to help out his maintenance, he was, according to country custom in those parts, boarded and lodged at the houses of the farmers, whose children he instructed. With these he lived alternately a week at a time, thus going the rounds of the neighbourhood, with all his worldly effects tied up in a cotton handkerchief.

That all this might not be too onerous on the purses of his rustic patrons, who are apt to consider the costs of schooling a grievous burthen, and schoolmasters mere drones, he had various ways of rendering himself both useful and agreeable. He assisted the farmers occasionally in the light labours of their farms, helped to make hay, mended the fences, took the horses to water, drove the cows from pasture, and cut wood for the winter fire. He laid aside, too, all the dominant dignity and absolute sway, with which he lorded it in his little empire, the school, and became wonderfully gentle and ingratiating. He found favour in the eyes of the mothers, by petting the children, particularly the youngest, and like the lion bold, which whilome so magnanimously the lamb did hold, he would sit with a child on one knee, and rock a cradle with his foot, for whole hours together.

In addition to his other vocations, he was the singing master of the neighbourhood, and picked up many bright shillings by instructing the young folks in psalmody. It was a matter of no little vanity to him on Sundays, to take his station in front of the church gallery, with a band of chosen singers; where, in his own mind, he completely carried away the palm from the parson. Certain it is, his voice resounded far above all the rest of the congregation, and there are peculiar quavers still to be heard in that church, and which may even be heard half-a-mile off, quite to the opposite side of the mill-pond, of a still Sunday morning, which are said to be legitimately descended from the nose of Ichabod Crane. Thus, by diverse little make shifts, in that ingenious way which is commonly denominated "by hook and by crook," the worthy pedagogue got on tolerably enough, and was thought, by all those who understood nothing of the labour of headwork, to have a wonderful easy life of it.

The schoolmaster is generally a man of some importance in the female circle of a rural neighbourhood, being considered a kind of idle gentleman-like personage, of vastly superior taste and accomplishments to the rough country swains, and, indeed, inferior in learning only to the parson. His appearance, therefore, is apt to occasion some little stir at the tea-table of a farm-house, and the addition of a supernumerary dish of cakes or sweetmeets, or, peradventure, the parade of a silver tea-pot. Our man of letters, therefore, was peculiarly happy in the smiles of all the country damsels. How he would figure among them in the church-yard, between services on Sundays; gathering grapes for them from the wild vines that overrun the surrounding trees; reciting for them all the epitaphs on the tomb-stones, or sauntering, with a whole bevy of them, along the banks of the adjacent mill-pond; while the more bashful country bumpkins hung sheepishly back, envying his superior elegance and address.

From his half itinerant life, also, he was a kind of travelling gazette, carrying the whole budget of local gossip from house to house; so that his appearance was always greeted with satisfaction. He was, moreover, esteemed by the women as a man of great erudition, for he had read several books quite through, and was a perfect master of

Cotton Mather's History of New-England Witchcraft, in which, by the way, he most firmly and potently believed.

He was, in fact, an odd mixture of small shrewdness and simple credulity. His appetite for the marvellous, and his powers of digesting it, were equally extraordinary; and both had been increased by his residence in this spell-bound region. No tale was too gross or monstrous for his capacious swallow. It was often his delight, after his school was dismissed of an afternoon, to stretch himself on the rich bed of clover, bordering the little brook that whimpered past his school-house, and there con over old Mather's direful tales, until the gathering dusk of evening made the printed page a mere mist before his eyes. Then, as he wended his way, by swamp and stream and awful woodland, to the farmhouse where he happened to be quartered, every sound of nature, at that witching hour, fluttered his excited imagination: the moan of the whip-poor-will from the hill side; the boding cry of the tree toad, that harbinger of storm; the dreary hooting of the screech-owl; or the sudden rustling in the thicket, of birds frightened from their roost. The fire-flies, too, which sparkled most vividly in the darkest places, now and then startled him, as one of uncommon brightness would stream across his path; and if, by chance, a huge block-head of a beetle came winging his blundering flight against him, the poor varlet was ready to give up the ghost, with the idea that he was struck with a witch's token. His only resource on such occasions, either to drown thought, or drive away evil spirits, was to sing psalm tunes;—and the good people of Sleepy Hollow, as they sat by their doors of an evening, were often filled with awe, at hearing his nasal melody, "in linked sweetness long drawn out," floating from the distant hill, or along the dusky road.

Another of his sources of fearful pleasure was, to pass long winter evenings with the old Dutch wives, as they sat spinning by the fire, with a row of apples roasting and sputtering along the hearth, and listen to their marvellous tales of ghosts and goblins, and haunted fields and haunted brooks, and haunted bridges and haunted houses, and particularly of the headless horseman, or galloping Hessian of the Hollow, as they sometimes called him. He would delight them equally by his anecdotes of witchcraft, and of the direful omens and portentous sights and sounds in the air, which prevailed in the earlier times of Connecticut; and would frighten them woefully with speculations upon comets and shooting stars, and with the alarming fact that the world did absolutely turn round, and that they were half the time topsy-turvy!

But if there was a pleasure in all this, while snugly cuddling in the chimney corner of a chamber that was all of a ruddy glow from the crackling wood fire, and where, of course, no spectre dare to show its face, it was dearly purchased by the terrors of his subsequent walk homewards. What fearful shapes and shadows beset his path, amidst the dim and ghostly glare of a snowy night!—With what wistful look did he eye every trembling ray of light streaming across the waste fields from some distant window!—How often was he appalled by some shrub covered with snow, which like sheeted spectre beset his very path!—How often did he shrink with curdling awe at the sound of his own steps on the frosty crust beneath his feet; and dread to look over his shoulder, lest he should behold some uncouth being tramping close behind him!—and how often was he thrown into complete dismay by some rushing blast, howling among the trees, in the idea that it was the galloping Hessian on one of his nightly scourings.

All these, however, were mere terrors of the night, phantoms of the mind, that walk in darkness; and though he had seen many spectres in his time, and been more than once beset by Satan in diverse shapes, in his lonely perambulations, yet day-light put an end to all these evils; and he would have passed a pleasant life of it, in despite of the Devil and all his works, if his path had not been crossed by a being that causes more perplexity to mortal man, than ghosts, goblins, and the whole race of witches put together, and that was—a woman.

Among the musical disciples who assembled, one evening in each week, to receive his instructions in psalmody, was Katrina Van Tassel, the daughter and only child of a substantial Dutch farmer. She was a blooming lass of fresh eighteen; plump as a partridge; ripe and melting and rosy cheeked as one of her father's peaches, and universally famed, not merely for her beauty, but her vast expectations. She was withal a little of a coquette, as might be perceived even in her dress, which was a mixture of ancient and modern fashions, as most suited to set off her charms. She wore the ornaments of pure yellow gold, which her great-great-grandmother had brought over from Saardam; the tempting stomacher of the olden time, and withal a provokingly short petticoat, to display the prettiest foot and ankle in the country round.

Ichabod Crane had a soft and foolish heart toward the sex; and it is not to be wondered at, that so tempting a morsel soon found favour in his eyes, more especially after he had visited her in her paternal mansion. Old Baltus Van Tassel was a perfect picture of a thriving, contented, liberal-hearted farmer. He seldom, it is true, sent either his eyes or his thoughts beyond the boundaries of his own farm; but within those every thing was snug, happy, and well-conditioned. He was satisfied with his wealth, but not proud of it, and piqued himself upon the hearty abundance, rather than the style in which he lived. His strong hold was situated on the banks of the Hudson, in one of those green, sheltered, fertile nooks, into which the Dutch farmers are so fond of nestling. A great elm tree spread its broad branches over it, at the foot of which bubbled up a spring of the softest and sweetest water, in a little kind of well, formed of a barrel, and then stole sparkling away through the grass, to a neighbouring brook, that babbled along among elders and dwarf willows. Hard by the farm-house was a vast barn, that might have served for a church, every window and crevice of which seemed bursting forth with the treasures of the farm; the flail was busily resounding within it; swallows and martins skimmed twittering about the eaves, and rows of pigeons, some with one eye turned up, as if watching the weather, some with their heads under their wings, or buried in their bosoms, and others, swelling, and cooing, and bowing about their dames, were enjoying the sunshine on the roof. Sleek unwieldy porkers were grunting in the repose and abundance of their pens, from whence sallied forth, now and then, troops of sucking pigs, as if to snuff the air. A stately squadron of snowy geese were riding in an adjoining pond, convoying whole fleets of ducks; regiments of turkeys were gobbling about the farm-yard, and guinea fowls fretting like ill-tempered housewives, with their peevish discontented cry. Before the barn door strutted the gallant cock, that pattern of a husband, a warrior, and a fine gentleman, clapping his burnished wings, and crowing in the pride and gladness of his heart—sometimes tearing up the earth with his feet, and then generously calling his ever-hungry family of wives and children to enjoy the rich morsel he had discovered.

The pedagogue's mouth watered, as he looked upon this sumptuous promise of luxurious winter fare. In his devouring mind's eye, he pictured to himself every roasting pig running about with a pudding in its belly, and an apple in its mouth; the pigeons were snugly put to bed in a comfortable pie, and tucked in with a coverlet of crust; the geese were swimming in their own gravy; and the ducks pairing cosily in dishes, like snug married couples, with a decent competency of onion sauce; in the porkers he saw carved out the future sleek side of bacon, and juicy relishing ham; not a turkey, but he beheld daintily trussed up, with its gizzard under its wing, and, peradventure, a necklace of savoury sausages; and even bright chanticleer himself lay sprawling on his back, in a side dish, with uplifted claws, as if craving that quarter, which his chivalrous spirit disdained to ask while living.

As the enraptured Ichabod fancied all this, and as he rolled his great green eyes over the fat meadow lands, the rich fields of wheat, of rye, of buckwheat, and Indian corn, and the orchards burthened with ruddy fruit, which surrounded the warm tenement of Van Tassel, his heart yearned after the damsel who was to inherit those domains, and his imagination expanded with the idea, how they might be readily turned into cash, and the money invested in immense tracts of wild land, and shingle palaces in the wilderness. Nay, his busy fancy already put him in possession of his hopes, and presented to him the blooming Katrina, with a whole family of children, mounted on the top of a waggon loaded with household trumpery, with pots and kettles dangling beneath; and he beheld himself bestriding a pacing mare, with a colt at her heels, setting out for Kentucky, Tennessee, or the Lord knows where!

When he entered the house, the conquest of his heart was complete. It was one of those spacious farm-houses, with high-ridged, but lowly-sloping roofs, built in the style handed down from the first Dutch settlers. The low, projecting eaves formed a piazza along the front, capable of being closed up in bad weather. Under this were hung

49

flails, harness, various utensils of husbandry, and nets for fishing in the neighbouring river. Benches were built along the sides for summer use; and a great spinning wheel at one end, and a churn at the other, showed the various uses to which this important porch might be devoted. From this piazza the wondering Ichabod entered the hall, which formed the centre of the mansion, and the place of usual residence. Here, rows of resplendent pewter, ranged on a long dresser, dazzled his eyes. In one corner stood a huge bag of wool ready to be spun; in another a quantity of linsey-woolsey just from the loom; ears of Indian corn, and strings of dried apples and peaches, hung in gay festoons along the walls, mingled with the gaud of red peppers; and a door left ajar, gave him a peep into the best parlour, where the claw-footed chairs, and dark mahogany tables, shone like mirrors; andirons, with their accompanying shovel and tongs, glistened from their covert of asparagus tops; mock oranges and conch shells decorated the mantlepiece; strings of various coloured birds' eggs were suspended above it; a great ostrich egg was hung from the center of the room; and a corner cupboard, knowingly left open, displayed immense treasures of old silver and well-mended china.

From the moment Ichabod laid his eyes upon these regions of delight, the peace of his mind was at an end, and his only study was how to gain the affections of the peerless daughter of Van Tassel. In this enterprize, however, he had more real difficulties than generally fell to the lot of a knight-errant of yore, who seldom had any thing but giants, enchanters, fiery dragons, and such like easily conquered adversaries, to contend with; and had to make his way merely through gates of iron and brass, and walls of adamant, to the castle keep, where the lady of his heart was confined; all which he achieved as easily as a man would carve his way to the centre of a Christmas pie, and then the lady gave him her hand as a matter of course. Ichabod, on the contrary, had to win his way to the heart of a country coquette, beset with a labyrinth of whims and caprices, which were for ever presenting new difficulties and impediments, and he had to encounter a host of fearful adversaries of real flesh and blood, the numerous rustic admirers, who beset every portal to her heart, keeping a watchful and angry eye upon each other, but ready to fly out in the common cause against any new competitor.

Among these, the most formidable was a burley, roaring, roystering blade, of the name of Abraham, or, according to the Dutch abbreviation, Brom Van Brunt, the hero of the country round, which rung with his feats of strength and hardihood. He was broad shouldered and double jointed, with short curly black hair, and a bluff, but not unpleasant countenance, having a mingled air of fun and arrogance. From his Herculean frame and great powers of limb, he had received the nick-name of BROM BONES, by which he was universally known. He was famed for great knowledge and skill in horsemanship, being as dexterous on horseback as a Tartar. He was foremost at all races and cock-fights, and with the ascendancy which bodily strength always acquires in rustic life, was the umpire in all disputes, setting his hat on one side, and giving his decisions with an air and tone that admitted of no gainsay or appeal. He was always ready for either a fight or a frolick; had more mischief than ill-will in his composition; and with all his overbearing roughness, there was a strong dash of waggish good humour at bottom. He had three or four boon companions of his own stamp, who regarded him as their model, and at the head of whom he scoured the country, attending every scene of feud or merriment for miles round. In cold weather he was distinguished by a fur cap, surmounted with a flaunting fox's tail, and when the folks at a country gathering descried this well-known crest at a distance, whisking about among a squad of hard riders, they always stood by for a squall. Sometimes his crew would be heard dashing along past the farm-houses at midnight, with whoop and halloo, like a troop of Don Cossacks, and the old dames, startled out of their sleep, would listen for a moment till the hurry scurry had clattered by, and then exclaim, "aye, there goes Brom Bones and his gang!" The neighbours looked upon him with a mixture of awe, admiration, and good-will; and when any mad-cap prank, or rustic brawl occurred in the vicinity, always shook their heads, and warranted Brom Bones was at the bottom of it.

This rantipole hero had for some time singled out the blooming Katrina for the object of his uncouth gallantries, and though his amorous toyings were something like the gentle caresses and endearments of a bear, yet it was whispered that she did not altogether discourage his hopes. Certain it is, his advances were signals for rival candidates to retire, who felt no inclination to cross a lion in his amours; insomuch, that when his horse was seen tied to Van Tassel's paling, of a Sunday night, (a sure sign that his master was courting, or, as it is termed, "sparking," within,) all other suitors passed by in despair, and carried the war into other quarters.

Such was the formidable rival with whom Ichabod Crane had to contend, and, considering all things, a stouter man than he would have shrunk from the competition, and a wiser man would have despaired. He had, however, a happy mixture of pliability and perseverance in his nature; he was in form and spirit like a supple jack—

yielding, but tough; though he bent, he never broke; and though he bowed beneath the slightest pressure, yet, the moment it was away—jerk!—he was as erect, and carried his head as high as ever.

To have taken the field openly against his rival, would have been madness; for he was not a man to be thwarted in his amours, any more than that stormy lover, Achilles. Ichabod, therefore, made his advances in a quiet and gently-insinuating manner. Under cover of his character of singing master, he made frequent visits at the farmhouse; not that he had any thing to apprehend from the meddlesome interference of parents, which is so often a stumbling block in the path of lovers. Balt Van Tassel was an easy indulgent soul; he loved his daughter better even than his pipe, and like a reasonable man, and an excellent father, let her have her way in every thing. His notable little wife too, had enough to do to attend to her housekeeping and manage the poultry, for, as she sagely observed, ducks and geese are foolish things, and must be looked after, but girls can take care of themselves. Thus, while the busy dame bustled about the house, or plied her spinning wheel at one end of the piazza, honest Balt would sit smoking his evening pipe at the other, watching the achievements of a little wooden warrior, who, armed with a sword in each hand, was most valiantly fighting the wind on the pinnacle of the barn. In the mean time, Ichabod would carry on his suit with the daughter by the side of the spring under the great elm, or sauntering along in the twilight, that hour so favourable to the lover's eloquence.

I profess not to know how women's hearts are wooed and won. To me they have always been matters of riddle and admiration. Some seem to have but one vulnerable point, or door of access; while others have a thousand avenues, and may be captured a thousand different ways. It is a great triumph of skill to gain the former, but a still greater proof of generalship to maintain possession of the latter, for a man must battle for his fortress at every door and window. He that wins a thousand common hearts, is therefore entitled to some renown; but he who keeps undisputed sway over the heart of a coquette, is indeed a hero. Certain it is, this was not the case with the redoubtable Brom Bones; and from the moment Ichabod Crane made his advances, the interests of the former evidently declined; his horse was no longer seen tied at the palings on Sunday nights, and a deadly feud gradually arose between him and the preceptor of Sleepy Hollow.

Brom, who had a degree of rough chivalry in his nature, would fain have carried matters to open warfare, and settled their pretensions to the lady, according to the mode of those most concise and simple reasoners, the knights-errant of yore—by single combat; but Ichabod was too conscious of the superior might of his adversary to enter the lists against him; he had overheard the boast of Bones, that he would "double the schoolmaster up, and put him on a shelf;" and he was too wary to give him an opportunity. There was something extremely provoking in this obstinately pacific system; it left Brom no alternative but to draw upon the funds of rustic waggery in his disposition, and play off boorish practical jokes upon his rival. Ichabod became the object of whimsical persecution to Bones, and his gang of rough riders. They harried his hitherto peaceful domains; smoked out his singing school, by stopping up the chimney; broke into the school-house at night, in spite of its formidable fastenings of withe and window stakes, and turned every thing topsy-turvy, so that the poor schoolmaster began to think all the witches in the country held their meetings there. But what was still more annoying, Brom took all opportunities of turning him into ridicule in presence of his mistress, and had a scoundrel dog, whom he taught to whine in the most ludicrous manner, and introduced as a rival of Ichabod's, to instruct her in psalmody.

In this way, matters went on for some time, without producing any material effect on the relative situations of the contending powers. On a fine autumnal afternoon, Ichabod, in pensive mood, sat enthroned on the lofty stool from whence he usually watched all the concerns of his little literary realm. In his hand he swayed a ferule, that sceptre of despotic power; the birch of justice reposed on three nails, behind the throne, a constant terror to evil doers; while on the desk before him might be seen sundry contraband articles and prohibited weapons, detected upon the persons of idle urchins, such as half-munched apples, popguns, whirligigs, fly-cages, and whole legions of rampant little paper game cocks. Apparently there had been some appalling act of justice recently inflicted, for his scholars were all busily intent upon their books, or slyly whispering behind them with one eye kept upon the master; and a kind of buzzing stillness reigned throughout the school-room. It was suddenly interrupted by the appearance of a negro in tow-cloth jacket and trowsers, a round crowned fragment of a hat, like the cap of Mercury, and mounted on the back of a ragged, wild, half-broken colt, which he managed with a rope by way of halter. He came clattering up to the school-door with an invitation to Ichabod to attend a merry-making, or "quilting frolick," to be held that evening at Mynheer Van Tassel's, and having delivered his message with that air of importance, and effort at fine language, which a negro is apt to display on petty embassies of the kind, he dashed over the brook, and was seen scampering away up the hollow, full of importance and hurry of his mission.

All was now bustle and hubbub in the late quiet school room. The scholars were hurried through their lessons, without stopping at trifles; those who were nimble, skipped off half with impunity, and those who were tardy, had a smart application now and then in the rear, to quicken their speed, or help them over a tall word. Books were flung aside, without being put away on the shelves; inkstands were overturned, benches thrown down, and the whole school turned loose an hour before the usual time; bursting forth like a legion of young imps, yelping and racketting about the green in joy at their early emancipation.

The gallant Ichabod now spent at least an extra half hour at his toilet, brushing and furbishing up his best, and indeed only suit of rusty black, and arranging his looks by a bit of broken looking glass, that hung up in the school house. That he might make his appearance before his mistress in the true style of a cavalier, he borrowed a horse from the farmer with whom he was domiciliated, a choleric old Dutchman, of the name of Hans Van Ripper, and thus gallantly mounted, issued forth like a knight-errant in quest of adventures. But it is meet I should, in the true spirit of romantic story, give some account of the looks and equipments of my hero and his steed. The animal he bestrode was a broken-down plough horse, that had outlived almost every thing but his viciousness. He was gaunt and shagged, with a ewe neck and hammer head; his rusty mane and tail were tangled and knotted with burrs; one eye had lost its pupil, and was glaring and spectral, but the other had the gleam of a genuine devil in it. Still he must have had fire and mettle in his day, if we may judge from his name, which was Gunpowder. He had, in fact, been a favourite steed of his master's, the choleric Van Ripper, who was a furious rider, and had infused, very probably, some of his own spirit into the animal, for, old and broken-down as he looked, there was more lurking deviltry in him than in any young filly in the country.

Ichabod was a suitable figure for such a steed. He rode with short stirrups, which brought his knees nearly up to the pommel of the saddle; his sharp elbows stuck out like grasshoppers'; he carried his whip perpendicularly in his hand, like a sceptre, and as the horse jogged on, the motion of his arms was not unlike the flapping of a pair of wings. A small wool hat rested on the top of his nose, for so his scanty strip of forehead might be called, and the skirts of his black coat fluttered out almost to the horse's tail. Such was the appearance of Ichabod and his steed, as they shambled out of the gate of Hans Van Ripper, and it was altogether such an apparition as is seldom to be met with in broad day light.

It was, as I have said, a fine autumnal day, the sky was clear and serene, and nature wore that rich and golden livery which we always associate with the idea of abundance. The forests had put on their sober brown and yellow, while some trees of the tenderer kind had been nipped by the frosts into brilliant dyes of orange, purple, and scarlet. Streaming files of wild ducks began to make their appearance high in the air; the bark of the squirrel might be heard from the groves of beech and hickory nuts, and the pensive whistle of the quail at intervals from the neighbouring stubble field.

The small birds were taking their farewell banquets. In the fullness of their revelry, they fluttered, chirping and frolicking, from bush to bush, and tree to tree, capricious from the very profusion and variety around them. There was the honest cock-robin, the favourite game of stripling sportsmen, with its loud querulous note; and the twittering blackbirds flying in sable clouds; and the golden winged woodpecker, with his crimson crest, his broad black gorget, and splendid plumage; and the cedar bird, with its red tipt wings and yellow tipt tail, and its little monteiro cap of feathers; and the blue jay, that noisy cox-comb, in his gay light blue coat and white under clothes, screaming and chattering, nodding, and bobbing, and bowing, and pretending to be on good terms with every songster of the grove.

As Ichabod jogged slowly on his way, his eye, ever open to every symptom of culinary abundance, ranged with delight over the treasures of jolly autumn. On all sides he beheld vast store of apples, some hanging in oppressive opulence on the trees, some gathered into baskets and barrels for the market, others heaped up in rich piles for the cider-press. Further on he beheld great fields of Indian corn, with its golden ears peeping from their leafy coverts, and holding out the promise of cakes and hasty pudding; and the yellow pumpkins lying beneath them, turning up their fair round bellies to the sun, and giving ample prospects of the most luxurious of pies; and anon he passed the fragrant buckwheat fields, breathing the odour of the bee-hive, and as he beheld them, soft anticipations stole over his mind of dainty slap-jacks, well buttered, and garnished with honey or treacle, by the delicate little dimpled hand of Katrina Van Tassel.

Thus feeding his mind with many sweet thoughts and "sugared suppositions," he journeyed along the sides of a range of hills which look out upon some of the goodliest scenes of the mighty Hudson. The sun gradually wheeled his broad disk down into the west. The wide bosom of the Tappaan Zee lay motionless and glassy, excepting that here and there a gentle undulation waved and prolonged the blue shadow of the distant mountain: a few amber clouds floated in the sky, without a breath of air to move them. The horizon was of a fine golden tint, changing gradually into a pure apple green, and from that into a deep blue of mid-heaven. A slanting ray lingered on the woody crests of the precipices that overhung some parts of the river, giving greater depth to the dark gray and purple of their rocky sides. A sloop was loitering in the distance, dropping slowly down with the tide, her sail hanging uselessly against the mast, and as the reflection of the sky gleamed along the still water, it seemed as if the vessel was suspended in the air.

It was toward evening that Ichabod arrived at the castle of the Heer Van Tassel, which he found thronged with the pride and flower of the adjacent country. Old farmers, a spare leathern-faced race, in homespun coats and small-clothes, blue stockings, huge shoes, and magnificent pewter buckles. Their brisk withered little dames in close crimped caps, long waisted short gowns, homespun petti-coats, with scissors and pincushions, and gay calico pock-ets, hanging on the outside. Buxom lasses, almost as antiquated as their mothers, excepting where a straw hat, a fine ribband, or perhaps a white frock, gave symptoms of city innovations. The sons, in short square-skirted coats, with rows of stupendous brass buttons, and their hair generally queued in the fashion of the times, especially if they could procure an eelskin for the purpose, it being esteemed throughout the country as a potent nourisher and strengthener of the hair.

Brom Bones, however, was the hero of the scene, having come to the gathering on his favourite steed Daredevil, a creature, like himself, full of mettle and mischief, and which no one but himself could manage. He was in fact noted for preferring vicious animals, given to all kinds of tricks, which kept the rider in constant risk of his neck, and held a tractable well broken horse as unworthy a lad of spirit.

Fain would I pause to dwell upon the world of charms that burst upon the enraptured gaze of my hero, as he entered the state parlour of Van Tassel's mansion. Not those of the bevy of buxom lasses, with their luxurious display of red and white: but the ample charms of a genuine Dutch country tea table, in the sumptuous time of autumn. Such heaped up platters of cakes of various and almost indescribable kinds, known only to experienced Dutch housewives. There was the doughty dough-nut, the tenderer oly koek, and the crisp and crumbling cruller; sweet cakes and short cakes, ginger cakes and honey cakes, and the whole family of cakes. And then there were apple pies and peach pies and pumpkin pies; not to mention slices of ham and smoked beef, together with broiled shad and roasted chickens; besides delectable dishes of preserved plums, and peaches, and pears, and quinces; with bowls of milk and cream, all mingled higgledy-piggledy, pretty much as I have enumerated them, with the motherly tea-pot sending up its clouds of vapour from the midst—Heaven bless the mark! I want breath and time to discuss this banquet as it deserves, and am too eager to get on with my story. Happily, Ichabod Crane was not in so great a hurry as his historian, but did ample justice to every dainty.

He was a kind and thankful toad, whose heart dilated in proportion as his skin was filled with good cheer, and whose spirits rose with eating, as some men's do with drink. He could not help, too, rolling his large eyes round him as he ate, and chuckling with the possibility that he might one day be lord of all this scene of almost unimaginable luxury and splendour. Then, he thought, how soon he'd turn his back upon the old school house; snap his fingers in the face of Hans Van Ripper, and every other niggardly patron, and kick any itinerant pedagogue out of doors that dared to call him comrade!

Old Baltus Van Tassel moved about among his guests with a face dilated with content and good humour, round and jolly as the harvest moon. His hospitable attentions were brief, but expressive, being confined to a shake of the hand, a slap on the shoulder, a loud laugh, and a pressing invitation to "reach to, and help themselves."

And now the sound of the music from the common room or hall, summoned to the dance. The musician was an old gray-headed negro, who had been the itinerant orchestra of the neighbourhood for more than half a century. His instrument was as old and battered as himself. The greater part of the time he scraped away on two or three strings, accompanying every movement of the bow with a motion of the head; bowing almost to the ground, and stamping with his foot whenever a fresh couple were to start.

Ichabod prided himself upon his dancing as much as upon his vocal powers. Not a limb, not a fibre about him was idle, and to have seen his loosely hung frame in full motion, and clattering about the room, you would have thought Saint Vitus himself, that blessed patron of the dance, was figuring before you in person. He was the admiration of all the negroes, who, having gathered, of all ages and sizes, from the farm and the neighbourhood, stood forming a pyramid of shining black faces at every door and window, gazing with delight at the scene, rolling their white eye balls, and showing grinning rows of ivory from ear to ear. How could the flogger of urchins be otherwise than animated and joyous; the lady of his heart was his partner in the dance; she smiled graciously in reply to all his amorous oglings, while Brom Bones, sorely smitten with love and jealousy, sat brooding by himself in one corner.

When the dance was at an end, Ichabod was attracted to a knot of the sager folks, who, with old Van Tassel, sat smoking at one end of the piazza, gossiping over former times, and drawling out long stories about the war.

This neighbourhood, at the time of which I am speaking, was one of those highly favoured places which abound with chronicle and great men. The British and American line had run near it during the war; it had, therefore, been the scene of marauding, and been infested with refugees, cow boys, and all kind of border chivalry. Just sufficient time had elapsed to enable each story teller to dress up his tale with a little becoming fiction, and in the indistinctness of his recollection, to make himself the hero of every exploit.

There was the story of Doffue Martling, a large, blue-bearded Dutchman, who had nearly taken a British frigate with an old iron nine-pounder from a mud breastwork, only that his gun burst at the sixth discharge. And there was an old gentleman who shall be nameless, being too rich a mynheer to be lightly mentioned, who in the battle of Whiteplains, being an excellent master of defence, parried a musket ball with a small sword, insomuch that he absolutely felt it whiz round the blade, and glance off at the hilt: in proof of which, he was ready at any time to show the sword, with the hilt a little bent. There were several more who had been equally great in the field, not one of whom but was persuaded that he had a considerable hand in bringing the war to a happy termination.

But all these were nothing to the tales of ghosts and apparitions that succeeded. The neighbourhood is rich in legendary treasures of the kind. Local tales and superstitions thrive best in these sheltered, long settled retreats; but they are trampled under foot, by the shifting throng that forms the population of most of our country places. Besides, there is not encouragement for ghosts in the generality of our villages, for they have scarce had time to take their first nap, and turn themselves in their graves, before their surviving friends have travelled away from the neighbourhood, so that when they turn out of a night to walk the rounds, they have no acquaintance left to call upon. This is perhaps the reason why we so seldom hear of ghosts excepting in our long-established Dutch communities.

The immediate cause, however, of the prevalence of supernatural stories in these parts, was doubtless owing to the vicinity of Sleepy Hollow. There was a contagion in the very air that blew from that haunted region; it breathed forth an atmosphere of dreams and fancies infecting all the land. Several of the Sleepy Hollow people were present at Van Tassel's, and, as usual, were doling out their wild and wonderful legends. Many dismal tales were told about funeral trains, and mournful cries and wailings heard and seen about the great tree where the unfortunate Major André was taken, and which stood in the neighbourhood. Some mention was made also of the woman in white, that haunted the dark glen at Raven Rock, and was often heard to shriek on winter nights before a storm, having perished there in the snow. The chief part of the stories, however, turned upon the favourite spectre of Sleepy Hollow, the headless horseman, who had been heard several times of late, patroling the country; and it was said, tethered his horse nightly among the graves in the church-yard.

The sequestered situation of this church seems always to have made it a favourite haunt of troubled spirits. It stands on a knoll, surrounded by locust trees and lofty elms, from among which its decent, whitewashed walls shine modestly forth, like Christian purity, beaming through the shades of retirement. A gentle slope descends from it to a silver sheet of water, bordered by high trees, between which, peeps may be caught at the blue hills of the Hudson. To look upon its grass-grown yard, where the sunbeams seem to sleep so quietly, one would think that here at least the dead might rest in peace. On one side of the church extends a wide woody dell, along which raves a large brook among broken rocks and trunks of fallen trees. Over a deep black part of the stream, not far from the church, was formerly thrown a wooden bridge; the road that led to it, and the bridge itself, were thickly shaded by overhanging trees, which cast a gloom about it, even in the day time; but occasioned a fearful darkness at night. Such was one of the favourite haunts of the headless horseman, and the place where he was most frequently encountered. The tale was told of old Brouwer, a most heretical disbeliever in ghosts, that he met the horseman returning from his foray into Sleepy Hollow, and was obliged to get up behind him; that they gallopped over bush and brake, over hill and swamp, until they reached the bridge, when the horseman suddenly turned into a skeleton, threw old Brouwer into the brook, and sprang away over the tree-tops with a clap of thunder.

This story was immediately matched by a thrice marvellous adventure of Brom Bones, who made light of the galloping Hessian as an errant jockey. He affirmed, that on returning one night from the neighbouring village of Sing-Sing, he had been overtaken by this midnight trooper; that he had offered to race with him for a bowl of punch, and would have won it too, for Daredevil beat the goblin horse all hollow, but just as they came to the church bridge, the Hessian bolted, and vanished in a flash of fire.

All these tales, told in that drowsy under tone with which men talk in the dark, the countenances of the listeners only now and then receiving a casual gleam from the glare of a pipe, sunk deep in the mind of Ichabod. He repaid them in kind with large extracts from his invaluable author, Cotton Mather, and added many very marvellous events that had taken place in his native state of Connecticut, and fearful sights which he had seen in his nightly walks about Sleepy Hollow.

The revel now gradually broke up. The old farmers gathered together their families in their wagons, and were heard for some time rattling along the hollow roads, and over the distant hills. Some of the damsels, mounted on pillions behind their favourite swains, and their light-hearted laughter mingling with the clatter of hoofs, echoed along the silent woodlands, sounding fainter and fainter until they gradually died away—and the late scene of noise and frolick was all silent and deserted. Ichabod only lingered behind, according to the custom of country lovers, to have a tête-a-tête with the heiress; fully convinced that he was now on the high road to success. What passed at this interview I will not pretend to say, for in fact I do not know. Something, however, I fear me, must have gone wrong, for he certainly sallied forth, after no very great interval, with an air quite desolate and chopfallen—Oh these women! these women! Could that girl have been playing off any of her coquettish tricks?—Was her encouragement of the poor pedagogue all a mere sham to secure her conquest of his rival?—Heaven only knows, not I!—Let it suffice to say, Ichabod stole forth with the air of one who had been sacking a hen roost, rather than a fair lady's heart. Without looking to the right or left to notice the scene of rural wealth, on which he had so often gloated, he went straight to the stable, and with several hearty cuffs and kicks, roused his steed most uncourteously from the comfortable quarters in which he was soundly sleeping, dreaming of mountains of corn and oats, and whole valleys of timothy and clover.

It was the very witching time of night that Ichabod, heavy-hearted and bedrooped, pursued his travel homewards, along the sides of the lofty hills which rise above Tarry Town, and which he had traversed so cheerily in the afternoon. The hour was as dismal as himself. Far below him the Tappaan Zee spread its dusky and indistinct waste of waters, with here and there the tall mast of a sloop, riding quietly at anchor under the land. In the dead hush of midnight, he could even hear the barking of the watch-dog from the opposite shore of the Hudson; but it was so vague and faint as only to give an idea of his distance from this faithful companion of man. Now and then, too, the long-drawn crowing of a cock, accidentally awakened, would sound far, far off, from some farm house away among the hills—but it was like a dreaming sound in his ear. No signs of life occurred near him, but occasionally the melancholy chirp of a cricket, or perhaps the guttural twang of a bull frog, from a neighbouring marsh, as if sleeping uncomfortably, and turning suddenly in his bed.

All the stories of ghosts and goblins that Ichabod had heard in the afternoon, now came crowding upon his recollection. The night grew darker and darker; the stars seemed to sink deeper in the sky, and driving clouds occasionally hid them from his sight. He had never felt so lonely and dismal. He was, moreover, approaching the very place where many of the scenes of the ghost stories had been laid. In the centre of the road stood an enormous tulip tree, which towered like a giant above all the other trees of the neighbourhood, and formed a kind of land-mark. Its limbs were vast, gnarled, and fantastic, twisting down almost to the earth, and rising again into the air, and they would have formed trunks for ordinary trees. It was connected with the tragical story of the unfortunate André, who had been taken prisoner hard by it, and it was universally known by the name of Major André's tree. The common people regarded it with a mixture of respect and superstition, partly out of sympathy for the memory of its ill-starred namesake, and partly from the tales, strange sights, and doleful lamentations, told concerning it.

As Ichabod approached this fearful tree, he began to whistle; he thought his whistle was answered: it was but a blast sweeping sharply through the dry branches. As he approached a little nearer, he thought he saw something white, hanging in the midst of the tree: he paused and ceased whistling; but on looking more narrowly, perceived that it was a place where the tree had been scathed by lightning, and the white wood laid bare. Suddenly he heard a groan—his teeth chattered, and his knees smote against the saddle: it was but the rubbing of one huge bough upon another, as they were swayed about by the breeze. He passed the tree in safety, but new perils lay still before him.

About two hundred yards from the tree, a small brook crossed the road, and ran into a marshy and thickly wooded glen, known by the name of Wiley's Swamp. A few rough logs, laid side by side, served for a bridge over this stream. On that side of the road where the brook entered the wood, a group of oaks and chestnuts, matted thick with wild grape vines, threw a cavernous gloom over it. To pass this bridge, was the severest trial. It was at this identical spot that the unfortunate André was captured, and under the covert of those chestnuts and vines were the sturdy yeomen concealed who surprised him. This has ever since been considered a haunted stream, and fearful are the feelings of the schoolboy who has to pass it alone after dark.

As he approached the stream, his heart began to thump; he, however, summoned up all his resolution, gave his horse half a score of kicks in the ribs, and attempted to dash briskly across the bridge; but instead of starting forward, the perverse old animal made a lateral movement, and ran broadside against the fence. Ichabod, whose fears increased with the delay, jerked the reins on the other side, and kicked lustily with the contrary foot: it was all in vain; his steed started, it is true, but it was only to plunge to the opposite side of the road into a thicket of brambles and alder bushes. The schoolmaster now bestowed both whip and heel upon the starvelling ribs of old Gunpowder, who dashed forward, snuffling and snorting, but came to a stand just by the bridge with a suddenness that had nearly sent his rider sprawling over his head. Just at this moment a plashy tramp by the side of the bridge caught the sensitive ear of Ichabod. In the dark shadow of the grove, on the margin of the brook, he beheld something huge, misshapen, black and towering. It stirred not, but seemed gathered up in the gloom, like some gigantic monster ready to spring upon the traveller.

The hair of the affrighted pedagogue rose upon his head with terror. What was to be done? To turn and fly was now too late; and besides, what chance was there of escaping ghost or goblin, if such it was, which can ride upon the wings of the wind? Summoning up, therefore, a show of courage, he demanded in stammering accents— "Who are you?" He received no reply. He repeated his demand in a still more agitated voice.—Still there was no answer. Once more he cudgelled the sides of the inflexible Gunpowder, and shutting his eyes, broke forth with involuntary fervour into a psalm tune. Just then the shadowy object of alarm put itself in motion, and with a scramble and a bound, stood at once in the middle of the road. Though the night was dark and dismal, yet the form of the unknown might now in some degree be ascertained. He appeared to be a horseman of large dimensions, and mounted on a black horse of powerful frame. He made no offer of molestation or sociability, but kept aloof on one side of the road, jogging along the blind side of old Gunpowder, who had now got over his fright and waywardness.

Ichabod, who had no relish for this strange midnight companion, and bethought himself of the adventure of Brom Bones with the galloping Hessian, now quickened his steed, in hopes of leaving him behind. The stranger, however, quickened his horse to an equal pace; Ichabod pulled up, and fell into a walk, thinking to lag behind—the other did the same. His heart began to sink within him; he endeavoured to resume his psalm tune, but his parched tongue clove to the roof of his mouth, and he could not utter a stave. There was something in the moody and dogged silence of this pertinacious companion, that was mysterious and appalling. It was soon fearfully accounted for. On mounting a rising round, which brought the figure of his fellow traveller in relief against the sky, gigantic in height, and muffled in a cloak, Ichabod was horror-struck, on perceiving that he was headless! but his horror was still more increased, on observing that the head, which should have rested on his shoulders, was carried before him on the pommel of the saddle! His terror rose to desperation; he rained a shower of kicks and blows upon Gunpowder, hoping by a sudden movement, to give his companion the slip—but the spectre started full jump with him. Away, then, they dashed, through thick and thin; stones flying, and sparks flashing, at every bound. Ichabod's flimsy garments fluttered in the air, as he stretched his long lank body away over his horse's head, in the eagerness of his flight.

They had now reached the road which turns off to Sleepy Hollow; but Gunpowder, who seemed possessed with a demon, instead of keeping up it, made an opposite turn, and plunged headlong down hill to the left. This road leads through a sandy hollow shaded by trees for about a quarter of a mile, where it crosses the bridge famous in goblin story, and just beyond swells the green knoll on which stands the whitewashed church.

As yet the panic of the steed had given his unskilful rider an apparent advantage in the chace, but just as he had got halfway through the hollow, the girths of the saddle gave way, and he felt it slipping from under him; he seized it by the pommel, and endeavoured to hold it firm, but in vain; and had just time to save himself by clasping old Gunpowder round the neck, when the saddle fell to the earth, and he heard it trampled under foot by his pursuer. For a moment the terror of Hans Van Ripper's wrath passed across his mind—for it was his Sunday saddle; but this was no time for petty fears: the goblin was hard on his haunches; and, unskilful rider that he was! he had much-ado to maintain his seat; sometimes slipping on one side, sometimes on another, and sometimes jolted on the high ridge of his horse's back bone, with a violence that he verily feared would cleave him asunder.

An opening in the trees now cheered him with the hopes that the Church Bridge was at hand. The wavering reflection of a silver star in the bosom of the brook told him that he was not mistaken. He saw the walls of the church dimly glaring under the trees beyond. He recollected the place where Brom Bones' ghostly competitor had disappeared. "If I can but reach that bridge," thought Ichabod, "I am safe." Just then he heard the black steed panting and blowing close behind him; he fancied he felt his hot breath. Another convulsive kick in the ribs, and old Gunpowder sprung upon the bridge; he thundered over the resounding planks; he gained the opposite side, and now Ichabod cast a look behind to see if his pursuer should vanish, according to rule, in a flash of fire and brimstone. Just then he saw the goblin rising in his stirrups, and in the very act of hurling his head at him. Ichabod endeavoured to dodge the horrible missile, but too late. It encountered his cranium with a tremendous crash—he was tumbled headlong into the dust, and Gunpowder, the black steed, and the goblin rider, passed by like a whirlwind.—

The next morning the old horse was found without his saddle, and the bridle under his feet, soberly cropping the grass at his master's gate. Ichabod did not make his appearance at breakfast—dinner-hour came, but no Ichabod. The boys assembled at the school-house, and strolled idly about the banks of the brook; but no schoolmaster. Hans Van Ripper now began to feel some uneasiness about the fate of poor Ichabod, and his saddle. An inquiry was set on foot, and after diligent investigation they came upon his traces. In one part of the road leading to the church, was found the saddle trampled in the dirt, the tracks of horses' hoofs deeply dented in the road, and evidently at furious speed, were traced to the bridge, beyond which, on the bank of a broad part of the brook, where the water ran deep and black, was found the hat of the unfortunate Ichabod, and close beside it a shattered pumpkin.

The brook was searched, but the body of the schoolmaster was not to be discovered. Hans Van Ripper, as executor of his estate, examined the bundle which contained all his worldly effects. They consisted of two old shirts and a half; two stocks for the neck; a pair of worsted stockings with holes in them; an old pair of corduroy small-clothes; a book of psalm tunes full of dog's ears; a pitch pipe out of order; a rusty razor; a small pot of bear's grease for the hair, and a cast-iron comb. As to the books and furniture of the schoolhouse, they belonged to the community, excepting Cotton Mather's History of Witchcraft, a New-England Almanack, and a book of dreams and fortune telling, in which last was a sheet of foolscap much scribbled and blotted, by several fruitless attempts to make a copy of verses in honour of the heiress of Van Tassel. These magic books and the poetic scrawl were forthwith consigned to the flames by Hans Van Ripper, who from that time forward determined to send his children no more to school, observing, that he never knew any good come of this same reading and writing. Whatever money the schoolmaster possessed, and he had received his quarter's pay but a day or two before, he must have had about his person at the time of his disappearance.

The mysterious event caused much speculation at the church on the following Sunday. Knots of gazers and gossips were collected in the church-yard, at the bridge, and at the spot where the hat and pumpkin had been found. The stories of Brouwer, of Bones, and a whole budget of others, were called to mind; and when they had diligently considered them all, and compared them with the symptoms of the present case, they shook their heads, and came to the conclusion, that Ichabod had been carried off by the gallopping Hessian. As he was a bachelor, and in nobody's debt, nobody troubled his head any more about him; the school was removed to a different quarter of the hollow, and another pedagogue reigned in his stead.

It is true, an old farmer, who had been down to New-York on a visit several years after, and from whom this account of the ghostly adventure was received, brought home the intelligence that Ichabod Crane was still alive; that he had left the neighbourhood partly through fear of the goblin and Hans Van Ripper, and partly in mortification at having been suddenly dismissed by the heiress; that he had changed his quarters to a distant part of the country; had kept school and studied law at the same time; had been admitted to the bar, turned politician, electioneered, written for the newspapers, and finally had been a Justice of the Ten Pound Court. Brom Bones too, who, shortly after his rival's disappearance, conducted the blooming Katrina in triumph to the altar, was observed to look exceedingly knowing whenever the story of Ichabod was related, and always burst into a hearty laugh at the mention of the pumpkin; which led some to suspect that he knew more about the matter than he chose to tell.

The old country wives, however, who are the best judges of these matters, maintain to this day, that Ichabod was spirited away by supernatural means; and it is a favourite story often told about the neighbourhood round the winter evening fire. The bridge became more than ever an object of superstitious awe; and that may be the reason why the road has been altered of late years, so as to approach the church by the border of the millpond. The schoolhouse being deserted, soon fell to decay, and was reported to be haunted by the ghosts of the unfortunate pedagogue; and the plough boy, loitering homeward of a still summer evening, has often fancied his voice at a distance, chanting a melancholy psalm tune among the tranquil solitudes of Sleepy Hollow.

Postscript

FOUND IN THE HANDWRITING
OF MR. KNICKERBOCKER

The preceding Tale is given, almost in the precise words in which I heard it related at a corporation meeting of the ancient city of the Manhattoes, at which were present many of its sagest and most illustrious burghers. The narrator was a pleasant, shabby, gentlemanly old fellow, in pepper and salt clothes, with a sadly humourous face, and one whom I strongly suspected of being poor, he made such efforts to be entertaining. When his story was concluded, there was much laughter and approbation, particularly from two or three deputy aldermen, who had been asleep the greater part of the time. There was, however, one tall, dry-looking old gentleman, with beetling eyebrows, who maintained a grave and rather severe face throughout; now and then folding his arms, inclining his head, and looking down upon the floor, as if turning a doubt over in his mind. He was one of your wary men, who never laugh but upon good grounds—when they have reason and law on their side. When the mirth of the rest of the company had subsided, and silence was restored, he leaned one arm on the elbow of his chair, and sticking the other a-kimbo, demanded, with a slight, but exceedingly sage motion of the head, and contraction of the brow, what was the moral of the story, and what it went to prove.

The story-teller, who was just putting a glass of wine to his lips, as a refreshment after his toils, paused for a moment, looked at his inquirer with an air of infinite deference, and lowering the glass slowly to the table, observed, that the story was intended most logically to prove,

"That there is no situation in life but has its advantages and pleasures, provided we will but take a joke as we find it:

"That, therefore, he that runs races with goblin troopers, is likely to have a rough riding of it:

"Ergo, for a country schoolmaster to be refused the hand of a Dutch heiress, is a certain step to high preferment in the state."

The cautious old gentleman knit his brows tenfold closer after this explanation, being sorely puzzled by the ratiocination of the syllogism; while methought the one in pepper and salt eyed him with something of a triumphant leer. At length he observed, that all this was very well, but still he thought the story a little on the extravagant—there were one or two points on which he had his doubts.

"Faith, sir," replied the story-teller, "as to that matter, I don't believe one half of it myself."

D.K.

PENGUIN 60s

are published on the occasion of Penguin's 60th anniversary

LOUISA MAY ALCOTT · *An Old-Fashioned Thanksgiving and Other Stories*

HANS CHRISTIAN ANDERSEN · *The Emperor's New Clothes*

J. M. BARRIE · *Peter Pan in Kensington Gardens*

WILLIAM BLAKE · *Songs of Innocence and Experience*

GEOFFREY CHAUCER · *The Wife of Bath and Other Canterbury Tales*

ANTON CHEKHOV · *The Black Monk* and *Peasants*

SAMUEL TAYLOR COLERIDGE · *The Rime of the Ancient Mariner*

COLETTE · *Gigi*

JOSEPH CONRAD · *Youth*

ROALD DAHL · *Lamb to the Slaughter and Other Stories*

ROBERTSON DAVIES · *A Gathering of Ghost Stories*

FYODOR DOSTOYEVSKY · *The Grand Inquisitor*

SIR ARTHUR CONAN DOYLE · *The Man with the Twisted Lip*
    and *The Adventure of the Devil's Foot*

RALPH WALDO EMERSON · *Nature*

OMER ENGLEBERT (TRANS.) · *The Lives of the Saints*

FANNIE FARMER · *The Original 1896 Boston Cooking-School Cook Book*

EDWARD FITZGERALD (TRANS.) · *The Rubáiyát of Omar Khayyám*

ROBERT FROST · *The Road Not Taken and Other Early Poems*

GABRIEL GARCÍA MÁRQUEZ · *Bon Voyage, Mr President and Other Stories*

NIKOLAI GOGOL · *The Overcoat* and *The Nose*

GRAHAM GREENE · *Under the Garden*

JACOB AND WILHELM GRIMM · *Grimm's Fairy Tales*

NATHANIEL HAWTHORNE · *Young Goodman Brown and Other Stories*

O. HENRY · *The Gift of the Magi and Other Stories*

WASHINGTON IRVING · *Rip Van Winkle* and *The Legend of Sleepy Hollow*

HENRY JAMES · *Daisy Miller*

V. S. VERNON JONES (TRANS.) · *Aesop's Fables*

JAMES JOYCE · *The Dead*

GARRISON KEILLOR · *Truckstop and Other Lake Wobegon Stories*

JACK KEROUAC · *San Francisco Blues*

STEPHEN KING · *Umney's Last Case*

RUDYARD KIPLING · *Baa Baa, Black Sheep* and *The Gardener*

LAO TZU · *Tao Te Ching*

D. H. LAWRENCE · *Love Among the Haystacks*

ABRAHAM LINCOLN · *The Gettysburg Address and Other Speeches*

JACK LONDON · *To Build a Fire and Other Stories*

HERMAN MELVILLE · *Bartleby* and *The Lightning-rod Man*

A. A. MILNE · *Winnie-the-Pooh and His Friends*

MICHIEL DE MONTAIGNE · *Four Essays*

JOHN MORTIMER · *Rumpole and the Younger Generation*

THOMAS PAINE · *The Crisis*

DOROTHY PARKER · *Big Blonde and Other Stories*

EDGAR ALLAN POE · *The Pit and the Pendulum and Other Stories*

EDGAR ALLAN POE, AMBROSE BIERCE,
    AND ROBERT LOUIS STEVENSON · *Three Tales of Horror*

FRANKLIN DELANO ROOSEVELT · *Fireside Chats*

WILLIAM SHAKESPEARE · *Sixty Sonnets*

JOHN STEINBECK · *The Chrysanthemums and Other Stories*

PETER STRAUB · *Blue Rose*

PAUL THEROUX · *The Greenest Island*

HENRY DAVID THOREAU · *Walking*

JOHN THORN · *Baseball: Our Game*

LEO TOLSTOY · *Master and Man*

MARK TWAIN · *The Notorious Jumping Frog of Calaveras County*

H. G. WELLS · *The Time Machine*

EDITH WHARTON · *Madame de Treymes*

OSCAR WILDE · *The Happy Prince and Other Stories*

The Declaration of Independence and *The Constitution of the United States*

Mother Goose

The Revelation of St. John the Divine

Teachings of Jesus

FOR THE BEST IN PAPERBACKS, LOOK FOR THE

In every corner of the world, on every subject under the sun, Penguin represents quality and variety—the very best in publishing today.

For complete information about books available from Penguin—including Puffins, Penguin Classics, and Arkana—and how to order them, write to us at the appropriate address below. Please note that for copyright reasons the selection of books varies from country to country.

In the United States: Please write to *Consumer Sales, Penguin USA, P.O. Box 999, Dept. 17109, Bergenfield, New Jersey 07621-0120.* Visa and MasterCard holders call 1-800-253-6476 to order all Penguin titles.

In Canada: Please write to *Penguin Books Canada Ltd, 10 Alcorn Avenue, Suite 300, Toronto, Ontario M4V 3B2.*

In the United Kingdom: Please write to *Dept. JC, Penguin Books Ltd, FREEPOST, West Drayton, Middlesex UB7 OBR.*

TRICKLE DOWN TYRRANY

ALSO BY MICHAEL SAVAGE

ABUSE

OF

POWER

MICHAEL SAVAGE

St. Martin's Paperbacks

This is a work of fiction. All of the characters, organizations, and events portrayed in this novel are either products of the author's imagination or are used fictitiously.

ABUSE OF POWER

Copyright © 2011 by Michael Savage.
Excerpt from *Betrayal of Trust* copyright © 2012 by Michael Savage.

All rights reserved.

For information address St. Martin's Press, 175 Fifth Avenue, New York, NY 10010.

Library of Congress Catalog Card Number: 2011019505

ISBN: 978-0-312-55301-2

Printed in the United States of America

St. Martin's Press hardcover edition / September 2011
St. Martin's Paperbacks edition / June 2012

St. Martin's Paperbacks are published by St. Martin's Press, 175 Fifth Avenue, New York, NY 10010.

10 9 8 7 6 5 4 3 2 1

Extremism in the defense of liberty is no vice!
Moderation in the pursuit of justice is no virtue!
—Barry Goldwater, 1964

Prologue

If the others knew what Abdal al-Fida was up to, they would kill him. Not fast, not pleasantly, and not just to make him suffer. These people killed the way others tweeted, to let people know they weren't happy. To discourage dissent.

To them he was simply a foot soldier, an expendable observer sent out to study the enemy, report, and await further instructions. Any deviation from that would be met with swift and brutal punishment.

But after three long weeks sitting in a cramped office cubicle doing routine computer repairs, Abdal was tired of waiting, tired of hoping the phone would ring. His beard was growing longer as the others busied themselves with endless debates and hand-wringing and second-guessing.

It's all in the hands of Allah anyway, he thought. *Why not be bold and trust in Him?*

He didn't want to believe it was a lack of nerve. That would be too discouraging. To have committed his life and energy to a cause, only to find out he was alone—

I refuse to believe that. But the thought was equally stubborn.

His mother once told him that he came into this world a squawking bird, violently flapping his spindly little wings as if his cage were too small to contain him. Maybe that was Allah sending a message as well, for he was no different now.

Abdal's faith in Allah's plan was absolute, and that was what gave him the courage to undertake what he was doing now. After that, proactivity became its own motor. Actions drove other actions and soon there was no changing course, no *desire* to reverse direction.

What would he tell them later? That contacting someone he knew here in America—someone who was well connected with the black market and was far under the radar—he had used his own money to procure the things he needed.

Building the device, as he'd been trained to do, had been simple. He was afraid he'd forget steps, have to improvise, but once he was focused everything came back to him. It was all he could do to keep his fingers from trembling with excitement as he dismantled the disposable cell phone he'd bought at a nearby Walgreens. He laid out the components, rewired connections, recalled with an almost rhapsodic joy the tart smell of the solder as he worked—

And as he sat in his small apartment he thought of Sara. He wondered if he should call her.

While he had no intention of taking his own life—unlike so many of his naïve brethren he was in no hurry to get to Paradise—he was aware that he might not survive the week. The only thing certain in war was that nothing was certain.

He smiled as he thought of the girl he had managed to grow so fond of. Not that he'd fought it. Every soldier needs a distraction, and they didn't come prettier than this one. But then something happened. It wasn't even part of his cover, an effort to blend in; it was genuine. Surprisingly, unexpectedly real. So real that he had broken other rules, had told her who he was and what he was about. She already knew what had happened to his family before he relocated from Karachi, and she understood the rage he carried with him every single moment of his life. Maybe that was one of the things he found so attractive: Sara shared much of that rage herself.

In the end, he decided it was best not to call her. Not until the deed was done. Not until she couldn't do the one thing no one else on earth could possibly have done: talk him out of giving San Francisco its very own ground zero.

PART ONE

Ride-Along

1

San Francisco, California

"Pump two," Leon said. "See it?"

"I see it," Jamal Thomas replied.

It was just after sunset and the battered old Camry was parked down the block from the Arco station on Mission Street. Jamal squinted through the dirty windshield at a shiny gray Land Rover that had just pulled up to the pumps. The driver had climbed out and crossed to the minimart, wallet in hand. Arab, from the look of him. Not just the skin color but the arrogance, the strut. He reminded Jamal of the movies he'd seen on YouTube of blacks in the 1960s, flexing their new legal rights, amped up by the power of numbers, ready for payback after centuries of being second-class.

"Why that one?" Jamal asked. "Why not a Benz or a Beamer?"

Leon shot him a frown. "This ain't *about* the car. It's about—"

"I know what it's about," Jamal said. "But we might as well wait for a sweeter ride."

Leon shook his head. Jamal continued to look out the window.

What this was about was Jamal and Leon trying to get the rest of the Sawyer Street crew to take Jamal seriously. Jamal was almost seventeen and even his brother, who was just three years older, still treated him like a wannabe. He'd spent two years selling apple jacks at school, but that wasn't good enough for them. It was time to prove himself. Show them he had a pair that clanged.

Jamal's hand was resting on his waistband, where he'd tucked the gun. Leon had given him a Glock 9mm for his birthday the week before, a bronze-colored beauty that came in a shipment smuggled from Vietnam, part of the old Ku gunrunning network. The weapon felt solid against Jamal's belly— not the weight of it but the coiled power, the right it gave him to enforce his will on some rich boy or a chump who looked at him funny or a blonde he just wanted because he wanted *that blonde*.

"Like a terrorist, man," Jamal said softly.

"What are you talkin' about *now*?"

"I was just thinkin' about how those guys feel when they *know* somethin' big is going down while everybody else worries about their own shit. That's got to be some heavy power trip."

"Yeah, well, you only have to worry about that Land Rover and not some damn 9/11."

"I'm on that," Jamal said. "Just sayin'."

Jamal was getting excited. Leon was right, but if power was the lesson of jacking a random car, he was ready to learn it.

They watched the Arab pump his gas, then get in and start the engine. The swarthy man fussed with the side-view mirror, adjusting it this way and that, then grabbed the wheel and rolled toward the exit.

Leon popped his transmission into gear, glanced at Jamal. "You ready?"

"I'm ready."

Leon shifted his foot from the brake to the accelerator and eased after the Land Rover.

They followed the Rover straight to the Loin—the part of the city that had long ago given itself over to liquor stores and strip clubs, where anything and everything was bought and sold, twenty-four/seven.

Jamal wondered what a well-off Arab was doing down here. If he was looking for action, all he had to do was pick up the phone. He didn't have to cruise through wine country. Maybe he had holdings here, invested some of that oil money in hookers and crack dealers.

An' the government tells us businessmen are responsible for everything that's wrong, he thought.

"Next red light," Leon said.

Leon's voice was soft, steady. It pumped Jamal up, like the gun. He wanted to impress his brother, win his respect.

A few seconds later the car came to a stop at Eddy and Larkin. The red light burned like the devil's own eye, fueling Jamal's own sudden, intense focus on the moment, the gun, the target—

"Go!"

Leon's voice broke through the near-hypnotic state. Jamal didn't think. He pushed open the door and jumped out, ripping the Glock from his waistband as he went, holding it against the driver's window, shouting, "Out of the car!"

The light turned and Leon roared past them, the Camry's tires shedding rubber. The Arab looked at the gun in horrified disbelief. Jamal slammed the window with the heel of his other hand, angled the gun menacingly.

"I said *out*! Do it *now* or you're a dead man!"

The Arab popped the lock and opened the door. He seemed resigned to losing his car. Jamal stepped back to let him out. Cars were beginning to pile up behind them. Jamal turned slightly so they wouldn't have a good look at his face.

"Don't shoot!" the Arab pleaded. "Take the car but don't kill me!"

"Shut up!" Jamal snarled as he drew back his arm and pistol-whipped the Arab.

The man fell to the asphalt, his arms fluttering like bird wings, his white button-down shirt a coat of feathers. *The Arab wasn't so tough now,* Jamal thought, *however much money he might have.* The young man sighted the gun on the man's forehead, above his big, frightened eyes.

Jamal heard more horns as well as people shouting. He should have just shot him—no talk, no knock-down, no *thinking.* Now, too many people were watching. He heard a siren in the distance. Maybe it wasn't for him, or maybe someone had already called the cops—

Jamal looked up the road, saw the Camry had pulled into an empty space curbside. It was too far to run. And he didn't want to leave empty-handed.

Okay, you didn't kill the guy but you can bounce with the car. He could still score points by leading the cops to the Embarcadero and putting the Rover in the bay, or maybe driving it into the hot new lounge of the Phoenix Hotel—

Shoving the gun back in his waistband, Jamal jumped into the Rover, slammed the door, and stomped on the gas. He shot through the intersection, unaware that the light had changed back, clipping a Prius and spinning it ninety degrees. Jamal caromed off into a double-parked yellow panel job with the words WONDER BREAD painted across the side. He saw the *R* and the *B* grow large and then the world got very loud as the sound of the impact, the screech of twisting metal, and Jamal's own scream blended into a single roar. He felt himself flying against the wind-shield as the rear end of the Rover went airborne and the thing flipped.

Jamal threw his hands out, felt his arms go through the suddenly liquid glass, felt countless pinpricks as the shards raked his hands and face and scalp. It seemed to take forever for the Rover to crash to the ground and everything to go still. In the cottony quiet that followed, all Jamal could hear was his own strained, wheezing breath and the throbbing blood in his ears. He was lying on his back, half out of the Rover, his head resting on the blacktop. He was looking back toward the front seat, which was upside down. Peripherally, he could see people ducking, shifting, reaching into the tangled metal that shielded him from the outside world. He couldn't move his head, couldn't feel his body, so he continued to stare ahead.

There was blood in his right eye. It swirled the driver's side in a ruddy haze, but his left eye was clear. That was how he saw the strange object that had been upended and was resting on the roof. It consisted of four . . . five . . . six two-liter bottles full of liquid and tied to one another with duct tape. They were anchored to a pair of propane tanks with more tape. Wires were strung from one of the tanks to a cell phone taped to its side.

A bomb. It was a *bomb*.

2

"You feel it?" Drabinsky asked. "The rush?"

Freelance TV producer Jack Hatfield barely heard
the man. As they blasted toward the crime scene, the
former firebrand talk show host—defrocked by a
fearful, powerful few—found himself thinking about
those long-ago days in Baghdad, days that were little
more than a distant wash of sounds and images. All
he really had left of the place was the shrapnel in his
right thigh and an instinctive reaction, a gut-tensing
alertness, to any sign or image that had Arabic or
Kurdish writing.

"I feel it," Jack said in a dry monotone. It reeked of
insincerity but Drabinsky didn't seem to notice. He
was in the moment, psyched and impatient. Jack understood; these were the times they'd trained for. For
Drabinsky, it was a chance to test himself. For Jack it
was part of a larger, frustrating picture of bailing

water instead of being able to get to the source and stop the damn flood.

They were barreling along Mission Street in a white Chevy Tahoe, the siren blaring, Officer Tom Drabinsky at the wheel—a lean cowboy with a leathery, sunbaked face.

Drabinsky was commander of the SFPD bomb squad, part of the city's Homeland Security Tactical Company, and Jack had been profiling the squad for nearly a week now. His time with them had been pretty uneventful so far—mostly interviews, each member of the team recounting past glories and talking him through the "what-if . . ." white papers they had studied.

"They're kind of like role-playing games, y'know?" one man had told him about those scenarios. *"They let you think about problems you might encounter and solve them before you have to."*

Sure, Jack thought. As long as you don't factor in the stuff that hits you square in the face when you're in the field: fear, pressure, the media watching you, and the fact that at the very least your job is on the line, at the most your life. . . .

Then just before dinner, Jack was putting together footage for the local CBS affiliate, something to help make the public aware of its role in watching and informing, when he got the call telling him it was time to saddle up.

"We're on," Drabinsky had said. "Where are you?"

Jack's heart had kicked up a notch. "At the marina, editing footage."

"A little out of my way but I don't want you to miss this. Be at the lot in twenty."

After he hung up, Jack immediately contacted his photographer Maxine and told her to meet them at the accident scene.

As Drabinsky maneuvered impatiently through traffic, Jack's mind went back to the first time he had been rushing somewhere, that morning in Baghdad when everything went wrong.

He was remembering Riley's face.

He saw that face in his sleep sometimes. The slack jaw, the glazed eyes, the dust-caked laugh lines around them. A dust that could neither be tamed nor conquered and had permeated every facet of their lives back then—two hotshot network news monkeys riding shotgun with the Second Marine Division, Riley always complaining that the desert was wreaking havoc on his video equipment.

Not that it mattered much.

Richard Edward Riley had the tragic distinction of being the second journalist killed during the early days of Operation Iraqi Freedom, and Jack had been right there when it happened. He could just as easily have been the third. One minute they were bumping along a deserted road and the next they were on the ground bleeding, their Humvee in pieces around them, Jack staring into the open, lifeless eyes of his best friend.

The details remained hazy, defensively isolated and contained by his mind, leaving the event with as much clarity as a half-remembered dream. Only the emotional and psychological pain were clear. Maybe that's why his mind occasionally returned to it for no apparent reason, with no apparent trigger. It was his subconscious trying to remember, trying to hide the hurt among some cold facts. Like putting ice on a swollen eye.

Of course, the company he was keeping could have something to do with it. Drabinsky's go-get-'em attitude reminded him of the marines who died that day. Tough, dedicated, counterintuitively marching into hell. Only the uniform was different. The SFPD bomb squad was full of that kind of men and women, the ones willing to risk their lives to keep Americans safe. And the people of San Francisco needed to know just how courageous they truly were. Instead, the rabid left wing harassed him endlessly.

Maybe they'd find out tonight. It was just too bad that a journalist's dream was often indistinguishable from the stuff that nightmares were made of.

"You alive over there?"

Jack smiled. "Sorry, Tom. I was off in the woods."

"Hunter or stag?"

"Hah. Good question."

"Well, come back home, Jack. We've gotta stay focused, top of our game. If something goes wrong, you need to know right away."

"Why? You ever see anyone outrun an explosion?"

"Of course not," Drabinsky said. "The survivors are the ones who smell things *before* they go bad. Any dope can run when it's too late."

Jack nodded. The commander wasn't talking out of

his ass. In his nearly forty years, he had known soldiers, cops, pilots who had the Spidey sense he was
talking about, an instinct for things that were slightly
off center. During a visit to southern China, Jack had
seen a demonstration in which a blindfolded Shaolin
kung fu master defeated two much younger men because he *felt* what they were about to do. When Jack
asked the sensei, through an interpreter, how he did
that, the man replied with a smile, "The gray hair."

Experience. There was nothing like it.

As Drabinsky pulled up to the nearest barricade, Jack
raised the Steiner Marine Binoculars he'd brought. It
was an ugly, surreal, yet strangely tranquil sight.

Big flatbed-mounted spotlights towered twenty feet
on either end of the street and illuminated the scene.
The bread truck lay angled toward the sidewalk. It
rested against a streetlight, half of one of its panels
caved in. Bisecting it was an overturned Land Rover,
its roof crumpled under its weight.

The street was empty, the cops maintaining a
by-the-book two-block radius from the site. All the
buildings and stores in a one-block radius had been
evacuated, though most were empty already due to
the hour.

Twenty-seven-year-old Maxine Cole showed up
while her boss was still studying the scene. Her press
pass was swung onto her back—where the camera
wouldn't hide it—and her video camera was already
hoisted onto a shoulder, floodlight on. Of Somali descent, she was a tall, city-born triathlete and one of

the best hose-n-go shooters Jack had ever known. She wet-kissed everything with her camera, missed nothing, and made editing a breeze.

"Sorry I'm late," she said. "Cops at the outside barrier didn't want to let me through. I tried calling you but couldn't get a signal."

Jack lowered the field glasses. "They've activated a cell phone jammer. Standard precaution."

"Oh. Right. Duh," she said as she shot.

Jack gestured toward the overturned vehicles nearly a block away. "The money shot is at the rear of that Land Rover. Can you manage it?"

"Not from this angle."

He turned to Drabinsky. "Can we go closer?"

"Only if you're suicidal. We're sending in the BDR."

As if on cue, the rear doors of a newly arrived van flew open and one of Drabinsky's men climbed out, put down a ramp, and started playing with the joystick in his hands. Jack saw a bright white light, heard a soft electronic whir as the bomb disposal robot glided out of the van and down the ramp toward the blacktop, looking like a RoboCop prototype on steroids.

Max got some footage of it making its descent. "So what's the story here? Somebody said something about a carjacking."

"Carjacking that went a little south," Jack told her.

"The perp?"

"Some fool EMTs went in and got him," Drabinsky said. He had been pacing back and forth, eyeball-

ing the crash. "They've got him at General. I don't
know anything else. One of the medics also tried to
pull the tag number off the Rover, but it was buried in
the bread truck."

"They get anything at all from the car?" Max
asked. Her questions weren't just for her own information; she was running sound and the bites were
often invaluable.

"You mean about the owner?" Drabinsky asked.

"That—or anything else."

He shrugged. "If they have, no one's told me. We're
just the garbage collectors. Last to know unless it
blows, as we say."

"Charming," Max said.

Drabinsky gestured to a portable computer stand
where a laptop had been set up. They walked over,
Max following everything through the eye of her
camera. The screen showed the view from a small
video camera mounted on the robot.

"We use the robot to tell us what we're up against.
If it's the real deal, we either blow it or I go in with
the suit to disarm the thing."

"What's the deciding factor?"

"Size. We'd just as soon not take out half a city
block if we can help it. If that thing is too big to blow,
I have to break out my suit and get all *Hurt Locker*
on it."

Jack watched the bot—the remote-controlled
robot—as it arced around and headed down the street,
Max videotaping its progress. It moved at a leisurely
pace, traveling about a block and a half before it came

to a stop two feet away from the rear of the Land
Rover. Jack glanced at the computer screen as the
joystick operator adjusted the angle and focus, zero-
ing in on the two-liter bottles—which, it was quickly
determined, were only the detonator. Under the upended dashboard were several bricks of plastic explosives, neatly bound together by det cord and at least
half a dozen detonators.

Jack's heart started to thump. This wasn't one of
the rusted-out IEDs the Explosive Ordnance Disposal units back in Iraq were tasked to deal with—
the kind that had derailed Jack's Humvee. This was
military-grade C4 that looked as if it had come fresh
out of the box.

Drabinsky said to his crew, "We got an eight-
hundred-pound gorilla, boys. No avoiding it. Time
to break out the demon."

"You're going in?" Max asked.

"No choice. Whoever was driving that car meant
business."

Jack's heart kicked up another notch, but for an
entirely different reason this time. It occurred to him
that what had started out as a routine profile for a
single night's airing and then online archiving had
blossomed into something much bigger. He was
working freelance on this, paying Max out of his own
pocket, and what he had here was a story that might
be important enough to put him back on the national
map. A potential terrorist attack in a major American
city. And he and Max were the only news personnel

who had been allowed inside the circle because Tom Drabinsky and he had hit it off, and that was the way the boss man wanted it.

But there was a downside. Because they'd hit it off, it was a friend who was walking into the hair-trigger kill zone, not some anonymous hero.

Jack watched as Drabinsky crossed to the Tahoe and threw the rear gate open. Two of his crew members joined him there and brought out a helmet and what Drabinsky had referred to as the "demon"—a personal armor suit made of thick padding, designed to withstand the force of an explosion. *"In theory, at least,"* Drabinsky had told him. They called it the demon because of the number of men who had died wearing one.

As Drabinsky suited up, Jack glanced to his right, toward a cluster of squad cars in the distance.

They had a person of interest in back of one of those cars. Not the bomber but someone who apparently knew the carjacker, had been trying to get to him immediately after the accident.

Jack turned to Max. He didn't have to tell her to keep the camera on Drabinsky. "Be back in ten," he said.

Max was surprised. "Where you going?"

"I want to try and find out who they've got in the car back there."

"You sure you don't want me there with you?"

Jack shook his head. "I want Tom to know he's got a lady in the lists."

"Sorry?"

"Jousts. Knights. Helped them focus. You didn't want to be unhorsed if a pretty eye was on you."

"Ah. Hey, do I get hazard pay for this?"

Jack smiled. "You're a newsperson covering news. Be grateful for the privilege."

Jack got lucky. There was a rookie uniform watching the SFPD's *guest,* as they called him. There's a myth that rookies tend to follow regulations. What they follow is experience and authority. They don't just give it up, though; most have to be wooed by guys who have been-there, seen-that.

Jack walked up, read the rookie's name tag, showed his credentials.

"Sorry, Mr. Hatfield, but we're not supposed to allow press near—"

"I'm not press, Officer Beckman, I'm a friend of Tom's," he said. Then he added pointedly, "Tom Drabinsky. The guy in the demon."

"Yes, sir. I know who that is."

Jack waved a hand toward the kid in the patrol car. "He give you any trouble when you took him into custody?"

"Nah. There were already a couple citizens keeping him in check."

"You find the owner?"

Beckman started to speak, then hesitated.

"Don't worry," Jack said. "We're off the record. I just want to know what's going on."

Beckman thought about it a moment then said, "Nothing on the owner."

"Who's this guy?" He indicated the kid in the car.

"Name's Leon Thomas. His younger brother Jamal was the jacker. He told us this was just an initiation, no one was supposed to get hurt, and his brother was going to abandon the car after a joyride."

"You believe him?"

"He's got a Big Block tat on the back of his neck," Beckman said. "Either he's a member of the gang or a serious wannabe. Their initiation is blood, not a carjacking."

"What did he say about the vic?"

"Only that he was an 'Arab-lookin' dude,' " Beckman said.

"Age? Clothing?"

"Twenties, well dressed."

The kind of guy who would probably slip through spot-check profiling, which the SFPD said they didn't do. The truth was, every metropolitan police department in the nation did it. Chances were pretty good that granny wouldn't be blowing up a street car unless she was wearing a head scarf, and Josh or Tyler was less likely to take out a federal building than Muhammad or Omar.

Jack was about to ask if he could talk to the kid when three black SUVs pulled up to the perimeter. A moment later the area was flooded with men in suits, one of whom—a hefty six-footer with the clean, resolute look of a *Mercury* astronaut—approached Beckman. "Where's the officer in charge?"

"Who are *you*?" Jack asked.

The suit reached into his jacket and brought out a set of credentials. Field Director Carl Forsyth, FBI. The agent in charge, by his manner. The man's eyes were still on Beckman. "Are you gonna point me in the right direction or does this loser do all your talking?"

"Whoa," Jack said. "What the hell is that supposed to—"

"You mean 'loser'? I know who you are. You used to have that show on TV, *Truth Tellers*."

Jack stiffened. "That's right."

"And you're still *working*? I figured we'd seen the last of you."

It was the kind of derision that Jack had gotten used to over the last couple years, but it had been a while since he'd encountered it. After losing his job at the network in a very public way—thanks to an orchestrated smear campaign that had pretty much destroyed his reputation and wrongfully painted him as a bigot—he had removed himself from the national stage, content to work in relative obscurity as a freelance news producer. He'd known he'd have to rebuild his reputation, brick by brick, and had spent the last few minutes feeling like he was back in the major leagues. But then a guy like Agent Forsyth came along and he sometimes wondered if it was worth it.

Beckman had caved, was pointing him in the di-

rection of the MCC—the mobile command center—
when someone near the bomb site shouted.

"Down! Everybody *down*!"

Without thinking, Jack grabbed the rookie and
dove toward the blacktop as a massive explosion
shook the ground, sending several tons of debris and
human body parts rocketing in all directions.

The shock wave blew over Jack, shattering car windows and taking down anyone who had been too
slow to react. He heard a low grunt nearby and,
through the haze of powdered debris, saw Beckman
lying facedown a few feet ahead, bleeding from the
base of his neck, a long gash having been ripped by
a chunk of cement. Muffled by the thick dust, the
roar of the explosion faded, leaving behind a low,
steady buzz in Jack's ears.

The whole world seemed to pause for a long moment, as if to take a deep breath, and he was once
again assaulted by that morning in Baghdad, his best
friend's blank stare vivid in his mind's eye. A vague
sense of panic welled in his chest, brought on by the
memory, his senses, and the unexpected chaos. But
he himself seemed unhurt and he forced himself to
remain calm and assess the damage around him.

One of the FBI agents was sprawled on the blacktop, out cold, his suit jacket askew, as the agent in
charge and the two uniforms slowly staggered to their
feet.

"My God," one of them muttered.

And that about summed it up.

Beckman stirred, groaned.

Jack got to his feet, simultaneously pulling a handkerchief from his pants and slapping it over his mouth and nose. He checked the rookie's wound. It didn't seem life threatening. He turned the man over, placed his head on the block that had hit him. He wanted to keep the flow of blood down, away from the wound.

"You okay?" Jack asked.

The rookie blinked several times, looking dazed. "I think so." He touched the side of his head, then the back. "I'm bleeding, aren't I? Feels like I blew out an ear—"

"That's just the concussion. You got clocked in the neck."

Jack gave him a pat on the arm. As he was turning to look back to where he had left Max he saw the door of the cruiser fly open and Leon Thomas stumble out. He was covered with a thousand tiny pieces of shattered glass but that didn't stop him from running into the man-made mist, his hands cuffed behind him.

"Hey!" somebody shouted—

—and Leon picked up speed.

He didn't get far. Twenty yards away a uniform broadsided him, taking him down like a defensive tackle, two more piling on for good measure. A moment later they had him on his feet, roughly shoving him toward another cruiser. One of them swatted him across the back of the head as they threw the door open and pushed him inside.

Even before the show was over, Jack turned away, shifting his attention to the center of the blast. The dust was starting to settle and through the haze he saw a crater. Half the building behind it was in shreds, a hotel that had been abandoned and was ironically scheduled for demolition. Though the spotlights had been taken out in the blast patches of fire were rising from the building and the shop beside it, lighting the night. A water main had ruptured in the center of the street and was spitting an ineffectual fountain toward the crater. Rivulets followed cracks in the asphalt, creating an odd, shimmering effect.

There was no sign of Drabinsky, his suit, or the robot.

Feeling dread, Jack scanned the perimeter, searching for Maxine. With relief that brought tears to his eyes, he saw her climbing to her feet, staring down at her battered video camera in limp shock.

As if suddenly remembering she had a coworker, she froze halfway to her feet, turned suddenly, and peered along the street. She made eye contact with Jack and, as though she had completed a minichecklist—camera, partner—she collapsed.

Dodging flaming pieces of fabric and paper that were floating carelessly from above, Jack made his way toward ground zero.

3

The line was picked up after three rings. The cell phones were encrypted using a Twofish algorithm and a 4096-bit Diffie-Hellman key exchange.

No one would be listening in.

"We have a problem," the caller said. "There was an incident downtown."

A pause. "The carjacking?"

"You heard about it."

"It's all over the news. Don't tell me that was us."

"The car was stolen from one of our assets, Abdal al-Fida. He decided to take a little trip off the reservation."

"What's our exposure?"

"He's alive but he isn't in custody, so I think we're in the clear. He outsourced the supplies he used, but that'll be taken care of by morning."

"Where is he?"

"Still in the city. He's been in contact and, to his credit, he seems remorseful. What would you like me to do with him?"

"What I'd like and what's prudent are very different things. Can we rely on his cooperation?"

"I think so."

"Good. I'd rather we not do this here. Wipe all trace of him and send him home. We'll deal with him later."

"Why not deal with him now?"

"He's one of Zuabi's recruits. Things could get sticky."

"What about the investigation? The scrutiny could compromise our operation."

"I'm aware of that, but it's too late to pull the plug. Point Justice in another direction and hand them someone of interest. Make sure it's homegrown. The White House will jump all over that."

"How can you be sure?"

"It's good PR. Better a few local crazies than some Islamic bogeyman." A pause. "Maybe we can even work this to our advantage."

"How?"

"Use it to tie up FBI resources while we do what has to be done. Zuabi says his man is already headed to Bulgaria to secure delivery."

"Who did he send?"

"The one I told you about, Hassan Haddad. The imam says he's his best soldier. Loyal, efficient, and deadly."

"He better be right. We can't afford any more mistakes."

"I'm with you. If anything goes wrong, we'll cut our losses and call it a day. Otherwise, we continue full steam and let the imam worry about this idiot al-Fida."

"Can Zuabi be trusted?"

"A little late to be asking that question, isn't it?"

"I wasn't worried till now. You realize however we distract them, the feds will heighten security across the board."

"They can trot out all the security they want," the voice said. "They still won't see us coming. No one will."

The woman in the security uniform smiled at him, but Abdal al-Fida had to wonder—was her smile genuine or was there something unspoken behind it? Something dangerous? Had someone at the terminal identified him, found something at the car, dug up a picture of him and sent it to every police department, every transportation center, every 7-Eleven?

He hadn't expected this, the paranoia. And perhaps he wouldn't feel it so strongly if the car hadn't sat there so long, if he hadn't screwed up. If he'd just done as he'd been instructed—

No, he admonished himself. *It was a good plan.*

He had intended to park the Land Rover in the underground lot of that absurd monstrosity of a federal building downtown, then wait for morning, when the place would be filled with enough infidels to send this fat, lazy nation a resounding message from Allah.

The afternoon before, Abdal had followed one of the blind fools who worked there to an apartment near Fisherman's Wharf—an elderly woman who wore the beleaguered look of a capitalist slave. Breaking into her car had taken him no time at all, and he'd found her electronic key card tucked into a pocket of the visor above the driver's seat. Stupid, trusting, *and* careless. It's a miracle the nation functioned at all.

In a way, this theft was an act of mercy. If she could not gain access to the parking lot the following day, her life might be spared.

Of course, in the end they were all spared, weren't they?

The black with the gun had seen to that.

Abdal cursed himself for allowing such an insignificant piece of trash to so easily take control of him. Finding the muzzle of a gun in his face as he waited for the light to change had been so unexpected that reason had fled. Ironically, his training had taken hold then: blend in. Don't create a scene. It took time for him to get to the rooftop of an unguarded building within a thousand feet of the target, to obtain an unobstructed transmit line from his phone to the one strapped to the primer bomb.

Allah had spared him, and for that he was grateful, but he had to wonder why. He'd never had any interest in martyrdom, but the shame he felt for this failure was worse than any form of death. He knew that those he worked for, those who at this very moment were probably shocked by his impulsiveness, his impatience—his *foolishness*—would kill him. The methods were still too horrible to contemplate. Yet he resisted the impulse to disappear. He also resisted the urge to rally his wits, to take his own life in an improvised act of terror. Allah did not smile upon cowards, and willful suicide with a tacked-on purpose was still first and foremost a means to escape punishment.

Besides, if he were meant to die Abdal preferred to do it in London, where he had lived for nearly twenty of his twenty-two years, in the comfort of his own home.

Within an hour of the disaster, he sent his primary contact an encrypted text message confessing his sin and begging understanding, if not forgiveness. Several minutes later he received a reply, instructing him to fly home via Los Angeles, where a reservation had already been made in his name. He knew full well that they would consult with Hassan before deciding what to do with him. That was something, at least. Hassan might choose to spare his life so he could surrender it with dignity.

Whatever the decision, Abdal would use the time he had left to make peace with his God.

He didn't want to risk stealing another vehicle, since the California Highway Patrol was particularly vigilant about watching for stolen cars. License-plate reading software gave them the ability to check over ninety percent of the vehicles on their freeway. So he booked bus passage down the California coast, arriving at Los Angeles International Airport at seven in the morning. He had no need for possessions but he had packed a small suitcase anyway, to avoid raising suspicion among the TSA profilers. Abdal kept a "ready bag" for that purpose, a carry-on stuffed with amenities, clothing, a nondescript novel, and a book of crossword puzzles.

A few minutes after his encounter with the security agent, Abdal was seated at the gate, his paranoia abated. If the woman had suspected anything he would never have gotten this far. She would have motioned one of the security guards over casually but with a hand gesture that indicated there was a problem, and Abdal would have been thrown to the floor, pinned there while another agent handcuffed him.

Instead, the woman went out of her way to be polite, to smile, to assure him she wasn't profiling. And in that way she let a terrorist through her checkpoint.

But that was not his concern.

All Abdal could think about now was not his mistakes, nor his certain death, only getting home to the woman he loved.

Getting home to Sara.

4

The FBI wasted no time instituting a media blackout.

They didn't call it that, of course. At an impromptu press conference near the blast site that night, with particles of dust still visible in the floodlights, newly appointed Mayor Daniel Maywood announced that the city of San Francisco was cooperating fully with the FBI and Homeland Security. However, due to the sensitivity of the investigation all inquiries were being routed to the FBI's press liaison—which Jack knew from experience was a deep black hole.

The public was assured that the federal government would spare no expense in finding out who was responsible for the blast, but until the investigation was complete, they would not engage in speculation.

Questions about Al Qaeda and other terrorist organizations were floated, but an FBI spokeswoman repeatedly explained that unless someone came forward to claim responsibility they may not know who was responsible for several days. At this point they didn't even know who the driver was, who owned the car, or what his target had been.

Figuring that out didn't take a Heritage Foundation think tank, Jack thought. The city's civic center was only blocks away, the fattest target on the route. But the feds had no intention of fueling rumors or causing concern that the center, or any other public space, was not safe.

The mayor had no comment about the assertion that a person involved in the carjacking had identified the driver as an Arab. He didn't want to speculate and create a reactionary spike against Muslim Americans.

When he heard that, Jack wished he had been there instead of riding in the back of an ambulance with Maxine. He would've gone on record as saying that he, for one, was tired of all the special-interest hyphenates and wished that any fill-in-the-blank Americans would be Americans first and something else second.

Even though that was the kind of thing that got you tossed off the air, he reflected. But it was worth it. People said he was insensitive and a racist. He said he was a patriot, which was different from most of the mainstream media who seemed to be happy watching the country perforate along ethnic borders like Spain or the former Soviet Union or Iraq.

Jack lived and worked on a fifty-nine-foot Grand Banks yacht in the Sausalito Marina where, as if reflecting the mood of the region, the wind and tides were making some pretty ugly chop. Still, he managed to snag a few hours' sleep around dawn then watched as local and national law enforcement across the country were put on high alert and did everything they could to create the impression of ensuring the public's safety. The President made an Oval Office speech the following morning, reminding the country of his commitment to keeping the citizens of the United States secure—and to raise his mortally wounded poll numbers—while politicos from both sides of the aisle clogged the cable news networks and talk radio with enough hot air to float a horseshoe. That bugged Jack the most. Despite the magnitude of what had happened, and the devastating scope of what had accidentally been avoided, the news coverage had no real depth to it, no dimension, no insight.

Only one thing resonated with him. At the center of the newscasts and speeches, the one piece that was never far from anyone's mouth was that while debris and shrapnel had caused several minor injuries, there had been only one fatality: Officer Thomas Drabinsky of the SFPD bomb squad, whose attempt to defuse the device had ended as he was en route to the target. There was one thing about him that no one mentioned, however, probably because it was too bizarre a thought for anyone to process. It was something he heard from the marines in Iraq and air force personnel when fighter pilots went down.

Tragic as the loss was, Thomas Drabinsky accomplished something that not a lot of people got to do: he died with his boots on and he would not be forgotten.

Jack had seen enough forgotten soldiers in his time. He'd tried to rectify this when he was still on the air, had used the last two minutes of his show to honor the fallen in Iraq and Afghanistan, to put names and faces to these men and women he so admired. It was a reminder to his viewers that the enemy they fought wasn't some abstract notion, but a real, living danger to the western world. Nine/eleven was a decade past, and too many of us were becoming complacent—including and especially our so-called representatives in Washington.

He had even started a fund, raising money for the kids of fallen vets, and for training guide dogs—by prison inmates, no less—to aid those who had left arms, legs, eyes, and ears in the Mesopotamian war zones.

Jack checked with the hospital at nine A.M. Max was sleeping and her injuries weren't serious. She had a gash on the side of her head that took twenty-seven stitches to close, but there was no concussion—her camera had taken the hit for her. It thanked her with a smack to the temple that looked, to Jack, like the recoil of a .357 Holland & Holland Magnum. However, he was not surprised when she called early in the afternoon and told him that she wanted to get to recuperate at home. What she said, actually, was, "The deductible on the health coverage I was forced to buy is going to kill me faster than my injuries, so get me out of here." She said she'd cleared it with her doctor, and calling a cab, Jack went and collected her.

After taking her home, putting her to bed, and making sure the nice old woman who rented her the attic space would look in on her, Jack went back to the boat and began editing the footage they'd shot over the last several days, retooling it to focus on Drabinsky himself. Nothing she had shot at the blast site had survived, but in the end it wasn't needed. The money shot was not the explosion, it was the proud, smiling face of the fallen warrior.

It took Jack most of the day to assemble it, and when he was done he realized he had something special. He also knew he could make anywhere from fifty to a hundred grand with the package, but decided to offer it to the networks free of charge. His entire reason for becoming a journalist was not to sleep on silk but to sleep well, knowing he had done the right thing.

This was the right thing.

Jack had known Tony Antiniori for a little over a year, but the moment he'd met the guy they'd felt an immediate kinship. And that was the kind of compliment he didn't hand out often.

A former Green Beret paratrooper, Tony had done three tours in Vietnam, had cross-trained as both a medic and a rifleman, and was still active in the National Guard, teaching combat medicine to young recruits headed to Afghanistan.

He was sixty-nine and still teaching field medicine to the young recruits. Maybe that was part of what kept him young, having to shame the know-it-all out of kids less than half his age. The other part was staying in shape. He was solidly built, more muscle than fat, but at first glance you'd never know that he was career military. He looked like a fugitive from a Fellini movie, his thick head of shoe-polish-black movie-star hair framing a tanned, creased, bearded face and wise but playful eyes. He kept his lanky, six-foot-four-inch frame in shape with a brisk morning flurry of push-ups, jumping jacks, and crunches every other day. Nothing high impact; just enough to get his heart rate up and help keep his cholesterol down. He dressed younger, too—casual, mostly turtlenecks and corduroys. And he dyed his white hair black, his one concession to vanity. If he squinted, he could still find and sometimes talk to the twenty-year-old who always wanted to be where he ended up.

That sense of accomplishment was the real reward, though sometimes there was unexpected blowback.

Tony had once told him the story of Beth Middleton, and how he was attracted to her the instant he saw her. The woman's smile hooked him and her tight jeans held him. Her quick wit did its job, too. In that sense he was not unlike most men: it was lust at first sight.

Beth was thirty years younger than him but something about her was much older. When they finally got around to talking about something other than medicine, he learned that she had grown up in a military family, moving from base to base, though she had managed to stick around the Florida panhandle, near Panama City, long enough to go to high school. Maturity was something he found in a lot of army brats. Because they never really got to put down roots, because they rarely got to make friends for very long, their lives were spent on the outside, reading when they were alone, watching when they were with people.

Beth's father had been a lieutenant colonel in the air force. He flew a hundred combat missions in Nam, in the F-4—a classy, long-range Mach-buster that was still being used in the Gulf War. The sky jocks always said that if you had to be away from home and honey, this was the baby you wanted to be with. Lieutenant Colonel Middleton apparently felt the same. He later became a flight instructor, keeping close to the Phantoms, married late, and had Beth even later.

She worshipped her father and craved his attention—which he obviously didn't bestow as readily or happily as he did lectures on the range of his big silver bird. Beth didn't have to say it for Tony to figure out that he was the reason she was attracted to older men. He didn't imagine he was the first.

After college she earned her master's in Arabic language studies from Texas A & M and, after hours, snagged a Ph.D. in MdS—Marquis de Sade. She liked to be dominated and humiliated, something Tony didn't know till later.

Although it was against military rules and regs they fraternized in the most intimate way. At first in his car and later in motels near the base in Sacramento. As they came to know each other better, she became more open about her desires.

At first Tony went along with the "game," as he called it, by tying her up and telling her she was a "dirty girl." But he—and his anatomy—quickly tired of the sport because he wasn't wired for it. He decided to self prescribe Levitra. He took it with a Coke from the vending machine outside their favorite cheap motel. When they got back to the room, Tony slipped into the bathroom. As he undressed he looked at his old friend in the mirror and was shocked to see it standing at the same angle as his seventeen-year-old self. And he didn't even have to squint.

In the months to come he would jokingly tell his friends about his experience, noting that, "I took that little orange tablet, looked at myself, and fell in love." It never failed to get a laugh.

The Levitra worked all right, except where it counted most: inside his head. This wasn't lovemaking, it was psychodrama. After a couple of months he found the sight and feel of the clothesline she carried in her bag to be a turnoff. It had the smell of the recent past but the less tangible odor of the distant past, a lack of attention from daddy. That was something he didn't want to be a part of.

The night he told her wasn't fun for either of them. Beth dropped her bag on the bed, crawled toward the pillows, and when he sat beside her she curled into a tight, fetuslike ball, covered her face with her hands, and began to sob, "Tell me I'm a bad girl . . . tell me I'm a whore!"

He gently lifted her hands and held them between his.

The light shone on her tears. The edge of the rope poked from the top of her bag like a fuse.

"Tie me up," she demanded. "Make me feel like the dirty slut I am."

"Not tonight, Beth," he said softly, cradling her to him.

She seemed to recoil slightly before yielding. "You'll be back?"

"Not tonight or ever again."

Tony missed what she made him feel, but not how she made him feel. On the other hand, after nearly seven decades, it was good to feel challenged. More than anything, that was what life had to be about.

As soon as he got back to the city that night, he immediately went to Peter and Paul Church in North Beach and begged Jesus to forgive his sin. Like millions of lapsed Catholics, Tony loved Jesus, admired the Church less, and was no longer constrained by the sexual edicts of a corrupt priesthood.

When Jack finished editing the footage of Drabinsky, Tony was the first person he showed it to.

"Damn if I don't have tears in my eyes," Tony Antiniori said.

"Thanks," Jack said.

"I mean it, that's a helluva tribute," Tony said. "You

think you'll run into any resistance from the networks?"

Jack shrugged. "My name isn't exactly welcome,
but considering what I've got here and the price I'm
asking, how can they refuse?"

"Because they're kind of like reverse terrorists,"
Tony said.

"I don't follow."

"They will blow up an entire network news division just to keep one guy from the spotlight."

Jack smiled. That was as good an assessment of
the network mind-set as he'd ever heard.

"They're putzes," Tony added for good measure.

"That's what my grandfather used to call my old
man."

"Your mother's father?"

Jack nodded.

"Because your dad wasn't Jewish?"

Jack shook his head. "No, because he was hoping
his daughter would marry up. In Granddad's mind,
watch repair didn't quite cut it. Even though my dad
loved it."

They were sitting in the aft salon of Jack's Aleu-
tian 59 he'd dubbed the *Sea Wrighter*. He and Rachel
had bought it during the real estate boom, with money
she made from flipping houses. Jack had been a live-
aboard for two years, since moving out of the house
in Tiburon he'd shared with his ex-wife. He often
marveled that his boat was almost double the size of
Hemingway's famous thirty-eight-foot *Pilar*. Named
for his second wife, Pauline, whose nickname was

Pilar, it was also the name of a pivotal character in *For Whom the Bell Tolls*. Built in Brooklyn, New York, in 1934 by the Wheeler Shipyard, it cost $7,455. Jack chuckled thinking about the 70-hp Chrysler Crown gasoline engine, which drove her at 8 knots with a top speed of 16 knots. Jack's Aleutian had two 1000-hp Caterpillar diesels, which could drive his forty-ton beauty upwards of 22 knots. Jack also had a small apartment in town but he rarely spent time there, preferring life on the marina instead. There was a sense of community here, of shared purpose, that you didn't get in the city.

Tony lived aboard the *Tarangi,* a thirty-two-foot Chey Lee clipper just three slips down—a slot he'd managed to score despite size restrictions when one of the larger boats pulled anchor. So a day wouldn't be complete without Tony at least popping his head in, and more often than not he brought along a bottle of wine. Tony considered himself something of a budget connoisseur and liked to share.

Jack preferred beer or a single malt himself. His favorite combo was a few '85 Glenrothes followed by a couple of cold Becks, but he indulged his friend's passion and usually gave in when offered a glass. Tony's selection tonight was an '04 Gaja Sori San Lorenzo, which he'd received in exchange for his mechanical skills on an Atomic-4 engine. They toasted Officer Thomas Drabinsky at the top; it was the first time since the blast that Jack had choked up. Something about the finality of the gesture, the acknowledgment that a life was over, his story had been told, The End.

Tony picked up on it and gave him a tight-lipped smile.

The wine was damn good and it lifted his spirits from the first sip. It tasted unlike any other heavy red. He savored the understated layers of currant and black cherry, with a tinge of coffee. But even his relaxed mind wasn't able to stray far from the events of the last twenty-four hours.

"Y'know, something's bothering me about this whole thing," Jack said.

"Talk to me."

"I watched that press conference twice and I still don't understand why the mayor and the FBI pushed aside the whole Arab connection."

"A problem with the source?"

"Who, the carjacker?"

Tony shrugged. "Maybe the kid was lying. Or could be he got it wrong."

Jack shook his head slowly. "They had to have pulled security video from the Arco station by now. If it's *not* true, someone would have said so. Maintain good relations with the Arabs and all that."

"So you're saying that the absence of a denial is as good as a confession."

"That is exactly what I'm saying."

"I like it," Tony said. "There's something else I like, too."

Jack looked at him. "What's that?"

"It sounds like you're finally getting your mojo back."

Jack considered that as he sat back. He let the wine and the cool afternoon breeze and the fellowship of a good friend remind him how sweet and precious life was. Even so, as Drabinsky had shown, there were qualities and ideals far greater than that, the need to do the right thing, the honorable thing, whatever the cost.

If an Arab had set the bomb, Jack wanted to know who and why. He wanted to find out why the authorities were tiptoeing around the monster who was at the center of their investigation. He wanted to know where the bastard was now and if he intended to try again. Not because he was a racist or hated Muslims as his critics had said, but because the elusive son of a bitch was a murdering terrorist. Tracking him down and exposing him was the right thing to do, whoever it pissed off.

"Yeah," Jack said at last. "The mojo is *so* back."

Jack Hatfield's fall from grace had been swift and brutal, and had come when he could least afford it. Already in the midst of his divorce, he was a year into a new contract hosting *Truth Tellers,* one of the top-rated opinion shows on the GNT cable news network, when he was blindsided by accusations that he was an unrepentent Islamophobe.

The accusations were nonsense, of course. Jack had long been a champion of religious freedom and free speech and anyone who watched his show knew

that. But the liberal media elite took it upon themselves to take his words out of context so they could
twist and amplify them. They went after him like a
starving jackal chasing an eastern cottontail.

As much as Jack believed in religious tolerance,
he drew the line at murder. And whether his detrac-
tors liked it or not, Muslim extremists were the face
of terror around the globe. Time and again they had
demonstrated a willingness to kill in the name of
Allah. Pointing out that simple fact, and suggesting
oh-so-gently that a few more imams should be speaking *against* the killing instead of getting wound up
stumping for a controversial mosque in the heart of
San Francisco did not even begin to rise to the level
of hate speech. The exact, very rational words that
started the anti-Hatfield fatwa were, "Hell, if these
guys did more of the first no one would ever complain about them wanting to do the second."

Jack knew he wasn't doing his career any favors
by compounding that statement with reports that the
mosque was being funded by a Saudi business consortium he believed had ties to a Wahhabi jihadist
organization called the Hand of Allah. Several
mosques funded by this same group had been built
in London and throughout the United Kingdom, and
Jack was convinced they were superficially mosques
and fundamentally training facilities for Islamofas-
cist sleeper agents. In the days that followed his initial
remarks, Jack regularly took Prime Minister Griffiths
to task for allowing these facilities to be built.

The last act of the drama occurred just ten days

after it started, when he held a *Truth Tellers* panel debate on the topic, bringing in participants from across the political spectrum. The debate was civil until Jack asked a simple rhetorical question:

"How would you feel if Muslim extremists got hold of a nuclear weapon?"

There was a momentary chill in the air, then one of the panelists—a supercilious professor of legal studies named Aldrich—said, "You're assuming that's even likely."

"You're naïve if you think it isn't," Jack told him. "And let's not forget what Abd al-Rahman al-Rashid told us. That while it's true that not all Muslims are terrorists, the majority of terrorists are Muslim."

"All right, but considering there are approximately one billion Muslims in the world, how exactly do you propose to stop them?"

"When you factor in the laissez-faire attitude of much of our country," Jack said, "the odds against us aren't good. But let's say, for the sake of argument, that just ten percent of those one billion Muslims are fanatic haters who would kill all of us at the blink of an eye. A matter of us versus them."

"And?"

"If it came down to it, would you rather see a hundred million of *us* killed, or kill a hundred million Muslims?"

Murmurs rose from the panel and Aldrich just stared at him with a self-satisfied grin. Within hours, a smear campaign was carefully orchestrated by a radical watchdog group called Media Wire, which spared no effort to grind Jack's reputation into the dust beneath its jackbooted heel.

HOST OF TRUTH TELLERS WOULD KILL A HUN-DRED MILLION MUSLIMS! was the headline tossed into the echo chamber, bolstered by an edited clip of the show that isolated his last words and removed all context. The distinction between true Muslims and those who perverted their faith to justify their violence—a distinction Jack always tried to make—was completely ignored by the media.

The man behind this campaign was a reclusive, Austrian-born billionaire named Lawrence Soren. The eighty-one-year-old had made his fortune by betting against national currencies. He profited almost a billion dollars on the British pound alone. Just after the catastrophic Japanese earthquake of March 2011 and the disasters in their nuclear power plants, he had shorted Tokyo Electric and made hundreds of millions on the tragedy. No government would stop this rapacious beast because he owned their leaders. He also had a controlling financial interest in several major news organizations in the U.S. and much of the world, including the recent acquisition of the company that controlled the majority of GNT's stock. By the time Soren was done, *Truth Tellers* had not only lost half of its sponsors but Jack was being told by the network that he had to apologize on air to the Muslim community or face immediate termination.

Because he felt he was innocent, not because he was afraid, Jack reluctantly tried an on-air explanation. It was exactly fifteen words long:

"It was not my intention to discredit all Muslims," he said, "only those who seek to harm us."

Before the night was out—before the show was over, in fact—he found himself as jobless as if he'd eaten apple pie off a map of Mecca. Trapped in a contract that kept him from moving his show to another network. *Time* magazine listed this sudden fall as one of the twenty biggest blunders in television history—a massive chunk of hyperbole if there ever was one. Anyway, to Jack's mind, standing up for his principles wasn't a blunder at all. He would lose sight of that for a while afterward, as he looked for a place to put his key, but that's the beauty about the truth: however long you turn away from it, it's still the truth and still there.

The final twist of the knife came three weeks later, when the British Home Office released a list of terrorists and criminals who were banned from traveling to the United Kingdom. To Jack's utter surprise *his* name was on that list. The home secretary hadn't bothered to include Osama bin Laden, but right there, front and center, was John Samuel Hatfield, former combat journalist and network news commentator, whose "radical and provocative statements" were deemed "a threat to public security."

Several weeks later, the *London Daily News* ran a story on the ban, revealing a series of illuminating e-mail exchanges between the Home Office and the

PM. What the newspaper uncovered was a case of political cowardice in the extreme. Jack Hatfield was being used to make the British government's bias against Muslims seem relatively tame and tolerant. This was the same government that many believed was instrumental in the concurrent release by Scottish officials of Abdelbaset al-Megrahi, a convicted terrorist who was responsible for the fiery deaths of two hundred seventy people on an airplane passing over Lockerbie.

Months later, it came out that the very home secretary who had banned Jack had been using government funds to support her husband's porn viewing habit.

When a reporter from a London tabloid had asked Jack for a newspaper quote, he said, "Her politics are more pornographic than any sex scene. What can be more obscene than the government of the U.K. refusing to deport radical Muslims who preach the overthrow of England, demand the introduction of Sharia law, and chant 'death to the queen,' all the while refusing to lift the ban against Jack Hatfield? I am the only member of the American media prohibited from entering the U.K. because of the degenerate political minds of the home secretary and her cohorts."

The hypocrisy of the U.K. and the weak-kneed sensibilities of his own nation were stunning, but with his credibility all but destroyed he was forced to surrender those battles, withdraw from the national scene, use his wits and skills and whatever closet supporters he had left—and thank God there were a bunch of them—to earn a living.

He did it alone, because his wife had withered under the scrutiny and catcalls, the burning bags of feces on the doorstep and the death threats on voice mail.

He made his deals in back rooms, wrote or produced anonymously because even his friends were afraid of Lawrence Soren, Muslim backlash, or both.

But he did it all, survived so he could get to this point.

Not to stroke his wounded pride, not to show a president or prime minster that *by God* he was right.

He did it for this one chance to help the nation save itself *from* itself.

5

Sofia, Bulgaria

The moment Hassan Haddad stepped off the elevator, he knew he was being watched.

It was a weeknight, and across the lobby the hotel lounge and casino were full of European and American businessmen, either drunk or getting there, planning their schemes to rape and pillage the country's economy as they gambled away their weekly salaries.

Both the hotel and casino were examples of the new Eastern capitalist vulgarity. Crowded craps tables, roulette wheels, and slot machines, surrounded by gold-inlaid walls and marble floors—all symbols of decadence and woeful immorality.

Then there were the Gypsy whores. Bulgaria didn't hide its perversions any more than it hid its corruption, and these brown-skinned Roma girls knew where the gold was. Nothing could be easier than picking off a pasty American salesman whose wife was nearly five thousand miles away.

Haddad understood the temptation these men felt. He had felt it himself, many times. Most of the girls were quite attractive, wearing short sheer dresses that clung to their skin and suggested at the pleasures that lay beneath. Just last night he had succumbed to the charms of one sloe-eyed beauty, taking her to his room where she had let him do things few women would ever permit. She had received him with such enthusiasm, such passion, that he had to wonder if, unlike so many of the whores he had spent time with, her pleasure was genuine.

Haddad was so surprised and delighted by the girl that he considered inviting her to accompany him home. It was an absurd, blasphemous notion, though it hadn't seemed so as she knelt over him.

After she was gone, he lay on the drenched bed sheets, thinking back to when he was a younger man, attending university in America. Like Bulgaria, there were no rules in the west, and the two girls across the hall from him, both as limber as gymnasts, had taught him how to please a woman. He often lay with them on their dorm room floor, watching them stroke and prod each other to a feverish frenzy—an education he wasn't likely to forget.

Haddad had applied those lessons last night and had been rewarded in kind. But shortly after the girl was gone he remembered who he was and why he

was here. Sending up a prayer, he asked for forgiveness, promising that he would never again allow himself to fall prey to such depravity.

It was a promise he wasn't certain he could—or
wanted—to keep. Nonetheless, women would not be
a priority. There was something more important he
needed to do.

The lounge and casino weren't the only sections of
the hotel that were crowded. Several businessmen sat
on chairs and sofas around the lobby itself, smiling
and laughing, deep in conversations that didn't interest Haddad.

What *did* interest him, however, was the lone man
sitting near the window that looked out onto a busy
street.

Turkish. Casually dressed in a sports jacket and
jeans. Neatly trimmed beard, after the current style.
Small but hard bodied, with a powerful frame that
clothes couldn't disguise.

Haddad had seen him the day before, amid the
crowd of commuters and tourists on the train from
Belgrade. They had not made eye contact, and at the
time he had thought nothing of the man. Had not even
considered that he was anything more than a weary
traveler, anxious to get to his destination. The fact that
he was staying at this very hotel had not been a concern.

Many people stayed here.

Yet now Haddad sensed that there was something
about the Turk that wasn't right. The way he kept his

gaze focused on the newspaper, never looking up, never showing any sign of curiosity about what was going on around him. A beautiful woman walked by but he didn't register even a flicker of interest.

So he was either a *luti*—a homosexual—or something else was going on.

Haddad knew quite well that surveillance was a skill that took cunning as well as patience. But the Turk was trying too hard to appear disinterested in his surroundings, and that was as much a giveaway as not trying hard enough.

That was how Haddad knew he was being watched. And this, unfortunately, *was* a problem.

Moving toward the lobby door, he checked the clock above the front desk. It was nearing eight P.M., and the man who called himself Chilikov would be expecting him soon. If he were late or arrived with an unwanted escort, Chilikov would disappear and that was unacceptable. These arrangements had to be concluded tonight or his schedule would be seriously compromised.

It had taken Haddad a considerable amount of time and money to cultivate a relationship with the Bulgarian, and he couldn't afford to start over. Normally, he would have sent someone else to handle this task but there was too much at stake.

So he had a choice. Lose the Turk—or kill him.

The meeting place was less than a mile away, a fifteen-minute walk. Haddad knew he could quickly hail a taxi and be there in less than five minutes, but taxi drivers had eyes and ears, and while the chances of anything coming of such a casual encounter were nearly nonexistent, he had always been a cautious man who preferred to travel on foot whenever possible.

After receiving Chilikov's text message this evening, Haddad had spent nearly an hour checking and rechecking the route to their meeting place using a portable GPS unit he'd picked up in Belgrade. He had found three possible routes to his destination and had memorized them all, certain that he would not be followed but prepared for the possibility.

Now that possibility was quite real.

Haddad stepped through the revolving door onto the sidewalk, paying no attention to the man as he passed but not overtly looking away as the Turk was doing. Because of that, Haddad was able to see, peripherally, what he needed to see.

Haddad moved with deliberation, never rushing. He was a tourist going out for a stroll, nothing more.

The Turk would know this was a lie, of course. But Haddad saw no reason to betray that he was aware of being watched. As he walked away from the hotel, he kept his gaze forward, never glancing back at that revolving lobby door but knowing that the Turk would soon emerge and head in his direction.

Haddad was relatively sure the man was working alone. The best surveillance is done in teams, the larger the better. The subject gets passed along like a baton, giving him less opportunity to make—or lose—a tail. But the modern spy tends to wear iPod earbuds or a Bluetooth, innocuous technology that keeps him plugged in to partners or HQ. Haddad's cursory look as he passed the Turk revealed neither of these. Besides, he'd been in enough of these situations to trust his instincts and they told him that the Turk was working alone.

The question was, who was he working *for*?

The Americans?

Haddad knew the CIA had a file on him—most of it fiction—and he knew they had followed him on occasion, a bit of information that had come to light when members of his cell tortured and killed one of their agents. But this man was not skilled enough to be CIA. His trade craft did not rise to their level. Nor did it rise to the level of Mossad. Besides, Jew or Druze, Haddad could detect an Israeli the way a rat smells cheese. It was in his DNA, millennia-old and infallible.

So who *was* this man? Could he be working for Chilikov?

No. The Bulgarian's loyalty had been bought and paid for, and it made no sense that he would jeopardize their arrangement. Chilikov was wise enough to know that should he ever betray Haddad, not only would he lose a large sum of cash but Haddad would slit his windpipe and leave him to die gasping in a river of his own blood.

But then, it didn't really matter who the Turk worked for. He was simply an annoyance to be dealt with.

Continuing to take his time as he walked, Haddad stopped to look in the store windows that lined the street. A bakery with samples of its baklava and garash. A clothing store full of well-dressed mannequins. A tattoo parlor with a flickering neon light, the quiet buzz of the needle emanating from an open doorway. All the while Haddad felt the Turk behind him, at least smart enough to keep his distance.

A small grocery stood on the opposite corner. Haddad crossed to it and went inside, assaulted by the bright fluorescent lights that hung high overhead, illuminating rows of crowded shelves. Most Bulgarians preferred to buy their fruit from street vendors, but there was a small display on the left side of the store and Haddad went to it, taking his time as he inspected a neatly stacked pile of blue plums.

Selecting two firm pieces of the fruit, he moved to the register and glanced casually out at the street as the clerk rang up his purchase. The Turk was nowhere to be seen but Haddad assumed he was out there.

He paid in cash, and after the clerk gave him his change she went to place the fruit in a small paper bag.

He stopped her.

Reaching across the counter, he tore one of the larger plastic grocery bags from its stand and dropped the plums inside.

The clerk didn't protest.

Thanking her in Bulgarian, Haddad pocketed his change then went outside. Still no sign of the Turk, but across the street was an unlit alleyway and Haddad was certain the man was waiting there.

Countersurveillance was a careful process that involved U-turns and double-backs, taking needlessly complicated routes to your destination. And given enough time, Haddad knew he could lose the Turk with relative ease. But that would only be a temporary solution to his problem. When he returned to the hotel his pursuer would be there again, feigning indifference behind a travel brochure or a magazine or a novel this time.

So Haddad decided to go with his second option. Death.

Crossing the street, he moved toward the alleyway knowing that the Turk would be on his guard, worried that he'd been spotted. But Haddad gave nothing away, reaching casually into his bag as he passed the alley without a glance and continuing up the sidewalk.

Selecting one of the plums, he bit into it and tasted the sweet, tart nectar. The near sensual delight of it reminded him again of the Gypsy whore and the realm of the flesh. It seemed strange to him that one pleasure should be accepted and the other considered sinful, but that only reminded him of how little time he had spent in religious study. It was something he promised to rectify when this matter was concluded, *inshallah*—if it were the will of Allah.

Continuing at his casual pace, Haddad finished the first plum, flicked the seed into the street, then took the second from the bag and consumed it in three quick bites. He could feel the Turk's presence now, matching his pace, so he picked up speed, widening the distance between them, then took a right onto an intersecting street.

There was less light here. One of the street lamps was broken, a bit of luck in his favor.

Moving even faster now, Haddad found his own alleyway and stepped inside, pressing his back against the brick wall as he quickly tied a knot in the bottom of the plastic bag.

A moment later the Turk came around the corner, his small form barely visible in the dim light. He stopped short when he saw no sign of his prey, swiveling his head to look up and down the street.

Haddad knew he had only seconds to do what needed to be done.

Stepping forward, he slipped through the shadows and moved in behind the Turk, then brought the knotted grocery bag up and over the smaller man's head, pulling it taut around his neck.

The Turk gasped as Haddad yanked him backward into the alley. The victim began to scratch at the bag but Haddad held fast. Haddad knew, if the man did not, that it took five seconds of breathing exhaled air to reduce a man's strength by half. The Turk gave up his attack on the bag and used what strength remained to swing his fists back, hitting and then clutching at Haddad's shoulders and face, trying desperately to break free. But his blows were weak and as the seconds ticked by the struggling Turk was reduced to long, sucking, guttural breaths.

By then, there was no air at all to be had. The plastic of the bag formed an ugly mask that clung to his open mouth and flared nostrils.

It was a death mask. After another moment he slumped to the alley floor—limp, listless.

Dead.

Haddad removed the bag, pressed two fingers against the man's neck and felt no pulse. But something was wrong, here. The Turk's skin was surprisingly smooth.

Too smooth.

Moving his hand upward, Haddad felt the jawline. There was no beard and the skin was far too soft.

Feminine.

With growing alarm he reached into the pocket of his own jacket, brought out the penlight he always carried with him. He flicked it on and shone it into the smaller man's face.

It wasn't the Turk at all.

In fact, it wasn't even a man.

To Haddad's surprise and horror he found himself staring into the glazed, lifeless eyes of the woman he had taken into his bed last night.

The Gypsy whore.

Ten minutes later, Chilikov said in Bulgarian, "You seem a bit out of sorts. Is it something I should be concerned about?"

"Everything is fine," Haddad assured him. "Let's get on with this."

Haddad spoke in Bulgarian as well—he knew six

languages fluently—and had he spoken the truth, he would have admitted to being rattled by the night's events. The Turk had not been working alone as he had thought. The Gypsy whore had been his accomplice. They had obviously tag-teamed him, and because of the Turk's smaller stature Haddad had mistaken the woman for him.

It was the kind of mistake he shouldn't make.

But worse, it also meant the Turk was still out there somewhere. And worse than that, it meant Haddad's instincts had betrayed him. Whoever these people were, he had allowed himself to be fooled by them. He wondered if he had made any more mistakes.

Had he said anything to the girl last night? Had he shared any secrets with her?

No. Of course not. He was much too careful for that. But what might she have observed and reported back? He *had* paraded around his room, preening like a proud lion, showing off for the girl, eager to prove to her that he was somehow stronger, better, more desirable than any man she had ever been with. He had left her alone, unwatched, when he went to the bathroom. The door had been ajar but a skilled operative could have used that time to check cell phone numbers, examine a passport, look for airplane tickets, perform any number of quick-assessment observations.

For all Haddad knew, the entire event might have been recorded. He hadn't bothered to inspect her bag.

Careless, cocky, *stupid*! That, Haddad realized

too late, was the difference between a woman and a plum.

After leaving the girl in the alleyway, Haddad had doubled back but saw no sign of the Turk. He had searched the pockets of the girl's jacket and jeans and had removed her shoes, checked the heels, examined her bracelet and watch and belt, but found no transmitters of any kind. She carried only a small-caliber pistol and a disposable cell phone that showed no record of calls.

Their operation was obviously low-tech, even improvised, but that revelation did nothing to ease Haddad's mind. If these people were to find out about his deal with Chilikov, there would be trouble indeed.

When he arrived at the meeting place—a car dealership seven blocks from the hotel—Haddad was three minutes late and saw no sign of the Bulgarian. But before he could curse himself again, a limousine pulled to the curb and its rear passenger window rolled down.

Chilikov's smiling face looked out at him. "Traffic," he apologized. "I'm glad you waited."

Anton Chilikov was a Cold War veteran who had embraced Bulgaria's transition from Communism to capitalism with enthusiasm. He had fingers in nearly every construction project in Sofia, and through his Russian friends, had control of an old Communist weapons dump, which was rumored to be a smorgasbord of Cold War–era military-grade artillery, much of it still functioning.

As the limousine idled, Haddad climbed inside and sat next to him. Opaque glass separated the driver from his passengers. Nothing happened for a long moment as the old man took stock of his companion in the near-darkness. Haddad knew that a skilled observer could tell a lot about someone in a seemingly casual encounter. Was he anxious, perspiring? Did he carelessly apply cologne that could be identified? If he was bearded, was it short in the style of a nationalist or full, suggesting a tribal affiliation? Did he look tired enough to make a mistake that could compromise them both, or did he appear well rested and alert?

Seemingly satisfied, the old man gestured to a small packing trunk sitting on the car seat opposite them.

"Ask and you shall receive," he said.

Shifting in his seat, Haddad leaned toward the trunk, then stopped and turned to Chilikov. In his eagerness he had almost forgot protocol.

"May I?" he asked.

Chilikov smiled. "By all means."

Haddad carefully flicked the latches, then lifted the trunk's lid and stared at its contents. His heart was hammering against his chest. He'd had his doubts about the Bulgarian, but, praise Allah, the old man had come through. Brilliantly.

"You understand, of course, that this is merely a duplicate," Chilikov cautioned.

Haddad regarded him unhappily. "I do not understand."

"It's proof that I'm a man of my word. The actual unit is en route."

Haddad's frown deepened. "It is the same?"

"Yes, but in order to meet your requirements I initiated shipping several days ago. I took it on faith that you'd make payment in a timely manner."

"How soon can we expect delivery?" Haddad asked.

"When you go to retrieve it, the item will be waiting for you. I will give you the pertinent information when it is necessary." He paused. "Now I believe you have something for me?"

Recovering from his disappointment, Haddad reached into his jacket pocket and pulled out a folded slip of paper. He handed it to Chilikov. "The number of the account. I'm sure you will find the balance satisfactory."

"I'm sure I will," Chilikov said.

Less than a minute later Haddad was once again standing on the sidewalk, watching the limousine drive away. He was relieved that the process was well along, that it had all worked out despite his mistakes.

He expressed his deep gratitude that night by reading the Koran instead of taking another Gypsy whore to his bed. He didn't need to make things easier for the Turk, though he was sure the man would try again.

And when he did, Hassan Haddad would not be merciful.

6

San Francisco, California

In the week following the blast, Jack found himself
between assignments. He spent much of that time
trying to get information from the FBI press office
about progress in the case, but they were as tight-
lipped as always. So he kept himself busy with idle
pursuits, drinking in the city he loved.

He enjoyed being downtown during the nine-to-
five hustle. The buses, the rush to the underground
BART tubes on Market. The girls hurrying to dates
with their girlfriends in this gay-friendly town where
straight men were as rare as eagles. He loved the loud
twitter of the green parrots of Telegraph Hill as they
alighted in tall trees near "bum park," adjacent to
the Embarcadero office towers, seeking shelter for the
night.

Sometimes Jack would marvel like a schoolboy at the great flock that flew outside the apartment he kept by the bay, chattering in a mad formation, racing to their next stop. He was amazed by the large number of green parrots in the wild flock, said to have grown from a single pair that had escaped captivity some twenty years back—parrots from South America. They had taken to the trees of Telegraph Hill and dispersed into other sections of the city.

Each little bird had its own personality, displayed as they sought friendship, a mate, food, warmth, acceptance, and a branch to sleep on. He loved to watch them clustering in the tall eucalyptus trees, chattering as they each found their toehold for the long cold night ahead—except for the outcasts among the flock, who were rejected because of a mere color differential and forced to seek shelter on a separate tree, like those homeless bums Jack stepped around.

Life's extras.

On Tuesday he went to visit Maxine to see how she holding up, and was surprised to find her anxious to get back to work. She had a couple of freelance jobs lined up for the following week but was hoping Jack had something for her as well. Jack admitted he hadn't been able to think about much more than the blast lately and said there was nothing in the works for now.

"How are you going to survive?" she asked, showing genuine concern.

"I've got a little cushion," he told her.

That was something he owed to his father. Not the

money itself but the idea of saving. He used to tell his son, *"You can always count on watches breaking. What you cannot rely on is people getting them fixed."* He watched his money carefully and the lesson wasn't lost on Jack. That was another area where his former wife and he had disagreed. She liked to indulge in the fashions of the moment, from expensive clothes to fancy restaurants. Jack didn't mind some of that, but as a treat, not a lifestyle. And it wasn't just her. That sense of entitlement, of rampant decadence, was everywhere.

Driving over the Golden Gate Bridge one night, Jack wondered about the decline of America. He couldn't believe that the entire bridge, this beautiful Art Deco structure, had been built in only two years. Such a feat would be impossible today. Considering the EEOC—the Equal Employment Opportunity Commission—the laws, the lawsuits, the regulations, the spotted owls, and the environment, construction would take forever. As with all those hypocrites the special interests had pumped up their own self-importance, inflated their own influence and resources, at the dearest price of all: the diminishing of America.

As he drove under the south tower, Jack looked up at the spires. He was one of the few civilians that knew there were elevators running inside of these spires, right to the top. An old bohemian friend from North Beach had been an iron worker on the bridge and once took Jack up to the top to see one of the most stupendous views in the world.

He'd felt as if he were only a step away from heaven.

On Friday, Jack and Tony walked to Pagliaci's on the Wharf—one of their favorite restaurants—taking the long way, up Columbus Avenue. On the way, they saw an old familiar face—Johnny Evans, retired SFPD. They nodded hello as they passed.

"Married three times," noted Jack when they were out of earshot.

"All brief wives," muttered Tony.

"Brief wives once made the briefs rise," Jack retorted. "Now they fill the court's briefs with lies."

Tony snorted a laugh. "A new mantra?"

"Not new," Jack said. "Just haven't thought about it for a while."

"Well, go easy on the Rachel juice. You don't want your ex-wife coming up on you."

"True enough. It's just that she's been on my mind."

"Because . . . ?"

"I think it's a default setting. Things come apart like they did the other day, it shoots me to my own blast zones—Iraq or Rachel."

"Familiar turf, stuff you've already wrestled with. Lets you get your footing to process new trauma."

"Something like that, I guess," Jack said.

The more he thought about it, the more Jack realized Tony had a point. Any time something bad happened, he went to the evils he already knew. It made sense.

Columbus crested near a Chinese herb store where

Tony bought a cure for prostatitis twenty years back. Small black pills. Took them for just four days. Never another ache. The instructions showed which herbs were in the pill and what each did in the body. The theory behind the cure was explained. The herbalist thought all prostatitis was first caused by an uncured venereal infection, a sort of latent gonorrhea. The pill contained a powerful antibacterial plant. It worked so well that Tony bought bottles for his friends, who were amazed by the results.

At the top of the hill, Jack and Tony both smiled inside at the view of the bay past Alcatraz to the green hills of Marin. It was one of those sunny but cool winter days where the water was "china blue," as Tony often described it. This was one of the *good* touchstones, a place Jack visited to purge the negativity. It was like those old World War II newsreels, *Why We Fight.*

This was why. His home. It never failed to raise his spirits.

At the restaurant on Fisherman's Wharf, where old-timers who still knew where to get the best seafood still ate despite the touristy nightmare they called the "redneck Riviera," Tony and Jack enjoyed a quick lunch. After a few glasses of wine, Jack became loud. Pointing through the large picture windows, he almost shouted at Tony. "Look, see over there, in Ghirardelli Square—that clock tower. Most clock towers, even our famous tower at Berkeley, they're all derived from Giotto's Campanile."

He went on while Tony stared at him. "Think about this, Tony. Built in the fourteenth century and how many thousands of structures have been derived from his genius design. What do we have now? Web designers, fake artists, no new music of any value. What will the derivatives be from this wasteland?"

Tony nodded as he devoured his scungilli. He was used to Jack's enthusiasms, and although he agreed with most of them, he had long ago decided that living well was, in fact, the best revenge.

The rest of Jack's nights were mostly spent kicking back on the *Sea Wrighter,* listening to the gulls in the harbor and the gentle lap of the bay. Tony always seemed to have a new wine sample. One night he brought a bottle and poured Jack a glass, saying, "Try this . . . tell me what you think."

Jack was a sipper not a twirler. Dry. Tannic. Ruby red.

"Good," he said. "Better than that other one— what was it, a Gaja? Did this one cost five hundred a bottle, too?"

"Thirty-five bucks with my BevMo discount," Tony said with a wry smile.

"Amazing. What is it?"

"It's French, from Bordeaux. St. Emilion. From the airplane manufacturer's estate. Château Dassault, 2005."

"How the hell do you find these?" Jack asked.

"Taste, my friend, taste. Gotta keep tryin'."

Amen to that, Jack thought as a long week drew to a close.

* * *

Nearly a week and a half after the blast, Jack was dreaming of a beautiful blue-eyed Czech woman he'd met at a bar in town, reliving in vivid detail the night they'd spent at her apartment in North Beach.

She was a stunning woman, with the longest legs Jack had ever seen close-up, and when she peeled off her dress, revealing that she had no tan lines whatsoever, he found himself instantly ready for her.

Jack had always been a proponent of the slow build but this woman had no interest in that. Before he could get his pants all the way off, she was reaching for him like a groupie with a rock star, pulling him to her bed, her body trembling, her breathing shallow, and a look in her eyes that said, *You can do anything you want to me, but do it* now.

Jack did, with fierce intensity as she clutched him to her, her breasts pressed against him, her nails digging into his back, her teeth scraping at his earlobe as she whispered softly to him.

The whispers were quickly replaced by moans that grew louder and more urgent with every passing moment—to the point where Jack thought he might be causing her pain. Finally she cried out, clutching him even tighter as her body stiffened, then shuddered in release. Jack soon followed, then collapsed against her, every nerve ending tingling. Then he rolled away from her and fell against the pillow, trying to catch his breath, and fell asleep.

He was awakened from his dream not by the rising sun but by a tongue licking his face.

Eddie. The eleven-pound bundle of trouble he'd inherited in the divorce.

When Jack realized what was going on he started to laugh. He had originally intended for Rachel to keep the little gray poodle, but after a series of nips, bites, and soiled rugs it turned out that Eddie was even less fond of her than *he* was and he happily retrieved the two-year-old dog. Ever since then Eddie had slept with Jack, always at his feet. Sometimes the little guy would moan in his sleep, sounding like a child having a bad dream, and Jack would only have to touch him gently with a toe to break the nightmare. Despite any macho posturing to the contrary, he always thought of Eddie as his guardian angel with fur.

Of course, a boat was no real home for an animal—even a ball of fluff not much bigger than a rabbit—but Eddie had adapted remarkably well, if you didn't count the annoying habit of waking Jack up at six A.M. every morning.

Sure enough, when Jack gave him a scratch behind the ears and glanced at the digital clock next to his bed it read 5:59.

Uncanny.

Jack had to wonder if Tony Antiniori had somehow put the dog up to this. The two had taken to each other like fellow conspirators when they were first introduced, and Tony would often look after Eddie while Jack was working, teaching him little tricks to keep them both entertained. Tony's father had been a dog handler in World War II, and had a Doberman during the Tarawa Campaign that had saved his life more times than he could remember. Those skills had been passed from father to son, so it wasn't much of a stretch to think that Tony was behind this particular stunt.

Tony often protested that Eddie was more trouble than he was worth, but Jack knew this was merely the old guy's way of proving that he was still a hard-ass. The truth was, they were both completely smitten with the shaggy little poodle, even if neither of them was willing to admit it out loud.

Dragging himself from bed, Jack adjusted the drawstring on his sweats, grabbed some change, then hooked Eddie to a leash and headed for the marina clubhouse. There was a patch of grass set aside specifically for this purpose, and it wasn't unusual for Jack to find several of his neighbors walking their dogs every morning.

Eddie never failed to bring a smile to their faces

This morning, however, the area was deserted, and Jack let the dog roam as he looked out at the morning sky and the bobbing boats on the marina.

Jack had always been awestruck by the morning sun on the bay. On calm days, when the water was flat, even a dim sun behind clouds and fog lit the surface in a light show unmatched by any digitally equipped house on earth. Here, or even in the cabin, as Jack peered out he inevitably found himself wondering about God, creation, the meaning of life, and all those grand, universal questions. In that sense he was a spiritual man. He knew that life did not end when we died—he had seen too many deaths in Iraq to take the NatGeo view of things.

No, the earth was not created from a ball of fire— God had created the earth and the heavens. No, we did not simply "expire" like a fly or seagull. We were judged by God and sent into the next world, judged for the things we did and the things we should not have done. Judged, too, for the things we did not do and should have done, for the things we said and should not have said, for the words we should have said and did not say. He was content to maintain his belief in an invisible God and conduct his life accordingly, and he was sustained by this faith. And while Jack himself steered clear of churches or temples, save the occasional wedding or funeral, he deeply admired those who regularly worshipped.

He believed that honorable houses of worship were the moral compass that kept society on the right track. Sure, he had met some "religious" people who were outright bastards. But, *so what*, he thought. Religion itself, God Himself, were the eternals. Some religious institutions had their share of shame and fraud but for Jack they were first and foremost the core of the family, the bricks of civilization.

And except for one religion they all seemed to preach tolerance for others. All religions had gone through their phases of crusade and persecution, but only Islam still openly preached conquest and conversion, especially the radical Wahhabi sect. They were antiwomen, antifreedom, anti-America—

Jack sighed, bringing his mind back to the morning as he walked Eddie back home.

It was a beautiful day, the air cool and crisp, and he was looking forward to his daily bicycle regimen. He was not a triathlete like Maxine—who was already back in training despite the stitches in her skull—but he was up to ten miles a day now, and enjoyed the feel of the wind and fog in his face and the burn in his muscles that told him he was alive.

Jack pulled on his running shoes and went back outside. He had always liked to stay in shape. Some of the best weeks of his life had been spent at a private boot camp in Florida, where he'd trained in hand-to-hand combat and tactical survival skills. The camp had been run by former Israeli commandos, teaching Krav Maga, a form of martial arts developed by the Israeli defense forces and involving grappling, wrestling, and ruthless striking techniques. It had none of the dancelike grace of kung fu, jujitsu, or some of the other styles Jack had seen. It was simply deadly, and that was good enough for him. There was a saying at the camp, that "a man who cannot protect his belongings owns nothing." That was true, and there was no greater confidence-builder than knowing that if your home were threatened, or you were up against the wall, you could snap a man's neck in a second or two. It was a skill Jack hoped he would never have to put to the test.

All of these thoughts instantly vacated his mind,

however, as he wandered over to the battered newspaper racks that lined the sidewalk near the clubhouse. That was where he always did his stretching exercises, but he froze when he saw the *Chronicle*'s headline framed in one of the windows:

SUSPECTS ARRESTED IN STREET BOMBING

The news was a complete surprise. The day before, he'd heard the first rumors of possible movement in the investigation, but he hadn't expected something so dramatic so soon. And as he scanned the column of words beneath the headline, he knew he'd been right to be bothered by this case.

Dropping his coins in the slot, he grabbed the paper, scooped up Eddie, then went back to the *Sea Wrighter* and quickly changed his clothes.

Fifteen minutes later he was driving toward the city.

Jack had always thought that press conferences were about seventy percent public relations and thirty percent verifiable truth, but when all was said and done, this one didn't even meet *that* narrow threshold.

Not that anyone noticed. Most of them were there to fill air time, column space, or blog pages. That wasn't anything new. Jack had noticed mainstream media reporters becoming oddly incurious over the years. No one dug for information anymore. They simply regurgitated press releases or drummed up controversy in the hope of pleasing their employers, who were busy trying to woo back the viewers or readers they'd lost to the Internet and talk radio.

Real news was a rare commodity these days, and rarer still were real journalists. The image of the investigative reporter who let nothing stand between him and his pursuit of the truth was seen mostly in movies and episodic television shows.

The lobby of the federal courthouse was jammed with people who *claimed* to be real journalists, but Jack could only count on one hand the number of them who truly fit that definition. He considered himself among their number, but was sure there were plenty of his colleagues who would disagree.

The conference began in the usual manner. A mix of uniforms and suits, feds, cops, and politicians flanking a single podium crowded with microphones. The chief of police stepped up and waited as the room grew quiet except for the steady click of digital single-lens reflex cameras.

After a moment, the police chief said, "Before we get into the reason we're here, I'd like to renew my condolences to the family of Officer Tom Drabinsky. His dedication to this city is unparalleled, and we'll all miss his good humor and unwavering courage in the face of danger."

A good start, Jack thought. The networks had all jumped at his tribute to Drabinsky, although most of them had edited the footage to fit their time slots, which wasn't uncommon. As he expected, the name Jack Hatfield was never mentioned.

Several of the uniforms behind the chief were

members of the SFPD bomb squad, and they lowered their heads in respect.

"A memorial service for Officer Drabinsky will be held at a later date, and the family has asked that the press allow them to mourn in private. I hope you'll all respect those wishes."

"Do you have that date?" a reporter asked.

The chief frowned. "I'll let the family decide whether or not they want to release that information." Several more reporters tried to jump in, but he ignored them and pressed on. "Now, I'd like to introduce Field Director Carl Forsyth, head of the FBI task force assigned to investigating this incident in conjunction with the Department of Homeland Security and the SFPD. He'll give you a rundown of the facts. Agent Forsyth?"

Cameras flashed as one of the suits stepped forward. He had the crisp but slightly bland demeanor of a typical FBI agent. Jack immediately recognized him as the agent in charge from the night of the blast.

Forsyth expressed condolences to the Drabinsky family on behalf of the federal government, dispassionately listed the names of his team, and thanked each of them for their swift and decisive work.

Then he said, "You've all read the release sent out by our press office late last night, so you know that our agents conducted a raid yesterday evening of a compound in the northern California border town of Higgston. We took into custody several suspects we believe are responsible for the failed bombing attempt last week."

The crowd erupted with shouted questions, but Forsyth held up a hand to silence them.

"Let me finish my statement and I'll answer all your questions." He paused as they settled again. "The compound is owned by a small paramilitary organization who call themselves the CDB or the Constitutional Defense Brigade, boasting about twenty-five members. As many of you may know, the leader of that group is under federal indictment for tax evasion and wire fraud and we believe the federal courthouse was the intended target of the bomber."

"What evidence do you have of their involvement?" someone called out.

Before the crowd could get fired up again, Forsyth once again raised his hand to keep them quiet. "During the raid, we found a cache of firearms and several bricks of C4 explosives and detonators, similar to those used in the blast. We also found a file containing multiple photographs of the target, three city maps focusing on the downtown area, and a GPS unit with travel coordinates to the courthouse. A similar GPS unit was found in the wreckage of the Land Rover.

"But the real kicker is a witness by the name of William Clegg, a resident of Higgston, who earlier this year attempted to join the CDB and was turned away. He claims that the group has been planning this operation for weeks." Another pause. "While it's ultimately up to the courts to decide guilt or innocence, we feel confident that with the evidence we've gathered, and with Mr. Clegg's testimony, each of our suspects will be spending a considerable time behind bars. I'll now open the floor to—"

The roar erupted before he had a chance to finish his sentence. Forsyth calmed them down again and said he'd take their questions one at a time, then pointed to a sultry blond correspondent for FOX News.

"Have any of the suspects confessed?"

"They're still undergoing interrogation," Forsyth said, "so I can't comment on that at the moment. Barring any legal restrictions, however, we'll be providing you with progress reports."

He pointed to a reporter from CBS.

"From the very beginning," the reporter said, "there've been rumors that this attack could be related to Islamic fundamentalists. Are you saying this is strictly homegrown?"

Forsyth nodded. "I won't deny that our first inclination was to look in that direction, but when Mr. Clegg came forward we quickly found out otherwise. This should probably serve as a lesson to us all not to prejudge such things. The world is full of dangerous people, and some of them are in our own backyard."

Maybe so, Jack thought, but the evidence Forsyth had mentioned was circumstantial at best. And relying on a local witness who hadn't been allowed on the inside, yet claimed to have inside information, strained credulity. Who was to say he didn't have a grudge?

As far as the firearms were concerned, if the feds

were to ever raid the apartment Jack owned near the Embarcadero they'd find enough legal weapons to equip a marine fire team—a collection he'd amassed over the last twenty years. Did that make him a terrorist?

The maps the feds had found could simply have been preparation for a trip to San Francisco to witness their leader's trial, and there might even be a logical explanation for the presence of C4 at the compound. A licensed demolitions expert would have the right to possess it, and any number of reasons to use it out there from construction to rock removal to movie special effects work.

Whatever the case, Jack wasn't willing to choke down any of this without a bit of resistance. Especially knowing what he knew about Leon Thomas's statement.

More hands went in the air and Forsyth made his choice.

"What about the minor who hijacked the car?" a reporter for the *Chronicle* asked. "Is he being charged with anything?"

Forsyth shook his head. "Not on a federal level. His involvement had nothing to do with the conspiracy itself, so no charges are anticipated. He's currently recovering from a busted arm and leg incurred in the crash and is in hospital room custody of the SFPD."

"I understand his brother has been released," the reporter said.

"He was arrested for allegedly aiding and abetting

the carjack and has been released to the custody of his parents on $25,000 bail. We'll leave it to the city prosecutor to sort out any crimes he may have committed."

Jack listened patiently as several more questions were asked and answered, all of them centering on the CDB. He kept waiting for someone to mention what he considered to be the gorilla in the room, but maybe he was the only one who actually saw it.

He raised his hand, only to be passed over several times by Forsyth, and he felt for a moment as if he were the scrawny kid in phys ed who was the last to be chosen for flag football. Back in school, Jack was usually the guy who *did* the choosing, but he now had a sudden understanding and sympathy for what those poor kids must have gone through.

Finally, when Forsyth had no choice, he called on Jack, saying, "Well, Mr. Hatfield, it's nice to see you're still among the living. Professionally speaking, at least."

The crowd laughed and Jack merely smiled. But it was nervous laughter, the kind you hear when a drunk uncle stands to toast the bride and groom at a wedding.

When they got it out of their collective system, Jack said, "I'm curious to know why there hasn't been any mention of the Arab reportedly seen by Leon Thomas?"

The crowd buzzed at the remark and there was a subtle shift in Forsyth's gaze. So subtle that most in the room had probably missed it, but Jack had been carefully watching for the man's reaction.

"An Arab, Mr. Hatfield?"

"I spoke to one of the first responders at the scene. An Officer Harold Beckman. He told me the carjacker's brother claimed the Land Rover was stolen from a man of Arabian descent."

Forsyth smiled. "We have yet to definitively identify the original driver, but we have every reason to believe that he's one of the men we just took into custody. And I assure you, there's not an Arab in sight."

"So you're saying Beckman was lying?"

"As I recall, Officer Beckman suffered a minor head injury in the blast, so I'm afraid his recollection cannot be relied upon."

Forsyth was about to call on another reporter when Jack interrupted. "Beckman told me this *before* the blast."

More muttering. The FBI agent shifted his gaze back to Jack and Jack could plainly see that he was seething inside. This was not information Forsyth wanted asked about or shared.

"If I remember correctly, you were also knocked down by the explosion. Maybe you're confused, as well."

"I don't think so," Jack told him. "And my memory's just fine."

Forsyth smiled again. It took some effort. "Or maybe you're just disappointed that our investigation hasn't turned up any Muslims for you to kill?"

The shot went straight to the heart, and after a split second of stunned surprise, the reporters around Jack laughed uproariously, nodding and shaking their heads.

It was, Jack had to admit, the perfect response. It immediately branded him a crackpot who shouldn't be taken seriously.

Jack thought of Tom Drabinsky and felt his own anger rising in his chest. He had a hard time believing the story this smug little jerk was selling, and he felt sick at the thought that Drabinsky's sacrifice might be explained away by a lie.

Something Jack had learned quickly as a combat journalist was that anything the commanding officers had to say should be taken with a heavy dose of skepticism. The soldiers on the ground were the ones who knew the truth, and that's who he needed to go to in order to find it.

He had no idea why the FBI would lie about this, but could only assume that they'd been unable to make any progress in the case and needed an easy scapegoat. Someone the President could point at to assure the public that the federal government was doing its job.

A quote from Isaiah came to mind: *"As for my people, a babe is their master, and women rule over them."* It was to this state America had fallen.

A few more questions were asked, but Jack tuned out the rest of it, knowing that it was just more nonsense. And when the party broke up, he immediately moved toward the podium, approaching Vince McElroy, one of Drabinsky's crew.

"Vince . . ." he said, keeping his voice low.

McElroy turned, not quite looking him in the eye. "Hey, Jack."

"What's going on here? Do you believe a word that guy said?"

McElroy gave him a halfhearted shrug. "We caught the bad guys. Isn't that all that matters?"

He started to turn away and Jack grabbed the sleeve of his uniform. "Wait a minute—wait. Are you telling me you're falling for this crap?"

"They've got the evidence, don't they? Besides, like Tom always said, we're just the garbage collectors. It doesn't much matter what we think."

Then he pulled himself free and walked away.

Jack was headed back to his car when his cell phone rang. He dug it from his pocket and checked the screen: Tony Antiniori.

"That was a load of bull if I ever saw one," Tony said. "And I've been around for a long, long time."

"You watch from the boat?"

"Yes, and I didn't much like what I saw. Wouldn't mind taking that FBI *strunze* straight up to the drop zone and letting go."

Jack smiled. "So what do you think we should do about it?"

"I've got an old pal who lives up in Higgston," Tony said. "I already gave him a call and he had some interesting things to say about the government's star witness."

"Like what?" Jack asked.

"You up for an early lunch?"

"Sure."

"Meet me at Pagliaci's in half an hour. We'll talk."

7

It was several months before Jack realized that Tony Antiniori had a limp. Only a keen eye could spot it, and when Jack finally did he wondered if it were a temporary thing.

They were strolling through North Beach at the time, doing the rounds of the local bars, when Jack noticed the hitch in Tony's step and said, "You hurt yourself?"

Tony immediately corrected his walk, and the limp all but disappeared. But when Jack gave him a quizzical look, Tony said defensively, "You spend enough time doing twenty-foot jumps out of a Huey Slick with sixty pounds of gear on your back, you'd be walking funny, too."

Jack didn't know the extent of Tony's injuries from his days in Vietnam and the Gulf, but based on the stories he'd told, the old guy had to be in constant pain. That he hid it all so well and still managed to maintain a relatively balanced disposition was a testament to pure will.

But that was Tony Antiniori.

Jack was sitting at his favorite booth at Pagliaci's on the Wharf, looking out at the bay and sipping a cup of perfect, nonbitter espresso, when Tony walked in, Eddie tucked under his arm. His limp was more pronounced than usual—a sign that he was hot and bothered about something.

He weaved through the maze of white-clothed tables, struggled into the leather booth across from Jack, and sat Eddie between them. The Pescatori brothers didn't normally allow dogs in their establishment, but for Tony they made an exception. The way Tony coddled Eddie, Jack sometimes wondered if what he was witnessing was a very slow, very deliberate dognapping.

Tony said, "The streets were packed with Euro-Peons. Did you order yet?"

Jack shook his head, then reached over and scratched Eddie under the chin. "Waiting for you two."

"I'm so steamed up right now, I'm not sure I can eat."

"Because of the press conference?"

Tony nodded. "Darleen spent the night, and we were in bed this morning when we watched it. Killed the mood the minute that FBI douchebag opened his mouth."

Tony may have had his injuries, but that had never slowed him down when it came to the ladies. Darleen was a neighbor and his latest hookup. And if Tony Antiniori had passed up a morning liaison because of a routine press conference, that was saying something indeed.

"You know me," Tony went on. "I may have my share of secrets, but I'm pretty much what you see. I didn't spend years in the jungle so some federal *strunzo,* a piece of shit, could lie to my face. I wanted to reach through my TV set and throttle that son of a bitch."

"Imagine how *I* felt."

"You ask me, the way he slapped you down only confirms he's a spokesmouth for some scumbag plot. Good thing I wasn't in that room."

Jack smiled. "Easy, boy."

"I mean it. I saw that video you made. Your friend Drabinsky reminded me of some of the men in my unit, and it just about kills me to see these people use his sacrifice to sell their fairy tale."

"I thought exactly the same thing."

"I'm not surprised."

Jack took a sip of his espresso. "So what did you find out about the government's star witness? Tell me about this friend of yours in Higgston."

"Met him years ago, while I was stationed up at Fort Lewis. He's Higgston born and raised and he's known this Clegg character since he was six years old. Says he's a drunk, a liar, and an idiot all rolled into one."

"But why would Clegg lie?"

"Why else?" Tony rubbed his thumb back and forth across his fingertips.

"You think somebody paid him off?"

"Makes sense to me. According to my friend, the Constitutional Defense Brigade is just a bunch of middle-aged tax dodgers sitting around bitching about the new world order. The only thing they've ever organized is a Saturday-night beer party."

"What about the C4 and the weapons?"

"My buddy says the guns are all legal and you and I both know the C4 could have been planted. And get this: William Clegg didn't try to join the CDB until two days *after* the bombing."

Jack immediately understood. "Someone manufactured a witness."

"That would be my guess. Nobody in the CDB can stand the guy. What does that tell you?"

"The CDBers get angry just hearing his name," Jack said. "On camera, it plays like they're angry about something else."

"Like having their ring busted up," Tony said.

"So why would anyone fall for this nonsense?"

Tony shrugged. "Same reason they always do. Everybody wants to believe. You've had some experience with that."

Jack nodded glumly, then took another sip of espresso. "I made a few phone calls, myself. Tried to get hold of Officer Beckman. Turns out he's on medical leave in Florida."

"That's convenient."

"No kidding. I saw his injury. Maxine took a bigger hit than he did and *she's* already back to running ten miles a day."

"So who else did you call?"

"Some of my old contacts at the FBI, but nobody seems to want to talk to me."

Tony gave him an amused look.

"No, not just because it's me." Jack grinned.

"The wall's gone up," Tony said, once again serious. "All because some punk said he thought the car belonged to an Arab."

"That's about the size of it."

Tony thought for a moment. "He had to tell them more than that."

"What do you mean?"

Tony leaned closer. The restaurant wasn't very crowded and he didn't want his voice to carry. "The carjack victim could have been Egyptian, Druze, Bahraini, and no one would give a damn. Or flip that around. What kind of Arab *would* the government care about?"

"Off the top, Saudi, Iranian—"

"Stop right there," Tony said. "That's the entire list. One a supposed ally, one an enemy. No one else could put a scare into Washington. Suppose the guy is GIP." Tony was referring to the General Intelligence Presidency, the Saudi spy network. "He goes rogue, plans an attack. The Saudis won't want that to become public knowledge. Spoils their image as being oh-so-damned-concerned about our security."

"Well, they are," Jack said. "Who's gonna bail them out when Iran goes nuclear."

"Exactly. My point is, that's one reason to hush things up. It would make the Saudis look bad. But that's not what happened."

"How do you know?"

"I made some calls. There has been no uptick in GIP activity here. Zero."

"So the Saudis are not looking for this mysterious Arab," Jack said.

"Right. And they *would* be—looking hard. Now, suppose the guy is Iranian. That would mean those bad boys aren't just shuttling weapons into Iraq anymore. They're active *here* and trying to blow a hole in one of our cities."

Jack sat back. "Interesting theory. But the Arab could also be an independent operator, a radicalized student, any number of things."

"Agreed, but that's not the point. Americans go right to the worst possible scenario, and a bunch of mini-Ahmadinejads running loose on our shores is one of those."

"I buy that. But what could this Leon kid have said that tipped them off?"

"Have you ever read any of the government white papers on Iran?"

"Not since I was stationed in the Gulf and they were part of the eyes-only press packets."

"Profiling has gotten a lot better since then. You know—the kind of stuff we're not supposed to be doing but are."

Jack laughed.

"I won't get into the psychology of it, but here's the shout-out for the young Iranian male," Tony said. "Neatly pressed button-down white shirt, long sleeved. Sunglasses, day and night. Beige or light-colored slacks. Loafers, no socks. Expensive gold wristwatch. Think you'd notice those things casing out a carjack?"

Jack nodded.

"That, my friend, is why the FBI thinks this guy is Iranian. Maybe they know more than that, maybe Leon's report and the explosion dovetailed with something they already knew, someone they were already watching."

"But it's enough to trigger a good old-fashioned multiagency cover-up," Jack said. "A bunch of local wackos seem a lot less threatening than an Islamic terrorist cell. And with only one man dead, people are bound to forget about this the minute some celebrity goes into rehab. It becomes a nonevent. And nonevents don't threaten political careers unless someone wants them to."

"Anybody ever tell you you're a cynical bastard?"

Jack smiled and was about to respond when a voice rang out from across the dining room, calling Tony's name.

They both looked up to see Danny Pescatori emerging from the kitchen with a grin on his face—a short, squat, powerful Sicilian who, along with his brother Carlo, had been running Pagliaci's for over thirty years now, ever since their parents had retired.

Pagliaci's on the Wharf was a San Francisco institution. It had been standing on this very same spot for nearly a century, serving Sicilian seafood that made your mouth water just thinking about it. It didn't hurt that it boasted a view of two dozen bobbing fishing boats, Alcatraz Island, and the bay, stretching past the Golden Gate Bridge to the Headlands.

Jack had been coming here for longer than he could remember, and always found it difficult to say no to the shrimp. The Pescatoris made sure that he got the "A" shack supply, which was reserved for family and friends. Shrimp that always smacked of the sea. Briny, not slimy.

But it was Tony who was the mainstay here. He'd practically grown up in the place and the Pescatoris always treated him like a brother. He knew more about the wharf and wharf politics than anyone really should, and had once said to Jack, "If I told you even a third of what I know, I'd be in cement shoes before you could peel one of those shrimp you love." In San Francisco, almost all Italians of a certain generation knew each other like extended family.

As Danny Pescatori emerged from the kitchen, he made a quick side trip to the front counter, then crossed the dining room toward them, waving a small card. "Hey, hey, Cousin, what did I tell you?"

Despite his mood, Tony's eyes lit up. "The gala?"

Danny reached the table and dropped an invitation in front of him. "Next Saturday night, VIP entry."

It was a black-tie dinner at the Legion of Honor

that promised appearanc
mayor, two senators, a ros
that would make Woodsto
and the President of th
$7500 a plate, only the

98

bull, and if t
ment, I ne
sky." "A

Tony had been angling for
months. Not because he particularly cared abo
ing—he wasn't a fan of the current occupant of the
White House—but because Darleen was hot to go
and Tony knew he had to try to get them an invite.

Not surprisingly, Danny Pescatori had come
through.

"I owe you, Cousin."

"Shut up, you. The day you owe me anything is
the day I retire."

The sight of the invitation must have perked Tony
up, because he suddenly declared that he was
hungry.

As usual, they both ordered off the menu, Tony
asking for Carlo's special seafood sausages, while
Jack decided to stick to the "A" shack shrimp,
drenched in marinara. He also ordered the pup his
usual hamburger.

The little guy actually licked his chops as if he
knew exactly what was coming.

When Danny went to put in the order, Jack said,
"So where were we?"

Tony sobered, pocketing his invitation. "Trying to
pin down exactly what the FBI wants to cover up."

"Well, whoever's behind it is crazy if they think
they've heard the last of it. We know their story's

here's any truth to Leon Thomas's state-
ed to find out. I owe that much to Drabin-

nd how exactly do you plan on doing that?"

"Same way I always have. Keep whacking at the piñata until it finally breaks."

"You may not like what you find inside," Tony told him. "Or worse yet, *it* may not like *you*."

"I've never let that stop me."

Tony nodded. "Fair enough. So what's your next step?"

Jack thought about it a moment. Then he said, "I think it's time to call Bob Copeland."

8

The Beat Café seemed like an odd place for a meet.

It was located next to a strip club in North Beach, and Jack thought of it as really nothing more than a hamburger joint with a gimmick. Done up like an old 1950s coffeehouse, its walls were adorned with huge photographs of beatniks, now long forgotten.

Pay a small fee and you could walk through the restaurant to the back, climb a set of wooden steps, and find yourself in a tiny "museum" full of more photographs, newspaper articles, and even furniture, all centering around the prehippie Beat Generation.

The museum had a kind of quiet, reverential charm, but was the last place Jack would have picked to rendezvous with a source. If anything, he would have chosen the Etna Café, which was just around the corner. At least you could get a decent drink there.

He checked his watch, a vintage Hamilton Gilbert

he'd inherited from his father that could well have been part of this museum.

It was nearly nine P.M.

He stood staring at a stark, moody portrait of an attractive blonde when he felt a presence next to him.

Bob Copeland.

"It's always about the girl, isn't it?" asked the rough, smoky voice. "Carolyn Cassady. She was the real driving force, you know. Married to Neal Cassady and sleeping with Jack Kerouac."

Copeland was a stout man with a bulldog face who had always reminded Jack of one of his heroes, Winston Churchill. Without the accent, of course.

"That must've made for an interesting home life," Jack said.

Copeland waved an arm. "All this nonsense destroyed Kerouac. He was a true American literary giant who despised the so-called Beat Movement that hacks like Ginsberg ruthlessly promoted." He looked at Jack. "Did you know Kerouac voted for Nixon?"

"I had no idea."

Copeland shrugged. "It's all ancient history. Which is what *we'll* both be a few years down the line. Think anyone'll ever erect a museum in our honor?"

"Doubtful," Jack said.

A former Defense Department official, Vietnam combat veteran, and a leading proponent of cyberdefense, Copeland was a member of a conservative think tank who divided his time between Washington and San Francisco—Jack's most reliable "anonymous" source back in the days of *Truth Tellers*. He had a direct line into the D.C. nerve center, and Jack had been all too happy to mine that connection.

The man also had a love affair with clandestine theatrics, which was why *he* always chose their meeting places. That usually meant the Museum of Modern Art, or the Academy of Sciences, but maybe Copeland was looking for a change of pace these days.

Jack couldn't be sure. He hadn't seen or heard from the man in over two years.

"You're looking pretty good, Jack. How you been?"

"Can't complain."

Copeland chuckled. "The hell you can't. You still getting death threats?"

"Nothing I can't handle."

"At least you've still got the old self-confidence. That and a pocketful of cash is all a man really needs. Everything else is dead weight." He shot Jack a glance. "Speaking of which, you see much of the ex these days?"

"Not really."

Jack didn't exactly think of Rachel as dead weight, but he had no interest in seeing her. Jack met her while doing a segment for one of his shows, *The World of the Runway Model*. She was tall, almost five foot nine, with raven hair and green eyes. After interviewing her for the program, he took her for a quick coffee at a local café in North Beach. She immediately struck him as more than just a body.

"What did you learn from your parents?" she asked him—out of nowhere, it seemed, but that was the way she was. Inquisitive in ways he never quite fathomed. And she was direct. There was nothing she would not ask.

They quickly became inseparable, joined in body and in mind. But they were also talkers, big-time, who hashed everything out—or talked it to death, whichever came first. In the end, they realized that neither of them was really listening to the other, two alphas competing for the same turf. At least he and Rachel had always had a wonderful time in bed, which is more than could be said for a lot of married couples. But they clashed just about everywhere else. After the divorce, he vowed never again to mistake an orgasm for a declaration of love.

"I hear she's dating a tax attorney," Copeland said. "That's gotta be a helluva letdown after the turbulent world of Jack Hatfield."

"What *is* this, Bob? *This Is Your Life*?"

"You've been underground for a while, my friend. I'm simply trying to get a feel for your state of mind."

"I haven't been under anything. Just making a living."

"Pickup stories and character profiles for the local affiliates? Not exactly GNT, is it? Makes me wonder what you might do to get back into their good graces."

As this was starting to sink in, Copeland moved to a glass display case that held a blue denim shirt. Reportedly Kerouac's.

Jack stared at him. "Are you trying to tell me something, Bob? Or is this just your usual schtick?"

"Careful. I'm not the enemy, remember? I didn't have to answer your call."

"I know. So why did you?"

He raised a shoulder and let it drop. "Loyalty, I suppose. I've always felt bad about what Lawrence Soren and his hatchet squad did to you. You're a man of integrity, and to see you attacked like that caused me considerable pain."

"Yet you never bothered to call."

Copeland smiled. "You know how it is in this business. Somebody slits your throat, everyone else is just trying to avoid the spray. It's never anything personal."

"Except to the guy who's getting his throat slit. So how about you cut the small talk, Bob. You wouldn't be here if you didn't have information to share. Did you look into what we discussed?"

Copeland nodded. "I did, just as you asked, and I found out that you're a tinfoil-hat-wearing lunatic who has no idea what he's talking about."

"Of course," Jack said. "And is that what *you* believe?"

Copeland eyed him sharply. "Come on, Jack, give me a little credit. Nobody spews that kind of venom unless they've got something to hide. Character assassination and misdirection are standard operating procedure these days. On both sides of the aisle."

"So you're saying this goes back to Washington?"

Copeland shook his head. "I'm saying no such thing, because I don't know. If there's anything more to that blast than what you learned from the press conference this morning, nobody's talking about it. And about all I could get out of one low-level administration lackey were a few choice words that would make my foulmouthed friend Dick Cheney proud."

Jack frowned. "So then why *are* you here, Bob? If that's all you've got, why agree to this meet?"

"Because I like you, Jack. I've missed doing business with you, and I think you may be right about this thing. And if you are, you deserve fair warning that you're about to swim upstream in dangerous waters."

"You know this for a fact?"

"No. Just a general feeling based on the reception I got when I started asking around about this alleged Iranian."

"Did anyone deny he *was* Iranian?"

Copeland shook his head.

"Who did you ask?"

Copeland sighed. "Come on, you know I can't answer that. You need to tread lightly, my friend. You already drew attention to yourself at that press conference. You didn't back down when that federal mouthpiece started in on you, and you kept asking questions when you didn't like his answers."

"That's my job," Jack said.

Copeland chuckled again. "Right. Which is how you got your name on another list. When someone starts acting like an actual reporter, the people I know tend to get nervous. They don't like real questions, hardball questions. They like reporters who get with the program. And I don't care *what* you're looking to find out. You start poking at a hornet's nest, you're bound to piss *somebody* off."

"Tell me something I don't know. Look, you're giving me nothing but generalities. Help me out here. Who do I need to be looking at?"

"Anybody and everybody, would be my guess. Try throwing a rock and see who throws it back. But make sure you're prepared to duck."

"And what about you? You just gonna watch or—"

"Give me *some* credit, Jack," Copeland said irritably. "I'll keep digging, as discreetly as I can. I'm curious, too, but I'm not interested in a suicide mission."

Jack nodded. "Thanks, Bob. I appreciate it."

Copeland gestured to the portrait of Carolyn Cassady. "She was something, wasn't she?"

Jack shrugged. "If you like the type."

"Oh, I do. Hell, if I'd been around back then, I probably would've made a move on her myself." He paused. "She wrote an autobiography, you know. I hear it's pretty good."

"Yeah?"

"I think Dark Nights still has a copy. You should grab it before somebody else does." He gave Jack a curt nod, then walked to the stairs and turned. "It might just open your eyes."

Then a moment later, he was gone.

Just Like Copeland to test a man, Jack thought.

Whenever someone's actions puzzled Jack, he sought answers in the Bible. He had read and re-read both Testaments, committing long passages to memory. And right now Job 18:2 came to mind, when Bildad said to his long-suffering friend: *"When will you put an end to words? Reflect, and then we can have discussion."*

Jack grinned.

The roles were a good fit.

He would reflect, then they would talk.

The Dark Nights bookstore was a San Francisco landmark, located just down the street.

The young woman at the cash register had so many tattoos and piercings that Jack had to wonder what had motivated her to mark and mutilate herself. Some fashion statements are permanent, and chances were pretty good that one day this girl would be a sixty-year-old grandmother wondering what the hell she'd been thinking.

Then Jack realized he sounded just like his old man, complaining about "kids these days . . ." It was the natural progression of things, he supposed.

He found the book Copeland had recommended, paid for it, then nodded good night and went outside and across the street to the Etna, where he found a table in back and ordered a single malt.

When it came down to it, *this* place was the real Beat Café. Kerouac had spent many a night here, getting polluted with Neal Cassady and the woman they shared. Jack honestly couldn't care less about these people, but Bob Copeland's suggestion that he buy a copy of Carolyn's autobiography had not been unmotivated.

So, as he waited for his drink, he opened the book—which she'd titled *Off the Road*—and carefully leafed through the fragile, yellowing pages, scanning them one at a time.

He got his first hit on page 94.

Halfway down, in an excerpt of a letter from Neal Cassady to Kerouac, a word had been neatly underlined in pencil:

operation

Jack knew full well that this wasn't some random marking, but was Copeland's handiwork, the result of his love for cloak and dagger.

He found the next one on page 98, at the end of another excerpt:

road

Then there was nothing for a few pages until he reached page 109, where the last word of the first paragraph was underlined:

show

His drink came, and he let it sit as he continued on through the remaining pages, one after another, all 355 of them. There were no more pencil marks to be found.

When Jack was done, he quickly went through it again to make sure he hadn't missed anything. Then he closed the book, knocked back his scotch, and felt its heat roll through him as he quietly contemplated Bob Copeland's message.

Operation Roadshow.

Jack immediately thought of a PBS television series that Rachel used to watch, where people brought in ancient household items to be evaluated by antiques dealers, in hopes of striking it rich.

He was pretty sure that Copeland's message had nothing at all to do with antiques.

Not even close.

But what, then, did it mean?

Jack spent most of the night trying to find out.

He got on his laptop back at the boat and hit Google and his usual go-to databases, checking news sources, public records, legislative filings, reference materials, freedom of information archives.

All he found was a single notation in the footnotes of an article about World War II, referencing a little-known intelligence operation called Roadshow, in which British spies attempted to infiltrate the German government and take it down from the inside. The operation had been a complete failure.

And so, apparently, was this search.

A couple hours before dawn, Jack looked down at Eddie, who was curled next to him on the bed. "What do you think, fuzzy? Are we being played?"

Eddie cocked an ear and tilted his head as if puzzled by the question, and Jack gave him a pat.

"My thoughts exactly."

Abandoning his task, Jack closed his laptop and then his eyes. He quickly fell asleep.

Before long, Jack was launched into a dream about Iraqi insurgents trying to steal his Humvee, which had a cache of explosives in back. His dead friend Richard Riley made an appearance—eyes as blank as ever—and so did Agent Forsyth, both of them coming and going as the dream shifted and morphed into a *Truth Tellers* panel discussion about Islamic fundamentalists and Beat Generation poetry.

He awoke at six A.M. with Eddie's usual face lick, and found the little guy wiggling around like crazy—which meant only one thing:

Tony Antiniori was in the vicinity.

Jack pulled on some clothes and found his friend topside, sitting at the dining table across from the galley, sipping a cup of coffee and reading the paper. Eddie immediately jumped into Tony's lap and let him scratch his ears.

"You look like hell," Tony said to Jack.

"Thanks, pal. You look rested."

"I had a good workout." He winked.

"Good thing I'm a gentleman or I'd ask for details."

Jack rubbed his face, trying to wake himself, then moved to the galley and poured a cup of coffee. Black, no sugar.

"How did things go with Bob Copeland?" Tony asked.

Jack took a long sip of his coffee. "He's an enigma. I wish for once in his life he'd get to the point instead of circling it. You ever heard of something called Operation Roadshow?"

Tony thought for a moment. "Not that I remember. What is it? Some kind of black op?"

"No idea. And I'm not even sure Copeland knows. But he went to a lot of trouble to put that phrase in my head, so I figure it must mean something."

"I can check around."

"Good luck. I tried, and all I found was some obscure World War II reference. Either this is something so far under the radar that it's out of our reach, or Copeland is playing mind games."

"Which do you think it is?"

"He may be annoying sometimes, but that's not usually his style."

"And you think this has something to do with the cover-up?" Tony asked.

"What I think is that all we've got is a hunch, based on speculation and hearsay, and unless we can get some solid information we're just spinning our wheels."

"So why not go to the source?" Tony asked.

"What do you mean?"

"Jamal Thomas or his brother. Ask flat out if they're sure about who was driving that car and whatever else they might remember."

Jack shook his head. "The brother's not talking and the cops have Jamal on lockdown. I tried talking to his brother's public defender a few days ago and got rebuffed. No way I'll ever get to those kids."

"Don't speak too soon," Tony said, then folded

the newspaper over and slid it across the table. "The story's buried on the second page, but I think you'll find it interesting."

Jack put his cup on the counter and crossed to the table, staring down at a single column, headlined CARJACKING SUSPECT TO BE RELEASED.

"Jamal's bail was set at 200K," Tony said. "His folks could barely afford the 25K they paid for Leon. His attorney filed a motion to reduce bail and the judge granted it."

"How much?"

"He'll be putting up ten percent with the bondsman, twenty thousand dollars. They're taking him home at the close of business tonight."

"Hold on," Jack said. "If his folks—"

"There's just a mother."

"Okay. If she was tapped out by Leon's bail, where's the twenty grand coming from?"

Tony tapped the tabletop. "Read the article. Says the bond is being put up by an organization called the Juvenile Defense Coalition."

"Never heard of it," Jack said.

"Apparently they're dedicated to keeping troubled teens out of jail because the poor things might actually have to take responsibility for their actions."

Jack nodded. "Better to have them out on the street where they can sell dope to school kids and break into their neighbors' houses, right?"

"Or steal cars from potential terrorists," Tony said.

Jack shook his head in disgust. He had no problem with the juvenile justice system treating kids like kids, but there was a point where you had to draw the line. Sure, some of them came from broken homes and had grown up in terrible environments, but that didn't really excuse the choices they made. And when it came down to it, the law-abiding citizens of this country were usually the victims of those choices.

Jack had come to believe that some people were just born bad. These kids knew damn well that what they were doing was wrong and couldn't care less.

So why should anyone else?

Of course, in this case the actions of a bunch of misguided do-gooders might actually work in Jack's favor. If the kid was due to be released, that meant access, and Jack might finally be able to talk to the punk.

Juvenile court records were routinely kept confidential in California, but Jack had managed to use a back-channel source to get a name and address, and he knew the kid lived with his brother and mother at the Sunnydale projects.

He had tried contacting the mother—Juanita Thomas—shortly after the blast, but her line was a constant busy signal, and he had assumed that he wasn't the only one looking to do a bedside interview with her son. But now that the focus of the investigation was a bunch of militia wannabes, most of Jack's colleagues would be centering their attention on the Constitutional Defense Brigade. Which meant, if he was lucky, he might just have the carjacker all to himself.

He looked at Tony. "You interested in a trip to Sunnydale tonight?"

Tony shook his head. "I'm headed to Camp Parks to run a training session. Gotta be up at dawn."

"So what—you're leaving me out in the cold?"

"I'd just slow you down anyway. I'm a doddering old man."

Jack stifled a laugh. "A doddering old man who thinks two hundred knuckle pushups on a hardwood floor are just a warm-up every morning."

"Sorry, Jack, but duty calls. Besides, if you're heading into Sunnydale, what you really need is a negotiator. Somebody who knows the area and is a helluva lot easier on the eyes."

Jack took a moment to process this. "Are you talking about who I think you are?"

Tony grinned. "As a matter of fact, I am."

9

London, England

"Someone followed me to Sofia," Haddad said.

He had waited for his imam for over an hour. It had taken some time to reach the decision to tell him about the Turk and the whore, but once Haddad had made up his mind he was anxious to be done with it.

When he first arrived, Imam Zuabi was away from the office and Haddad had grown more and more impatient with each passing minute. He had been to the Muslim Welfare Center and Mosque many times since the day it opened, but events of late were taking their toll on him and he felt little comfort within its walls.

When Zuabi returned, the sun had gone down and it was time for *Maghrib*—evening prayer. So the two went to the *wudu* room together and quietly washed their bodies before heading upstairs to kneel before Allah.

Afterward, they returned to Zuabi's office, and after a few brief pleasantries Haddad broke the news.

"I think they may have traveled with me on the plane to Belgrade," he said. "That is the only explanation I can think of for their being there. But I wasn't aware of them until after I arrived in Sofia."

Zuabi considered this. "Do you know who they were?"

Haddad shook his head. "A Turk and a woman, that's all I can tell you. I thought she was a Gypsy, but now I'm not so certain."

Haddad saw no point in mentioning their night together. The whore lingered in his memory as an effigy of dangerous lust and blind, stupid, dangerous trust. The pleasures he had enjoyed, and they were considerable, were swallowed in a swamp of disgust and self-reproach.

Zuabi frowned. "This is a concern, Hassan. If someone knows about our plans, they could destroy everything we've built. I assume you took care of the matter?"

"The woman," Haddad said. "But the Turk got away. And I can't be certain how much he knows."

Zuabi's frown deepened. "Our friends won't be happy about this. They'll want assurances that we haven't been compromised. Our relationship is already on shaky ground after the incident with Abdal."

Zuabi often spoke of their "friends," but had never bothered to give Haddad details about who they were.

The Hand of Allah had several sources of revenue, much of it funneled through charities around the world, but *these* particular friends—or benefactors—continued to remain anonymous to Haddad, an endless source of frustration for him. Did Zuabi not trust him? Was he not, after all, one of the Hand of Allah's most dedicated soldiers?

But like any good soldier, he remained silent, not allowing himself to ask the questions that so plagued him.

Instead he said, "Is it necessary for them to know?"

Zuabi thought about this a moment. "I don't suppose there's any point in raising an alarm until we understand who we're dealing with. You continue as before and I'll look into the matter. If you see this Turk again, find out what you can and then kill him."

"What about Abdal? Have you decided what to do with that fool?"

Haddad had only learned about the disaster in San Francisco upon his return to London, and had been relieved to hear that the Americans believed the incident had originated locally. Abdal al-Fida had recently returned to London himself, and if it had been up to Haddad he would have killed him within moments of his arrival.

But Zuabi was apparently leaning toward benevolence.

"He's quite contrite about the whole incident," the old cleric said. "He has promised to do anything he can to remain in our favor."

"He's a liability," Haddad said. The words were

softer than he had intended, since he himself had made a few bad calls of late.

Zuabi nodded. "But I see no reason to let him believe that. Fear has a way of loosening a man's tongue. If he continues to believe he is safe with us, he'll remain faithful to the cause." He paused. "And he *is* the son of one of my dearest friends. I've known him since he was a boy."

"Is it wise to let sentiment guide us?" Haddad pressed. "We could arrange an accident—"

Zaubi's eyes narrowed slightly. "Do not worry. Abdal will be dealt with when the time is right."

"And the woman he's been seeing? Will she be dealt with, too?"

"We're not savages, Haddad. Abdal may be impulsive, impatient, but he's not stupid. The woman is a mere distraction. A Yemeni girl. I've looked into her and she knows nothing about us."

"And if you are mistaken?"

Anger flashed in the man's eyes. "Are you questioning my judgment?"

Haddad made it a habit to question *everyone's* judgment, including his own, but he immediately backed down.

"No," he said softly. "Of course not."

The anger was gone as quickly as it had appeared, and Zuabi rose from behind his desk. "Then I believe we're done here." He gestured for Haddad to accompany him to the door. "There's much to do before you travel, my brother. This Turk aside, I trust everything else is in order?"

"Yes. It's all falling into place. I'll be leaving again in a few days."

"Good," Zuabi said, then smiled. "I look forward to the moment we can stand here together and celebrate the defeat of the infidels."

"As do I," Haddad told him. "As do I."

He was waiting for his train when he thought he saw the Turk again.

Haddad stood close to the tracks at the Westminster Underground Station, listening to the voices of waiting passengers reverberate against the walls, when he caught a glimpse of movement at the far edge of the crowd.

Small. Dark hair. Flash of a beard.

Nothing particularly noteworthy, of course. There were at least half a dozen such people here. But the figure he saw had a way of carrying himself that reminded him of the man he'd spotted on the train from Belgrade and in that hotel lobby.

An instant later the man was gone, swallowed by the crowd, and Haddad wondered if his imagination were getting the better of him. He'd barely seen a face, and what he *had* seen could be anyone. Anyone at all.

But he didn't think so.

His instincts may have failed him somewhat in Bulgaria, but he had the same feeling now that he had then: that he was once again being watched.

And he knew who the watcher was.

He didn't take a second look, however, instead

keeping his eyes on the tunnel, waiting for his train to arrive. If the Turk remained in that same general area he'd be entering just three cars down.

Haddad wasn't foolish enough to make the same mistake twice. He assumed the Turk wasn't working alone. The Gypsy whore had been replaced by someone new. Someone who would also be on this platform, a rooks-on-king move modeled after the game of chess: one rook could be blocked, lost, or avoided by the king but not without remaining vulnerable to the other.

The woman standing next to him, perhaps? The old man stooped over the water fountain? The curly-headed college student with an e-book reader?

It could be any of them. Or none. The only way to find out was to leave this place and see who followed.

But he didn't leave immediately. Instead he waited several minutes until his train finally glided up to the platform, its brakes hissing. The doors opened and the crowd began pushing through them, anxious to find seats.

Haddad moved along with the other passengers, then hung back suddenly and turned, heading for the stairs.

He didn't wait to see if he was followed.

When he reached the street, Haddad immediately ducked into a nearby pub—the Old Town Brewery—and stood near the front window, watching the underground steps less than two hundred yards away.

A moment later a man emerged from the stairwell

and bounded to the top of the steps, out of breath, his head swiveling, his eyes frantically searching the crowded sidewalk. There was no question about it now.

It was the Turk.

As the man's gaze shifted to the pub, Haddad stepped back from the window to avoid being seen. The place was dimly lit and the shadows hid him well.

But the Turk must have had instincts, too. He knew that Haddad couldn't have disappeared that fast unless he'd taken refuge in one of the nearby stores. And the darkness of the Old Town Brewery was the most likely candidate. Fixing his gaze on the front doorway, the Turk headed straight for it.

That was Haddad's cue to move.

The pub was sparsely populated with ruddy-faced businessmen and their whorish companions. Haddad weaved his way through them to the back, counting the seconds it took, then ducked through a doorway marked TOILETS and found himself in a dim hallway lined with old black-and-white photographs of London.

The men's room door was less than two meters away.

Haddad knew that the Turk would check back here. It made sense. He immediately flattened against the wall and waited, mentally calculating the time it would take his pursuer to step inside and cross to the back. It had taken Haddad about twenty seconds, and the Turk was moving as quickly, with purpose.

In less than fifteen seconds the Turk stepped into the hallway, apparently expecting his quarry to be in one of the rooms, behind a locked door, perhaps trying to get out through a window.

He wasn't. Haddad was facing the hallway door.

As the door swung outward Haddad lunged, grabbing the Turk by the collar. Spinning the smaller man around, he shoved him to the left so that he crashed through the men's room doorway. The Turk's eyes went wide in the grimy white light as he stumbled back and slammed against a stall door. Haddad pinned him there with a forearm pressed hard across his exposed throat.

"Who are you?" Haddad demanded in Turkish. "Why are you following me?"

The Turk made a sound in his throat but nothing came out. Haddad released the pressure and the man spat at him. Haddad spun him around again and shoved him hard against the door. The Turk couldn't get out and now no one— including his partner— could come in. With one fluid motion, Haddad pulled a butterfly knife from his back pocket and flicked it open. The two metal pieces that sheathed the double-edged blade rotated around their pivot pins and snapped together, forming the hilt.

He pressed it to the Turk's Adam's apple. "Answer me or you'll bleed out on a dirty bathroom floor. *Who* are you working for?"

"N-no one," the Turk sputtered. "I—I wasn't following you, I only came here to use the—"

Haddad pushed the knife into the soft flesh of the man's throat. Blood began to trickle around the steel blade.

"You think I'm a fool?" Haddad hissed. "I saw you in Sofia, sitting in the hotel lobby. And on the train before that. How do you think your whore wound up with a plastic bag over her head?"

"I—I don't know what you're *talking* about!"

"Stop insulting me with *lies*!"

Haddad withdrew the knife, grabbed him by the collar again, and jerked him onto his knees. The Turk cried in pain as his kneecaps slammed into the bathroom tile. Haddad again put the knife to his throat.

"I won't ask again," Haddad said. "Who are you and why are you following me?"

But the Turk said nothing and that was the wrong strategy to employ. Haddad had no qualms about making good on his threat. The only question was how much of his head would still be attached to his body when Haddad was done.

"You've made your choice," Haddad said under his breath. He put a thumb and index finger into the man's eyes, pressed back so his head was against the door and his throat was exposed, then pressed the blade to flesh.

The Turk stiffened. "Wait! *Wait!*"

Haddad stopped. Waited.

The Turk's voice trembled. "I was telling the truth.

I . . . I don't work for anyone. I was following you because I want to join you."

That surprised Haddad. "What are you talking about?"

"I want to join your cause."

"Why didn't you say so back in the hotel? Why did you hesitate with a knife to your throat?"

"I wanted to be sure in Sofia. Here, I wanted you to see I had courage."

Haddad laughed. "And what about the woman in Sofia? Did she want to join me, as well?"

"She was no one. A simple whore. I saw her go to your room so I hired her to follow you from the hotel."

"More lies," Haddad said.

"No . . . no, I'm telling the *truth*! I know all about the Hand of Allah. I know all about your operation."

Haddad hesitated. "And what operation would that be?"

The Turk paused a moment, lowering his voice almost reverentially as he suddenly spoke English. "Roadshow."

Haddad stared at him for a long moment. He had no idea what the Turk was talking about. He had his orders, but he knew of no operation by that name.

But what startled him was that he'd heard the word before. Spoken by Imam Zuabi during a telephone conversation several weeks ago as Haddad had waited outside his doorway. He could remember nothing else about what had been said; it hadn't seemed important. But that word—now that he'd heard it again—came back to him with clarity. And it troubled him.

Was this something else Zuabi was keeping from him?

He looked at the Turk. "This is nonsense. There is no Operation Roadshow."

"Why would I lie? You have my life in your hands."

Haddad pressed the knife against the Turk's throat again as if to prove that point. "Then where did you hear about it?"

"I . . . I don't remember. On the street. People talk . . ."

"What people?"

"I told you, I don't remember."

"And I don't believe you," Haddad said. "Tell me now or I swear to Allah—"

Suddenly, the Turk brought his left elbow up hard, digging it into Haddad's chin. Pain tunneled through Haddad as he stumbled back, loosening his grip on the knife. Before he could recover, the Turk jumped to his feet and shot a hand out, grabbing hold of the bigger man's wrist, twisting so that the joint was bent with the force of the Turk on one side, the weight of Haddad's body on the other. It was a basic combat technique, simple and debilitating.

The nerves inside Haddad's arm caught fire and the knife fell free, clattering on the floor.

The Turk may have been small, but that was an advantage in the confined space. Throwing another elbow, he connected with Haddad's temple, causing both ears to ring. Then he squirmed around him, kicked Haddad from behind—sending him belly-down on the floor—and made a mistake. Instead of running out the door, the Turk looked for the knife.

It was under Haddad.

Scooping it up and scrambling to his feet, Haddad spun and tackled the Turk by the legs, taking him down just short of the door. Rolling the Turk over, he straddled the man, pinning his arms with his knees as he pressed the knife against the smaller man's jugular.

"Why were you following me?"

"Die in hell!" the Turk spat, struggling beneath him.

Haddad smacked him across the face. *"You first! Tell me who you work for!"*

Suddenly, to Haddad's surprise, the Turk stopped fighting. There was a quiet rage in his eyes and Haddad knew he would get nothing from him.

Nothing at all.

The Turk said softly, "May Allah condemn you for what you are about to—"

Haddad didn't let him finish the sentence.

He uttered a prayer as he thrust the knife into the man's throat, dragging it deeply along the jawline.

10

San Francisco, California

"So what is this, Jack? Some kind of black thing?"

Maxine no longer had stitches in the side of her face, but the mark they'd left behind still looked raw and painful. She was driving at a fairly good clip, headed south on Van Ness, Jack in the passenger seat.

"What do you mean?" he asked.

"You think because I look like everyone else in the hood, I've got the key to the kingdom?"

Jack could tell by the tone of her voice that she was only half serious, but now that she'd put it out there he had to respond.

"Correct me if I'm wrong," he said, "but you *did* grow up in the Dale, right?"

Max stopped at a red light. "Fourteen years of

hell before my mom got a job that paid her enough money to move us out of that dung heap."

"So what's the problem? This is more about knowing the territory than anything else. Although you have to admit this Jamal kid is more likely to talk to you than me."

She gestured to the side of her face. "You almost got me killed once. Isn't that enough?"

Jack smiled. "We run into any trouble, I figure they'll be too mesmerized by your beauty to do anything stupid."

"They call that a bulletproof marshmallow," she said.

"Say again?"

"Someone soft and tasty that they're not going to hurt."

"I like that," Jack said. "Besides, you know how to handle yourself."

Max had proven that more than once. Most recently, when she was shooting footage of the dock workers' strike, one of the union apes had threatened to hurt her and break her camera. The moment the goon made his move, Max sidestepped him and drove the ridge side of her hand into his exposed Adam's apple without skipping a beat—or losing a frame.

She shot Jack a look. "You're on crack, you know that? Have you ever even *been* to Sunnydale?"

"It's not part of my usual routine, no."

"So you really have no idea what you're asking me to do here."

Jack had to admit he didn't. He'd heard stories about the place. But he'd also spent time on the streets of Baghdad, so how bad could it really be?

"Besides, what makes you think the kid will be up and about?" she asked. "Hasn't he got a couple of busted limbs?"

"Yes, and that's why he'll be out struttin'."

"I'll bite. How do you figure that?"

"The kid was obviously trying to impress a gang," Jack said. "He blew it, totaled the jacked car and didn't waste the owner. Two strikes. So how does he save face?"

"By sucking up the pain and showing off his injuries."

"Exactly," Jack said.

Max shook her head. Jack didn't know if she admired his thinking or just thought he was crazy.

"You didn't have to come along, you know," he reminded her. "You could've stayed home."

Max sighed. "*Somebody's* gotta protect you from yourself. And when have I ever told you no?"

"I can think of a couple times."

The light turned green and Jack saw a flicker of a smile on Max's lips as she rolled her eyes, then faced forward and hit the gas. "You're lucky I did, Casanova. You wouldn't know how to handle me."

Jack grinned. "Neither will the gangstas in Sunnydale."

It was less than half an hour before sunset when Max turned onto Sunnydale Avenue. Jack immediately understood her trepidation and started having second thoughts about asking her to come along.

The place was a lot worse than he had expected.

The Sunnydale Projects were built during the Second World War as military housing—a square mile of sturdy new cinder-block buildings sandwiched between the McLaren Park golf course and the Cow Palace, home to the Grand National Rodeo.

The place was turned into low-income housing in the 1970s, but the buildings were never renovated. By the time Max was born, what was left were several blocks full of decrepit, tumbledown hovels with peeling paint, bad plumbing, worse electricity, and enough rats and roaches to keep a fleet of exterminators busy for a dozen years.

Now, despite promises by government officials to clean the place up, the Dale was considered one of the top ten areas to avoid in the city, where murders were frequent and muggings were an everyday occurrence. Over sixteen hundred people were crammed into these neighborhoods, many of them for generations. And most of them wouldn't be leaving anytime soon.

By day the place was pretty much a typical ghetto, with mothers or grandparents watching young children who amused themselves with whatever was handy, younger teens hanging out against cars or on stoops after school; by night it was hell on earth. Bus drivers and cabbies routinely avoided it, and even the cops were scarce.

Jack suddenly understood why.

The moment they made the turn he felt tension in the air—a lot of it coming from Max herself, whose body seemed to have stiffened as she gripped the wheel.

He knew her mind was flooding with bad memories.

"I must be outta my head," she muttered, her tone different now. The reality of the place weighed her down.

Jack looked out at the rows of dilapidated buildings, the graffiti, the bars on the windows, the laundry hanging in the yards, the sidewalks and streets eerily empty.

No kids. No couples out for an evening stroll. Even the dogs had stayed inside.

The only sign of life was a handful of teens clustered around a muscle car in a distant parking lot, their gazes on the street, as if keeping watch over their territory. This was a neighborhood under siege.

"You're right," Jack said. "I never should've asked you to come along. If you want to turn around I won't hold it against you."

"How magnanimous of you."

"I mean it, Max. Turn the car around. I'll do this alone."

"You really *are* on crack. You go in by yourself, you might not walk out."

"It's gotta be done," he said.

"Why? Is talking to this kid really that important?"

"I told you, I need to know exactly what he saw." He gestured. "If I can't get you to turn around, at least pull over and I'll walk from here. And if I'm not back in twenty minutes, or you run into any trouble, get to safer ground and call the cavalry."

"You're assuming they'd come," Max said.

She pulled to the curb across from the Little Village Market and let the engine idle, glancing at that cluster of gangbangers, who were now less than a block away.

"I can't let you do this, Jack. It's not worth it."

"Don't worry," he said, "I brought protection."

Lifting his shirt, he reached to the holster resting against his right hip and pulled out a Smith & Wesson Magnum .357 AirLite. Because he was a celebrity who was known to have fielded a substantial number of death threats, he'd long ago been granted a conceal and carry permit by the Marin County sheriff.

The AirLite was compact yet deadly.

Max's eyes widened slightly at the sight of it. "Just because you spend time at a shooting range, doesn't mean you're a badass. You pull that thing, you better be ready to use it or you're likely to get five more stuck in your face. These boys don't fool around."

"Neither do I," Jack said, then tucked the gun back into its holster and popped open his door.

Jamal Thomas lived with his mother and brother in a small apartment on Sawyer Street.

Jack consulted the GPS map on his cell phone and saw that he had two blocks to travel from where Max had parked her car. Unfortunately, the only way to get there was to go straight past the kids in the parking lot, and he had a feeling that the moment Max pulled to the curb they'd noted the intrusion on their turf.

Max is right. You are *on crack,* he thought.

But Tom Drabinksy's face kept drifting through his mind, and Jack knew the only way he'd make any headway with this story was to talk to Jamal. He might come away from the encounter with nothing to show for it, but at least he had to try.

He walked up the street, heading straight for the parking lot. He decided to try the open and friendly approach. It probably wouldn't work, but neither would ignoring them or coming in hot.

The kids—some of them no older than sixteen—had been laughing and chattering until Jack stepped into the lot.

The oldest of the kids came forward. Jack recognized him.

"You and your girlfriend make a wrong turn, homey?" He laughed. It was more of a statement than a question. The kid was trying to see into Maxine's car as he approached but the dark window showed only a vague silhouette.

Jack slowly reached into his shirt pocket and brought out a set of credentials. His old GNT identification card, which had expired two years ago. He didn't expect these kids to recognize him, but they'd surely recognize the network he once worked for.

"I'm with GNT News," he said.

The kid gave the card a cursory glance, then looked back down the block toward Maxine's car. "I don't see no camera truck. How you gonna put me on *Tee Vee*?"

"The cameras come later," Jack said. "I'm what they call an advance man. I'm here to set up an interview with a kid named Jamal Thomas, lives on Sawyer Street. You know him?"

The kid stiffened. "Nah."

That was it? Jack thought. *No negotiation, no shakedown?*

"You sure?" Jack pressed.

That seemed to trigger something in the kid.

"Man, why don't you jus' turn 'round and go back to where you from?"

"Why?" Jack asked. He spoke in a voice that was loud enough for the others to hear. "What are you scared of, Leon?"

The kid snapped forward like he was a shooting guard for the Warriors. He was in Jack's face almost as fast as Jack's hand was on the .357. The move did not escape the kid's notice. If he had a piece he wouldn't be able to get it in time, and it was too dark here for the rest of the gang to see.

"How do you know me?" Leon asked.

"I saw you in the car the day of the explosion," Jack said. "I was the guy talking to Officer Beckman."

Leon nodded, drew back. "I ain't scared," he said defiantly.

"Not of me, no," Jack said, offering him a bone. His hand moved from under his shirt. "What happened? Did someone do something to Jamal?"

"Like you don't know."

"I don't," Jack said. "Jesus, man, I'm trying to *help* him."

"Right."

"What else would I be doing here with just my associate in the middle of the goddamn night?"

Leon considered this.

"Tell me what happened. Please."

The kid spat to the side to show the others that he was okay, that he was in charge and unafraid. "What happened? Jamal was outta the hospital for what, not even half an hour, when they came to see him."

"Who did?"

"I don't know *who*," he said. "They come off Bay Shore in a big black Escalade, poundin' on the door and—"

He was cut off by the shriek of a siren as an ambulance blasted up the avenue and streaked past them, making a left turn on Sawyer. The kids whipped their heads in its direction then started piling into the muscle car.

One of them shouted, "Come on, man, let's check this out."

Leon glanced in the direction of the ambulance. The glow of a distant streetlight, one that wasn't broken, showed he was wearing a funny expression, something between anger and concern. He ran to the car and jumped inside, its tires squealing as it tore out of the parking lot.

Jack waited until it was around the corner, then started out after it.

11

"My baby! They killed my baby!"

By the time Jack reached the muscle car it was parked out in front of one of the tenement houses. The ambulance sat in the middle of the street, its red strobe flickering, curious neighbors spilling from their homes to see what the commotion was.

The paramedics were already rolling a gurney out a doorway, the small body on it covered with a sheet.

Jack checked the address. It was Jamal Thomas's apartment.

An emaciated but not unattractive woman in her early forties stood on the sidewalk, her arms stretched toward the gurney, her face twisted in agony as Leon held her back.

"My baby!" she cried, her high, shrill voice full of raw emotion. "Why did they kill my baby?"

She tried to wriggle away but Leon held tight, his

own face slack with shock and grief as he stared at the gurney, tears running down his cheeks. The other kids stood around him, open-mouthed, looking much more like children than gangstas, their bravado overwhelmed by the tragedy of the moment.

Jack quickly assessed the scene, and as the paramedics reached the rear of the ambulance he approached the one nearest the doors and showed him his GNT credentials. "What happened here?"

The paramedic waved him away. "Stay clear."

"Have the police been notified?"

"Soon as we got the call."

"What's the C-O-D? Was he shot?"

The guy hesitated, as though sizing Jack up; he seemed to decide it might not be a bad idea to keep a potential ally on hand.

The EMT shook his head. "Overdose."

"Like hell!" Leon shouted, gently passing the crying woman into the arms of one of his friends. "I already told you, Jamal wasn't no junkie!"

"Okay, man, take it easy," the paramedic said.

"Yo, man, that's not good enough," Leon snarled. He drew a Glock from the back of his waistband and crossed the sidewalk. "You take it back! You *apologize* to my mother!"

"I'm sorry!" the young man said. "I take it back!"

The other EMT had stopped moving the gurney. He edged behind the ambulance. Jack positioned himself between Leon and the other paramedic.

"Leon, listen to me—put away the gun," Jack said. "I want to find out who did this but we need to *talk*."

"The *cops* did this. That's who killed my brother."

"How do you know? Do you have any names, descriptions? Are there any witnesses?"

Jack couldn't make a grab for the Glock. Leon's finger was on the trigger, and though they were backing off, moving behind cars, there were too many people standing around to risk an accidental discharge. Instead, Jack ignored the gun. He'd had weapons pointed at him before, and they were never the threat. The man holding it was. If Jack stayed calm, chances were fifty-fifty he could talk Leon down. Or at least delay him until his mother realized what was happening.

Jack looked into Leon's eyes and held them. They were bloodred in the flashing light of the ambulance, still clouded with tears.

"Talk to me, Leon," he said calmly.

"The cops," he said, sobbing but still pointing the gun. "They came in our house and put Jamal down like a dyin' dog."

"If we're going to prove that, I need details," Jack said.

"Man, you need to go *away*!" one of the kids shouted.

"Me, too?" came a voice from the middle of the street.

They all looked over as Maxine came walking from out of the darkness. If she wasn't exactly an angel, she was the closest thing Jack had ever seen.

"This is my associate Maxine," Jack said. "You saw her in the car. Remember?"

Leon kept the gun on Jack while he looked at Max. "Yeah."

"Leon, if you want to show your brother respect, then let the paramedics do their job while we go inside and have a nice calm conversation," she said. "Think you can manage that?"

Leon looked at her. Then, choking back a sob, he wiped tears from his eyes with the back of his gun hand. He nodded.

"Great," she said.

The apartment was a cluttered, two-bedroom disaster in serious need of a handyman. Cracked ceiling. Dents and scuff marks on the walls. A battered oven in the small kitchenette with its door hanging lopsided, probably unused for months.

From the looks of things, Juanita Thomas wasn't much of a housekeeper, and judging by the drug paraphernalia scattered across the worn coffee table, she wasn't much of a mother, either.

Jack and Maxine exchanged looks the moment they entered the place. Max's expression said, *See, I warned you.* Jack's replied, *Did I say I doubted you?*

But he wasn't here to judge anyone, just to get information. It took Max a little more persuasion to get Leon to sit down with them—minus his gang—but the kid finally came around. In fact, now that his rage had given way to sadness, now that he didn't have to put on a tough-guy show for the gang, he seemed grateful to have someone to talk to.

As they entered, Leon escorted his mother into

the bedroom and closed the door behind him. Jack
and Max were silent as they waited, Jack feeling the
walls of this depressing dump close in on him. He
caught Max flash a look at the water stain on the ceiling, the dark, mildewed rot around it.

"You made it out," Jack said in a voice barely
above a whisper. "This isn't your life anymore."

"But it's theirs," she said sadly.

There was no disputing that. Jack was trying to
imagine where Mrs. Thomas got Leon's bail money.
Either she had the cash on hand for drugs, got it from
selling drugs, or went into hock with a pusher who
would have her on her back till it was paid back with
interest. Or maybe Leon would knock over a 7-Eleven.
Roll some tourists on Market Street. There were all
kinds of opportunities for people who had nothing
to lose.

A moment later Leon came back out. "I gave her
medicine to calm her down," he said. "She needs to
sleep."

They didn't ask what he had given her. They didn't
have to.

"What about you?" Max asked. "You feeling any
calmer now?"

Leon dropped into a threadbare armchair and
lowered his head slightly, trying to hide the tears that
were forming again.

These guys are always different when you get them
alone, away from their posse, Jack thought. The
tough talk, the gestures—it was all for show, like a
peacock fanning its tail feathers to seem bigger.

"He was just a stupid runt," Leon said. "Never hurt anybody. Not even—"

Leon stopped himself.

"Not even the guy he was supposed to pop on the Tenderloin?" Jack asked.

Leon looked up sharply. "A dude gotta know how to survive," he said. "Off this block, another thug's turf, you choke, you dead."

"Did you see what happened that night?" Jack asked.

Leon didn't answer.

"You stopped at a light," Jack prompted. "That's how it's done, right?"

"Yeah."

"What happened then?" Max asked.

Leon took a tremulous breath. "Jamal got out and I drove ahead. I looked back an' the Arab dude was gone and Jamal was swervin' through traffic. I saw him hit—*wham, wham*—an' I went back. But I couldn't get him out. Next thing up, I was bein' hustled into a cop car."

"You never saw the Arab again?"

Leon shook his head.

"What about today?" Jack asked. He moved around the coffee table and sat on the sofa. "Tell me about the cops in the Escalade."

Leon took another breath. "I picked Jamal up when we got the okay. He was all smilin' even though he was in a wheelchair and me an' a nurse had to carry him into the car." He smiled. "Banged him up, tryin' to fit him an' crutches." The smile faded. "Then, 'bout an hour before you guys showed up, some cops come poundin' on the door."

"You saw this?"

"I heard 'em when Mom let 'em in. I was in the bedroom with Jamal. He was talkin' about wantin' to go to the lot, show his badass casts, an' I told him I'd think about it. I took off out the window."

"Why?" Jack asked.

" 'Cause I heard them ask where I was."

"Really?" Jack said. "Leon, I need to ask you something. Were you ever picked up on a gun charge?"

"What that got to do with anything?"

"Humor me."

"Yeah, sure, once, two years ago," Leon said. "They couldn't prove shit."

No, Jack thought, *but it would show up on your rap sheet. If they were coming for Jamal they'd want to know where his pistol-packing brother was.*

"How do you know they were driving an Escalade?" Maxine asked.

"Saw it parked out front, one of 'em standing next to it. I called Mom on the cell, but she said they went into the bedroom and closed the door. Tol' her they had to ask Jamal a few questions. Jus' like you."

"And you're *sure* they were cops?"

"What else?"

"Were they in uniform?"

"Suits, man," Leon said. "Black. Plainclothes. I *know* the law and they was it."

"No, Leon," Jack said. "They were bigger than cops."

Leon made a face. "What the hell that s'posed to mean?"

"The EMT said they phoned in the OD. That was at least a half hour ago. The Tenderloin Station is, what, five minutes from here? You've got the largest concentration of parolees in the city with nonstop patrols. Don't you think they'd *be* here by now?"

"They don't give a damn 'bout us, and Jamal was already dead—"

" 'Officers shall investigate and complete Juvenile Disposition Report Form 8716,' I think it is, 'and get a statement from the parents and/or guardian in the event of a suicide or accidental death of a person or persons under the age of eighteen,' " Jack said. "They didn't always come to bail out my ass, either, so I memorized the codes."

Leon and Max both looked at him.

"This is *not* a situation someone would slough off unless someone high up told them to do it," Jack said, adding pointedly: "Someone high up told them to stay away. What happened when you got to the lot?"

"After a while I called Mom again and she said they was gone and Jamal was resting," Leon said. "I figgered he just pass out, y'know what I'm sayin'?" His manner was different now, cooperative and even contrite. "Next thing I know, you two show up and there's an ambulance." He averted his gaze again, sniffed back tears. "I get here an' paramedics are already about, 'Jamal OD'd' and Mom is screamin' that the cops kilt him. She said she came into the bedroom and found a needle lyin' on the bed beside his *mouth*." Leon glared into space. "My kid brother stuck himself under the tongue, right, 'cause his arm was in a cast? Is that *real*? We kept drugs on the nightstand so we could shoot up before bed! That's *bullshit,* man!"

"Isn't that how you put your mother to sleep?" Maxine asked.

Leon shifted uneasily.

Jack leaned forward. "Are you sure Jamal didn't take drugs?"

"I told you, man, that kid was clean. Maybe smoked some weed, but that was it."

They were all silent a moment. There were a lot of pieces now, but they still didn't fit. *Try throwing a rock and see who throws it back,* Bob Copeland had told Jack. What kind of target did they have?

"The guy standing next to the Escalade," he said to Leon. "Did you get a good look at him?"

The kid shrugged. "Good enough, I guess."

"Can you describe him for me?"

Leon dug a hand into his pants pocket. "Don't need to."

He brought his cell phone out, pressed a few buttons, then handed it to Jack.

A video started playing.

Maxine moved around next to him and they watched together, a dark, shaky shot of the tenement house from about half a block down, a tall, muscular guy in sunglasses standing near the hood of the SUV, looking off toward Jamal's apartment.

Professional, Jack thought. But definitely not a cop, from the looks of him—local *or* federal.

So who was he?

The video cut to black and Jack punched a button to play it again.

"What do you think?" Jack asked as the image replayed.

"I think it's amazing what you can shoot on a cell phone these days. That's HD quality. Maybe I should chuck the vidcam."

He made a face but he let it pass. That was Max's way of blowing off tension; she'd earned the right tonight.

"Why, what do you think?" she asked.

"If I had to guess I'd say private security."

Max squinted slightly, concentrating. "Y'know, there *may* be a way we can find out."

"How?"

She pointed at the Escalade. "We don't have a view of the license plate, but you see that little rectangle in the corner of the driver's window?"

Jack looked, nodded. "Parking sticker."

"Right. And I bet if I dump this video into my system at home, I'll be able to enhance it enough to get a fix on that sticker. At least tell us where they park their car."

"It's a start," Jack said, then shifted his gaze to Leon. "Is there some way you can transfer this video to Max?"

He shrugged. "E-mail."

Jack nodded. "Good. I don't know who's behind

all this, Leon, but I'm gonna do everything I can to find out."

"Why?" the kid said. "Why do you even care?"

Jack studied him grimly. "Because that's just who I am."

12

After they left Leon, Jack and Maxine walked along the street unassaulted and climbed into her car. Two of the gang members had been watching it for them. The kids left wordlessly when they arrived.

They both needed a drink so they made their way to the nearest bar, found a booth, and ordered the best scotch the place had to offer. Jack liked Glenrothes single malt scotch but it was hard to find. He usually settled for Jameson 12, Irish whiskey.

Jack was working on his third when his cell phone vibrated against his thigh, telling him he had a text message. He pulled it from his pocket, glanced at the screen, and saw that the sender was Bob Copeland.

The message was short and simple:

1600 hrs MOMA

Jack did not bother to reply. Copeland wouldn't expect or even want one. He knew that Jack would be waiting for him at the Museum of Modern Art at four P.M. tomorrow, so there was nothing else to be said. But Jack was happy to hear from him. Copeland would only be requesting another meet because he had new information.

"Who's that?" Max said, glancing at the screen as he put away his phone. "One of your many conquests?"

Jack looked at her and grinned. "You know I only have eyes for you."

"And for some reason they keep staring at my chest. Men are so predictable."

"Well, you know how I feel about sex, Max, don't you? 'The position is ridiculous, the relief momentary, and the results catastrophic.'"

She laughed. "Yeah, I've read Chesterfield, Jack. But I think that's probably the scotch talking, Don Juan. Or maybe you're just turned on by the fact that I saved your hide tonight."

"Not that I don't appreciate it," Jack said, "but I had the situation under control."

Max cocked an eyebrow, giving him a playful look. After working together with her for the past few months, Jack recognized it as the expression she wore when she was having fun with him.

"What you *had*," she said, "was a near-death experience. If I hadn't come along when I did, you would've been riding in the back of that ambulance with Jamal Thomas."

Jack played along, not bothering to mention that he could have taken Leon with a Krav Maga move— step in, push the gun arm to his chest with your own perpendicular forearm, hold it there while you take a second step behind him, then snake that arm up and across his throat and put him in a chokehold. The way they were standing, however, the EMT would probably have taken a slug or two in the chest.

"Are you purposely trying to deflate my sense of masculinity?" he asked.

"I don't think that's possible. Let's just call it a dose of reality."

Jack was about to respond when they heard a beeping sound. It was Maxine's turn to grab her cell phone. She checked the screen and suddenly got serious. "Leon finally sent me the video."

"Good. You really think you can blow it up?"

"Blowing it up isn't the problem," she said. "It's the resolution I'm concerned about. Even though it's HD, there's no telling what we'll have once the image is triple its size."

"So it's a crap shoot."

"I've got a few high-end tools I can use to fill in some of the pixels, but no guarantees."

Jack nodded. "You have an ETA?"

She smiled. "I could be working on it right now if you weren't busy trying to get me drunk and figure out how to take advantage of me."

Jack grinned again. "A man's gotta do what a man's gotta do. Sometime tomorrow then?"

"I'm working another shoot in the morning, but

I'm pretty sure I can have a yea or nay for you by the time you get back from that little rendezvous with your hottie. I'll call you the minute I do."

Max dropped him off at his boat around eleven P.M.

After a halfhearted attempt to invite her in—an attempt that went down in flames, as he knew it would—Jack bid her farewell and climbed aboard the *Sea Wrighter*. He wasn't two steps on deck before he abruptly sobered.

Someone had been here.

Boaters tend to have a kind of sixth sense when it comes to knowing their space has been invaded—maybe because there's often so little of it—and Jack had no doubt in his mind that he'd had a visitor tonight.

Tony?

Not likely. He would have left for Camp Parks hours ago.

Carlos Rodriguez, the kid Jack had hired to wash his boat? Carlos was an illegal and Jack had been trying to help him gain citizenship—although he was convinced that the illegal problem, coupled with corporate welfare, were two things that were surely and swiftly sinking this country.

But Jack wasn't without his sympathies, especially toward a young man he knew wasn't afraid of hard work. His own grandfather, a Russian immigrant, had taken a similar path, working long, backbreaking hours to raise his family, and had spent many years living in poverty on New York's Lower East

Side. Jack saw the same thing in Carlos that he saw in his own family and people. A sense of pride and a willingness to make sacrifices.

But Carlos only came to wash the boat on Tuesdays, and wasn't due again until next week. So, if not him, and not Tony, who was the intruder?

And, more importantly, was he still here?

Jack glanced up toward the flybridge but saw no sign of movement up there. As a precaution, he pulled his .357 from its holster then quietly unlocked the starboard pilothouse door and slipped inside, carefully surveying the room. He left the lights off, leaving only the pale moonlight to guide him, but as far as he could tell, there was nothing out of place.

Yet that feeling of invasion persisted.

What was worse, Eddie would usually be leaping at his feet by now, over and over until Jack caught him in his arms. But there was no sign of him.

Jack's gut tightened and a fresh wave of uneasiness rolled through him. He was tempted to call out to the little guy but he remained silent. If anyone was in here, there was no point in announcing himself.

Instead, he stepped past the helm to the port door.

It was unlocked.

Jack *never* left his doors unlocked. Not while he was gone.

For a moment he considered backing out completely and waiting in the darkness on the dock for someone to emerge. But an unlocked door was merely proof that someone had *been* here, not that they'd stuck around. And he was worried about Eddie.

Turning, he checked the salon, watching the darkness for any sign of movement, listening for any sounds of breathing, but there was a stillness in the air that told him it was empty. He moved down the short set of steps and crossed through to the aft cabin, which was also empty.

Taking his cell phone from his pocket, he hit the flashlight app and the screen glowed. He shone the beam up the spiraled wooden stairway and cautiously climbed the steps to the flybridge, but there was no sign of anything amiss. A moment later he was back inside the pilothouse and headed down to the lower deck. He took the steps cautiously, keeping the .357 at the ready. He had no qualms about doing whatever was necessary to protect himself.

When he reached the companionway he stood very still, listening. The boat gently rocked and the only sound was the quiet lapping of the bay against the hull. No sign of Eddie down here, either.

So where *was* he?

Dread washing through him, Jack used his cell phone flashlight again, keeping the beam low as he worked his way around to the guest stateroom, bracing himself for a surprise attack. But the cabin was clear—no bogeymen in the shadows, no sign of a disturbance.

Turning, he was about to check the second guest stateroom when he noticed that the door to the head was ajar. He supposed it could have come loose somehow, but he doubted it, and he wasn't prone to leaving the door unlatched.

Tightening his grip on the .357, he approached the head carefully, half expecting to find someone hiding in there. But when he gently pushed the door open and shone the light inside, he discovered the small bathroom and shower stall empty.

But his instincts had been right. Someone *had* been in here.

In the light of his cell phone he saw a noose hanging from the shower head.

An empty noose that had been fashioned from Eddie's leash.

Tony was half asleep when Jack called.

"Do you have any idea what *time* it is?" he groaned. "I got training in the morning. I'm trying to get some shut-eye."

"Sorry, man, but is Eddie up there with you?"

"Up *here*?" Tony said groggily. "What the hell are you talking about? Why would I bring him up here?"

"You two seem to be attached at the hip lately, so I was hoping you took him along for the ride."

The grogginess in Tony's voice abruptly disappeared. "Jack, what's going on?"

"Someone broke into the boat and Eddie's gone. And I'm not sure I want to tell you what I found in the head."

"You think they *took* him?"

"Or worse. He's nowhere around." The dread Jack had felt earlier was rolling around in his belly like a bad stew. "I've tried calling him but he doesn't come."

"Wait a minute," Tony told him. "Hold on—"

"What—?"

"Go into your stateroom."

"What? Why?"

"Just do what I tell you. This is something me and Eddie wanted to surprise you with."

"What the hell are you—"

"Just *do* it, Jack. Trust me."

Jack hesitated a moment, still battling his rage, then did as he was told. He had already turned on all the lights, in hopes of spotting the little guy cowering in a corner, but grew more and more alarmed when he couldn't find him.

"You in there yet?"

"I'm here," Jack said.

"All right. Now say, 'FIDO.' "

"What?"

"FIDO," Tony told him. "It's an old military acronym. 'Fuck It and Drive On.' Trust me, just say it. And say it loud."

Jack hesitated, wondering what Tony was up to. "All right. . . . FIDO."

The moment the word was out of his mouth he heard Eddie's familiar outsized growl coming from somewhere near the bed. The one he normally reserved for strangers. It was muffled, but clear, and Jack moved quickly to a low, narrow cabinet on the port side.

When he opened the cabinet door, he found Eddie lying prone inside the tiny space, stretched out flat like a platypus.

"You've gotta be kidding me," Jack said, relief washing through him.

"A little self-preservation measure, in case someone ever broke in. I noticed the door on that cabinet was spring-loaded, so I started working with him about three weeks ago."

"Thank God you did," Jack said. He tucked the phone under his chin and pulled Eddie into his arms, letting his friend lick at his face. "I was worried sick about him."

"No kidding. You ready to tell me what you found in the head now?"

Jack gave the dog a quick back scratch, above the tail, then set him on the bed. "A noose made out of Eddie's leash."

"What the *hell*? Did you call the cops?"

"For what? They'll just file a report and call it a day." Jack sighed. "I'm used to death threats but this is a little too close to home. And I'm not entirely convinced it's the work of one of my garden-variety stalkers."

"Then who?"

"Good question. Bob Copeland told me I should watch my back, and after what happened to Jamal Thomas tonight—"

"What happened?"

Jack gave him the rundown on the trip to Sunnydale, Jamal's overdose, and the men in the black Escalade. "The kid's brother got one of them on his cell camera and Maxine's gonna see if she can identify the parking sticker on the car."

"Jesus," Tony muttered. "Sounds like we got this thing right. You and Eddie better not sleep on that boat tonight."

"This was just a warning, Tony. If somebody wanted me dead, they would've stuck around instead of playing games."

"Okay, but humor me. Get the hell out of there. Go to a hotel or hit up Maxine. Or your ex. She's got plenty of room in that big house you left her."

"I don't think the tax guy she's been dating would approve," Jack said.

"Do you care?"

Tony was right. About all of it.

"Okay. I'll make sure we get to safer ground. When are you due back?"

"Sometime tomorrow night."

"Good," Jack said. "See you then. Now get back to sleep."

"Keep your powder dry."

Jack nodded. "I always do."

13

Jack thought of his apartment on Union Street as his Fortress of Solitude. The only people who knew he owned it were his real estate broker, the bank, and his former wife—and he wanted to keep it that way.

He hadn't even told Tony. Jack kept it separate from his everyday life, a place where he could seek refuge, to reflect and reminisce.

A twenty-two-story sixties-era complex right off the Embarcadero, it was just a block from the bay. The beauty of the building was that there were four or five entrances and exits on various floors, and he sometimes marveled at how difficult it would be for any of the "progressives" who had threatened him over the years to stalk him here.

You could elude a rampaging army in this place.

He inwardly thought of the complex as a mini-UN. It was populated by a variety of people of vari-

ous nationalities, and riding the elevator to the
twentieth floor was often an education in cultural diversity. One day he'd be smiling and winking at a
Norwegian child in a stroller and the next he'd be
chatting with a businessman from Tokyo.

The view from his window was spectacular. Facing north, it looked out across the bay. And just beyond the Richmond Bridge, you could see the East
Brother Light Station, a small island lighthouse that
had been in operation for over a hundred and thirty-
three years.

Jack had spent part of his honeymoon on that is
land, staying at the bed-and-breakfast there. And
while he had found the place charming, Rachel had
complained that they were too isolated to have any
fun—beyond the bedroom, that is. Jack loved and
could enjoy the birds, the bay, even the winds. That
contrast in their attitudes was one of the many reasons they were no longer married.

As with many marriages, Jack and Rachel stopped
sleeping together years before the sex stopped. They
had side-by-side separate beds, and later they slept
in separate bedrooms.

He liked to watch movies on TV, she liked to read.
He went to bed early, she read until after midnight.
He got up at first light, she slept until eleven. He was
obsessed with politics and TV news, she found this
too predictable. "What's the point of getting excited,"
she used to say to him, "they're all liars and you can't
change a damn thing."

The sex between them had been great for years,

endless and heated. But Jack wasn't made for marriage. It was a strain on his nature. He couldn't conform to another person's needs and wants.

The only interest he really had was his own ego. He believed he could make the world a better place. She was cynical about "the good guys winning."

But she was loyal and faithful. That kept them together. Nothing entered her life that she did not want to be there. She had an iron will.

Jack both admired her for that and was repelled by it. Being married to a Margaret Thatcher was no picnic, he would say, while admiring the iron lady's strength. Her love for him blinded her to what she considered his egotism and his other flaws and quirks.

His father had warned him, "Two rules, Jackie boy, never, ever agree with a friend who leaves his girlfriend and puts her down. They'll get back together and blame you. And one other thing: never touch another guy's girlfriend. Ever." He never cheated on her and he never put her down. Even after the divorce.

But Rachel ignored Jack's work. She rarely commented on any of his broadcasts or even his columns. This was her way of hurting him. When at first she did not leave him because of his habit of withdrawing into himself, she left him in a more fundamental way, abandoning him where it hurt the most. Ignoring the things he was proudest of.

Eventually, they both wanted more than a memory of how things were.

Much of Jack's past was here in this apartment.

After the divorce, boxes that had been stored in his garage in Tiburon had been dragged out and sifted through, yielding a collection of mementos he had gathered over the years:

Some of his childhood toys made of metal, his favorite a vintage 1940s Indie 500 racing car, number 54. It had a real gas engine that he still liked to inspect, marveling at how his country had gone from leading the world in technology to becoming a nation of Web designers and welfare recipients—all in his own lifetime. Another toy was a model airplane gas engine. "The drone" still had the same wooden propeller he had cranked as a small boy. Sometimes he wound it just to hear the sucking sound of the piston gasping for air.

Then there was the set of encyclopedias that his mother had scrimped and saved to purchase for him when he was ten years old. The track and football trophies from high school. His college diplomas. His journalism and broadcasting awards.

And, of course, the battered helmet he'd worn on assignment in Iraq, reminding him just how close he had come to dying there.

He kept them all neatly on display, for *his* eyes only. Because when it came down to it, who else really cared? Rachel hadn't. His parents were no longer alive. And while Tony and Maxine had turned out to be great friends, Jack wasn't yet ready to share this part of his life with them.

The truth was, Jack Hatfield was something of a loner. He missed some of the friends he'd made at

GNT—friends who had largely abandoned him out of concern for their own careers—but he had never had much trouble spending time with himself.

Just as Tony Antiniori hid his limp, for fear it might signify weakness, Jack did his best to disguise what really amounted to a mild case of Asperger's syndrome—an aversion to social interaction. He craved order in the world. Anyone with a keen eye would notice this.

When he was a child he would line his shoes up under his bed, only to become upset if he ever found them out of place. He kept weekly journals of his activities, developing skills that served him well in his older years as a reporter. And taking on a career as a war correspondent was his own personal version of therapy, plunging him into a world of chaos in hopes that he might somehow make sense of it and find a way to rid himself of this demon.

Over the years this desire for order had dissipated somewhat, but every so often it flared up again, as it had tonight when he thought Eddie was missing, or a week ago when Tom Drabinsky met his fate, or two years ago when the life he'd built came crashing down around him. Jack's orderly world had been disturbed, and Tony had been right when he'd suggested that he get away from the boat for the night.

Because here, in his Fortress of Solitude, surrounded by the comforts of his past, he could shut out the noise and finally breathe free. He had often felt Isaiah applied to his life as it did to so much else: *"He was despised, and forsaken of men, a man of*

pains, and acquainted with disease, and as one from
whom men hide their face; he was despised, and we
esteemed him not."

Across from Jack's bedroom was the room in which
he kept his gun collection. He locked them in a huge
gun safe that had taken four men to muscle into his
apartment.

He preferred weapons that were precise and reliable, like the Colt Combat Commander .45 automatic,
with its sheer stopping power and deadly accuracy at
short range; the SIG-Sauer .380, a precisely machined
German pistol known for its smoothness of operation; and, as a final back-up "shoe gun," he relied on
his Kel-Tec Crimson Trace, which was the size of a
pack of cigarettes and weighed only a few ounces.
This little tiger held a six-round clip and fired a .380
round. Big enough to save your life, small enough to
slip into a shirt pocket.

Then there were the rifles and shotguns. A
12-gauge Model 870 Remington Express Magnum;
a Colt AR-15, which shot the .223 rounds first de-
ployed in Vietnam as a fully automatic; and a Ruger
Mini 14, .223.

Next to the display case was his father's old worktable. His old man had been an horologist who made
a living fixing rich men's watches, and had passed
much of his knowledge on to Jack. The hours spent
learning about winding wheels and barrel bridges
and balance screws and regulators had been some of
the best of his childhood. There is nothing like

watching a master at work, and nothing like the pride from knowing that master is your dad.

Over the years, Jack's interests had expanded from watches to clocks. His father said he'd moved backward, because clocks were larger and easier to repair, but Jack loved the sound of the bells when they struck on the half and on the hour.

Winding one particular wall clock seemed to re-set his mind. It was his favorite, a walnut German Berliner made by Kienzle in 1880. The brass face was embossed with a winged angel, the pendulum driven by an eight-day spring-wound movement that played the Westminster chimes on the half hour. Jack often smiled at the irony of being banned from entering Britain as he listened to the harmonious gongs.

He kept that clock in his living room now, and made sure to rewind it every time he came here. Like a diligent child, he listened attentively, counting the rings each and every time, careful not to overwind or run past the stops.

And every time he reset it, he thought about the internal clocks inside each of us. A clock for the heart. Another for the mind. And the final chime—was it set by fate or by circumstance?

After his father died, Jack had taken custody of the old man's worktable and tools. The day he moved into this apartment, he'd brought them here as a kind of shrine to his old man.

Nights like this were rare, but when he had them he always found comfort sitting here in this darkened room under the glow of his father's magnifying lamp, Eddie curled at his feet, as he quietly worked on the Hamilton "Gilbert" he'd inherited.

Like the Berliner, it was an exquisite timepiece, circa 1952, with a rectangular face and a solid fourteen-karat yellow gold case with nineteen jewels. He always kept it serviced, cleaning and replacing parts as necessary, and in all the years he'd owned it, he'd never once let it wind down.

Jack's relationship with his father had been a difficult one, but he'd loved the man fiercely and this was the only way he knew to keep his spirit alive.

He sat at that worktable for several hours, laboring quietly as he thought about the events of the past week. He was carefully buffing out a small scratch in the watch's crystal when his cell phone rang.

It was nearly three A.M. and the sound startled him.

Who would be calling him at this time of morning?

Setting the watch down, Jack fumbled the phone from his pocket, checked the screen, and saw that the number was blocked. He pressed the receive button, put it on speaker, and placed the phone on the desk. "Hello?"

There was static on the line, followed by a moment of silence, then a slurred but familiar voice said, ". . . Hatfield? 'Sat you?"

Bob Copeland. He sounded as if he might be drunk.

". . . Hatfield? . . . You there?"

It was unusual for Copeland to be calling him directly like this. With his penchant for secrecy, their normal mode of communication was a text message—like earlier tonight—and Jack had no doubt that those messages went through half a dozen encryption filters before they reached his phone.

"Yeah, Bob, it's me. What's going on? Are you okay?"

". . . What?"

The static flared up again and if Copeland said anything more, Jack missed it. "Bob? Did you hear me?"

". . . Can't find my other shoe . . . Where the hell is my shoe?"

Definitely drunk, or even drugged—although Copeland had never struck Jack as a big fan of pharmaceuticals.

"Listen to me, Bob. Tell me where you are. Are you at home?"

More static.

"Bob?"

"Upstream, Jackie boy . . . Definitely upstream . . . Gotta get out of here . . . Gotta look after the twins . . ."

Jack had no idea what Copeland was talking about, but if he wasn't at home, he definitely shouldn't be driving.

"Whatever you do," Jack told him, "don't get behind the wheel. You hear me? Leave your car where it is and call yourself a cab."

". . . What?"

"Call a cab, Bob. I mean it. Promise me you won't drive."

". . . No driving," Copeland murmured, his voice sounding distant, as if he'd lowered the phone. ". . . Can't find my goddamn shoe . . ."

Jack was about to insist he let him pick him up, when the line clicked and the phone went dead.

Damn.

Jack sighed. He knew Copeland had a reputation as a hard drinker, but had always thought of him as a man in control. And a drunken phone call at three in the morning was completely out of character.

He tried to think of who he might call to get Copeland some help—family or something—but when it came down to it, Jack really didn't know all that much about him. Especially after two years of no contact.

As he racked his brain trying to figure out who he might call, the phone rang again.

He clicked it on. "Bob? Is that you?"

No static this time, but no response, either.

"Bob?"

Several seconds ticked by, then the line went dead, and Jack silently cursed again, wishing there was some way to find out where Copeland was. Maybe call the police to make sure he didn't wind up in a gutter somewhere.

But what would he tell them?

Where would they start looking?

Then it struck Jack. What if there was more to this than a night of simple overindulgence? After what he'd found hanging in his shower, he had to wonder if it was possible that this was some kind of a cry for help.

Could Copeland be in a different kind of trouble?

But when Jack thought it through, that didn't make much sense. If Bob Copeland were in danger, why would he be calling in a drunken stupor? And there were plenty of people he could call besides Jack. The guy had once worked for the Pentagon, for God's sake.

This was a simple case of drunk dialing, is all. And there's nothing worse than a drunk dialer.

Maybe Jack wasn't the only one who had demons to contend with. He just hoped the guy got home safely and was sober enough to make their meeting tomorrow.

They had a lot to talk about.

14

Jack went back to the *Sea Wrighter* the next morning. When he stepped onto the deck, he discovered he'd had another visitor in the night. He found a package about the size of a shirt box, wrapped in brown paper and tucked against the starboard pilothouse door. There was no name, no address, no writing of any kind.

Odd, he thought. What the hell was *this* all about?

He raised it slightly, feeling with his fingers for a minelike depression plate underneath. Nothing. He kept it level as he raised it. There was no lopsided weight to indicate packed explosives, no faint chemical smell, no ticking, no wires that he could see under the wrapping. Snatching it up, he let himself in, then moved into the galley and laid it on the table. He tore away the brown paper. All he found inside was a

briefcase containing a swath of papers. Government
authorization forms, from the looks of them, generated by the Department of Defense.

Jack paused when he saw them.

Was this something he should be looking at?

The authorization involved a special transport mission. On August 20 of this year, a shipment of highly
classified experimental hydrazine-based rocket fuel
was to be carried from a facility Jack wasn't even
aware of, designated by number only. For security
reasons, the fuel would be traveling by tanker truck
rather than the usual rail transportation.

According to the timetable, part of that journey
would involve passing over the Golden Gate Bridge
at approximately 2200 hours that night, and Jack got
the impression that the Bridge Authority had not
been notified of this shipment. The truck itself would
be marked as a milk tanker.

In other words, this was a so-called black shipment. Okay; Jack had no doubt that happened all the
time.

The question was, why had this package been left
on his deck, and who had left it?

Searching through the package again, Jack found
a business card for a Linda Hodgkins of the Department of Defense. After mulling it over, Jack flipped
open his cell phone and called the number.

It was picked up after three rings. "Yes?"

"Is this Linda Hodgkins with the Department of
Defense?"

A hesitation. "Yes, who is this?"

"Ms. Hodgkins, my name is Jack Hatfield and it seems a package of yours has been left on my boat. Would you know anything about that?"

A longer hesitation. "Copeland said you can be trusted."

"You know Bob Copeland?"

"Yes, I wanted him to take the briefcase but he told me to leave it on your boat."

"Maybe you'd better back up a bit and tell me what this is about."

She hesitated again, as if trying to gather her courage, then she said, "Yesterday afternoon my colleagues and I went to lunch at Fisherman's Wharf and we left some sensitive materials in the back of our van. Somebody broke in and took everything except that briefcase, including a classified laptop computer."

"Okay," Jack said. "So what does this have to do with Copeland?"

"We've already been burned and are looking at some serious disciplinary action. I went to Bob for help and he suggested I stash the briefcase and documents in case I ever need to use them for leverage."

"And he told you to give them to me?"

"Yes. He said he was too hot to be hanging on to them for now and that you're the most trustworthy person he knows. But when I went to your boat you weren't there, so I left them by the door."

"Something *that* sensitive," he said. "You just leave it like a UPS package."

"That's exactly right," she replied. "It's called a

Poe Drop, after Edgar Allan. From 'The Purloined Letter.' Hide what people are looking for in plain sight and they'll never see it."

"If you say so. What are you expecting me to do with them?"

"Just keep them safe until Bob can take possession of them. That's all I ask."

"Okay," Jack said. "I think I can manage that."

"Thank you. Now, I really have to go. I don't want to be on this line any longer than necessary."

Then she abruptly hung up.

Jack stared at the phone for a moment, wondering how this played into everything that had happened so far, but couldn't for the life of him make a connection.

Just another typical bit of Bob Copeland cloak and dagger, he supposed.

Taking the papers from the briefcase, he stuffed them into a manila envelope and put them in the safe in his cabin.

Yet another question to ask Copeland when he saw him this afternoon.

At ten past four, Hatfield stood in the central atrium of the Museum of Modern Art wondering if Copeland would ever show.

After the events of this morning and that bizarre phone call last night, he was concerned about the guy. Shortly after the second call, he'd remembered that Copeland had a house in San Mateo, and before going to bed, he'd called every number listed in the book. But all he'd succeeded in doing was pissing off a bunch of half-asleep strangers.

Jack sent his friend several text messages during the day, using their usual contact number, but so far there had been no response. Not that this was all that unusual. It often took Copeland a while to get back to him. And based on the guy's behavior this morning, Jack wouldn't be surprised if he was still passed out somewhere, in an alcohol-induced coma.

But none of this made him feel any better. He liked Copeland and hated to think of him that way. There were, of course, other matters to consider. Copeland wouldn't have requested this meeting if he didn't have information, and Jack was curious to know what that information was.

Like the building itself, the atrium of the Museum of Modern Art was a thing of beauty. Jack had always had a soft spot for great architecture, even if his knowledge about what was stored inside this place was limited. Fine art was more Rachel's territory, and in their ten years of marriage they'd come here several times to see various exhibits.

The place had been a San Francisco icon for nearly two decades, and still had that edgy, modernistic look that made it stand out in a crowded urban environment. The atrium was cavernous, boasting a huge, tubular skylight, and you couldn't help having a feeling of awe every time you entered the place.

Unless you had other things on your mind.

Jack checked his watch. Four-twenty, still no Copeland.

He stood there wondering if he should stick around a while longer or call it a day. Maybe check in with Maxine, see how the video was coming. Just as he made up his mind, his cell phone rang.

It was Tony.

Jack clicked it on. "Hey, Tony, I can't really talk right now. I'm in the middle of—"

"You'll want to talk about this," Tony said. "Are you near a TV?"

"No, why?"

"Your friend Bob Copeland is all over the news."

Jack's gut tightened. "What do you mean? We're supposed to be meeting right now. I'm standing here waiting for him."

"Yeah, well, you'll be waiting forever," Tony said. "Copeland's dead."

15

It didn't take long for the smear job to start.

Bob Copeland himself had said it best: "Nobody spews that kind of venom unless they've got something to hide."

His body was found in a landfill in Oakland, when the driver of a garbage truck dumped his load for the afternoon. Copeland came tumbling out like an oversized rag doll, his three-piece suit stained and askew, one of his shoes missing, and enough bruises on his body to suggest he'd been beaten pretty badly.

The part about the shoe hit Jack hard. He couldn't purge his friend's slurred voice from his head, talking about the shoe, and he kept second-guessing himself, wondering what he could have done to prevent this from happening.

"Don't start the blame game," Tony told him.

But the truth was, if Jack hadn't contacted Copeland in the first place the man might still be alive.

The initial reports on Copeland's death were sketchy, but as the night wore on more and more sordid details came to light, and the more Jack heard, the more he wanted to break his TV.

Those initial reports had told of Copeland's service in Vietnam, his work with the think tank, the Pentagon, and the two Bush administrations, his dedication to cybersecurity, and his regular appointment to the board of trustees for the San Francisco War Memorial and Performing Arts Center.

In other words, Bob Copeland was a patriot, through and through. An outstanding human being on just about every level.

But once the news had gotten that part out, they were done with it and quickly moved on to the more salacious details, half of which seemed to have been cooked up by a bad mystery writer.

Every time you changed the channel there was a slightly different version of events. But as far as Jack was concerned they'd all gotten it wrong. This was, the news insisted, the story of a man who had had a mental breakdown, distraught over a lawsuit, a dispute with his neighbor about the building of an addition to the house across the street from his home in San Mateo.

According to police, several incendiary devices—smoke bombs, it turned out—had been set off at the construction site shortly after midnight, and they claimed they'd found Copeland's cell phone buried under some construction debris.

Early the next morning Copeland was caught on video wandering the aisles of an Oakland convenience store, walking with a limp and missing that shoe. The proprietor said he was so drunk and disoriented he'd taken him for a homeless guy and had kicked him out.

There were conflicting reports on whether or not the police believed Copeland was murdered or his death had merely been an accident.

Some department spokesmouth—who seemed to have come from nowhere, and had no forensics credibility whatsoever—publicly made the claim that Copeland's bruises were consistent with a fall. But the cops soon realized that nobody believed that a guy Copeland's size—no matter *how* drunk he might have been—could accidentally fall into a chest-high Dumpster, and his death was officially ruled a homicide.

The question was, who had done it and why? The police weren't talking, but according to reports, they were working on the theory that Copeland had gotten drunk and run into a gang of muggers or drug addicts who robbed and killed him before hastily disposing of the body.

The story was ludicrous, of course, but all the news channels seemed to be eating it up. The Big Bad City and all that. Stay in your homes and lock your doors. Derelicts and gangbangers want your wallets.

Oh, and don't forget to stock up on breakfast cereal and toilet paper.

Jack had contacted the Oakland Police about the phone call from Copeland this morning, but their interest in his story was minimal-bordering-on-nonexistent, and Jack doubted there would ever be a follow-up.

The only ones making any real noise about the whole thing were the talk radio hosts and their listeners. Many of them were convinced that there was a cover-up afoot, and Jack certainly couldn't disagree. But all they had were theories, from a mob hit to an SEC investigation conspiracy—and Jack knew the truth.

Bob Copeland had been killed by the very same people who had killed Jamal Thomas. The same people who had broken into his boat and put that noose in his shower stall. The very same people who were behind William Clegg and his ridiculous charge against the Constitutional Defense Brigade.

The way Jack saw it, those smoke bombs had been used as a distraction while Copeland was kidnapped from his home. He'd been drugged and interrogated and somehow managed to escape before he was found again and promptly eliminated.

Now three people were dead, and Jack was convinced it was all because of the message Copeland had left for him in Carolyn Cassady's autobiography.

All because of Operation Roadshow.

* * *

"So here's what I started with," Maxine said.

Jack had phoned Tony and asked his friend to meet him at Max's place. He didn't tell him why and Tony was hooked. The two were looking over her shoulder as she punched a key on her computer. The large rectangular monitor on the wall came alive with the video that Leon shot with his cell phone. The image seemed less shaky than before, and on the big screen the guy with the sunglasses was easier to distinguish. About forty or so, with a muscular frame and a military bearing. And to Hatfield's mind, there was something off about the guy. Call him crazy, but the man didn't strike him as American.

South African, maybe?

"He looks private," Tony said, confirming Jack's earlier assessment. "Definitely no amateur."

They were all sitting in task chairs, surrounding Max's desk in her video editing booth, which was really nothing more than a spare apartment bedroom jammed full of specialized electronic equipment.

"This is normal HD resolution," she said. "I applied a stabilizing filter to steady the image and try to cut down on Leon's crappy camerawork. If he'd been thinking, he would've included the Escalade's license plate and saved us all a lot of trouble."

"If wishes were horses," Tony murmured . . .

Max looked at him as if she had no idea what he was talking about, then pointed to a corner of the screen.

"That right there is our target," she told them. "Looks like a standard parking sticker, about half the size of a playing card. It's hard to tell from this distance, but I'd say that that black-and-white blob is probably a logo of some kind. And that's what I went to work on."

Jack clucked in disgust. "I still can't believe how ballsy these guys are. Broad daylight and they don't give a damn who sees them."

"I already told you," Max said. "People in that neighborhood make a habit of *not* seeing things. And even if someone picked up the telephone, who would listen? A teenage kid died of an overdose. Case closed."

Jack felt the rage building inside of him again and wanted very badly to put his fist through a piece of Max's equipment. He knew that the same thing would eventually be said about Bob Copeland's death. In the end it would be blamed on misadventure in the City by the Bay, a drunk wandering off the beaten path, then everyone would forget about the guy.

Case closed.

"Anyway," Max said, "back to our parking sticker."

She stabbed a key and the video image froze. Shifting her hand to a small dial next to her keyboard, she carefully rotated it and stepped backward through several frames until she found the cleanest—and clearest—of the lot.

"So then I doubled the magnification," she said, punching another key.

The image doubled in size and Max adjusted the frame, centering the Escalade's windshield on the screen. Everything was bigger, all right, but it was also a lot fuzzier, and it still wasn't big enough to make out what was printed on the parking sticker.

"Anyone feel the sudden need for Lasik surgery?" Tony asked.

"Like I said to Jack last night, real life isn't like the cop shows on TV. We can't just zoom in on a pin head and read the inscription written across it. There's a little thing called pixilation that gets in the way. The more we magnify the image, the worse it gets. Especially when it originates on video."

Jack nodded. "Video shot on a cell phone, no less."

She punched another key and the image zoomed in even closer, now centering the parking sticker in the middle of the screen. All Jack could see was an unidentifiable black-and-white mass that could have been just about anything.

"So," he said to her, "is that your not-so-subtle way of telling us this is a bust?"

Max shook her head. "I didn't call you here to waste your time. We're fortunate enough to live in a day and age when there are a lot of technical geniuses out there, doing what they can to fix problems like this."

"Meaning what?" Tony asked.

"Meaning I have software that can help. We'll never be able to get this sticker to the point it can be read, but we can do a lot better than *this*."

Jack huffed impatiently. "How about we get to the

bottom line already? Do you have something solid or not?"

Max arched an eyebrow at him. "No need to get snippy, Mr. Hatfield. I know you're hurting, but believe it or not, I'm trying to help."

Jack sighed. "Sorry, Max. I just want to know who these assholes are."

"We all do," Max said, then punched another key.

The screen went blank for a moment, then the image returned, the black blobs starting to shift a bit and take on shape. They gradually grew sharper, but even if he squinted at it, Jack still felt as if he were looking at a Rorschach ink blot behind a wall of pebbled glass.

Tony said, "Looks to me like your technowizards need another trip to the drawing board."

"Be patient," Max told him. "I'm not done yet."

She hit a few more keys, typed in some numbers, and the image continued to shift, taking on more form and substance. When she was done, they were still blobs, but the blobs were defined enough to make a bit more sense out of them. A few nearly discernible numbers, the letters *B* and *C*, and—

"Is that some kind of animal?" Tony asked, pointing to the left side of the screen.

"That was my thought," Max told him. "And I'm afraid this is about the best we're gonna get out of this image."

"So it *is* a bust," Jack said. "We've got nothing."

Max sighed. "Is that what I have to look forward to when I grow up? Zero optimism?"

"Honey, I hate to break it to you," Tony said with a suggestive leer, "but you're *already* grown-up."

Max rolled her eyes. "Oh my God, there are *two* of you." She looked at him. "You know, you're supposed to call a doctor if that thing lasts longer than four hours."

Tony's jaw dropped slightly. A man without a comeback. He wasn't used to Max's quick wit.

Despite himself, Jack laughed as Max gestured to the screen.

"Here's the thing," she said. "That may not look like much to us, but a computer looks at it differently than we do. I'm pretty sure there's enough here for an image recognition program to find a match."

"Pretty sure?" Jack said.

"As sure as I can be about this stuff. I took the liberty of sending a copy of this to a friend of mine, an MIT grad who has some state-of-the-art recognition software—stuff he's developing himself—and he's promised to e-mail me the minute he finds something."

"So how does this software work?"

"Without pounding you over the head with a lot of technical details, it interprets the pixels as numerical data, looks for patterns and sequences, then scours the Internet and several image databases, searching for the same or similar data."

"I think I'll stick to boat repairs," Tony said.

"It's not as complicated as it sounds."

"When I was your age, young lady, we barely had ATMs. And I still haven't gotten used to *those*."

Jack laughed again, but he knew Tony was only half kidding. It was a miracle the guy had a cell phone, considering his aversion to anything you couldn't fix with a torque wrench.

Max was about to respond when her computer dinged and a pop-up with a winged envelope appeared on-screen.

"Speak of the devil," she said, then clicked on the envelope and quickly scanned the e-mail. "Looks like we're in business, gentlemen. He found a match."

She clicked again, opening the e-mail attachment, and a new image filled the screen. Jack frowned, thinking there must be some mistake.

"This can't be right," he said quietly.

It was a black-and-white rendering of a lion and a unicorn flanking a coat of arms. The lion was wearing a crown.

The image was one that Jack was all too familiar with.

It was the seal of the British embassy.

16

Jack stared at the two images side by side—the blowup and the e-mail attachment—and the only conclusion he could draw from this was that the parking sticker had come from the local British consulate. And that raised more questions than it answered.

"How accurate is your friend's software?" he asked.

Max gestured toward the screen. "Pretty damn accurate, I'd say."

Tony nodded. "That's definitely a match."

"So whoever drives that Escalade works for the San Francisco BC?"

"Unless it was stolen," Max said.

Jack shook his head. "I doubt it. And judging by the guy in the sunglasses, we aren't talking about office drones." He looked at Tony. "What do you think? Consulate security?"

"Hard to say. Could be full-on Security Services. MI6 or special ops. I trained with some of those guys in the eighties and I can tell you firsthand they mean business."

"This doesn't make any sense," Jack said. "Why would the Brits be involved in this?"

"Maybe these guys are freelancing, borrowed the company car," Tony suggested.

Jack thought about this, then looked at Max. "How are your friend's hacking skills?"

"Nonexistent," she told him. "He's strictly a software tech."

"What about that guy you said you dated a few years ago? Made a living hacking college transcripts."

"Dave Karras? Genius and loser, all rolled into one. Why do you think I dumped him?"

"You still have his number?"

It took Max a moment to realize what Jack was asking of her, and her expression soured. "Uh-uh, no way. Not gonna happen."

"Come on, Max, I want to see what we can find out about these guys."

She shook her head. "Forget it, Jack. I'm not contacting that freak."

"Not even for me?"

Max turned to Tony. "You want to help me out here, stud?"

"Are you kidding?" Tony said. "I'm on *his* side."

* * *

From all appearances, Dave Karras *was* a freak.

He came to the door wearing a ratty bathrobe and boxer shorts, with three days' worth of stubble on his chin and unruly black hair in serious need of a shampoo and rinse.

The cramped apartment behind him was barely a step above Juanita Thomas's, and Jack thought if he ever saw the guy on the street, he'd be carrying a cardboard sign: WILL HACK FOR FOOD.

Karras was what Max had described as a grad school dalliance, memorable for all the wrong reasons. And Jack had a difficult time picturing the two of them together.

Maybe he'd been a little more presentable back then.

"Where's Maxie?" Karras asked, looking crestfallen when he didn't see her standing in the hallway with them.

Max had finally agreed to set up the meet but had declined to be part of it. She'd told Jack she wasn't interested in taking a trip down memory lane and had wished them luck.

"She sends her regards," Jack said, then pushed his way into the apartment, Tony at his heels.

"Okay. Fair enough. Whatever." Karras stepped aside, a small frown on his face. "Make yourself at home."

The words were laced with mild sarcasm, but even if they'd been genuine Jack couldn't imagine how anyone would ever manage it. This was not exactly a homey environment. There was little furniture to speak of, and the center of the room was dominated by a large, cluttered computer desk sporting three monitors, one of which was open to a Web site featuring several busty women playing topless beach volleyball.

In their brief phone conversation, Jack had learned that Karras was now making the bulk of his living hacking gambling sites and giving himself modest winnings at Texas Hold'em. Judging by Karras's environment, Jack felt he should give himself a few more royal flushes. That, Karras explained, would raise automatic red flags. Which might explain why he'd agreed to meet with them.

Jack and Tony surveyed the room for a place to sit, but the old, deflated bean bag chairs didn't look particularly inviting so they both opted to stand.

After closing the door behind them, Karras got straight to the point. "Max says you've got a job offer."

"That's right," Jack said.

"My services start at two grand, cash only, and I don't do banks, military defense, or intelligence agencies. Too much of a risk. That work for you?"

The fee was less than what Jack had been expecting, but Karras obviously wasn't a greedy man. According to Max, he had the ability to make himself a millionaire at the stroke of a key but he avoided temptation. Why he *chose* to live like this was anyone's guess.

"I think that works," Jack said. "Although scrounging up cash at this time of night could be difficult."

Karras shrugged. "Don't worry about it. You're a friend of Maxie's, I'll trust you. I'll even give you a discount, you get her to deliver it to me."

No chance in hell that would ever happen, but Jack smiled and nodded. "I'm sure she'll be happy to."

The prospect seemed to make Karras's day.

"Good," he said, crossing to the chair at his computer station. He sank into it and stabbed a key, making the porn site go away. "So what's our target?"

"I need to look at some personnel records."

"Corporate?"

Jack shook his head. "Government."

"Hmm," Karras said. "That gets tricky. Foreign or domestic?"

"The local British Consulate."

Karras's eyebrows went up and for a moment Jack thought he was about to refuse. But he had only been thinking, apparently, for an instant later he shrugged it off. "Easy as making white rice."

Jack was surprised. "How do you know? You been in there before?"

"I've made a few exploratory trips."

"Why?"

Karras shrugged. "Why not? I like challenges, so I go looking for them."

Jack regarded him critically. "But why the British Consulate?"

"The U.K.'s Terrorism Act of 2000 made hacking an act of terrorism," he said. "I keep checking to make sure I'm not on any of their watch lists."

"By committing the very act that would *put* you on the list," Jack said.

"Yeah. How else?"

Jack held up his hands. "Beats me. I'm already *on* that list, so I'm not one to judge. You were saying, about challenges?"

"Right. The BC's firewalls are state-of-the-art, but the biggest vulnerability of any organization is people and training. No matter how many times you pound it into an employee's head to create strong passwords and keep them secure, there's always some fool who doesn't listen. It's an IT manager's nightmare."

"Which you use to your advantage."

"Little social engineering and I'm in. And once I'm in, that sucker is mine." He jabbed a key with his index finger and the screen on his right came to life with a list of files. "I think I have a password that's current."

Tony, who had been looking disappointed ever since the porn site was banished from view, said, "You keep this stuff on file? What if you get raided?"

"Kill switch," Karras told him as he scrolled through the files. "I can fry every single one of my hard drives in about thirty seconds flat. You'd need a forensics miracle worker to figure out what was on them." He found what he was looking for and opened the file. "Here it is. Hermione10."

"Hermione?"

"Yeah, daughter. Women tend to use their kids' names, pet's name, or mother's name for their password, in that order. God bless Facebook, it's like a big, fat password directory."

"Pretty scary when you think about it," Jack said.

"Best not to," Tony suggested.

Karras typed something and a network portal blossomed on his center screen showing the British embassy logo. The lion and the unicorn.

Navigating to the local consulate's page, he called up the log-in box, typed in the name, *Winterbottom, Jane,* the password, *Hermoine10,* then punched the enter button and waited.

"Let's hope she hasn't changed it," he said.

Jack almost hoped she had, simply because he couldn't believe how lax people were about their security. There were office towers in the city that changed their elevator passwords every twenty-four hours, but during that time handed them out to every pizza delivery man and overnight delivery service that came by. Unless he was honest or a complete moron, that gave potential intruders a full day to get in and out of so-called high-security buildings.

A moment later Karras was inside the network and zipping around it like a bee on a hillside. Opening a command window, he started typing again. It all looked like gibberish to Jack, so he just waited as Karras did his thing.

Tony said, "You got something to drink? This looks like it could take a while."

Karras gestured. "Beer in the fridge. Make it two."

"Three," Jack said.

Tony disappeared around a corner, made some

noise, then brought the beers and went back for a couple of dinette stools to sit on. They drank and watched as Karras typed, Jack trying not to think about how much jail time they'd all be facing if he got caught.

Karras seemed to read his mind.

"Don't worry," he said, "I'm covering my tracks as I go. They'll never even know we were in here."

"Famous last words."

"An expression coined, I'm guessing, by someone who wasn't very good at what he did," Karras said.

A moment later Karras jabbed a key and a list of names filled the screen. "Gentlemen, I give you the employees of the San Francisco British consulate. You interested in anyone in particular?"

"Security staff," Jack said. "I was hoping for ID photos."

"I think I can arrange that." Karras typed in a few key words and hit enter, then a dozen names and faces popped up. "There you have it. The SFBC security staff."

Jack and Tony leaned forward, studying the photos. Jack didn't see anyone who looked even remotely like the guy in sunglasses.

"You see him?" he asked Tony.

Tony shook his head then sipped his beer.

"Okay, so he's not security. Let's go through the rest of the staff, department by department. All the males."

"Your wish is my command," Karras said.

They spent the next few minutes going through each of the employee photos, working their way from the lowliest maintenance worker to the consul general himself.

Still no sign of Sunglasses.

"I guess we got it wrong," Jack said to Tony.

"Or they're MI6, which means they wouldn't be in this system." He turned to Karras. "Any chance you can hack into the British security services?"

Karras balked. "What did I say when we started—"

"That you like money and challenges. Another grand?"

Karras still didn't bite. "You got a couple weeks and a safe house in Brazil? Those people have firewalls on top of firewalls and enough booby traps to discourage even the most aggressive attack. Getting past them would take a lot more than social engineering and, like I told you, I don't do intelligence networks."

Jack sighed. "So we're at an impasse."

"Not necessarily. This guy you're looking for— what made you think he works for the consulate in the first place?"

"Long story."

Karras took a sip of beer and nodded. "Sure, sure—need to know. But just because his file isn't here today, doesn't mean it wasn't here yesterday or a week ago. Could be he quit or got fired."

Jack immediately understood. "Archives."

"Most organizations keep their employee files for

years. I could go back a couple months, look for recent terminations."

"Do it," Jack told him.

Karras called up another command screen and
went to work. A few moments later, he said, "Looks
like there's only been three terminations processed
in the last year and a half. All female. But there *is*
something a little strange here."

"What?"

"Some data remnants that look like they were
purged from the personnel database a little over a
week ago. Could be an employee record and it might
be your guy."

"Can you access it?"

"Data only completely disappears when you nuke
the drive. So, yeah, I'm pretty sure I can pull something up. But give me a few minutes."

He went at it, working the keyboard furiously, all
of his concentration focused on that center screen.
Jack and Tony were about halfway through their second beers when he finally came up for air.

"Success," he said. "It's only a partial, but at least
I've got a name and a photo for you."

He stabbed a key and the file opened up on-screen.

The employee was male, but it wasn't Sunglasses.
Not even close. However, the photo stirred something inside Jack and he felt his heart kick up a notch.

"You say this was purged about a week ago?"

"Give or take."

Jack stared at the screen. Could it really be who
he thought it was?

"What's wrong?" Tony asked. "You know this guy?"

"No, but I know someone who might." He looked at Karras. "Can you download this photo and send it to a cell phone?"

He was already maximizing a snip program to copy the photo without leaving a fingerprint.

"Just give me the number."

Jack did, then dug out his phone and dialed the number himself. After three rings the line picked up and he said, "This is Jack Hatfield. I'm gonna send you a photo. I want you to take a careful look and call me back, okay?"

He got the answer he was hoping for, then clicked off.

"Jack, what's going on?"

"I'll explain in a minute," he said, staring intently at the computer screen as he waited for his phone to ring. A moment later it did, and he answered quickly. "Is that the guy? The one you and your brother saw at the Arco station?"

"It's him," Leon replied.

"You're absolutely sure?"

"I'm sure," Leon said.

Jack thanked him, then clicked off, turning to Tony. He gestured to the face on the screen. Dark, Middle Eastern descent. The name next to it read ABDAL AL-FIDA and listed him as a computer maintenance technician.

"He's the one," Jack said. "The reason for the cover-up."

"The Iranian guy?"

Jack nodded. "That's why they wiped him from the database." He paused, not quite believing what he was about to say. "The bomber was working for the Brits."

17

"This has to be a mistake," Tony said, staring at the screen.

As much as Jack wanted to believe that, the proof was right in front of them. Abdal al-Fida was an employee of the British government. And his previously deleted personnel file had been flagged to indicate that he'd been living here on a G-2 diplomatic visa. He lived at an address in Newham, London, and had arrived in the U.S. less than a month before the carjacking.

"I wish it *was* a mistake," Jack said. "But what we have here is a major embarrassment to the Brits, and they're doing whatever it takes to make it go away. Could you imagine the shit storm they'd see if it came out they had a terrorist on the books?"

"They couldn't have known what he was up to."

"Which makes it even more embarrassing. The

guy was obviously a mole and that means they've had a serious security breach. Not something they'd want made public."

Tony looked doubtful. "So they send in MI6 to clean up? There's gotta be more to it than that. They killed a teenager, for God's sake. And what about Bob Copeland?"

Jack was a strong believer in Occam's razor, that the most obvious explanation was usually the best one. But Tony had a point. Had Copeland been killed simply because he'd discovered a security breach? Or was there another reason altogether?

Like Operation Roadshow, he thought.

The Home Office was overly sensitive to criticism, but would they go this far to protect themselves?

"Um, what *exactly* are you guys getting me into here?" Karras said, suddenly looking very nervous. "Maxie never mentioned anything about bombers and dead teenagers. Maybe you two should leave."

Jack ignored him and got to his feet, started pacing. He needed to think about this.

Tony gestured to the screen. "Whatever the case, this guy's probably buried in somebody's backyard by now. And without him, what do we have?"

"More speculation," Jack said.

"Exactly."

"Guys—" Karras said.

Jack didn't seem to hear him.

What if this al-Fida guy isn't dead? What if he immediately fled for home after botching the bomb-

ing? It didn't seem likely, but Jack would be stupid not to check into it.

Karras got to his feet now. "I mean it," he insisted. "I don't want anything to do with whatever you're into. You need to get out of here."

Jack stopped pacing and turned to him. "Fine, but one last thing. Would you be able to hack into an airline and pull up their flight manifests for the last week or so?"

"Sure, but that doesn't mean I *want* to."

"I'll triple your fee."

"Hey, money isn't every—"

"What about some intel about Maxine?"

Karras hesitated. "What kind of intel?"

"Coming to you was *her* idea," Jack lied. "She has all kinds of regrets and if she finds out you went that extra mile for us she'd probably be real appreciative."

"Really?"

"Haircut and a shave and—who knows?"

He could see that the prospect excited Karras. The guy hesitated a moment longer then sat back down. "Quadruple the fee."

"Done."

"What airline do you want to start with?"

"What else?" Jack told him. "British Airways."

It took Karras a while to find what Jack was looking for, but his instincts had proven right and they didn't have to leave the British Airways network to prove it.

There was a flight out of LAX to London the day after the carjacking, and Abdal al-Fida was one of the first class passengers. The ticket had been charged to the British embassy's travel account. This didn't mean al-Fida was still alive, but the possibility existed and that was enough for Jack to hang his hopes on.

Twenty minutes later he dropped Tony off at his car outside Maxine's with promises that they'd reconvene at the *Sea Wrighter* after he'd picked up Eddie. But as he drove toward his apartment he decided to take a detour to the Arco station on Mission, the place where Jamal and Leon had first seen al-Fida. It was nighttime; the same attendant might be on duty.

The guy at the register was nodding off, a travel magazine in his lap, open to a story about Amsterdam.

Jack rapped on the countertop and he came awake with a start. "Uh?"

"GNT News," Jack said, showing him his expired credentials. "Were you working here the night of the bombing?"

The counterman blinked a couple times to clear the cobwebs, then hastily set the magazine aside. "Uh, yeah. Yeah, I was here. Why?"

Jack brought out a copy of al-Fida's personnel photo that Karras had printed out. "Do you remember this man? He would've stopped for gas shortly before midnight."

The counterman squinted at it. "Do you know

how many people come in here every night? I guess I coulda seen him but I don't remember."

"What about surveillance video?"

The man looked up like he was Eddie asking for more spaghetti. Jack had expected that. He flipped a twenty onto the counter. The man laid a hand on it and swept it off like a croupier.

"It's on a forty-eight-hour cycle. It would've been erased by now." He paused. "But it's funny you ask, because the feds were in here looking for it last night, right after my shift started."

Jack was surprised. "Did they say why?"

"Just that they were looking for a suspect in a bank robbery. But they didn't show me any pictures or anything. They made me play the video back, like they thought I was lying."

"And you're sure they were FBI?"

He looked at Jack blankly. "The head guy flashed a badge."

"Did you look at it closely?"

His expression told Jack it was obvious he hadn't. *Typical.*

"What did they look like?"

He shrugged. "Like feds. What are they supposed to look like?"

"Did you see what kind of car they were driving?"

"I think it was an SUV of some kind."

"An Escalade, maybe? Black?"

He shrugged again. "Could be. Don't quote me."

"I won't," Jack promised. "Thanks for your time."

He pocketed the photo then went back to his car and sat for a while. He had been hoping to get confirmation that the man Jamal and Leon had seen really *was* Abdal al-Fida, but he'd known it was a long shot. Leon had sounded sure on the phone, but Jack wasn't completely comfortable hanging an entire theory—as thin as it might be—on the word of a grieving teenage carjacker. Any good attorney would tell you that eyewitness testimony is rarely reliable, even though a shocking number of people have gone to jail because of it.

But then why else would the British consulate delete al-Fida's file? Why not just archive it like the others? And why fly him out of the country immediately after the blast?

Jack started his car and pulled out of the gas station, easing into the flow of traffic.

Too many questions, he thought. *Too many questions and not nearly enough answers.*

Jack had traveled only a few blocks when he saw the Escalade in his rearview mirror.

A little less than a block behind him, it was hidden by several other cars. The darkness and the shining headlights made it difficult to see, but every once in a while they'd pass through a brightly lit area, illuminating the SUV as if it were standing on a showroom floor.

Jack knew there were bound to be other Escalades on the road, that this could be nothing more than paranoia at work, but it looked just like the car in the video—and he had a very strong feeling there was a Brit behind the wheel. There was something about the way he was maneuvering, the slightest hesitation, as though he were consciously trying to remember which side of the road he had to be on.

They weren't trying very hard to conceal themselves, but there was no reason they should. They didn't know about Leon's video, so they couldn't know that Jack was on to them. He wasn't sure when or where they had picked him up, but if they saw him coming out of the Arco station they had a right to be curious.

Hitting the accelerator, he quickly changed lanes, cutting in front of a Nissan Sentra and getting an angry blast of horn for his trouble. Glancing in his mirror, he saw that the Escalade hadn't reacted. It kept a steady pace about six cars behind him.

Could he be wrong? There was one way to find out.

At the next intersection, Jack made an abrupt left turn and picked up speed, dividing his attention between the road ahead and his rearview mirror. Several seconds ticked by and no sign of the Escalade, but just as he was about to chalk this up to an overactive imagination, the car came barreling through the intersection in hot pursuit.

The driver was handling the vehicle more aggressively now, and Jack knew without a doubt that he was in trouble. Tightening his grip on the wheel, he punched the accelerator and weaved between two cars, hearing more horns in his wake.

He took a sharp right at the next intersection, and again picked up speed, blasting past several more cars. He was half a block in when he saw the Escalade again, tearing around the corner behind him.

But as he continued up the street, it suddenly occurred to him that he was making a mistake. He shouldn't be running from these people at all. This was his chance to find out what was going on.

Sure, it could be dangerous, but part of the reason he'd gone to his apartment last night was to prepare for just such a possibility. Unless you were a theater critic or society reporter, journalism was a dangerous racket.

Zipping past several parked cars, he screeched to a halt under a pool of light at the corner, cut the engine, and snagged the trunk lever as he jumped out. He moved quickly to the rear of the car and threw open the lid, then popped the latches on the rifle case inside and took out his Remington shotgun, which was loaded with 12-gauge rounds designed to mince a deer.

It was overkill, but that was the point.

By the time he turned around, the Escalade was on top of him.

Jack perched himself on the lip of the trunk and laid the rifle across his forearm, making it clear that it wouldn't take much for him to swing it into action.

The Escalade came to an abrupt halt about twenty yards away and sat idling for a moment. Jack squinted, trying to make out the faces behind the windshield, but the car's headlights prevented it. Several seconds ticked by, and he kept his gaze steady, doing his best to hide the effects of the adrenaline pounding through his veins.

Then the passenger door opened, and a man of about forty climbed out. He wasn't wearing sunglasses, but Jack recognized him just the same. He closed the door then slowly moved forward and stopped in front of the Escalade's bumper, spreading his hands to show they were empty.

"The weapon isn't necessary, Mr. Hatfield." His accent, not surprisingly, was decidedly British. "All we want to do is talk."

"All I want is to stay alive," Jack said. "And answers to a few questions. I figure I've got a better chance at both if I'm heavily armed."

"Spoken like a true American."

"Thanks," Jack replied.

He hadn't meant it as a compliment and Jack's proud response caused him to start visibly, as if he weren't so sure the "American" *wouldn't* pull the trigger.

"So?" Jack said. "How about those answers?"

"I'm not quite certain what it is you think is going on here, but whatever it is you're mistaken," the man said.

"Is that why you're following me?"

"We mean you no harm."

Jack stifled a laugh. "I know of at least two dead people who would disagree."

"You think that has something to do with us?"

"Not 'think,'" Jack said.

"And who might these people be?"

Jack sighed. "Don't waste my time, all right? I know you're MI6 or special ops, and I know you were at Jamal Thomas's house yesterday. So why don't we cut through the bull. You can start by telling your name."

"Adam Swain," he said.

Jack had no idea if the name was real—somehow he doubted it—but it would do for now.

"And you're right," Swain continued. "We *are* MI6."

"Okay, Adam. Now what's so important to the Home Office that you had to execute a fifteen-year-old kid?"

Swain's eyebrows went up. "Execute? Hardly. We're not in the child-killing business. From what I've been told, the poor little bastard died of an over-dose."

"Helped along by you."

Swain smiled. "You watch too many television shows, Mr. Hatfield. All we did was talk to the boy. Nothing more. Just as we're talking to you. If you want to blame anyone for his death, blame that fright-ful mother of his and that filthy sty she raised him in. It's a wonder he survived this long."

"He had a busted arm and a limited radius," Jack said.

"He was also in a lot of pain," Swain replied. "Maybe his mother wanted to ease it. Or maybe she just didn't want to *deal* with it."

Partly true, but Swain's condescension rankled

Jack. "What about Bob Copeland? Do we blame that on *his* mother?"

"I have no idea who you're talking about."

"I told you not to waste my time."

"And I don't intend to," Swain said. "But I don't know anyone named Copeland."

"You don't watch the news?"

"BBC America, and this Mr. Copeland didn't turn up there."

Also possible, Jack had to admit.

"I'm not a big fan of fiction, Mr. Hatfield. But I *did* catch that press conference two days ago, and I heard the questions you asked. If you're as good at what you do as I've been told you are, then you've undoubtedly discovered our friend Abdal al-Fida by now."

Jack was surprised. He had been holding al-Fida as one of his trump cards and hadn't expected Swain to bring him up.

Swain must have seen this in his expression because he smiled again, saying, "Yes, that's right. I have no problem admitting—off the record, of course—that Mr. al-Fida was driving that Land Rover. And I have no problem telling you that we fed a cover story to the FBI and the local police. But we had good reason for that. Al-Fida is not what you seem to believe he is."

"And what would that be?"

"A terrorist."

Jack couldn't stifle the laugh this time. "So he was driving around in a car full of C4 just for the hell of it?"

Swain was silent for a moment. Then he said, "What I'm about to tell you is highly classified."

"I'm sure it is."

"Which means I have to be able to trust you, Mr. Hatfield. I need assurances that you'll keep it to yourself."

Jack considered his options and how little information he actually had. This Swain could be lying, of course. But if he wasn't—

"All right," Jack told him. "You have my promise."

"Nothing gets written, aired, or anonymously blogged. Your word."

"Cross my heart," Jack said.

Swain studied him for what must have been at least thirty seconds, as if weighing whether he should continue or simply turn around and leave.

Jack waited patiently. More than anything, the man's hesitation gave this the veneer of truth. But only the veneer. This kind of hesitation was Intelligence 101, the act of pretending to let someone in on a big secret. That was half the battle in convincing them the information was accurate.

Swain finally said, "Abdal al-Fida is an MI6 asset. For the last two years he's been working for us as a deep cover mole, infiltrating one of the most ruthless Islamic extremist organizations in the world."

"Which is?"

"I'm not at liberty to say more than that. But that carjacking was an unfortunate incident that essentially put him—and us—out of business for the time being."

"I'm not sure I understand," Jack said. "Why was he driving a car full of C4?"

"He had just taken delivery of it and was headed for a rendezvous with members of his cell. If we hadn't rushed him out of the country when we did, they would have executed him for his—let's call it initiative."

"You mean launching an attack on his own."

"Just so. That particular cover story was hatched to prevent the cell from knowing that we were on to them."

"But the whole thing about the hicks up north, the Constitutional Defense Brigade. Wouldn't that whole thing signal the enemy that something was being covered up? *They* know who was driving that Land Rover . . . *I* know who was driving that Land Rover . . . they'd have to figure the FBI knew it, too."

Swain smiled again. "The CDB arrests merely confirm their faith in the investigative incompetence of American law enforcement. They have, after all, been operating here with impunity for nearly two years."

Jack considered that, and on the surface the story seemed at least semiplausible. And if he were a trained seal like so many of his colleagues, he might have taken Swain's word for it and called it a day.

But Jack wasn't in this for the fish. And Swain's version of events left too many questions unanswered— not the least of which was, if the driver of the Land Rover was merely making a supply run, why had those explosives been fully wired for detonation?

Abdal al-Fida wasn't headed to a rendezvous, and that fact alone was enough to put Swain's story in the "doubtful" category.

How stupid did this guy think he was? It was time to play his second trump card.

Tightening his grip on the Remington, Jack said, "So tell me something."

"Haven't I already told you enough?"

"Yeah, well, I'm hoping for something that resembles the truth, this time." He paused. "What does any of this have to do with Operation Roadshow?"

There was a shift in Swain's gaze, a nearly imperceptible widening of the eyes that told Jack he'd struck a nerve, just as he expected he would. And Jack couldn't help but enjoy the surge of satisfaction he got from catching the man off guard. Not just because he had surprised Mr. "Swain," but because it validated the impression that this guy was not truly a big boy.

The smugness that had permeated the entire conversation abruptly disappeared. Swain's expression went flat, and his next words were clipped and passionless, as if he were prepping for a kill.

"Tread carefully, Mr. Hatfield. This line of inquiry will get you nothing except, perhaps, an early grave."

Start throwing stones and see who throws one back.

Jack's palms were sweating. He shifted the Remington in his hands to reassert his grip. "Is that what you told Bob Copeland?"

"I should warn you," Swain said, "that at this very moment there's a sniper crouched in the back of our truck pointing an extremely accurate weapon at your head." He gestured to Jack's shotgun. "All it takes is my signal and before you can squeeze off a single shot your brains will be splattered all over the boot of your car."

Jack's throat tightened. Was this a bluff? A shooter would have to aim a little high to account for the downward deflection of the bullet caused by the Escalade's windshield, but a basic armor-piercing round would certainly do the trick.

Bye-bye Jack Hatfield.

"So why am I still standing?" he said.

"Two reasons," Swain told him. "First, we have no real desire to clean up another mess in a less than optimal location. Not here, not now. And second, as sad as this may be, you don't really pose all that much of a threat to us."

"Meaning what?"

"Despite what my own prime minister might think, you have no credibility, Mr. Hatfield. I think that was proven by the derision at that press conference. No one took you seriously then, and there's no reason they would now."

"Yet here we stand," Jack said.

"Because I want you to understand the gravity of the situation in which you've found yourself. Trust me, if you continue to pursue this line of inquiry we *will* consider you a genuine problem and react accordingly. Is that understood?"

Jack stared at the Escalade's windshield and considered calling Swain's bluff. But he decided not to push his luck. The man was right about one thing: not here, not now.

"Understood," Jack said tersely.

Swain smiled again, but there was no humor in it. "Excellent. I'm glad we could come to this agreement."

Then he turned, went back to the Escalade and climbed in. A moment later, the SUV shot backward, quickly turned around in an empty space, and disappeared up the street.

It was only then that Jack realized he was trembling.

Returning the Remington to its case, he closed the trunk, then climbed back behind the wheel.

Contrary to what he'd told Swain, he had no intention whatsoever of adhering to their so-called agreement. And he knew Swain wouldn't, either. When the time and environment were right, those men would strike again and Jack could only assume that he'd be the victim of a sudden heart attack or a tragic accident.

Worst of all, he still knew nothing about Operation Roadshow. And with Bob Copeland dead, there was little chance of him learning anything more.

He halfway considered calling the one man who had stuck by him during the *Truth Tellers* debacle— Senator Harold Wickham—but if Wickham were to start digging like Copeland had, who was to say he wouldn't wind up suffering the same fate? Jack couldn't have that on his conscience.

As he started the engine, he pulled his cell phone out and hit speed dial. A moment later, Tony Antiniori answered.

"I was getting worried," his friend said. "Where the hell *are* you?"

It was amazing how reassuring it was just to hear Tony's voice. Part of it was the fact that it was Tony himself, but part of it was having a friend on deck with him during a blow. Someone watching his back.

"I got sidetracked," Jack told him. "I think it's time for me to get a little more proactive with this story."

"What does that mean?"

There was only one way Jack knew to make any leeway here and hopefully get the information he needed.

"I'm going to London," he announced.

To which Tony replied, "I don't think so, Jack."

PART TWO

Vigilance

18

London, England

Ever since his return from the United States, Abdal al-Fida knew he had been living on borrowed time.

His contact in San Francisco had been vague about what might happen to him, and it would be up to the imam to decide whether he was to live or to die for his transgression. Abdal had received this news with trepidation, of course, but his meetings with his imam had given him hope. They had prayed together, and in the light of day he felt optimistic about his fate. He had sworn his undying allegiance to the Hand of Allah and begged for forgiveness, promising that he would never again fall prey to his impatience, and his own self-interest.

But with each night's darkness came uncertainty. He would lie in his bed with Sara pressed against him, feeling the Newham cold seep in through his bedroom window, and anxiety would burrow into the pit of his stomach, the feeling that he would not be alive much longer.

Abdal would never have survived such torment if it had not been for Sara. She knew exactly who he was and what he believed, and what he was willing to do to further those beliefs. But she had not asked questions when he returned. She had only soothed him when he needed soothing, giving him pleasure while asking little in return. The Koran gave sexual freedom to men, saying, "*Women are your fields: go, then, into your fields whence you please.*" He had not known another Muslim woman like her, devout in her beliefs yet willing to love. But there must be others. In the Muslim world, the surgical restoration of virginity was a thriving business.

And if she *were* a sinner, the sin they shared was so sweet and exhilarating that Abdal could not imagine why Allah would condemn it. Surely they would be forgiven once they married.

Assuming he lived to see that happen.

Abdal had not told Sara about his mistake in America, how he had jeopardized months of planning with his impulsiveness. He couldn't let her know that he was a failure, a disgrace, even though he was certain she would not think less of him for it. She knew what had been done to his family and she understood his pain. But he could not risk seeing even a hint of disappointment in her eyes—not judgment, but simple regret for his inability to exact vengeance against those who had harmed them.

Abdal felt her warmth in the darkness, her *life*. He had fallen in love with Sara the instant he saw her and he remembered that moment with great clarity.

It was late afternoon just six months ago, and he was in the tube, headed home after work. The train had pulled into the Charing Cross Station and the doors opened, letting in a rush of commuters. With them came what he could only believe was an apparition—a woman too beautiful to be real.

Yet she *was* real. And as she timidly pushed her way through the crowd, moving in his direction in search of a place to sit, Abdal jumped to his feet, gesturing for her to take his place.

She had smiled at him then, a smile like a warm breeze, and Abdal had stared at her so long and so hard that she finally looked away in discomfort.

He had cursed himself for making her feel that way. No one should—ever.

Abdal had never been awkward around women, but there was something about this one that both unnerved and fascinated him, and he could not bring himself to speak to her. To apologize for his rudeness.

Still, he wanted to ride past his stop, just to be near her a bit longer, and it had taken all his will to leave that train when he arrived at his station in Newham.

He saw her the next day. And the next. He didn't

know whether it was coincidence or the work of Allah, but they somehow managed to share the same car for nearly a week. On the fifth day, after he had once again surrendered his seat to her, *she* was the one to speak.

"My name is Sara," she said softly, once again offering him that warm smile. "Since you've been so kind to me, I thought you should know."

Names had never meant much to Abdal. They were merely labels used to identify people. But Sara's name was like a song to him. The sound of it, as it was released from those beautiful lips, washed over him as if it were sent from heaven. A message from Allah that there was something special about this woman. Something beyond her beauty.

Sara. Sara Ghadah.

Abdal's own name caught in his throat as he struggled to respond, but he finally managed to get it out, and what followed was a flood of words he had no memory of. Whatever he said to her, it made her laugh and that could only be good.

For the next several days they sought each other out on the train until Abdal finally found the courage to ask her to dinner. They went as soon as they left the train, and only then did Abdal realize that Sara was just as eager to know him as he was to know her.

They ate at a small café near Hyde Park, a meal that lasted much longer than it should have. It was a traditional halal meal, which was more and more common in London, offered by merchants who prized profit over indignation toward the Muslim population. They had lamb with a white bean and risotto mix on the side, finishing with fruit. While the food was mediocre, every bite seemed exquisite because he was sharing it with her.

Afterward, they walked in the park, talking. Abdal told her about his job repairing computers in a small government office, but he didn't mention the strings that had been pulled to get him that job, nor the parts of his background that had been carefully erased and rewritten.

Sara worked in a small office at the College of Islam, processing applications for new enrollees. She had immigrated from Yemen when she was nineteen after tragedy struck her family. Her brother—a young man who had given so much to her—died in an explosion, an innocent victim. Her desire to come here was fueled by the fact that it was the new battleground for their faith. The city, awash with Muslims, was sometimes referred to as Londonistan. It was meant as a pejorative, but both Abdal and Sara found it inspiring, proof that they had a home here and that there were those who feared their presence.

You do not wait for the enemy to come to you, Abdal believed.

It was not until they shared their first night in bed that Abdal confessed there was much more to him than a simple computer repairman. That he was one of Allah's chosen who had killed in His name.

And would surely do so again.

But Abdal did not tell Sara about the Hand of

Allah. He had been sworn to secrecy by those who had recruited him, and he told her that the trip to America was for business. She suspected he had ties to a group of freedom fighters, but she didn't push for details—not then. She merely told him how proud she was of the work he did, calling him her *aswas jundi*.

Her brave solider.

But Abdal didn't feel very brave these days. In the week since he had returned to Newham, he spent most of his time praying, hoping that Allah—and Imam Zuabi—would spare him. He didn't want this for himself only. As much as he had come to depend on Sara, he knew that *she* needed him as well.

And then he discovered the dark side of that need, and of keeping his secret.

Abdal went to her flat after she'd failed to answer her cell. It was the longest, most agonizing journey of his life. He had knocked on her door, again and again, and was ready to force it open when she finally let him in. She was wearing nothing but a bed shirt, her face pallid, her beautiful brown eyes puffy from crying.

"What is it?" he said with alarm. "What happened?"

Sara fell into his arms and sobbed against his chest, and Abdal stood there feeling helpless, wondering what terrible thing could have happened. When she finally calmed down, they sat on her sofa and she told him that a student at the college—a student she had helped enroll—had been found stabbed to death. A young man from Lebanon who had wanted nothing more than to further himself. A young man who had reminded her of her brother . . . and of Abdal. She said she couldn't stop thinking about what it would be like to lose him. She had looked directly into his eyes as she said this, and Abdal fought to keep from looking away, afraid she might see the truth behind them.

"I'm not going anywhere," he told her.

But as the lie escaped his lips he felt ashamed for deceiving her, for his inability to tell her that his future was uncertain at best . . .

She had kissed him, then. Brought those beautiful lips to his, and as if trying to bury one emotion with another, she kissed him harder, letting him know that she needed to be loved. She lay back on the sofa, pulling him toward her, unbuckling his belt as he slipped his hands beneath her bed shirt, sliding them along her ribs.

He felt her excitement, her hand gently squeezing him, as the other hand pushed his pants to his knees.

Getting to his feet, Abdal quickly shed his clothes, then grabbed the bed shirt and pulled it over her head, exposing her flawless flesh. He had never seen a body more perfect. Had never known a woman who enchanted and possessed him so completely.

And as he guided her down to the carpet he wondered, *Is this our last time?* Would there even be a grave for her to stand over, or would he simply disappear?

Concentrating on the sound of Sara's moans, the

feel of her hands gripping his back as their bodies moved together, he tried to drive these thoughts from his mind.

She was getting close. She ran her hands up behind his neck and pulled him toward her, kissing him hungrily as her muscles tightened. Her breathing stopped as she squeezed her eyes shut then let go, a long, guttural moan filling his ears. Then Abdal joined her, pulling her close as he released himself.

A moment later they lay still on the carpet, their breath labored, Abdal still struggling with his dark thoughts.

Before he could stop himself, he said, "I didn't go to America on business."

"I know," she said softly.

Abdal was surprised. "But how?"

"I'm not stupid, Abdal. I know what you believe in, and I know you're working with people who believe the same. You've been planning something together for several weeks now."

He must have looked dumbfounded.

"You never tell me about the texts you receive," she explained. "You do not speak to friends, do not appear to *have* any. You scan a restaurant, a park, the underground when we first arrive as though looking for someone—someone you hope not to find. You are not just a private man, Abdal, you *work* at it. You cultivate anonymity."

He was stunned. She was better at this than he was. Abdal had never suspected *she* was studying *him*.

"Can't you see that's why this student's death upset me so?"

"Yes," Abdal said. "Yes, of course."

"I don't understand why you feel the need to keep it hidden from me," she went on. "We both want the same thing. As the Koran tells us, *'A life for a life, an eye for an eye, a tooth for a tooth, and for wounds . . . retaliation.'* We both want retaliation."

He nodded. She had obviously spent a lot of time considering this.

"I want to help you, Abdal. I want to be part of what you're part of. To be one with you, just as we are when we make love. And if you're to die, I want to die alongside you."

These last words struck like a dagger. He had been on the verge of telling her everything but stopped himself, hard. It was one thing to risk his own life. He wouldn't risk hers as well.

"I only hide these things to protect you, Sara."

"You think I need protection?" she said sharply.

"It isn't that," he said. "I can't bear the thought of anything happening to you. I won't take that chance."

"That is my decision to make."

"Sometimes we are too close to our feelings to think rationally—"

"That too is Allah's way. He will guide me. He knows that what we seek is right."

Abdal was quiet for a moment. Then he said, "I'm sorry, Sara. I won't. I *can't.*"

She said nothing. Not with words. She just got to

her feet, grabbed her bed shirt and disappeared into the bathroom.

Abdal waited several minutes, then pulled his clothes back on, went to the door, and knocked.

She didn't answer, even after he called out her name.

A moment later the shower started and he knew she wanted nothing to do with him for the rest of the night.

She was, he thought, preparing herself for the inevitable.

Perhaps she was wiser than he.

Perhaps he should prepare himself as well.

Hassan Haddad stood in the shadow of a large oak tree, watching the woman's window. It was dark up there, though he had an idea what was going on. He had seen Abdal's woman enter the place two hours earlier. Sara Ghadah. He had followed her from the College of Islam where she worked, and he could only assume that they weren't playing backgammon. He had seen Abdal arrive an hour later. He stayed for an hour more and had just left.

Alone.

Haddad was leaving the country soon, and there were things to be done, but this was the second night in a row he had come here. The second night in a row he had followed the woman. The second night in a row he had seen that fool Iranian come and go.

The first time he saw Ghadah, Haddad felt she was possibly the most alluring woman he had ever seen.

It struck him as odd that she would be attracted to the likes of a weakling like Abdal. What could he possibly offer a woman like this?

It was then that Haddad became suspicious of her. He had decided that there must be another explanation for her presence in Abdal's life. Yet when he had checked into her background he discovered nothing unusual. She had been born and raised in Sanaa, Yemen, and for nearly nineteen of her years she was a good Shia girl. All of that changed when her brother was killed by a pair of Sunni radicals in a small flourish of sectarian violence.

After immigrating to London nine years ago, Ghadah had held a number of jobs, finally settling as an enrollment counselor at the college a few months before Abdal became part of her life.

Despite this, Haddad couldn't shake the feeling that there was something wrong about her. He had tried to tell this to Imam Zuabi a few nights ago, but the old man had dismissed him, just as he had dismissed Haddad's pleas to handle the Abdal matter itself in an efficient and expeditious manner.

Zuabi's reluctance to deal with an old friend's son was understandable but ultimately reckless. Abdal had not only brought shame to the Hand of Allah, he had jeopardized their entire mission. At least Haddad had cleaned up his own mess, with the Turk. Actions such as the failed attack in San Francisco should not—*must* not—go unpunished.

It was times like these that Haddad wondered about his imam. Did Zuabi no longer possess the strength it took to be a leader? Haddad had known the old man for many years, had studied under him since he was a boy, and it pained his heart to think that his imam may have outlived his usefulness.

But no, he told himself. Zuabi was in charge, and Haddad had a task to complete.

Even so, before he left for America he knew that he would have to learn more about this woman, and to do what Zuabi had so far failed to do: bring honor back to the Hand of Allah. The only questions that remained were how to do it. Where to do it.

And to whom.

19

Tel Aviv, Israel

"Welcome to the city that never sleeps," the Reb said, as they exited the highway.

Traffic was light on the new express lane into Tel Aviv and the drive in from Ben Gurion International Airport had taken them only twenty minutes. Rabbi Mel Neershum had come in from San Francisco on an earlier flight—to make the appropriate arrangements for Jack's arrival—and had picked up his friend in an old family heirloom: a '66 Ford Anglia he'd borrowed from his cousin Ohad.

Jack had known Neershum for many years now. They'd met through a mutual acquaintance, Bill Hicks, a private detective. Hicks and Hatfield frequented the same restaurant, a place on Columbus, the North Beach Restaurant, where they both liked

to eat at the bar as they watched the crowd coming and going while they talked what they called
"the unholy trinity": sports and politics and religion.
The city's ruling elite still ate there. Pelosi, Brown,
the former mayor. All the known and hidden power
brokers.

One night Hatfield brought up his disenchantment
with the Catholic church (echoing his father's own
discontent), and complained that it had lost its edge
and become too pacifist—no fire, no brimstone.

"If you're looking for fire and brimstone," Hicks
said, "you should check out my old friend Rabbi
Neershum. Toughest Jew I know."

The more he heard about this "rebellious rebbe"—
hence, the Reb—the more curious Jack got. Although he'd been raised Catholic, he'd always been
attracted to his mother's history and culture, so a
few days later he set up a meet with Neershum, discovered a kindred soul, and the two became instant
friends. And when the Reb found out Hatfield had
Jewish blood, he insisted Jack join him and his friends
on Friday nights for prayer, vodka, and a home-
cooked meal—an invitation Jack had accepted more
than once.

Hicks had been right. Neershum *was* a tough old
Jew.

The product of an Orthodox day school, the Reb
had fallen out of love with Judaism in his late teens
and, much to his parents' dismay, decided to rebel.

He was a hippie in the sixties. Later a boxer. Then,
in his middle years, he rediscovered his roots with a

fierce passion and spent five years studying Jewish law at a rabbinical seminary in New York. This was followed by a year in Israel, before returning to San Francisco as an ordained rabbi. He soon married the love of his life, Miriam, and fathered two sons and three daughters, all now grown.

The Reb was a "black hat," a Chabad-Lubavitch Chasid, who often spent weeks at a time in Tel Aviv.

Jack himself hadn't been here in years. The last trip was with his mother, who was seventy years old at the time, and they'd come to visit family that Jack hadn't even known existed—and hadn't spoken to since.

The first thing he noticed now was how much the place had grown. Comparisons to New York were no longer as laughable as they'd once been. Tel Aviv was a thriving metropolis perched on the edge of the Mediterranean, and everything about it screamed big city.

"So where are we headed?" he asked Neershum as they took the exit.

"First, we do something about those clothes." Jack was wearing jeans and a suede leather jacket. "You want to blend in with us, you'll have to look the part."

The Reb himself was wearing a traditional dark suit and black felt fedora, although he'd substituted a more manageable suit coat for the *kapote*. The longer coats were reserved for Shabbat, the day of rest and reflection.

Hatfield had once asked him why Chasidic Jews always wore dark clothing, and Neershum explained they were more concerned with what was on the inside rather than what was fashionable. In fact, these Chasids wore nineteenth-century Polish business garb. They were stuck in a fashion time warp.

"I'm not so sure about blending in," Jack said. "If I dress like you, I'll probably look more Johnny Cash than Menachem Schneerson."

The rabbi smiled. "Bring a guitar, you'll get all the girls."

Jack's decision to come to Tel Aviv had grown out of necessity.

Logically, as he told Tony, he should have followed the trail to London. But Tony had brought up the obvious sticking point.

"How do you plan on doing *that,* genius? Last I heard, you were still on the home secretary's hit list."

"Rules are meant to be broken," Jack told him.

"And *why* London?" Tony asked. "I understand about the consulate connection—"

"It's more than that," Jack said. "This guy Swain had MI6 all over him."

"And you know that how?" Tony asked.

"Those boys worked the Gulf War," Jack told him. "I saw a lot of them. They've got big personalities because they've got the international beat. They're not like MI5, quietly and discreetly keeping eyes and ears on the home front. MI6 has to bully their way into places where they might not be welcome."

"Fair enough. That still doesn't explain why you need to go there."

"Whether Swain is British intelligence or an independent contractor, whoever got to him and his team is *back* there. I need to follow the trail. Lift the rocks. There isn't time to wait for them to come to me. Besides, I'd love to find the one honest person in the Home Office who had the courage to say I wasn't a terrorist, that I never incited violence, and that the whole banning thing could backfire."

"Who said that?"

"I don't know," Jack said. "It was in an e-mail my London solicitor uncovered. Written anonymously by someone in the Brown government. I'd like to find that person to prove I'm innocent of the charges."

"I'm sure," Tony said. "But it's still moot. The minute you step on British soil they'll deport you."

"That might not be a problem," Jack said. "What if John Samuel Hatfield never goes anywhere near England?"

"I'm confused."

"What if Hatfield takes a vacation in Israel and Jacob Samuel Heshowitz makes the trip to London instead? Flies right out of Ben Gurion International?"

Tony was silent a moment. "You have a way of arranging that?"

"I'm pretty sure I know someone who does."

It hadn't taken much convincing to get Rabbi Neershum involved. The Reb was rumored to have connections to both Mossad and the Israeli mafia, and while he wasn't a violent man he'd never shied from a good fight. He was also known to quote Rabbi

Meir Kahane, the founder of the radical Jewish Defense League who was assassinated in a Manhattan hotel room in 1990 by persons unknown.

"Every Jew a twenty-two," the Reb had said more than once.

A staunch proponent of the Second Amendment, the Reb had always supported a well-armed citizenry, which he believed was the only way to keep another Castro or Stalin or Hitler or Chavez from rising in America.

"The one thing that stops an evil government from seizing total power," he once told Jack, "is fear of millions of armed citizens. The Brits learned that lesson a couple hundred years ago."

Yet despite this tough talk, the Reb was genuinely a kind and friendly man. He acted as a missionary to fallen Jews he met in the streets of San Francisco, trying to bring them back to God. He'd saved many a drugged-out soul over the years, and they loved him for throwing them a spiritual life preserver when they were drowning.

In some ways, Jack was in need of a life preserver himself. And once he told his story, the Reb was all too happy to help.

"Try to look more serious," the man behind the camera told him. "When was the last time you saw someone smile in a passport photo?"

Jack put on his best poker face. Hadn't even realized he was smiling. He certainly didn't feel much like it, standing there stiffly in his new suit with a black fedora perched atop his head. It didn't help that the Reb had supplied him with a fake beard made by a wigmaker so that Jack could blend in with the rest of the Lubavitchers. The beard was surprisingly realistic, using human hair woven into a special netting, but the glue they'd used to secure it with was itching his skin like crazy.

He thought of Bob Copeland and the man's love of cloak and dagger. Jack did not share that love.

The flash went off, Jack certain he looked appropriately dazed, then the man behind the camera— a Russian Jew named Falkovsky—popped out the data card and crossed the small room to a computer station.

"Your timing is good," he told them. "Two years from now, who knows if I'm still in business?"

"Why is that?" the Reb asked.

Falkovsky, who worked out of a camera store, was an old-school documents forger who found the advent of computer technology a godsend. What had once taken him hours of precise work using special inks and printing presses could now be handled by a standard PC in about a third of the time.

"Biometrics," he said. "The government is pushing for biometric passports and working on a slow roll-out to establish a database over the next couple years. There's no final decision on whether they'll implement, but some intelligence experts are worried that if they do, it'll compromise their ability to operate. And I don't need to tell you what it will do to me."

Jack had heard about this. The "e-passport," as it was called, used smart card technology to store standardized biometric information, including facial, fingerprint, and iris recognition. And intelligence agencies had a right to be worried. If these types of passports were adopted universally, they'd not only be virtually impossible to forge, but any leaks of biometric data could potentially put an agent traveling under a false identity in danger of being discovered by the enemy. All the phony beards in the world wouldn't disguise them.

Fortunately, this wasn't a concern for Jack right now. Jacob Samuel Heshowitz would be traveling with what, to the naked eye, looked like a standard-issue Israeli passport, properly distressed and carrying several travel stamps.

His cover story was simple. Heshowitz was a Borough Park Lubavitcher who had moved to Tel Aviv a year ago and sought citizenship under the Law of Return. A frequent traveler, he applied for and received an Israeli passport shortly after his arrival in the country.

The Reb had assured Jack that the passport would be flawless. Falkovsky—whom he'd met through one of his Mossad contacts—was *very* good at what he did.

The Russian pushed the camera's data chip into a slot on his computer, then sat down.

"Give me about two hours," he said, and waved them away.

*   *   *

Several hours later, after dinner had been served and the dishes cleared away, Jack and the Reb sat at Cousin Ohad's dining table, admiring Falkovsky's handiwork, Jack happy to be rid of the beard for the time being.

"What did I tell you?" Neershum said. "The man's an artist."

"He should be, for the price I paid. You sure you don't have any qualms about all of this?"

The Reb gave him the look he always gave when Jack asked stupid questions. "Do *you*?"

"Not really, no."

"Good. We're at war, my friend. It may not feel that way sometimes and that in itself can be a problem, but it's real, and real people die as a consequence—something you know better than most."

"I can't argue with that," Jack said.

"This man you seek, I can assure you *he* has no qualms about breaking laws to further his goals. He'd just as soon see people like you and me buried under a pile of rubble." The Reb absently stroked his beard. "No matter what a man's ideology or religion may be, when he's faced by a fanatic with a knife in his hand he should cut him down. No amount of reasoning will dissuade the true believer."

"There are people who would disagree."

The Reb leaned forward in his chair now, his gaze intense. "Then they deserve to die. They look at terrorists and genocide as abstract notions, lessons in history that fall on their ears like some ancient melody that no longer has any relevance. They comfort themselves with trivial entertainments, but how do you think they'd feel if that knife was pressed to their throats?"

"Ready to fight back."

"Yes, then. *Then,* when it's too late." The Reb paused, leaned back again. "So I think God will forgive us for breaking a few rules for the greater good."

He got to his feet, grabbed his glass from the table and drained the last of his potato vodka from the Ukraine. Clean. No hangover.

He let loose a satisfied sigh as he set the glass down again. "To bed," he told Jack. "Tomorrow is a big day and you need rest. I only wish I were going with you."

Jack finished his own glass. "You still can."

The Reb shook his head. "This is a one-man job. I'd only be in your way."

"I doubt that," Jack said, getting to his feet. "But I understand. Are you heading back to San Francisco tomorrow?"

"Ohad has invited me to stay a while. I think I'll stick around, enjoy the family." He smiled. "Thank you for the holiday, my friend."

Jack nodded and shook his hand. "Good night, Rabbi."

"Lailah tov."

/

Jack traveled with a group of ten, all Lubavitchers who were flying to Bristol, U.K., for a week-long sojourn—friends of the Reb who were happy to have Jacob Heshowitz's company, no questions asked.

Despite knowing that he blended in, Jack felt conspicuous. The fake beard didn't help, especially since it was itching twice as much as the day before. He caught a glimpse of his reflection as he moved with the others past a phalanx of armed guards to the airport terminal doors, and what he saw made him feel naked, like a high-school kid in the halls without pants.

He half expected one of the guards to pull him away and interrogate him, but they merely glared. That was the first line of security: to look intimidating and see who started to perspire. Jack couldn't afford to; the spirit gum holding his beard would come loose. Fortunately, to them, Jack was part of a group of men no different from a thousand other such groups that would pass through these doors in the coming weeks. They dismissed him as harmless.

The group's flight wasn't scheduled to depart for three hours. Jack had been warned that airport security measures at Ben Gurion International were quite different than they were in the U.S., and he and the Reb had spent much of the previous night going over how Jack should act and what he should say.

As they moved into the check-in line, Jack was approached by a pleasant-looking woman in uniform. The Israelis called this second line of security, somewhat jokingly, "the Fisher of Men." The surly-faced guards made you uneasy. This was the one who reeled you in.

She spoke Hebrew. "Passport and ticket, please."

Jack's facility with the language was limited to a

few brief phrases he'd learned from his mother and grandfather, and a couple the Reb had taught him last night. But he'd been assured that Tel Aviv was a melting pot, that most Israelis spoke English, and a relocated American with limited knowledge of the native tongue wouldn't raise too much of a red flag. He could easily be a drifter who had only recently rediscovered his faith.

Taking his ticket and the forged passport from his inner coat pocket, he handed them to her, telling her he preferred to speak English.

She glanced at his suitcase, carry-on, and passport, then directly at him. "Where did you live before you moved to Tel Aviv, Mr. Heshowitz?"

"Brooklyn," he said. "Borough Park."

"I have family there. What area did you live in?"

"Near Eighteenth Avenue," he told her. "Although I only spent about three years there. I was raised in California."

As he spoke, she didn't stop looking into his eyes. He knew he was being profiled, that she was trained to search for any signs of distress, and he did his best not to show her any.

His biggest concern was the beard. The wigmaker's artistry was nearly as flawless as Falkovsky's, but he couldn't help worrying that this woman could see right through it. He just hoped his concern wasn't showing in his eyes.

"Are you traveling alone?" she asked.

He gestured to the other Lubavitchers around him,

grateful for the momentary break from her gaze. "We're all together."

She gave the others a cursory glance, then looked at his ticket and said, "I see you're flying to Bristol today."

"Yes," he said.

Back to his eyes again. "And the reason for your travel?"

"Worship. We'll be visiting the Bristol Chabad."

Her gaze was unwavering, as if she *wanted* to find something suspicious—was just looking for an excuse to pull him into a back room somewhere and have him more thoroughly interrogated.

"And your luggage. Has it left your side today?"

"No."

She stared at him a moment longer, Jack imagining the worst, then she suddenly handed him his documents.

"Have a pleasant trip," she said with a warm smile.

When she moved on to the next person in line, Jack felt relief wash through him. There was still baggage screening and other checkpoints to get through, but the toughest test had been passed.

Now, if only he could get his chin to stop itching.

20

London, England

The flight to Bristol was mercifully uneventful.

Except for a moment prior to takeoff, when his fellow Lubavitchers started to pray together, there was nothing unusual about it. Jack had been warned of this and had joined in as instructed. As he genuflected and bobbed in prayer with the others, he felt out of place, like a conservative at Harvard.

After they landed, the group sailed through customs and immigration without a snag. Jack bid his escorts farewell, then traded dollars for pounds at the airport exchange and caught a cab to the Bristol Temple Meads railway station. He had a flashback to a story he'd once reported on about an undercover cop in San Francisco posing as a Chasid. The guy was spying on Israelis who were spying on us when he was assaulted by skinheads in a hate crime. His beard came off and his attackers were so stunned he was able to take them out with ease. There was no avoiding the publicity, which the SFPD used to its advantage: they said the guy was working to secure the safety of the Jewish community. He even got a citation from the Israeli ambassador.

In the men's room, Jack stuffed the hat and the beard in his small carry on, happy to finally wash the residue of the glue off his face, then smoothed back his hair, went to the ticket window, and bought passage to London.

Three hours later, as the train rolled into Westminster, Jack's mind flashed memories of his week here with Rachel. They both thought they were in love at the time—who knows, maybe they were—and had wandered the streets of central London for hours, absorbing the sights and sounds, hitting all the usual tourist spots: Westminster Abbey, Buckingham Palace, and of course, Trafalgar Square, with its beautiful fountains and majestic mid-nineteenth-century architecture. London had a unique vibrancy to it that was exhilarating, and it pained Jack to know that he was no longer welcome here.

Jack hired a cab and took a short ride to the Beresford Hotel. As they rumbled along Rochester Row, Jack looked up at Big Ben towering over the city and marveled at its overpowering beauty. Its movement was famous for its reliability, but when he checked it against the Hamilton Gilbert on his wrist—which he flawlessly maintained—he was surprised to discover that the great clock was off by a minute.

Jack suddenly felt uneasy. It was strange how psychological triggers worked. The need for order flared up inside him, and he realized he had been so focused on his mission, so alert, that he had neglected to maintain balance. He should have grabbed some sleep on the train. He should have given himself some downtime. Being so deep in something made you question the instincts you were trusting, made you second-guess your actions, made you wonder if you'd thought the whole thing through enough.

He had been so thoroughly guided by Bob Copeland's sensible one-line mantra that he never thought that the trip to London might be too impulsive.

Listening to the hum of the engine, he closed his eyes and imagined the perfect mechanism of the watch on his wrist, or the Berliner on the wall in his apartment, letting the *tick-tick-tick* in his mind center him. It had been a long and stressful day and his first order of business had to be to get some rest.

The Beresford Hotel was an old redbrick monstrosity that had once been a school dormitory and looked it. Jack knew he wouldn't be spending much time here, but he needed a base of operations that would take cash for a couple nights and ask no questions.

The room he rented wasn't much bigger than a walk-in closet, with a lumpy twin bed and a rattling radiator, and the only plumbing available in the room itself was a dingy sink with rusty fixtures.

Throwing his suitcase on the bed, he peeled off his clothes, wrapped a large but rather gray-looking towel around his waist, then went down the hall to the communal bath and took a scalding hot shower to wash away the day.

Fifteen minutes later, he climbed onto the bed and slid between the sheets, letting the last of the tension drain from his body, the *tick-tick-tick* still in his mind as he fell into a deep, dreamless sleep.

It was dark outside when Jack hired another cab to take him across the Thames to East London. According to Abdal al-Fida's personnel file, he lived in the Forest Gate section of the borough of Newham, an area known for its ethnic diversity and high concentration of Muslims.

Isaiah once again came to mind: *"They come from a far country, from the end of Heaven . . . to destroy the whole Earth. . . ."*

Jack had no way of knowing if al-Fida still lived there, or was even alive at this point. This entire enterprise was a huge gamble. But he had to try, for the sake of Bob Copeland. And Tom Drabinsky. And Jamal Thomas.

But most of all, he was here for his own sake. For that burning need-to-know that had consumed him ever since Drabinsky went up in that blast.

Jack hadn't called his show *Truth Tellers* simply because it sounded good. Truth was the fire that

fueled him. He'd spent his entire career cutting
through the layers of horse manure that people often
used to hide or deflect responsibility for their actions,
always searching for the truth they were trying to
hide. His interviewing style was direct and sometimes confrontational, but never without empathy,
and he often thought of himself as "good cop/bad
cop" rolled up into one. He believed truth was liberty's Siamese twin, not her cousin. When truth was
absent, liberty followed.

Jack suspected that Adam Swain's cover story
about al-Fida being an MI6 mole was yet another
layer he had to cut through. And the only way he
knew to do that was to confront al-Fida himself.

He had the cab driver drop him off in front of a
small pub on St. George Road, which was sandwiched
between a Laundromat and a Classic Kitchens store.
He went inside and ordered a pale lager, taking a
few minutes to again center himself and weigh his
options.

According to Google Maps, al-Fida's flat was located about two blocks down, in a modest Victorian-
style building across from St. Angela's Ursuline
School. Deciding the direct approach was probably best—just knock on the door and start asking
questions—Jack drank his lager in three quick gulps,
then threw some money on the table and went back
outside.

As he stepped onto the sidewalk, he nearly col-
lided with an olive-skinned man with a wispy goa-

tee. The man was moving briskly, obviously in too much of a hurry to see Jack coming. For a moment Jack thought it might be al-Fida himself.

But no—this man's face was older and more angular than the one in the personnel photograph, and Jack dismissed him as just another resident of the area. He muttered a quick apology that got no response, then crossed the street and headed in the direction the man had just come from.

Less than five minutes later he found al-Fida's building and stood in the shadow of a large oak tree, next to the beige brick wall that bordered St. Angela's.

He knew that al-Fida lived in Unit 2, which faced the street, but the window was dark now and it looked as if no one were home.

Jack tilted his watch toward the light of a street lamp and checked the time.

Nearly nine P.M.

Too early to go to bed, he thought, unless al-Fida was an early riser. Tucking his hands in his pockets, he leaned back against the wall and waited, hoping a car would come along at any moment and deposit al-Fida at his front door.

He was still waiting forty minutes later, increasingly convinced his target was either out for a late-night rendezvous or wasn't coming home at all.

Jack was betting on the latter.

So what should he do? Abandon this whole crazy idea or ratchet it up a notch? He may have been without a witness—or suspect—to interview, but there was no telling what the man's flat might reveal. Jack hadn't scooped up a handful of paper clips at the business center for nothing. Plan B had been in the back of his mind all night.

He didn't fancy himself a burglar, but he'd assisted in a few break-ins as a kid, when he and his friends got their kicks rummaging around in homes, raiding refrigerators and purposely rearranging furniture. They were harmless pranks, but Jack wasn't particularly proud of that time in his life. His father hadn't been too thrilled when he found out about it, either, and Jack could still vividly see the disappointment in his old man's expression, and the verbal tirade he had to endure because of it.

His dad wasn't likely to approve now, but the Reb's words about the greater good kept circling through Jack's mind. After waiting another half hour, as windows went dark up and down the street, he checked for any unwanted eyes, then crossed to al-Fida's building and went to work on the entryway door.

Getting into the flat was easier than he expected. Picking a lock wasn't exactly like riding a bicycle, but with patience he was able to make do with a couple of the unfolded paper clips. The main parts of this type of lock are small pins. All he had to do was simultaneously push the ones on top up and the ones on the bottom down and the lock popped open. He credited his work with watch mechanisms for his success. Fortunately, he hadn't encountered any curious neighbors from across the hall in the process.

Pushing the door open, he listened carefully for any sounds of activity, but didn't hear any. Stepping inside, he quietly closed the door behind him and looked around at what appeared to be a modest one-bedroom flat. There was enough light from the street lamps outside to reveal that al-Fida had decent taste in furniture, but the place had a kind of stark, spare coldness to it that didn't particularly appeal to Jack.

Not that it mattered.

The living room was to his right, and a small uncluttered kitchen to the left, and beyond that was a narrow hallway that undoubtedly led to the bedroom. He was hoping to find a computer desk out here, but no such luck.

Jack crossed to the hall and stopped, listening carefully for any sounds of breathing or soft snores that might indicate that al-Fida was at home and asleep.

Nothing.

The bedroom was at the far end of the hall. As he worked his way toward it, he stopped at a door that hung ajar about halfway there. He carefully pushed the door open and checked inside. It was too dark to see much, so he fumbled for a light switch and flicked it on.

It was a walk-in closet but there was nothing hanging inside. No shelves or storage boxes. The closet was completely empty except for a compass and a mat on the floor. Set in a round brass frame about the size of a pocket watch, the compass was a qibla indicator, pointing the user toward Mecca. It lay in a corner of the closet, with a prayer mat carefully placed in proper alignment behind it. The order displayed impressed Jack. He could see how the simplicity and order of the Islamic faith appealed to so many.

This was al-Fida's prayer room. A small, clean space free of distraction that he undoubtedly used several times a day.

The compass was compact enough to be used for travel, and its presence here led Jack to believe that al-Fida hadn't left London. Which meant if he wasn't dead, he might walk through his front door at any moment.

Flicking off the light, Jack continued down the hall to the bedroom. There was another window back here that opened onto an alleyway with very little light coming in. He didn't want to turn on the overhead for fear someone might take notice, but he could hear the hum of a computer and was able to make out the edges of a monitor sitting atop what looked like a small desk in the corner of the room.

Stepping past the neatly made bed, he moved over to the desk, nudged the mouse with his finger, and an iMac screen came to life. He was hoping to do a thorough search of al-Fida's desk drawers and hard drive, but what he saw on the screen stopped him cold.

It was open to a word processing application. And

typed at the very top of the page were two simple words:

Forgive me

Jack's jaw tensed.

This looked suspiciously like a suicide note.

His heart racing, he spun around, looking past a closet slider to a closed door that was now illuminated by the light from the computer screen.

A bathroom, no doubt.

And then he saw it—a tiny sliver of light coming from the crack beneath the door.

Someone was in there. And he doubted they were using the facilities.

Grabbing a lamp as a weapon and moving away from the desk, Jack hurried to the bathroom and yanked open the door, freezing in motion at the horrific sight inside.

The tub was full, and Abdal al-Fida lay chest-deep in the bloodied water, his eyes staring blankly at the ceiling—eyes that reminded Jack of his old friend Riley after their Humvee was ambushed. His dark skin had a pale cast. Both arms were concealed in the murky red water and there was no visible wound that Jack could see.

Jack took in a sharp breath but didn't rush forward to check his neck for a pulse. There was no point. Al-Fida was dead.

There was nothing to be done for him now. Jack

also knew that he needed to get out of here, but there was something he wanted to check first. He was about to go back to the desk when he heard a sound from the living room—the rattle of keys and the front door being pushed open.

"Abdal?" a voice said. "Abdal, are you home?"

It was a woman. She sounded concerned.

Then a moment later she was inside and moving down the hall.

21

"Abdal?" she said again.

British accent, but not quite. Something else in there.

By the time she stepped into the bedroom, Jack was already cramped inside al-Fida's slider, nestled amid the hangers full of clothes, the door open just a sliver so he could see what he was dealing with.

She flicked the light switch, saying, "Abdal? I've been calling all night! Why didn't you answer your—"

She halted, leaving the question unfinished when she saw that the bed was empty and neatly made.

She glanced around the room. "Abdal?"

Like many Muslim women, she wore a *hijab* on her head, a scarf that covered her hair, ears, and neck and shoulders. She had a regal look about her, with flawless skin, an angular, almost perfectly sculpted face, and large brown eyes. Her dress was modest

and loose-fitting and hid her body, but Jack had
no doubt she was exquisitely proportioned. Despite
his predicament—and what he'd just seen in that
bathroom—Jack found her beauty mesmerizing.
There was a faint smell of aloe—hand lotion, he
guessed—which only added to her exotic appeal.

As she moved farther into the room and turned toward the bathroom, Jack wanted to call out to her, to
protect her, warn her away, keep her from seeing that
horrifying tableau inside. But he hesitated and then
it was too late. Her eyes widened slightly as she took
in the bloody tile and al-Fida's body, frozen in death.

To Jack's surprise, she didn't break down. Didn't
even utter a sound. She just stared at al-Fida for a
long moment, then reached into her purse and took
out a cell phone.

She didn't use it immediately. Instead she stood
there quietly, still staring at al-Fida, looking more
disappointed than bereaved. Jack had no idea what
her relationship was to the dead man, but the fact
that she'd had keys to his flat seemed to indicate that
they were close.

Yet there was no sign of tears in her eyes.

Was she in shock?

Keeping her gaze on the body, she took a deep
breath and shifted her shoulders as if preparing for
something. Then she punched in a number, a short
one, and put the phone to her ear.

Jack could hear it ringing even in the closet. And
when the line was picked up, the woman began to
cry—so abruptly it startled him.

Her voice choked with emotion, she said, "Please . . . please . . . you have to help me. My boyfriend—I think he . . . I think he's killed himself."

Jack watched in astonishment as she answered a few questions between sobs, trembling uncontrollably as she gave al-Fida's address to the person on the line.

Then she hung up—and the moment she did, her demeanor abruptly changed again, the tears vanishing, her expression blank and unmoved by what lay before her.

Dropping the cell phone into her purse, she crossed to the bedroom doorway, flicked off the light, and went back out to the living room.

By the time the police and ambulance arrived, Jack was back outside.

After the woman left the bedroom, he climbed out the window then moved down the alley to the adjoining street and worked his way back around to the front of the building.

Waiting in the shadows under the oak tree, he watched the drama unfold. Neighbors awakened at the screech of approaching sirens and the flashing of lights against windowpanes. Soon the street was filled with people, and as the police and paramedics rushed in through the building's entrance, Jack couldn't help but think about the scene outside Jamal Thomas's apartment.

The window was lit now and he saw the woman crying again as she pointed them toward the hallway.

She had called al-Fida her boyfriend, but her initial reaction to his death seemed to belie that. As much as Jack would have liked to attribute her behavior to shock, the changes in her demeanor were simply too abrupt to be believed.

She was acting. And doing a very good job of it.

So who the hell was she?

Jack had assumed that with al-Fida dead, his search for answers had come to a hard stop. But this woman's puzzling reaction raised new questions, and her association with al-Fida, whatever it might be, was bound to be significant in some way.

Was it possible that Swain had been telling the truth? That al-Fida was an MI6 mole and this woman was part of the cell he'd infiltrated?

No. That explanation didn't make any more sense now than it did before.

Jack knew he needed to talk to her.

He stayed in the shadows, unnoticed by the police or the neighbors. If anyone *were* to notice, they'd only look at him as yet another rubbernecker—or whatever the British equivalent of that was. As they carted al-Fida's body out on a stretcher and loaded him into the back of the ambulance, Jack saw the woman standing in the window again, watching as they closed the doors.

A uniformed police officer was questioning her now, notepad in hand, and the woman played her part to perfection. He couldn't hear what she was saying, but he didn't doubt that her words were halting, filled with just the right amount of emotion, as she told them about al-Fida's depression and the loss of his job, or whatever story made sense of the note that was left on his computer, and what they'd found in that bathroom.

But Jack knew this wasn't suicide. He was convinced that, just like Copeland and Thomas—and just as Swain had threatened to do to *him*—Abdal al-Fida had been disposed of for the sake of expediency. He was a liability that had to be silenced.

Jack felt no love lost for a man who could very well have been planning to kill thousands of Americans, but the thought of yet another death rankled him.

When would these people stop?

And what the hell were they hiding? No matter how many times Jack ran the chain of events through his mind, however often he stopped to reexamine an event or a fact or even a half-cocked *assumption,* he still couldn't make any sense of it.

By the time the ambulance left and the police finished taking the woman's statement and started wrapping things up, the neighborhood crowd had already lost interest and people had wandered back into their homes. From the shrugs and brief conversations and lack of anything approaching shock or sorry, Jack gathered that not many people had known al-Fida.

Before long, the woman was back at the window, watching the last of the police cars drive away. Jack decided to give her a few minutes before he crossed the street and knocked on the door. But to his

surprise, when the lights of the last police car had
faded, she immediately doused the light and a few
moments later emerged from the entryway of the
building. She stepped out to the sidewalk, stopped,
and once again pulled the cell phone from her purse.

Jack quickly stepped backward, moving deeper
into the shadows beneath the oak tree, hoping she
didn't look his way. But she seemed intensely pre-
occupied as she put the phone to her ear.

Despite the distance between them, he could
clearly hear her when the line was answered and she
said, "There's a problem. We need to talk."

She listened for a moment, then hung up, dropping the phone back into her purse as she started up
the sidewalk in the direction of the pub.

Jack waited until she was about half a block away,
then started out after her.

22

The woman caught a train at the Upton Park underground station. She took the Hammersmith and City
Line toward Liverpool Street. It was nearly half past
midnight as she boarded a car along with a handful
of others.

Jack had to run to get in before the doors closed.
He took a seat, careful not to glance in her direction
as she headed for the opposite end of the car and sat.

He kept his gaze forward, trying to catch his breath
as he puzzled over who this woman was and what she
was up to.

"There's a problem. We need to talk."

She was certainly no girlfriend—although he
couldn't be sure her alleged boyfriend knew this.
They had obviously been intimate enough for her to
feel comfortable walking into that flat, and Jack had

a feeling al-Fida would have been just as surprised by her reaction to his death as *he* was.

But she also didn't seem to be aligned with Swain and MI6, or whoever had killed the terrorist. Otherwise, why would she have shown up at the flat at all? Why would she have notified the police and made that phone call when she left?

What was the *problem*?

Who did she *need to talk* to?

Jack sat there through stop after stop—West Ham, Bow Road, Mile End, Stepney Green—running various scenarios through his mind. Once again, none of them fit. Too many missing pieces. It was starting to agitate him.

About fifteen minutes into the ride, the woman got up from her seat as they approached Whitechapel Station. Watching with peripheral vision, Jack waited for her to pass as she moved to the doors in preparation for the stop. Chancing a glance as she walked by, he noticed that she was no longer wearing the *hijab*. She had removed it in the train, revealing a head of luxurious dark hair that only enhanced her beauty, and he once again felt that tug of attraction, a stirring of feelings he was hard-pressed to describe. Some women just had a certain thing, a star quality, and she had it in spades.

As she waited for the train to slow, he casually got to his feet behind her—just another passenger anxious to get home.

The train pulled into the station, its brakes hissing, then finally eased to a stop and opened its doors.

The woman and three other passengers stepped through to the platform and Jack followed, moving with the group toward a flight of stairs, but lagging behind slightly to put some distance between them.

A few minutes later he was outside the station and on the street, the woman several yards ahead of him, walking through an empty car park toward a narrow road flanked by blocky brick factory buildings the color of sandalwood.

The road was dimly lit and sparsely populated, and judging by the graffiti Jack saw scrawled across a Wholesale Fabrics building to his left, it was one of the poorest of East London neighborhoods.

The only thing he knew about Whitechapel were stories of Jack the Ripper, who had used this area as his hunting ground over a three-year period in the late nineteenth century. The streets the Ripper had roamed were very different than these, but you couldn't walk along here without thinking about his brutal butchery and the hysteria surrounding it.

The woman didn't seem bothered, however. She kept moving at a steady pace until she reached the end of the block and turned left.

Jack hurried to catch up, slowing again as he made the turn and saw her about forty yards ahead. She moved past a darkened dry cleaning store, then a low wall—which he soon discovered offered a view of the train tracks—then crossed to her right at the intersection and turned down Whitechapel Road.

Again he sped up. He wasn't in the habit of

stalking women, but that's exactly what he was doing right now.

He thought of Jack the Ripper again and shuddered.

When he finally did turn the corner, she walked briskly past a row of closed shops—a kebab house, a stereo store, a real estate agency—

Near the middle of the block she took a sharp left, moving into an alleyway. Jack crossed to her side of the street, but again he held back. He knew that stepping into that alley might alert her to the fact that she was being followed, and he didn't want to tip his hand. Or find her waiting for him with a .45.

Waiting what he hoped was enough time, he continued toward the alley and made the turn. It was short and narrow and came to a dead end at a graffiti-scarred wall.

The woman was nowhere in sight.

Where the hell has she gone?

In the wall to his right was a dilapidated metal door marked EXIT ONLY. Jack moved to it, checked the knob.

Unlocked.

He stood there a moment, thinking about what he might be getting himself into, wishing he had his .357.

Well, you don't, he thought. *How badly do you want more pieces of the puzzle?*

He took a calming breath then pulled the door open.

When he got inside he heard music. The steady

thump-thump-thump of a bass drum. A short set of cement steps led downward toward a narrow hallway, lit by a flickering fluorescent light.

Jack navigated the steps and headed toward the end of the hall, its walls and ceiling adorned with enough Day-Glo graffiti to trigger an epileptic seizure. There was an adjoining hallway to the right. He took it.

At the far end was another metal door, a large skinhead in a muscle shirt sitting on a wooden stool next to it, his beefy face expressionless. He was the kind of "soccer thug" whose ancestors had exploited the world and built Britain. Now the government hated and suppressed his breed, permitting Muslim thuggery to reign. A nation that attacked itself this way was a nation with a political autoimmune disease.

The skinhead's face didn't change as Jack approached. He merely extended a hand, palm up, and said, "Twenty quid."

"Did a woman just go in here? Beautiful. Dark hair."

"Twenty quid or sod off," the guy told him.

Jack took a twenty-pound note from his jacket pocket and handed it to him. The guy inspected it in the dim light then got off his stool, stuffed the bill into his back pocket, and wordlessly reached for the doorknob.

"Take your pick," he said.

As the door swung open, Jack was accosted by a wall of sound, the music slamming into him like a living force, so loud that his eardrums immediately began to throb in pain.

Beyond the doorway was a small brick warehouse filled with flashing lights and writhing bodies, moving to the beat of the music. Most of the dancers wore typical street clothes, but some of the woman had skirts so short with necklines so low they flirted with public indecency.

Not that Jack was complaining.

It was a good old-fashioned rave, and for a moment he wondered if he'd made a mistake. Surely this couldn't be where the woman had gone—no good Muslim girl would be caught dead in a place like this.

But then, based on what he'd seen so far, Jack wasn't entirely sure she *was* a good Muslim girl. And what was the alternative? There was no place else for her to have gone.

Jack moved inside, pushed past a couple in a clinch, then stepped onto the main floor and scanned the sea of bobbing heads for any sign of her. He was too jet-lagged to make more than a poor stab at dancing, doing only as much as it took to blend in. The strobe lights didn't help much, and after a full minute of searching, he was convinced he'd lost her.

Had he missed something in the alleyway? Another door, maybe?

His question was answered a moment later. At the far side of the warehouse, on a raised platform that looked like an old loading dock, the woman emerged from a doorway. A cardboard sign marked TOILETS hung above it.

No longer wearing the shapeless dress she'd worn at al-Fida's flat, she now sported clothes that could easily have been hiding beneath that dress—a dark pullover sweater and a pair of blue jeans. He had been right about the woman. Her body *was* spectacular.

She eased up to a rail along the edge of the loading platform and looked down at the dance floor. It was hard to see her face clearly in the intermittent light, but judging from the way she carried herself—no bobbing head, no shake of the shoulders to match the beat—Jack figured she had as much interest being in this place as he did.

She'd been standing there for less than a minute when a slender, curly-headed white guy sidled up next to her and smiled, making his best play.

Who could blame him? She was a knockout. She was also way out of his league.

Jack watched them, thinking he was about to see the guy go down in flames. But to his surprise the woman leaned toward Curly and whispered something into his ear.

Did she know him?

"There's a problem. We need to talk."

Curly's smile disappeared as he listened attentively. Then he nodded and whispered back, gesturing toward another hallway at the back of the warehouse.

When he was done, the woman gave him a dismissive push then shoved away from the rail without another word. Curly lost himself in the crowd. She headed toward that hallway.

Jack didn't waste any time. Threading his way

through the crowd of dancers, he moved in her direction, reaching the far edge of the dance floor just as she disappeared from sight. He glanced toward the loading platform to see if Curly was still there, but the guy was long gone.

Then someone grabbed Jack's arm.

He spun around, expecting to see Curly, but was surprised to find an attractive blonde in a black bustier and fishnet stockings smiling at him. The bustier barely contained her, and her eyes had the glassy, faraway look of the perpetually stoned.

"Hey, luv, where you going? Let's dance."

"Some other time," he said, and pulled his arm free.

This time it was Jeremiah that came to mind: *"For my people are foolish, they know me not; they are wise to do evil, but to do good they have no knowledge."*

Then he was up a short set of steps and heading into the hallway, which was dark because of a broken light fixture.

There was movement to his left and he hesitated when he saw two dark figures—then realized it was the clinching couple from the dance floor. They hadn't bothered to find a motel room, their silhouettes moving rhythmically to the music.

He hurried past them and saw a door marked EXIT.

Pushing through, he found himself in another alley that ran the length of the building and then some, opening out to streets on either side. But there was no sign of the woman, and Jack was quickly coming to the conclusion that he wasn't very good at this stalking thing.

Which way had she gone?

Making his choice—there was a faint floral scent in the air, possibly the hand lotion he had smelled earlier?—he went to his right and hurried toward the street, not slowing this time as he reached the mouth of the alley. Moving onto the sidewalk, he swiveled his head, glancing both ways, and was relieved to find her walking about a quarter of a block away to his left.

Dry skin, he thought gratefully. A woman's vanity can be dangerously second nature.

As he moved out after her, she crossed the street again and disappeared into yet another alley.

What the hell was she up to?

Jack waited for a couple cars to pass, then followed. The way the alley was situated, there was very little light in there and he hesitated, once again wishing he had his .357 on his hip. Those years as an embedded reporter in Iraq had made firearms seem like part of a man. More often than not he was allowed to carry weapons in hairy situations. It was against the regs, but so was a lot of what happened in war. His third arm was an M249 light machine gun, fussy with sand but it took care of them; a Beretta M9 was his fourth hand, making up for a lack of stopping power with smooth, semiautomatic action that put a lot of those little balls into an enemy. Being unarmed felt like an unnatural state of being.

Plunging forward, he walked briskly, looking toward the other end of the alley. Jack didn't see the woman. That was the first inkling he had that she was the cat and he was the mouse. But he had gone this far—

Halfway through, the building to his right gave way to a small car park—probably an employee lot. It was empty and lit only by a single incandescent bulb that burned over the building's rear door. A faded sign under the bulb read CG & SONS FINE GARMENTS.

Had she gone in there?

Jack was about to move toward the door when a figure stepped from the shadows next to him and pressed the muzzle of a Browning Hi-Power 9mm to the side of his head.

He froze. Slowly, he shifted his gaze to her.

There was a gun at his skull, the safety probably off, an anxious and unsentimental finger on a hair trigger, yet he couldn't help thinking she was even more mesmerizing up close and personal.

Ridiculous, but there it was.

Her face was a mask. Hardened. Unflinching. In these kinds of situations, it was best to let the person with the firepower do all the talking.

"Why are you following me?"

"I saw you at the club and—"

Gunmetal and perspiration produce a distinctive

odor. It was in the air now and it overpowered the fading smell of aloe. The smart-aleck act was not going to buy him anything.

She pressed harder. She knew what she was doing. She didn't lean into the gun like an angry street thug. She knew he would feel the increased pressure against his skin, understand that it meant her center of gravity was off, realize that if he were willing to risk it he could step from the line of fire, pivot, grab her wrist, and hurl her off balanced self against the wall. It was basic self-defense.

So much for the stuff you can't *do,* he thought.

"*Who* do you work for and *what* do you want?" she demanded.

She was getting impatient but she wasn't quite there. He had a little wiggle room. He hoped so; he was betting his life on it.

"I could ask you the same thing," Jack said.

"Except you're the one following *me,* remember? Although you're not very good at it. I spotted you back at the train station."

"That shows what you know."

"What do you mean?"

"I had you way before that," he said. "I was in Abdal al-Fida's flat when you found him."

That caught her off guard. Her dark eyes widened. "That's impossible."

"I was hiding in his closet. I saw that show you put on when you called the police. Pretty good performance as a grieving girlfriend."

She pressed the Hi-Power against his temple—
hard, like it was a drill bit. He'd pricked her pride.
Now she was off balance.

"Did you kill him?"

Jack frowned. "Hell, no. I wanted to *talk* to the
guy."

"Why?"

"Because of what happened in San Francisco. I
know al-Fida was behind it and I'm trying to find
out who he works for."

She considered this. "You're a Yank."

"Through and through."

"*Who* are you?"

"A reporter," Jack told her, just as squealing tires
announced the arrival of a dark SUV in the alley. Its
headlights washed across them. The woman flinched
and Jack took his shot. He stepped sideways, simultaneously grabbing her wrist and twisting it away
from her. Only she didn't release her hold on the gun
as he'd expected. She yelped and swung a fist toward
him, landing a blow to the side of his head.

He stumbled sideways, caught off guard by her
power.

Another SUV roared in from the opposite side, and
the alley was soon flooded with men, automatic weapons in hand, heading straight for Jack and the woman.
More surprised than hurt by her punch, Jack kicked
her legs out from under her, grabbed the Browning
with his right hand, then spun toward one of the approaching gunmen. He slammed the heel of his left
hand into the gunman's nose and the guy howled

and went down as Jack raised the Browning. But before he could make use of it, three more men were grabbing hold of him. The butt of a rifle slammed into the back of his head and his cranium exploded in pain. The world went red and he stumbled as the men started pulling him exactly where he didn't want to go—to the ground, where his chances of survival were nearly nil. You can't grapple with men who are beating you.

He tried to fight, but there were too many of them. Then the rifle butt slammed him again, and the next thing Jack knew he was spiraling down a long black hole.

23

Jack awoke to the sound of screaming.

A woman's screams of pain, the kind of pain that comes from teeth being extracted without Novocain, or fingers being cut off with wire clippers. Her high-pitched wails echoed mournfully down a long hall-way.

Then they stopped, abruptly, followed by the sound of her sobs as she gasped for air.

Jack had a bag over his head—burlap, from the smell of it—and he had no idea where he was. He was sitting in a chair with a sagging wicker seat, his wrists tied to the slats that comprised the seatback. The chair was not bolted to the floor but even if he could hop it around, where would he go? His mouth tasted of blood, and his tongue was sore, which meant he'd managed to bite it during the struggle in the alleyway.

Worse yet, his head was throbbing and the room seemed to be spinning slowly. Around and around, like a Ferris wheel. He thought he might throw up.

But at least he was alive.

For now.

Listening to the woman sob. And he knew she wasn't acting this time, a turn of events that surprised him.

Back in the alley he had thought she was with the gunmen—had attacked her because of it—but he'd obviously been wrong. And now that he knew better, this knowledge begged yet another question:

Had those gunmen been after him or her?

Someone said something to her—it sounded like English, but with the accent and echo he couldn't be sure—and she responded. Her words were slurred and unintelligible from this distance. She sounded defiant, however, as if she were refusing to give in. Jack had no idea what they were doing to her, but he had a pretty good imagination and a very strong feeling he'd find out soon enough.

But before he could start feeling sorry for himself, the woman's screams rang out again as she endured another round. Her wails increased in pitch and intensity and Jack strained against his bonds, wanting desperately to break free. He thought about those dark eyes filled with anguish, with pain. He didn't know anything about her yet he wanted to help.

Her screams went on almost too long to bear—then suddenly she was silent. Eerily so. No sobs this time. No defiant words. Jack knew she had either passed out or was dead.

As he considered this, a metal door clanged down the hallway, opening, hitting a wall, then closing. Whoever had thrown it open wasn't happy. Voices drifted toward him as two pairs of footsteps reverberated against the walls, moving in his direction. He wrestled with his bonds again, trying to loosen them, the rope cutting into his flesh, rubbing his wrists raw. There was nothing in the Krav Maga training manual to deal with this, except for the rubber-encased, bite-activated potassium cyanide pill that Mossad operatives carried between cheek and jaw like chewing tobacco. Which he didn't have.

Then a door in front of him clanged open and a voice said, "Your girlfriend is a stubborn little tart, Mr. Hatfield. I've seen men twice her size break under half the stress."

Jack would know that smarmy voice anywhere. It was Adam Swain.

A hand grabbed the burlap bag and yanked it from his head. Swain stood near the door and another man, an ape Jack recognized from the attack in the alley, tossed the bag aside. He stepped back, standing to Jack's right. He was carrying a black baton.

They were in a cell of some kind, the cement floor filthy, a tattered mattress atop a rusty bed frame against one wall. The walls were mottled with peeling green paint, the room illuminated by a single work light attached to a portable battery.

Jack guessed that they were in an abandoned hospital of some kind. Judging by the reinforced doors, it was probably a psychiatric facility.

He felt gutted and he was scared. Not Iraq-scared, where the enemy just wanted to kill you. This was semipersonal. They were going to want him to talk. It was a strange sensation: a strange calm settled over him as he literally felt his ego and id go to opposite sides of his head, the first curious to see if the other would break. He felt his id manning up.

"Is she dead?" Jack asked.

Swain ignored the question. "You don't look surprised to see me. You assumed we'd keep an eye on you?"

"Of course. I'm not stupid."

"You almost fooled us in Tel Aviv with your little black hat routine. Very clever."

"Apparently not," Jack said.

Swain was flipping through the Israeli passport Jack had been carrying. He dropped it and smiled. "Don't be too hard on yourself. We're professionals, after all, and at least you tried." He waved a hand. "And you're here, aren't you? In England. Which I'm sure the home secretary would be delighted to know."

"What can I say? I like a challenge."

"So I see," Swain said. "But what about our agreement? I told you what would happen if you broke it."

"Yeah, and I feel bad about that. I probably should've stuck around San Francisco so you could arrange a Dumpster death, or maybe toss me in a bathtub and slit my wrists."

Swain's eyebrows went up. "You're assuming that was us?"

"Who else?"

"I just found out about al-Fida myself. Terrible way to go. Not that I really give a toss."

"I thought you said he was an asset. Was that a lie?"

Swain didn't answer.

Jack pushed. "So, if *you* didn't kill him, who did?"

Swain smiled again. "Not everything is black-and-white, Jack. There are politics to consider. Protocol. There's a very delicate balance at work here, and a lot of people involved. Dealing with a mongrel like al-Fida is below my pay grade."

"Should I be flattered?"

Swain shrugged. "I don't give a damn."

"What about Bob Copeland? Was *he* flattered?"

"He made the mistake of associating with the wrong people, just as you have."

"So why don't you kill me. Get it over with."

Swain huffed a dry chuckle. "I'd think you would have figured it out by now, considering what you just heard. My job isn't simply to eliminate a problem but to extract information and respond accordingly."

He nodded to the other man, who tucked the baton into a loop on his belt and disappeared into the darkness behind the work light. Jack flexed his wrists again, trying to pull a Houdini, stretch the ropes just enough to slip free. He heard the voice of his deceased father admonishing him, *"Don't be a jack of all trades, Jack, and a master of none. Learn some-*

thing well." One thing Jack knew well was the art of the long struggle, the art of war.

Swain pointed a Glock at him. "You see, old boy, killing you quickly would defeat the whole purpose of this exercise."

Jack's heart started to accelerate. The show was over. Ego and id were merging again. He had no idea what they were about to do to him, but he had the feeling the next screams he heard would be his own.

The thug came back carrying a bucket full of water, and Jack felt dread sluice through him.

"Look," he said to Swain, his heart about ready to burst through his chest. "I don't know what kind of information you're hoping to extract from me, but I've got nothing. I only came here on a hunch."

His wrists were burning, but he didn't stop flexing, relaxing, flexing, relaxing. The rope was starting to loosen. Not much, but it was a start.

"That may be true," Swain said, "but I have to be certain, Jack. Especially considering the company you've been keeping."

"The girl? Just another hunch. I don't even know her name."

"Yet the moment I walked into this room, the first thing you did was ask about her. I could hear the concern in your voice."

"She was screaming, for God's sake! She's a human being."

"An attractive one," he said. "Though not for much longer. We're just resting her for act two. Your capacity for empathy is admirable, but you can understand

why I have to find out if there's more to it than that.
And then, of course, there's Operation Roadshow.
That's a very sensitive subject in my world."

"What does the woman have to do with it?" Jack
asked. Despite what was about to happen, he couldn't
help himself.

Swain was surprised as well. "You amaze me.
Here you are about to feel more pain than I'd wish on
any human being—well, almost any—yet you keep
asking me questions. At what point do you stop being
a reporter?"

"When I know the truth."

Swain nodded. "All right, then. Here's your truth."

He gestured and the thug swung his arms, throwing the bucketful of water, drenching Jack's hair, his
jacket, his shirt, his pants. Then the thug pulled the
baton free and flicked a switch in the base. It was an
electroshock device. The click was the loudest, most
terrible sound Jack had heard since the explosion in
Iraq. It even beat the bomb back home because it was
all about *him*.

He'd heard of the Chinese using these batons
against practitioners of Falun Gong, jamming them
into their prisoners' mouths and letting loose as much
as 250,000 volts of electricity. It was the torturer's
preferred method because it reportedly didn't leave
telltale marks.

He worked his wrists urgently, trying to loosen
the damn rope. Ironically, the blood from the wounds
that caused was helping to soften them. The wrig-
gling was subtle, would look to the other men like

anxiety, like panic—if they bothered to look. The room was poorly lit and their eyes were on his face, his pain. It helped that the chair was worn from repeated sessions like this one. Jack guessed that people had fallen over, taking the chair with them. The wood was slightly splintered, the armrests rough, providing an abrasive surface for his purposes. Whether it would be enough to cut through in time, or at all, was another matter.

"There's something that might interest you," Swain said. "Something you learn by trial and error. You know why we tied you to the armrests?"

"To keep me from punching you in the balls?"

"That, yes," Swain said. "We found that when we tied peoples' hands behind the chair, they arched their backs and fell over. This way, they kind of crumple in on themselves."

"Thanks for sharing . . ."

"You're welcome."

". . . but you're wasting your time," he said to Swain, panic rising in his chest. His rapid breathing helped to cover the tactical back-and-forth, side-to-side motion of his wrists. "I swear to you, I don't know any—"

The ape touched the tip of the baton to Jack's abdomen, letting loose a wave of agony that swept through every bone, every muscle, every blood vessel and nerve ending in his body. It caused his legs to twitch, not kick, an involuntary muscular reaction. He had no control over them, over his bowels, over anything. The closest he had ever come to feeling anything like this was when he accidentally touched the exposed prongs of a plug in the wall. But that had only been an instant of pain. This didn't stop. This burned every piece of him without letup.

He gritted his teeth against it; that lasted no more than a second or two.

Then he began to scream.

24

The ape withdrew the baton and Jack's body went slack, the relief so sweet he wanted to kiss the guy for being merciful.

He felt strangely weightless. He could barely breathe and his abdomen throbbed. He felt as if a hole had been burned right through it.

"Operation Roadshow," Swain said. "Tell me what you know."

". . . Nothing." Jack managed, spewing strings of saliva. "Just the name . . ."

"You'll have to do better than that. I'm told Mr. Copeland called you the morning he died. And I can imagine he was quite talkative."

Jack shook his head. "He was drunk . . . drugged . . . He wasn't making any sense . . . talked about a shoe."

He added any useless information he could re-member, trying to buy time.

Swain nodded, but clearly didn't believe him. "Who else did you tell about it? Who are you work-ing with?"

"No one . . ."

"Not even your friend from the yacht harbor? Or the black bird with the nice big neddies? You spend a lot of time with those two. Not that I can blame you in her case."

Jack thought of Tony and Max and felt panic ris-ing. ". . . They're just friends," he murmured. "She takes video . . . he watches my dog . . . they don't know anything . . ."

"I really wish you'd be more forthcoming."

Swain flicked two fingers at the thug and the baton touched Jack's belly again. Jack wailed, pride gone, dignity evaporated, his body stiffening against the pain as it raced through him. And just when he thought his skin might rupture, the ape pulled the baton away, well-being immediately flowing through him.

Jack didn't know how much more of this he could take. Two hits and he was about ready to sign over all of his real estate. His body ached from head to toe, his muscles twitching uncontrollably. He'd com-pletely forgotten about loosening the ropes at his wrists.

He thought about that poor woman in the other cell, how this was a strangely bonding experience. He realized that if she wasn't dead, it was a miracle.

"Anything else you want to share?" Swain asked.

"I swear to you . . ." he wheezed, "I don't know anything. . . ." Jack didn't even recognize his own damn voice.

"Then what are you doing in England, Jack?"

"A fishing expedition . . . That's all . . . I was . . . I was . . ." He thought for a moment he was going to pass out.

"You were—"

"Following al-Fida . . ."

Swain nodded, then flicked his fingers again. Jack tried to brace himself for the impact, but there was no preparing for something like this. The baton touched his neck now, and a whole new level of pain shot through him. Flaming fingers reached into his brain, his lungs, rammed down to his stomach. He swore he could feel the shape of his own navel, ringed by fire. He felt himself slipping into darkness, running away to escape this agony.

Then it was done and a hand slapped his face, keeping him from passing out. He jerked his eyes open and, through the smear of tears, found Swain crouched in front of him.

"Not as easy as you thought, is it? Playing the crusading journalist. You'd think all those years, working all those wars, would've toughened you for this. But all I'm seeing is a weak little wanker about to piss his trousers."

"I think . . . I already . . . did. . . ." Jack gasped.

His arms felt like putty, but the cockiness of this son of a bitch pushed the right button. Jack rallied himself and started working his wrists again. If he could just get a hand free, he'd slap this prick so hard it would take a brain surgeon to repair the damage.

"Last chance, Jack," Swain said. "Tell me what you know and who you're working with or my associate here will see to it that your last hour of life on this planet is filled with more pain than you can possibly imagine."

"I already told you . . . I don't know anything . . ."

"I wish I could believe you," Swain said. "Truly. But I suppose there's one way to find out." He paused. "Do you ever watch films, Jack? Go to the cinema?"

The question was so random that Jack didn't have a response, but Swain didn't seem to expect one.

"When I was a child," he continued, "I saw a little English film on the telly about a man who hunted witches. Vincent Price roaming the countryside in search of demonic evil. Very traumatizing for a six-year-old. *Witchfinder General,* it was called."

"Is that you?" Jack asked, trying to buy more time as he worked the ropes. "Shouldn't that . . . be . . . *Spookfinder General*?"

"Cute," Swain said. "I'll always remember a scene where Price trussed up a woman who vehemently denied practicing witchcraft, and unceremoniously threw her into the river. Told his men, if she survives, she's a witch. If she drowns, we'll know she's telling the truth." He paused. "Typical British irony, don't you think?"

"That's not the word I'd use," Jack replied.

Swain stood, smiling down at him. "No matter.

I'm going to take a page from Price's book. I'm going to stand here, and let my associate do what he does best. And if you die without telling me exactly what I need to know, I'll have to assume you aren't a liar after all. So apologies in advance if I'm mistaken. But if I'm not, do be sure to let me know."

He stepped back now, leaning against the wall as he nodded to the ape. But then a cell phone rang and Swain put up a finger, stopping him. After all, he couldn't let Jack's screams interrupt his call.

Swain took the phone from his pocket and answered it. "Yes?"

He listened a moment, then murmured a response and clicked off.

"Seems I'm being called away," he told Jack. "Which is a shame, because I felt we were about to come to an understanding. If nothing else, I would have enjoyed the show."

He turned to his man and gestured, and the two of them moved to the door and spoke quietly. Jack kept working on the ropes, ignoring the burn in his wrists, and finally, thankfully, felt them give again, offering him even more room. Whether or not it was enough to get a hand free was another question.

As he continued to work, the two men broke from their huddle and the ape stepped over to him again. With a self-satisfied look, Swain was out the door and gone.

"Looks like it's just you and me, mate," said the ape. "And I'm not nearly as agreeable as Mr. Swain."

He flicked the switch on the baton.

"They say these things never leave marks, but if you know how to use them you can cause quite a lot of painful scarring." His smile widened. "I think most people are put off by the smell of burning flesh, but I've always found it invigorating."

Events happened quickly. As the baton was lowered toward his crotch this time, Jack screamed and pulled and managed to rip his right wrist free of the rope. His arm swung up, slamming the thug in the side of the head. His muscle coordination was a mess and the blow didn't land with nearly the power he hoped. But it was enough to throw the guy momentarily off balance.

Jack was still tied to one of the armrests. That worked in his favor. He got up and swung the chair around hard, and the ape went down like a sack of grain. He lost the baton when he hit the concrete floor. Jack raised the chair high and smashed it down on the bastard's shoulder, shattering it and freeing his other arm. While the man lay there moaning, Jack recovered the baton.

He stopped himself from using it. The baton was the ape's way, it was Swain's way. He didn't want to be like them. He threw it down, kicked the ape in the head to make sure he would stay put—*that* was Jack's way. Then he crouched and went through the thug's pockets. He found car keys, a handkerchief, a cell phone, his Hamilton Gilbert, and a wad of folded pound notes—*his* money, no doubt, taken from him along with the watch while he was passed out. There was no wallet or ID, a sign that someone didn't want to be identified. If these people really *were* MI6, Jack had the feeling they were working off the grid.

There was also no gun, which puzzled Jack. He'd expect a guy like this to carry one, but maybe he preferred his trusty magic wand.

Jack picked up the passport where Swain had dropped it. He pocketed the watch, phone, bills, and keys. He tore the handkerchief in half and wrapped it loosely around his bloody wrists. He looked for something to tie the ape's hands, but there was only the man's shirt. He decided that the time it took to bind and gag the guy was better spent getting the hell out. He gave the ape a parting kick in the ribs and moved to the doorway.

His escape hadn't brought anyone coming, and Jack guessed that no one was nearby. He carefully peered into the hall.

It was too dark to see much of anything.

Taking the cell phone out, Jack turned it on and shone the beam down the hallway. There were several doors with windows dotting each side and he knew he'd been right, that this was once the psychiatric ward of a hospital. From the run-down look of it, the place had been abandoned at least a couple of decades ago. At the far end was an elevator, a stairwell next to it. A straight line and he'd be down those stairs and out the door, assuming none of Swain's men tried to block his path.

But he couldn't leave without checking on the woman. If she was alive, he needed to get her out of here.

He moved from door to door, shining the light through the windows, and finally found her in the cell nearest the stairwell. She was tied to a chair, her head hanging forward and canted to one side, her dark hair wet and stringy. Her sweater, shirt, and bra had been stripped away, exposing her naked torso.

Jack thought he saw movement there, the subtle rise and fall of her bare chest.

Throwing the door open, he stepped inside, quickly untied her and slapped at her face. "Wake up," he whispered. "Come on . . ."

She didn't respond.

He slapped her again, giving it more force than he would have liked, but she finally stirred and blinked up at him with dull, nearly lifeless eyes, not really registering who he was or what he wanted from her.

Searching the floor, he found her sweater, snatched it up, and quickly pushed it down over her head. Then he shoved her arms into it and pulled her to her feet. "Can you walk?"

She seemed to understand but her legs were trembling and she stumbled, losing her footing. She fell against him and he held her steady, but his own legs weren't quite back to normal yet and they swayed together, like a pair of saplings in a storm, her face falling against his neck.

He felt the heat of her breath. ". . . Who . . . ?" she croaked. "Who . . . are you . . . ?"

"The guy who was following you. Remember?"

She stiffened slightly, but he pulled her close in the hope of reassuring her. "Don't worry," he said. "I'm not one of them. I'm a friend."

He had no way of knowing if that was true. She could well be a terrorist sympathizer or an extremist herself. But right now she was simply a human being who needed his help, and Jack decided they'd sort out the rest later.

She started to straighten now, as if she were regaining strength, and he shifted her around, supporting her by the armpits. "We need to get out of here. Can you walk?"

"I . . . I think so. . . ."

They took a step together toward the door and she stumbled again, but Jack steadied her and kept moving them forward. Then they were out the door and headed toward the stairwell, Jack once again using the cell phone as a weak flashlight. Now that her legs were moving the woman seemed to be regaining even more strength.

"This probably isn't the time for introductions," he said quietly, "but I need to call you something. What's your name?"

"Sara," she told him.

"Nice to meet you, Sara. My name is—"

A roar of anger reverberated off the walls as the ape crashed into the hallway behind them. Jack spun around and saw the quick flash of a muzzle—

The world exploded in gunfire.

25

"Down!" Jack shouted, pushing her forward.

Sara didn't need any encouragement. She dove toward the stairwell before Jack had managed to douse the cell phone light.

The good news: the ape was firing crazily into near darkness, making no attempt to aim—which wasn't surprising, if he felt anything close to the way Jack did. The guy was running on rage and adrenaline.

The bad news: he had a gun and Jack didn't. And a stray bullet didn't discriminate. Jack had no idea where the gun had come from, but that didn't really matter much at this point. He also guessed he should have tied the bastard up.

Hindsight.

Sara was on her belly and clambering down the stairs, Jack close behind her. As they tumbled onto the landing, he jumped to his feet and pulled her up. They took off running as fast as their wobbly legs could carry them. They hurried down several more flights, occasionally gripping the rusty metal rail, struggling not to fall as the ape thundered down the stairwell after them, shouting in fury.

One floor, two floors, three floors, four floors—

—and then they were at the bottom and Sara lost her footing and yelped as her legs flew out from under her. She went sprawling, grunting in pain as she skidded across the dilapidated tile.

Jack ran after her and pulled her to her feet. "You okay?"

"I'll live," she told him. "Which is more than I could say an hour ago."

He thought he detected the faintest hint of gratitude in that remark; it gave his stamina a much-needed shot.

They heard the ape no more than two floors above. Jack glanced around, trying to get his bearings. It was marginally lighter down here, moonlight coming in through broken windows, and he saw they were in the hospital lobby, about twenty yards behind the reception counter. The place looked as if it had been hit by a hurricane, trash and debris strewn across the floors, the walls and ceiling battered by years of neglect and bad weather.

The main entrance was twenty yards to the left of the reception counter, at right angles. The doors that once filled the double-wide frame were missing, leaving behind a gaping rectangle, the floor in front of it littered with broken glass. Outside, punctuated by distant street lamps, the pale moonlight shone down on a gravel drive, three cars parked haphazardly near the entrance—two of which he recognized from the attack in the alley.

Three cars.

The ape wasn't alone.

As if on cue they heard a crash in the long hallway behind them, light spilling through an open doorway as more of Swain's men emerged from the room beyond. Glancing at the cars again, Jack remembered the keys he'd taken off the ape, then grabbed Sara's hand.

"Come on!"

They stumbled toward the main entrance, Jack pulling her along, using momentum more than anything else to carry him. They passed the reception counter, ducking low to use it as a shield, just as a shot cracked, splintering wood. Sara yelped and Jack jerked her sideways, then started zigzagging, trying to make them as difficult a target as possible. He stayed close to the benches in the waiting area as they afforded some protection from the gunmen.

Shots gouged the seatbacks, causing the chairs to rattle on their metal bases. Their shoes crunched glass and then they were outside and headed for the cars—two SUVs and a BMW behind them. Jack yanked the keys from his pocket as they ran. He jabbed at the buttons on one of the keys and the BMW *chirp-chirped* as its doors unlocked.

Swain's men were shouting behind them. More

shots pinged off the asphalt and the SUVs as Jack instinctively darted toward the left side of the vehicle, then suddenly remembered he was in England. Swearing, he pulled open the rear door and shoved Sara in, then got into the front seat and scrambled across it. He got behind the wheel and jammed the key into the ignition.

A shot shattered the rear window and Sara yelped again, glass showering around her, as Jack started the engine and stomped on the accelerator.

He had no idea where they were. A wooded area, surrounded by thick trees that looked malevolent in the moonlight. From the outside the hospital looked old, very old. It was a majestic, neglected relic from another century, from the shameful era of the Bethlem Royal Hospital, also known as Bedlam.

But where he was didn't matter. There was a driveway ahead of them, and a road beyond and Jack drove as fast as he could to get to them.

Checking his rearview mirror, he saw Swain's men spilling from the hospital entrance and running toward the remaining cars. But he already had a fairly good lead on them and it wasn't likely they'd catch him.

Shooting out to the road, he picked up speed then blasted past a row of old country houses and disappeared down a tree-lined street into the early morning darkness.

The sun was coming up by the time they reached Central London.

Jack had used the GPS on the cell phone to chart the course, then memorized the route and tossed the phone into the street as they rolled through a suburban neighborhood. If these guys really were MI6, he had no doubt they'd be able to track the thing.

So be it. Even if the spook patrol found them they would probably give Jack some space, the way Swain did in San Francisco. Intelligence ops were like vampires: they preferred the night, the shadows. Especially now, when anyone with a cell phone could be a journalist.

Sara hadn't said a word during the drive, and when he turned to check on her he found her flopped across the seat, passed out. He didn't blame her. He was halfway there himself. He wondered for a moment if she had been hit by a bullet or a piece of shrapnel kicked up by the gunfire, but he saw no sign of blood. When they stopped at a light he reached back and touched her neck, found a steady pulse.

So he drove, too exhausted to think about much more than the mechanics of his journey—left turn, right turn, brake, gas, brake, check the mirror for any sign of hostiles. . . . It took special concentration because he wasn't used to driving on the opposite side of the road.

When they got to central London he didn't go back to the Beresford Hotel. Although he had checked in under a false name, he couldn't risk Swain showing up there, so he headed into Paddington and found a place that made the Beresford look like Buckingham Palace.

He left Sara in the car as he checked in, then woke her enough to get her into the rickety elevator.

"'Ard night?" the round, scruffy concierge chuckled.

"The girl likes her scotch," Jack said, affecting a British accent. He didn't want to make the same mistake he did with Sara, tipping his nationality. Just in case anyone asked.

Jack got her into the room and onto the bed, its springs groaning noisily as she sank onto it. Then he went back to the car, drove for several blocks, and abandoned it in the car park of another, much larger hotel. That would keep the bastards busy for a while.

When Jack got back to the room, Sara was out again—which didn't surprise him—so he drew the curtains to mute the morning sun, then sank into the threadbare armchair across from her and allowed himself to doze.

A couple hours later he heard her stir and opened his eyes. She still had her head on the pillow, but she was staring at him.

"We were interrupted," she said. "You were about to tell me your name."

Jack smiled. "Jack Hatfield. Nice to meet you."

She haltingly pulled herself upright, as though testing her stamina each step of the way. Without a shirt or a bra, her sweater clung to her in a way that made it difficult for Jack not to look. The room was a little cold and it showed, but he was a gentleman and averted his gaze. He couldn't help but wonder what kind of danger, what kind of physical duress, it would take for a man *not* to think about sex. Obviously, he hadn't reached that threshold.

"You ready to talk?" he asked. "I'm sure you have as many questions as I do."

"I don't know if anything I have to say would make much sense at the moment."

"You seem fine to me."

"Thanks to you," she said. "And I mean that. Thank you. You could have left me with those sadists but you didn't."

"Not part of my DNA," he said. "And you're welcome."

She offered him a wan, fragile smile. A grateful smile. It was restorative, not like the hardened mask he'd seen in al-Fida's flat and in that alley.

But, he reminded himself, he still didn't know what she was about and who she worked with.

Sara's smile faltered as she stared at him with those dark, vulnerable eyes. "Why do I feel like I've seen you before?"

Over the years, Jack had got that a lot, though mostly in the States. People seeing him on television and remembering his face but not quite able to place him.

"I told you, I'm a reporter. I used to have a show on GNT, although I don't think there's much chance you'd ever see me on this side of the Atlantic."

Something shifted in her expression as a memory came to the surface. "Hatfield," she said. "Of course. Brendan told me about you."

"Brendan?"

"A colleague. He showed me one of your videos on YouTube. You're the one the Home Office banned from traveling here, one of Copeland's friends."

The name landed like a depth charge in Jack's brain. He sat upright. "How do you know Bob Copeland?"

She must have sensed a threat from him, because she put her hands up as if to reassure him. "He was a friend," she said. "When we heard about what happened to him, we were devastated."

"We?" Jack had no idea what to make of this. "Sara, I think you'd better explain."

"I don't know how much I can tell you," she said. "We've already been compromised, and if you were to report anything about—"

"*Report* anything? Are you serious?" Heat rose in Jack's chest. "This isn't about my job. I don't have a clue what's going on here yet it's cost me two friends and nearly my own life—"

"You're not the only one who has lost friends and nearly his life," she said.

Right, he thought. He remembered her half dead in the chair. He sheathed his claws.

"A man who was like a brother to me was found dead in a pub toilet, his throat slit. And a woman I was close to was suffocated in Bulgaria."

"I'm sorry," Jack said. "That still doesn't tell me how you know Bob Copeland. What do you mean, he was a friend?"

She lowered her head a moment as if to gather her thoughts. Probably trying to decide how much she should tell him. "You may have a hard time believing this, but I'm a field agent for Interpol."

He looked at her as if she had said she was one of Santa's elves. Not because there weren't women agents but because the FBI and MI6 were already folded into this thing. Now Interpol?

"Okay," he said. "You're Interpol. And?"

"For the last two years I've been working with a small, international task force, trying to gather information about an extremist Muslim group called the Hand of Allah."

Jack knew the name well and his reaction made it obvious.

"I see you've heard of them."

"An offshoot of Al Qaeda, way under the radar. I used to talk about them on my TV show, but I wasn't sure anyone was listening. People wanted to believe we had this stuff under control."

She nodded. "A lot we do . . . some we do not. The Hand of Allah is among the latter. Their leader is a nasty piece of work named Faakhir Zuabi, who reportedly used to rub shoulders with Khalid Sheikh Mohammed, bin Laden's chief of operations.

"After Mohammed was taken into custody, Zuabi went out on his own. Since then he's had his fingers in more death and destruction around the globe than we can track, all the while sitting comfortably in a mosque in East London—not that the British authorities want to believe this. He's spent the last several years getting cozy with the elites in this country, financing campaigns of people who are sympathetic to Muslims."

"You have people like that here?"

Sara made a face.

Jack realized he'd stepped in it.

"Not all Muslims want to be witness to the downfall of Western Civilization," she said. "Some of us are quite fond of it, in fact."

"Sorry," Jack said, though he wasn't sure he meant it.

Her expression relaxed. "But it goes much deeper than political influence."

"What do you mean?"

"Abdal al-Fida was one of Zuabi's followers, but he also worked for the British government. My job was to gather information from him about the Hand of Allah."

Jack looked at her, thinking she must have had a very powerful motivation beyond a sense of duty to voluntarily lie down with a known terrorist. He imagined she'd had to take many long, hot showers after their time in bed to wash away the taint. Her stone-cold reaction to al-Fida's so-called suicide suddenly made all the sense in the world.

"What kind of information were you hoping to get?"

"Names, places, anything actionable. But he was also a computer technician and we thought he might be our back door into the government's counterintelligence network."

Jack frowned. "Why would you want access to that?"

"To explore. We think that over the last several years, helped by the politicians who were in their pocket, the Hand of Allah has been slowly infiltrating the British government with hadist sleeper agents like al-Fida. Particularly the Home and Foreign Offices. All the way to the top. Which means they'd have access to and control of the counterterrorist branches, like MI5 and—"

"MI6," Jack said. "Adam Swain."

She nodded. "He and his gang of thugs may not look like your average Muslim radicals, but they are sympathizers. We believe they were bought off by some very deep pockets."

"And you think Zuabi's behind all this?"

"Without a doubt," Sara said. "But he's very clever about it. He keeps everything on a need-to-know basis. I don't think even his own men—the true believers—are aware of how far this reaches. Even though al-Fida worked for the government, I never got the impression he knew anything about Swain and the others. Zuabi likes things fragmented so that it's not so easy to connect the dots."

"That still doesn't tell me about Copeland. How did he fit?"

"Copeland was working with us," she said, "a clandestine consultant, I'd guess you'd say."

Jack nodded. Typical Bob. "So he knew about al-Fida all along."

"Al-Fida—and several others."

"What kind of 'others'?" That didn't sound good.

"When Abdal left for California a few weeks ago, he didn't say anything to me about his real purpose in going there because that would have betrayed his oath to Zuabi. But I knew that his trip wasn't for consulate business, so we started taking a closer look. We discovered that the Home Office had sent several employees to San Francisco over the last two years, all Muslims, all traveling on diplomatic passports."

"A sleeper cell?"

She nodded. "We think they're planning something in the U.S. That exploding Land Rover was a good indication that we're right. Al-Fida was like a child, no impulse control and a desire to be patted on the head—I can certainly attest to that. When he went off the rails, the Hand of Allah had to scramble to cover their tracks. They couldn't afford for him to expose them and interfere with their real objective."

"So why didn't they just kill him?"

"I suppose Zuabi had his reasons," Sara said. "Perhaps he wished to allow a loyal follower to make peace with God or take his own life. That would have been honorable. Either way, after Abdal returned to London he was very subdued. If not for me, for wanting to spend more time together, I believe he would have died by his own hand."

"Not that I believe Swain, but he told me that killing al-Fida was not on his to-do list."

"That may be true," she said. "I think Abdal was killed by a man who is devoted to Zuabi, another true believer."

Jack suddenly remembered the guy he nearly bumped into last night as he left the pub near al-Fida's house, a dark, angular-faced man with a wispy black goatee who had seemed to be in a hurry. Jack had thought the man was just another Muslim resident of the neighborhood, but maybe he was wrong.

"You have a name?" he asked.

Sara hesitated.

"Maybe I know him," Jack prodded.

"Hassan Haddad," she said. "He's one of the Hand of Allah's top soldiers, recruited when he was a child by Zuabi himself. Very skilled, quite ruthless. We picked him up on a cell phone call, tailed him for several days, followed him to Bulgaria where we think he may have been in contact with an arms merchant named Anton Chilikov. We don't know if any purchases were made, but Haddad killed one of our agents to prevent us from finding out."

"The girl who was suffocated?"

"Yes," Sara said. "Someone I recruited." A faraway look crept into her eyes and Jack knew the loss must have been difficult for her.

"So where is this Haddad guy now?"

She quickly refocused. "We're not sure. We lost him here in London, after he killed another one of our agents."

"Jeez. The guy sounds like a one-man jihad."

"Well said. That's why we think he's the point man on whatever Zuabi's planning in San Francisco, and we're assuming he'll be headed there soon."

"On a diplomatic passport, no doubt."

She nodded. "Bob Copeland was our man on the ground over there, but with him gone we're not sure who we can trust."

Jack wondered why Copeland hadn't been more forthcoming. Then again, the way things were looking back in San Francisco, Sara was right. If Zuabi's people had managed to infiltrate the British government, who was to say they weren't working on the Americans as well. So Copeland had to play it sly, as he always did.

As if reading his thoughts, Sara said, "He told us about you. Copeland."

"It would have been nice if he'd told me about *you*."

"We instructed him to be cautious," she replied. "You're a journalist. We did not know whether you would put a story, a scoop, above a principle."

"I remember when those two went hand in hand, when members of my profession kept D-day a secret and hit the beaches with the first wave," Jack said.

"That's the reason I'm telling you all this now. Copeland insisted that you might be a valuable asset down the line."

"Down to the wire, you mean."

"That, too. And it may not be far off." She eased herself forward wearing a grave expression. It was as though she were telling herself she had rested enough. More than anything, that gesture told Jack how little time might be left. "Abdal al-Fida thought I was just like him, a die-hard extremist. He may not have told me much, but he once said that the infidels would soon see destruction that would dwarf 9/11."

"You're talking nukes."

"I am. You're aware of the recent leak of diplomatic documents revealing that al Qaeda was sourcing nuclear materials and hiring scientists to build dirty bombs for use against Americans. Jack, al Qaeda isn't nearly as well connected and well funded as the Hand of Allah."

"Operation Roadshow," Jack said ominously.

She nodded. "Coming to a city near you."

26

Eurostar, London to France

It was late afternoon and they were aboard the Eurostar, a high-speed train that connected London to Paris through the Channel Tunnel.

Once they'd gathered their strength and left the hotel, Sara had taken Jack to an old boxing gym near the Tower Bridge where the task force kept private lockers—both men's and women's—in case of an emergency.

The men's locker contained identification documents, money, and prepaid cell phones, along with a toiletry kit and several changes of clothes. The IDs were useless to Jack—he still had his Israeli passport with him, and it would have to do. He found a pair of slacks and a shirt that fit, and a suede leather jacket that was much like the one he'd left with Rabbi Neershum in Tel Aviv.

He also found a small theatrical makeup kit, a savvy addition to the provisions. There was a passable beard inside. That would save him having to explain why his passport showed him with a beard while he had just a stubble. He would put it on at the terminal; it wasn't something he just wanted to spring on Sara.

After a hot shower, he put on the new clothes then retrieved his father's watch from his old pants pocket and strapped it to his wrist.

He found Sara in the gym, watching a couple of over-the-hill boxers jab at each other in the ring. She had also showered and changed, now wearing dark jeans, a tight gray T-shirt, and a black leather jacket, her hair pulled back in a neat ponytail—every bit the modern woman.

The gym was crowded and several of the men were staring at her. As Jack approached her, he didn't need them to remind him how stunning she was, and it was difficult for him to look at her without wanting her. Especially now that he knew she was on the right side of this fight. He wasn't sure if he was imagining it, or it was just wishful thinking, but she seemed to appreciate what she saw in front of her as well.

She continued to be all business, however. After they left the gym, she called Brendan Lapworth to let him know she was still alive.

"Who?" Jack asked as they took a cab to the terminal.

She quietly explained that the man Jack had seen Sara talking to at the rave—Curly—was a hardened former Central Scotland Police constable named Brendan Lapworth who had been working antiterror for at least a dozen years. He was Sara's task force leader, and had been on the other end of the line when she made her call outside of al-Fida's flat.

"There's a problem. We need to talk."

"When I realized I was being followed," she told Jack, "I knew I had to warn him off. Too many of us have been getting ourselves killed. We were supposed to rendezvous again after I either lost you or took care of the situation. But that obviously didn't happen."

Jack raised an eyebrow. "Took care of the situation? You mean shoot me?"

"If it came to that, yes."

His brain didn't know if that should excite him or be a deal-breaker. Fortunately, his body didn't give a damn.

"When you said you were in Abdal's flat I thought you might be working for Zuabi," she told him. "A homegrown terrorist. Of course, I didn't know who you were, then."

"Believe me, I didn't know what to make of you, either. That little crying act was quite a show. You were very convincing."

"I've had a lot of practice," she said softly.

Without having said a word, Sara and Jack adopted the roles of lovers on holiday. They boarded the Eurostar to Paris and spent the nearly three-hour ride trying to get as much sleep as possible. They both still felt the lingering effects of the ape's magic wand, and Jack only wished he'd been a little more thorough with the guy and put him out for good.

Maybe that's the difference between us and them, he thought. People like us were raised to be empathetic and understanding, to use violence as a last option, always looking for reasons *not* to kill. But mercenaries like Swain and his men, or extremists like Zuabi, looked at people as nothing more than a way to earn a buck, gain power, make a political point, or achieve some false religious nirvana that really had nothing to do with God at all. They used greed and faith as weapons, their concern for humanity never stretching beyond the limits of their own selfish interests.

Jack remembered what the Reb had said about al-Fida at Cousin Ohad's dining table.

"He'd just as soon see people like you and me buried under a pile of rubble."

Thugs like Swain and Zuabi and al-Fida and Haddad had no qualms about killing. Why, Jack thought, should he?

Because that's one of the only things that separates human beings from animals, he reminded himself. And if that didn't matter, then the bad guys had already won.

As it said in Jeremiah, *"In truth, in justice, and in righteousness; then shall the nations bless themselves by him. . . ."*

Paris, France

"Good to see your bonnie face again," Lapworth said to Sara, with only a hint of the rolled *r*s that signaled a Scottish burr. "We were afraid we lost you."

"You nearly did," she told him. "If it weren't for Jack, I'd be rotting in a chair right now."

Brendan Lapworth had picked them up at the Paris train station, the Gare du Nord, in a battered Citroën Berlingo panel van. Up close, Jack noted that the curly hair was flecked with gray, and there were lines in Lapworth's ruddy face—the roadmap of a hard life. But his eyes were clear and blue and unflinching.

Jack sat in the backseat, watching the sun drop below the horizon as he absently wound his watch. Ironically, his last visit to Paris had been for a story, when the city was plagued by Muslim riots. It occurred to him that, except for the trip to London with Rachel, most of his world travel had been accompanied by war or political upheaval.

At some point in his life he'd have to take a *real* vacation, assuming the world would still be around when he was ready for one. Considering what was going on these days, the machinations of Islamic extremists, the anger back home, the turmoil in the Middle East, it sometimes seemed to Jack as if we were already in World War III and losing.

These thoughts aside, Jack had always loved Paris. From the iron-lattice splendor of the Eiffel Tower to the street side cafés and the Gothic majesty of Notre

Dame Cathedral, the city hummed a romantic, old-world European tune, while managing to feel modern and vibrant and alive. As they drove through the traffic-clogged streets, he allowed himself to fantasize about an alternate life. A life in which he took a small apartment and spent his evenings at the Café de Flore, drinking real Chablis as he watched the carefree young French women stroll by.

As Lapworth drove, he said, "Good to meet you, Hatfield. You did real good by Sara. Bob Copeland told me you're one of the good guys."

"So was Bob," Jack said, shaking off his reverie. "How did you meet him?"

"He was a consultant on a cybersecurity case I handled when I was still a constable," Lapworth replied. "We found we had mutual interests and stayed in touch. You can't know how much his death angers me."

"I think I can imagine."

Lapworth nodded. "'Tis good to have you with us. What we lack in number, we make up for with passion."

An odd statement, considering the size and scope of Interpol.

"And hopefully we'll take down a few terrorists in the process," Jack said.

"More than a few. I look forward to the day when every one of these bastards is either dead or wasting away in prison."

"That's a pretty tall order."

Lapworth shrugged. "I've always dreamed large."

It suddenly struck Jack that, like Sara, Lapworth seemed to have reasons for his work that went deeper than a sense of duty. There was a forcefulness to his words that spoke of an underlying rage, anger that had probably been cultivated by some tragedy in his past. Jack understood the sentiment, but he sometimes wondered if such feelings clouded one's judgment.

"Where are we headed?" Jack asked.

"To our command station," Sara said. "We're in an apartment complex that was scheduled to be gutted and renovated until the investors backed out. Now it's just sitting there. We had to tap a neighboring building for power, but it works well for us."

That also struck Jack as a little strange. Why would an organization with a fifty-million-dollar annual budget put its agents up in a building scheduled for demolition, especially with their main headquarters not that far away? Then again, from what he'd heard so far, this task force sounded like a ragtag operation trying to remain as invisible as possible. Maybe the fewer ties they had to the mother ship, the better.

Interpol wasn't a policing body. It was primarily a communications liaison between law enforcement agencies around the world, but Jack was well aware that some of the "advisors" they contracted did a lot more than give advice.

Lapworth made a turn down a desolate cobblestone street and pulled to the side of the road in front of a five-story limestone building that was fronted by a high chain-link fence. Sara popped open her door and got out, gesturing for Jack to follow. When Jack closed his door, Lapworth hit the gas and headed down the street.

"Where's he going?" Jack said.

"To a garage down the block. He'll be along in a minute."

She gestured for him to follow again and they moved to a gate secured by a chain and padlock. She punched in the combination then unhooked the lock and swung the gate open, ushering him inside.

The sun was all but down now, and with little light to guide them they walked along a short stone path toward the building entrance. When they got close to the lobby doors, a hard, sinewy man emerged, an HK IAR slung over his shoulder.

"It's all right, Ethan, it's me," Sara said.

The man named Ethan relaxed, nodded. "Good to see you back. We thought you were dead." He shifted a hard gaze in Jack's direction. "Who's this?"

"The reason I'm not," she told him.

Ethan quickly patted Jack down, then pulled a radio from his belt and spoke into it, saying, "Two coming up."

As it squawked in response, Sara pushed the lobby doors open and Jack moved with her.

"An Infantry Automatic Rifle," Jack observed.

"Sorry?"

"That's what your friend Ethan was carrying," Jack said. "I don't believe that's standard Interpol issue."

"As I've said, this is not a standard Interpol operation."

They continued down a dingy hallway to a set of wooden steps, Jack once again wondering why the unit was housed here. Nothing about this struck him as part of a sanctioned operation, Interpol or otherwise, and he was beginning to wonder if he'd been too quick to trust these people.

They started up the stairs, but as they reached the third-floor landing, Jack abruptly stopped.

"We're on the fifth," Sara said, gesturing him upward.

"I think I've gone far enough."

"What's wrong?"

Jack stared at her. "You've been lying to me, haven't you? You people don't have a thing to do with Interpol."

She didn't have to respond. Her face said everything.

Jack turned, looking down the stairwell toward the first floor, where Ethan now stood, staring up at him suspiciously, his hands on the weapon.

Sara touched Jack's arm, squeezing it. "It's all right, Jack. You're safe here."

"Then why did you lie to me?"

"Because I wanted you to trust me. Take me seriously. I *was* with Interpol, but I left the agency some time ago."

"Then who the hell *are* you people?"

"Survivors," she said.

"Of what?"

"Each one of us has a different story. Brendan lost his wife in the London subway bombing and Ethan lost both his children to a suicide strike in Israel."

"And you?"

Her eyes clouded. "Not now," she said.

Jack decided not to push. He saw real pain in those eyes and backed off. "So you're vigilantes."

"In a sense. But I wouldn't put it like that. We're all former law enforcement, counterterrorism specialists. We became unhappy with the red tape and the shifting politics and the inability of our governments to handle this crisis. These fanatics need to be stopped, so we're doing what we can on our own."

"How many of you are there?"

"Two years ago there were over twenty of us. Now there are twelve. Life expectancy isn't one of our strong suits, as you well know."

"So how the hell do you expect to accomplish anything?"

"We have hundreds of contacts all over the world. People in law enforcement who are sympathetic to our cause. People like Bob Copeland who are willing to help." She squeezed his arm again. "People like you."

"People who hate terrorists, sociopaths, and flat-out liars, you mean?"

She was silent.

He looked down at her hand. Soft. Delicate. A hand that should be painting a picture, or playing the piano. But her grip was firm, and he knew from experience she was capable of striking a solid blow.

He looked into her eyes again. "You should have told me all this from the start."

"I know," she said. "I'm sorry."

She was a very good actress, he knew that from experience, too. But there was a sincerity in her expression that was tough to fake.

"The fifth floor, you said?"

She nodded. Without saying another word, they continued up the steps.

As they reached their destination, Jack heard voices and saw another man standing guard in the hall, his cold eyes assessing them as they emerged from the stairwell.

He nodded to Sara. "Welcome home."

Sara smiled at him and patted his shoulder as she passed, then took hold of Jack's arm again and pulled him toward a lighted doorway.

They stepped into what had once been a decent-sized Parisian apartment, but was now a fully functioning antiterrorist command center. There was a large white board to Jack's right, with the words *HAND OF ALLAH* written across it in red marker.

Several photographs were taped below this. Surveillance shots of Adam Swain, Abdal al-Fida, an older Middle Eastern man standing outside a mosque—Faakhir Zuabi, no doubt—and assorted other Arab faces, including one Jack recognized: the man with the wispy goatee he'd nearly bumped into outside the pub.

Hassan Haddad.

He was angry that he hadn't known who Haddad

was at the time. If he had, there might be one less terrorist in the world.

There were multiple computer stations scattered about the room with men and women manning them. One screen showed night-vision security video of the front, back, and sides of the building, while another was open to a screen that Jack remembered from his own explorations—the British embassy personnel files.

Another screen was open to what looked like an Arabic-language chat group, and the guy sitting in front of it—a squat, swarthy man with biceps the size of grapefruits—was typing away furiously.

The other people in the room were an eclectic mix of ethnicities and nationalities, all deeply focused on their tasks. A woman with short-cropped red hair, a spray of freckles, and startling blue eyes glanced up, offering Sara a relieved smile as she got out of her chair and pulled her into a hug.

"Thank the Lord," she said in a heavy Irish accent. "Brendan told us you called and I've been praying ever since."

Now others turned, greeting Sara with a smile or a quick hello before giving Jack a slow, suspicious stare. Sara introduced him to the group, rattling off names to fit the faces, but all he got from them were a few grudging nods. He felt like the new kid at school that everyone was curious about but no one wanted to commit to.

A man with a graying beard and horn-rimmed glasses—Alain, if Jack remembered correctly—

looked up from his station and called across the room.

"Sara, your intel on Abdal was excellent. I was able to get into the home secretary's internal network and I think I may have found something of value."

"What?" she asked.

He tossed a small object to her and she looked down at it in her palm—a USB data key. "Encrypted e-mails from one of Zuabi's moles, sent over the last week."

"Encrypted? That's unusual."

"Oui," Alain said. "This is why they caught my attention. And even more unusual is that the e-mails were sent to an employee of an American firm called Allied Harbor Associates."

"Which is?"

"They handle port operations in our country," Jack told her. "They took over the contract after the Dubai controversy a few years ago."

The redhead frowned. "Dubai controversy?"

"Yeah. I blew the lid on it when I had my TV show back in the States." He saw the blank stares. "That's what I used to do—hosted a talk show that held the powers that be accountable.

"The contract was originally handled by a British firm called P & O, but when they sold all their assets to Dubai Ports World, concern about port security in our country became a political football. Most people thought handing control to a UAE-based company was extremely risky, if not outright idiotic. Including me."

Sara nodded. "So Allied took over."

"Right," Jack said. The others were listening as well. This seemed to be earning him points. "The political pressure forced DP to sell all their U.S. assets to a company called American International. They, in turn, quietly sold it to Allied."

Anyone who was paying attention knew that port security in the U.S. was a joke, even after the SAFE Port Act was passed by Congress. There were far too many shipping containers moving in and out of the country, and no workable method of keeping track of them all.

"And who owns Allied?" Sara asked.

"That's where it gets interesting," Jack said. "The majority stockholder is an old friend of mine. A naturalized citizen named Lawrence Soren. Originally from Austria. The guy's a billionaire and a propagandist extraordinaire, and has definite Marxist leanings."

"And he's a *friend* of yours?"

"I was being facetious. The guy destroyed my career." He gestured to the USB key. "I'll be curious to see what's in those e-mails. They could be confirmation that Zuabi's moles aren't limited to the British government. Soren may have a traitor in his midst, which wouldn't surprise me. His extremism has made him enemies."

"It will take some time to find out what is in them," Alain told him. "As I said, they are encrypted, and it may be hours before I break the—"

A harsh voice cut him off. "What's going on here? Who *is* this man?"

They turned to find a brutish-looking German with a crew cut standing in the doorway, frowning at Jack.

Jack held out a hand, about to introduce himself, but the guy ignored him. "Did anyone sweep them?"

"Relax, Reinhardt," Alain said.

"Relax? That's how errors are made." The man came into the room now, looking like an angry bulldog. "How many times do I have to tell you, we sweep everyone. No exceptions." He scooped a security wand from a nearby table then gestured to Jack and Sara. "Against the wall."

Sara gave Jack a look that said, *What can you do?* But considering the number of people they'd lost over the last two years, Jack couldn't blame the guy. He moved to the wall, placed his palms against it, and spread his legs.

Reinhardt flicked a switch on the wand and started with Jack's shoes, slowly moving up the inside of each leg, the torso, the neck and shoulders, then up each arm.

When he waved it over Jack's right wrist—over his Hamilton Gilbert—the wand began to beep. Loudly.

The entire room went quiet, heads turning in reaction to the sound. Without missing a beat, Reinhardt produced a gun and pressed it against Jack's head.

"The watch," he demanded. "Take it off."

Sara just stood there looking stunned and Jack was flabbergasted.

With horror, he thought:

Swain. While I was out, he had my watch. Has he been tracking us all this time?

"Take it off!" the bulldog roared.

But before Jack could comply a radio squawked nearby. Brendan Lapworth's frantic voice came over the airwaves—

"Shut her down! We're under attack!"

As one, all eyes shifted to the computer screen showing the infrared security cameras as a team of black-suited commandos spilled from a van then crashed through the chain-link gate—

—and shot Ethan and Brendan down in cold blood.

27

Chaos.

That was the only word to describe it.

The room erupted in shouts and scrambling bodies. Alain quickly moved from computer to computer to shut them down, as people hurried toward windows and doors. Reinhardt's expression was pure fury. He slammed Jack across the back of the head with his gun, then stepped back and was about to pull the trigger when Sara shouted.

"No!"

She smashed into their leader, knocking him against the white board. He went down with a crash and she grabbed Jack's arm, pulling him toward the doorway.

"Run!"

Jack's head was throbbing as they flew through

the hallway, shouts echoing around them. The commandos were inside the building and storming up the stairs, firing indiscriminately at any movement they saw.

A bullet gouged plaster above Jack's head and Sara steered him through a doorway into another apartment, pulling him into the bathroom.

She pointed toward the ceiling. "Up there. Open it!"

Gunfire echoed in the hall as Jack jumped onto the toilet, unlatched a square hatch above it—an air vent—and threw it open. The space was just big enough for him to fit through.

"Go!" she said.

Jack hoisted himself up and through to a slanted slate rooftop. He turned and reached back inside and Sara got onto the toilet and grabbed hold of his hands. He pulled her up, paused just long enough to drop his beloved watch through the opening, then quickly closed the hatch.

Down in the street, several more vans and French police cars screeched to a stop in front of the building, uniformed officers piling out, weapons at the ready. Whatever lie they had been told—undoubtedly by MI6—they had swallowed it whole.

The rooftops of Paris were like no place else on earth. For as far as Jack could see in the moonlight there were no flat surfaces, just a maze of slants and protrusions, gullies and pipes and television antennas—*visual* disorder but beautiful, as if the city had been designed by a mad genius.

Sara got to her feet and started across the slanted roof, gesturing for Jack to follow. But that was easier said than done. She seemed to have a path mapped out, grabbing onto landmarks along the way—a pipe here, a chimney there, the occasional satellite dish— and Jack could only stumble along after her, his head throbbing, trying his best not to slip and fall.

When they were halfway across, the hatch popped open behind them and they heard a shout, the voice familiar—

"Sara! Sara!"

Coming to a stop, they turned and saw Alain climbing from the hatch as he called to her.

"I had to wipe all the computers," he said. "The key—tell me you still have the key!"

She patted her pocket. "Yes, yes. Now hurry!"

Alain started forward as a shot rang out behind him. His spine split in a burst of blood, the impact pitching him onto the slanted rooftop. He threw his hands out, scrambling for purchase—more twitching reflex than anything, Jack knew—but then his face went blank and his body flopped and rolled, tumbling over the side of the building into the darkness below.

Sara screamed, moonlit tears filling her eyes— genuine tears—as one of the commandos hoisted himself through the hatch.

Jack put his hands on her shoulders and gently nudged her forward.

"Go! *Go!*"

Sara didn't need further prompting. She turned

and continued toward the edge of the rooftop, picking up speed. Jack did his best to keep up with her.

The adjoining building was only four stories high, but Sara didn't let that slow her down. She leaped onto it without hesitation, grabbing a fat ventilation pipe as she landed. Jack followed, his shoes slipping from under him as he hit the second rooftop. He fell onto his side and nearly went tumbling, but managed to grab Sara's extended hand, got hold of the pipe, and steadied himself.

Another shot cracked, the bullet ricocheting wildly. Pulling himself upright, Jack got back to his feet and hurried after Sara as she yanked open the roof-access door of the building and disappeared inside. A moment later they were on the stairs, spiraling quickly toward the ground floor. When they reached it, breathing heavily, Sara cautiously opened a squeaking door into a narrow, cobblestone alleyway. She looked, then exited. As Jack followed her outside, she stopped and turned, her eyes still full of tears.

"Give me that bloody watch," she said, still trying to catch her breath.

"I left it in the bathroom so they couldn't track us," he said.

She looked at him suspiciously.

"They were shooting at me, too!" he reminded her.

"Alain was one of my dearest friends," she said.

"I'm truly sorry," Jack told her. "But I didn't set you up, if that's what you're thinking. You think I want to see another 9/11? I was *had*, Sara, just like your agents who died in the bathroom, in the alley. Like you were when they killed Abdal. It happens."

She looked at him with angry eyes but didn't seem to have a response. She gestured toward the roof. "They'll be across soon. There's a garage around the corner, where Brendan left the van. Let's hope they haven't found it."

She turned and hurried through the alley.

Jack followed her, unable to fathom how any religion, any philosophy, any political goal, was worth what this had already cost.

And it was still just the opening salvo.

They were blasting through the streets of Paris in the Citroën, Sara behind the wheel. She'd found the key in a small magnetic box under the rear bumper, and so far the journey had been uneventful, no sign of anyone in pursuit.

Sara was angry and heartbroken, but had that slightly shell-shocked look that Jack had gotten so used to seeing during his days in Iraq.

"They're dead," she said. "Probably every last one of them. All because of that bloody watch. All because I brought you there."

"Believe me, Sara, I didn't know about the tracker. How could I? You think they strapped me in that chair for the fun of it? You must have heard my screams."

"I was out. I didn't hear *anything*."

"Then you'll just have to trust me."

"Why should I?"

"The same reason I trusted you, even when you were lying," he said.

She suddenly crushed the brake, pulling to the side of the road. "Get out of the car!"

"Sara, you've got to look past this."

"Out!"

It killed him to see her in such pain. He sat there a moment, just staring at her, wanting her to change her mind, but she didn't say another word. Angrily, he opened his door and got out.

She hit the gas even before he had closed the door, blasting down the street on squealing tires, as Jack watched in dismay. But as she approached the intersection she abruptly stopped, the van's brake lights glowing in the darkness. The horn let out a short, angry blast and then she just sat there, the engine idling.

Jack jogged unsteadily to the van, still not quite having found his land legs after their across-the-rooftop run. He opened the passenger door to find her just sitting there, her eyes clouded, trying her best to keep from crying. One death can produce an anesthetic reaction that allows someone to function through a short period of mourning. But multiple deaths are like a landslide: *it* controls *you*. The hardened façade she usually presented was starting to crack and it took everything she had to hold back.

"It's okay," he said. "It will *be* okay if we don't give up."

"I don't know if I can do this anymore."

"I know," he said.

"It's what you said. Every time one of us falls I feel it all over again. The loss, the self-doubt, the questioning, wondering what I might have done to foresee this, to *prevent* it."

"You're not a professional. Neither am I. We're making this up as we go along. Those guys." He indicated the enemy with a backward jerk of his head. "They have years of training, limitless resources, and vastly superior numbers. It's amazing you've gotten this far."

His words seemed to cut through the grief and remind her why they were here. She wiped her eyes. The gesture was transformative: he saw the old Sara return.

He didn't want to intrude on her sorrow but he knew they couldn't stay here much longer. They needed to get rid of the van. The alert would have gone out and the police would be searching for them. Terrorists on the run, that's the story MI6 likely fed them. Dangerous extremists who needed to be shot dead on sight.

Still, he sat there saying nothing, suddenly aware that despite knowing her for less than twenty-four hours he'd never felt this way about a woman. Not about Rachel or any of the one-nighters he picked up since the divorce.

And then the sadness seemed to pass. She put her hands back on the wheel.

"I'm sorry," she said. "I know this wasn't your fault. You couldn't have known what they'd do. But *I* should have anticipated it."

"Shoulda, woulda, coulda. *This* is where we are. Do we sit here or do we go and get those sons of bitches."

"I'm trying to figure out *how*," she said. "The team is gone, the computers. All we have is the USB key, and even if we manage to get the information off of it, it could be worthless."

"You ever hear of the wasp strategy?" Jack asked.

"The wasp? Like the insect?"

"Yeah. How do you kill eighty people and destroy fourteen tons of hardware with something that weighs a fraction of a pound?"

She nodded. "Set a wasp loose in the cabin."

"Exactly. We have to be wasps," Jack said. "You said you have contacts around the world."

"Yes, but we kept all our information on our hard drives. That's why Alain wiped them."

"You told him you have the key—"

"But I have no idea where he kept the backups," she said. "I was a field operative, not a techie. I wouldn't even know where to start."

"We still have the encrypted e-mails Alain gave you," Jack said.

"Right. But the key word is *encrypted*. Do you know anyone we can go to?"

Jack thought about the Reb, wondered if he should call him. But most of his people were in Tel Aviv, and getting there would take too long. Encrypted or not, he didn't want to chance sending data over the Internet.

"Not in Europe," he told her.

She paused, a sudden light in her eyes.

"What?"

"I work at the College of Islam. That was my cover. There's a student there—a young man who's brilliant with computers. In fact, if I remember correctly, he's even done some work with codes. Maybe *he* can help us. He's Muslim and he's very religious, but he's not like Zuabi. He's a good man."

"Can he be trusted?"

"I think so. What choice do we have?"

"None, at this point," Jack said grimly. "Let's just hope he agrees to help."

"He will," Sara said.

Jack didn't know whether she was alluding to the flirtatious stick or ballistic carrot approach. Not that it mattered.

Right now, nothing mattered but stopping Zuabi.

28

London, England

It was a cardinal rule of intelligence work that Sara *had* learned: if your cover has been compromised, either go deep undercover or hide in plain sight.

Going to ground was not an option.

Fortunately, Sara and Jack looked a mess and stank of perspiration from the torture, their flight, days without a shower. Any description MI6 might have sent out barely applied to the dirty, disheveled couple who showed up for the train ride back to London. They had taken the precaution of having a drink so their breath suggested a night of heavy partying. And they acted the part as they purchased tickets with the cash Jack had been carrying.

They reached London without a hitch and cabbed to the school.

The young man's name was Faisal al-Jubeir.

He couldn't have been more than twenty-six years old, and was an inch taller than Jack, with dark skin and a thick black beard. He seemed a bit irritated as he opened the door at nearly one in the morning. The moment he saw Sara his annoyance evaporated. He didn't even seem to see Jack, not at first.

"Ms. Ghadah," he said in surprise. "Sara. What are you doing here?"

"I'm sorry if we woke you, Faisal."

"Actually, no. I was studying for—" He paused, frowning at her. Like everyone else, he saw and was mesmerized by Sara's face in those first moments. "Your clothes, your *hijab* . . . where are they? Why are you dressed like that?"

"It's a long story," she told him.

"Are you all right?"

"I'm fine, but I desperately need your help."

He looked confused. "*My* help?"

"May we come in?"

He hesitated, glancing at Jack as though seeing him for the first time. Then he stepped back and opened the door wide. "Of course," he said. "Come in."

"Thank you, Faisal."

They stepped into a clean but modest flat full of furniture that looked as if it had come with the rental. Cheap but functional. There was a small kitchenette with a dining table in front of it, the table cluttered with books and spiral binders, illuminated by a reading lamp. It was like being in a neat version of

Max's hacker friend Dave Karras's place, with one exception: among the books was *Fundamentals of Islamic Philosophy*. Jack felt his gut tighten ever so slightly.

Amid the clutter was a laptop computer with a screensaver showing photographs of an attractive Arab woman and a small boy.

"Faisal, this is my friend Jack."

"Assalamu alaikum," Faisal said, and they shook hands, each man assessing the other, Jack wanting to trust him and fighting the sense that he shouldn't. He supposed it all boiled down to whether or not this young man's idea of Islamic philosophy was similar to al-Fida's and included killing in the name of Allah.

Sara had assured Jack that Faisal wasn't a radical, but then Sara herself had spent nearly a year pretending to be something she wasn't, as had Abdal and God knew how many others. Jack was still trying to adjust to the fact that there was a president of the United States with a middle name Hussein. Who was to say this guy wasn't pretending as well?

Faisal gestured to the sofa. "Sit. Please."

They sat and Faisal took a chair opposite them.

Sara leaned forward. "I know it's late. And I know you're not used to seeing me like this. I could probably give you some excuse as to why we're here and look the way we do, but you've always struck me as a man of principle so I think it's best to be truthful."

"Yes, of course. Islam teaches us to strive always to excel in virtue and truth. But you're starting to frighten me."

"It's a frightening world," Jack said unhelpfully. But it had to be said. Everyone was a soldier for one side or the other, whether they liked it or not.

Sara reached into her pocket and pulled out the USB key. "This," she told him. "There are some encrypted e-mails on it that I'm hoping you can crack."

"Me?"

"I know how talented you are, Faisal. I know you've helped some of the teachers with their computers. Other students. And I know codes are one of your hobbies. I remember it from the essay in your application packet."

He shrugged. "I know a few things." He looked at the key suspiciously. "Who do these e-mails belong to?"

Sara fixed those beautiful but firm eyes on the young man. "Have you ever heard of a group called the Hand of Allah?"

His expression became restless, anxious. It was obvious he had. "Now you truly *are* frightening me. What are you involved in?"

"Trying to stop them," she said frankly.

Jack was watching the young man's face carefully. Nothing changed. That was a good sign. There was no, *"Aha! I've got you! You've fallen into a Hand of Allah trap!"*

"We believe the e-mails come from a member of that group," Sara went on. "Someone high within the home secretary's office."

"What?" Faisal exclaimed. "That's absurd! And why would *you* have them?"

That was sincere, Jack decided. He was beginning to feel better about this guy. Now all they had to do was get him to cooperate, to risk his life.

Sara was quiet a moment, as if looking for a way to explain it all. "Faisal, I'm not exactly who I seem to be," she said. "You think of me as the quiet Muslim girl who works in the office, the girl you sometimes talk to during your lunch hour, but I only took that job as a cover."

"Cover?" He looked nonplussed. "Cover for what?"

"I'm part of a counterterrorism unit. Or at least I was until tonight. The Hand of Allah hit us hard, in Paris. Jack and I made it out with just this key."

"This is incredible," Faisal said. He smirked. "Surely this is a joke. A prank. And I've fallen for—"

"Believe me, I wish it were," she said.

"So you're not Muslim?"

"I *am* Muslim, but this isn't about religion. Religion is just an excuse these radicals use. You are part of our community. You should know that."

"Of course," he said. It was almost an apology.

Jack thought of all the heartache the U.S. Congress got for its radicalization hearings of American Muslims. Dammit—a lot of ordinary folks *did* know more than they let on.

"Look," Sara told him, "I'm sorry to spring this on you but we really do need your help." She waved the key in front of his face. "Will you try to decrypt this, or not?"

He looked at the floor, at a photograph on his desk, at the floor again, then at Sara. He took a long, slow breath. "If I do as you ask, who's to say that the next knock on my door won't be the Hand of Allah? I have a wife and young boy back home."

"No one knows we've come here, and there's no reason they should. You have my promise that this will remain between us. You, Jack, and me."

Still, he hesitated.

"We really do need your help, Faisal," she went on. "The Hand of Allah is planning an attack. A massive one, and that can only be bad for all of us."

"Not just Muslims," Jack added. "We're talking about the future of Western Civilization here. Your own son's future."

Faisal still looked torn. Jack wasn't sure whether he'd help or kick them out. Apparently, Faisal wasn't sure, either. But then he took the USB key from Sara and got to his feet, moved to his laptop on the table.

He pushed the key into a slot and waited for the file system to recognize it. Then he called up the e-mails and studied them.

Time crawled. Jack was tired and he felt sleep encroaching, his eyes shutting. He may even have drowsed off. He didn't know how much later it was when Faisal finally spoke.

"This is very sophisticated," the young man said. "I have some code decryption software that might help, but even with that it could take hours to break this."

"But it's possible?" Sara asked.

"If the software can ferret out the proper keys,

yes. But I offer no guarantees." He paused. "You swear to me no one knows you're here?"

"In the name of Allah," she said.

He studied her carefully, as if weighing her sincerity. Then he slowly nodded. "You may as well make yourselves comfortable. We are in for a long night."

Sara was asleep on the sofa, Jack slumped in the armchair across from her, only half awake, when Faisal said, "I know who you are, you know."

That got Jack's attention. He pulled himself upright unsure what to expect.

Faisal sat at the dining table, reading one of his textbooks. A clock on the wall said it was approaching two A.M. The decryption software had been running on the laptop for close to an hour, numbers and symbols skittering across its screen.

Faisal looked up from his book. "It took me a while to remember you. I saw your photograph in the newspapers some time ago. There was an article about the home secretary banning you from travel to this country. You're an American television host."

Jack shrugged. "Close enough."

"I remember because we talked about you at the college. About the things you've said, your hatred of Muslims. Your desire to kill a hundred million of us."

Jack didn't like the direction this was heading. "That was taken completely out of context. I don't hate all Muslims."

"Just a few, then?" It was an accusation, not a question. "I saw the mistrust in your eyes when you first looked at me."

"You have to understand my perspective," Jack said. "There are a lot of radicals out there. Like the Hand of Allah. People who want to destroy America."

"Yes, and that's why I agreed to help you and Sara. But don't you see that when you say such hateful things, it makes men like me feel as if you're talking about *us* as well."

"I understand, but it's a very delicate balance. And I'm sure you have even more to fear from radicals than I do."

"You're a hundred percent right about that."

He was quiet a moment as he closed his book and stared at the laptop, watching the software do its magic. Then he said, "But it isn't just the radicals. My mother is Indian, and my father is Pakistani, and our extended family is a mix of many different beliefs. Some are *liberal* Muslims, and they may well be the worst curse there is."

"Worse than those who want to kill people? Bomb them?"

"I don't condone such actions, and I never will. But the liberals are nearly as dangerous in their own way. People who think that pornography and degeneracy and gay marriage are normal, acceptable. To my mind, that's a bigger threat to the stability of Pakistan and the world than anyone can imagine."

Jack relaxed a bit and had to stifle a smile. He

almost felt as if he were in a bar back home, talking American politics with Tony or the Reb.

"When I'm not at school," Faisal said, "I work in a mobile phone store. There's another man who works there, a fundamentalist Christian, and we've had many conversations about our beliefs. And when it comes to social values, family values, we're in total accord. We agree on almost everything with regard to how life should be led."

The laptop beeped and he checked the screen, then typed in a quick entry and started it running again.

"The point I'm trying to make to you," he said, "is that there are many varieties of Muslim, just as there are Catholics or Jews. There are Muslims who are not religious, yet use Islam as a political weapon. They have no interest in following the teachings, yet they're willing to kill for their own self-advancement. Do you realize that in some of our Muslim schools— right here in England—they're teaching young students how to properly chop off the hands of thieves?"

"You're kidding me."

"I wish I were. It's right there in their textbooks." He paused, clearly disturbed by the thought. "But there are other Muslims, like me, who are *very* religious yet have no taste for violence, no desire to harm anyone. While I may detest what the liberals believe, and think that their view of society is dangerous, I don't want to hurt or convert them, I simply want to be left alone. There are many of us who feel that way."

"And how do you feel when one of these radicals sets off a bomb?"

"Just as frightened as you do. Just as terrified." He paused. "Why wouldn't I be?"

"Point taken," Jack said.

"What I want to stress to you is that when you go on television and speak of Muslims, you should be very careful to separate us, not lump us all together."

"That's true, but this isn't one sided, you know. How do you think it feels when Americans are all seen as infidels?"

"Those who say such things aren't speaking for me," Faisal told him. "All I really want is peace throughout the world. That's all any true Muslim wants. We believe in the blessed words of all of the prophets, from Moses to Jesus. We respect others and their religions, and all we ask is that they do the same in return."

Jack knew all of this, of course. But it didn't hurt to have a face to attach to it. He had stereotyped Faisal, mistrusted him, the moment he'd walked in the door. And he regretted that.

"That's good to hear," Jack said. "And you're right. I *will* be more careful."

Faisal nodded, satisfied to have had his say. He rose from his chair and gestured to the laptop. "This will take some time and I need to sleep. I'll check its progress in the morning."

"Thank you, Faisal. I know you didn't have to help us, and I appreciate what you're doing."

Faisal gestured to Sara stretched out on the sofa.

"She looks comfortable there, but you can't sleep in that chair. I have a spare bedroom for when my family arrives. There's a bed. You are free to use it."

Then he stepped into the hallway and disappeared.

29

Exhausted as he was, Jack couldn't sleep.

It was nice to be on a mattress again, and have the warmth of a working radiator, but he spent the next two hours unable to stop *thinking*.

There were big thoughts. He was unable to put aside the pieces of the puzzle, the disaster waiting for so many people if he failed. His tired brain told him to drop the whole thing in the lap of the FBI or the CIA but he didn't dare. For one thing, they probably wouldn't believe that "wacko" alarmist Jack Hatfield. For another, by the time that machine got into motion and up to speed, the event could well be in their rear-view mirror.

There were smaller thoughts. He wept inside for his watch, violated by Swain and necessarily discarded like so many other parts of his life. He kept telling himself that it was only a watch, that he'd always have his memories, the good and the bad. It was like death. Be happy for the time you were together, the memories you built, rather than mourn the future that was never guaranteed.

Yet that watch had brought him comfort so many times over the years. A sense of calm. There was nothing that could ever replace it, and he cursed Swain for using him, for knowing instinctively that Jack would never leave something so valuable behind and using that knowledge against him.

Against all of them.

He remembered the violence and death that had descended on that apartment house and was overwhelmed by survivor's syndrome. He took no solace in his own relative comfort and security. Despite his admonitions that Sara not blame herself for what had happened, Jack couldn't fight off his own guilt. People had died because of his failure to realize he'd been used. And it was quite possible that many more would die before they saw an end to this.

"Stop it," Jack finally said through his teeth. "You're going to *save* lives!"

It was a tragic corruption of his comment about preferring the death of a hundred million Muslims to a hundred million non-Muslims. The lives of dozens of people had to be surrendered in the hope of sparing millions more.

That was the math of modern-day antiterror activities. It was only a waste if he failed. That kept returning him to the biggest thought of all:

"The infidels will soon see destruction that will make 9/11 seem like child's play."

Operation Roadshow, coming to a city near you.

When? How? That question had yet to be answered.

Jack was finally starting to drift off when he heard the faint flush of a toilet down the hall. A moment later a silhouette appeared in the bedroom doorway—Sara, barely visible in the light from the window.

"You left me alone," she said softly.

"You looked peaceful. I didn't want to disturb you."

"Probably happy to be rid of me for a while."

"Never," he told her.

She came into the room. "I said some terrible things to you last night. Sometimes I speak without thinking."

"You've already apologized for that, even though you didn't need to. You had a right to be upset. We both did. Nobody should ever have to see what we saw."

She closed the door behind her now, then moved to a small television in the corner and turned it on, tuning it to an Arab station, which was playing only Arabic music at the moment. Jack wasn't sure what she was up to but he didn't protest when she came over to the bed and lit the scented candle that was sitting on the nightstand. Her long brown hair was highlighted against the window and he saw a light snow falling outside.

He didn't know if he should trust this, or her motives. It didn't matter. He instantly felt himself stirring.

"I don't want to be alone right now," she said, then reached a hand under the back of her T-shirt and unfastened her bra, dropping it to the floor. Her breasts shifted, reacting instantly to the brush of the fabric.

He didn't look away this time. "Neither do I."

"I want to forget for a while, Jack. Can you help me do that?"

"You have no idea how much I'd like to try."

He hadn't bothered to take off his clothes before lying on top of the bed, and she came to him, reaching for his belt and unbuckling it. She unfastened his pants and pulled them away, freeing him, then took him in her hand, gently kneading him as she leaned forward and kissed his lips.

Then she pulled away, whispering softly against his cheek. "Make me forget, Jack. Please make me forget."

As he drew her nearer and removed her T-shirt and panties, she began to moan deeply and loudly. Loudly and deeply. In the midst of their heat, such a state of abandon was reached that the normally voyeuristic Jack, who liked to watch himself make love, actually fell from the bed onto the hot radiator. But, like the Indian fakirs who can be on a bed of nails without later showing puncture marks, Jack did not scorch or burn, nothing visible remaining except a small soreness days later.

Once he was inside her, she began to cry and shudder in a series of small convulsions. He had never been with a woman who reacted like this and was both surprised and excited by her abandon.

Her cries became veritable screams as she moaned, and her eyes became glassy with passion. As Jack continued to bring Sara to an increasingly greater state of tension and release, tension—a violent begging for release and then the convulsive wave—her screaming became threatening.

He tried to quiet her by putting his hand over her mouth while continuing to stroke with his loins and lips.

"Quiet, quiet," he tried to command hoarsely. "Faisal will hear you."

He reached for her T-shirt and couldn't believe himself as he pressed it over her mouth, holding it down hard against her lips by pressing it against the sheets, one hand on each side of her face.

Their hips were in perfect synchrony and she continued her cries and screams, now muffled beneath the shirt, as Jack made love to her as he had never made love before. Sara bucked and arched and was in a world he could never see.

Then it was over and they collapsed onto the bed, sweating, chests heaving. Sara rolled toward him and snaked a hand across his chest as she nuzzled his neck.

"Thank you," she murmured.

"You don't know how long I've been wanting to do that."

She smiled, kissed his neck. "It couldn't have been that long. We barely know each other."

"This'll sound crazy," he said. "But I think I've wanted you most of my life. Even before I knew who you were."

"Well, I'm here now," she said, then moved atop him, reaching a hand down to take hold of him again. He put his arms around her, running his own hand along her spine, brushing his fingertips across her flawless skin—

—until he felt something there and suddenly stopped: the long thin puckered flesh of a scar, just above her right hip. He hadn't seen or felt it before, had somehow missed it in the darkness and the heat of the moment.

"What's this?" he said, before he realized the words were out of his mouth.

She stiffened against him now and he knew he'd made a mistake. She rolled away from him and stared at the dark ceiling, as all of his efforts to make her forget vanished in that instant.

She seemed to go away for a while, lost in a memory, then said, "You asked what happened to me. What made me join Brendan and the others."

"I'm sorry, Sara. Really. You don't have to tell me if you don't want to."

She turned toward him and ran her hand along the side of his face. "I *do* want to tell you. I want you to know everything there is to know about me."

He studied her. "I'm listening."

It took her a moment to gather herself. "When I

was a young girl in Yemen, I was just like Abdal al-Fida. A true believer. I think that's why it was so easy for me to convince him that we were kindred spirits. I knew that fervor, that hatred. It was a hatred that had been nurtured in me by my own father." She paused. "But I was female, and sickly, and when my brother Kafir was born all of my father's hopes for a great soldier of Allah landed on him.

"But Kafir was an unusual child. Intelligent, very wise for his age. And he was a disappointment to my father because he didn't share our passion. He was always questioning us. Why did we believe the things we did, when a careful reading of the Koran showed that it clearly preached peace?"

Tears filled her eyes now. "My father beat him, but Kafir never gave in. Never compromised his own beliefs. And I found myself coming to admire him for it.

"When I turned seventeen," she continued, "I got very sick. One of my kidneys failed and the other required regular dialysis, and it was clear to the doctors that I needed a transplant. Neither my father nor my mother were a match, and the thought of going to a thirteen-year-old boy seemed wrong somehow. But Kafir volunteered—*insisted* on taking the test—and when the results came back it turned out that he was the perfect donor.

"Two weeks later I had this scar, this gift from my brother. Without him, I wouldn't be here."

She paused again, as she wiped her tears with her forearm. "A year went by and both of us had grown strong again, bound together not just by blood, but by flesh as well. Then, on a warm afternoon, Kafir left school early one day. Call it fate or coincidence or simply bad luck, but as he walked past a synagogue a car parked in front of it exploded, taking half the building and my brother along with it."

"My God," Jack said.

"No," Sara told him. "Not God. Not Allah. This was simply the work of men, men like my father whose hatred was so strong that it took the life of an innocent young boy. A boy who had more potential, more nobility, in his small body than any of them would ever understand."

Jack held her as she sobbed. Her tears were warm and dear against his chest. As much as their love-making, that gift of trust was precious.

"Did they find the bombers?" he asked.

Sara collected herself. "No. And that is the sick-ness of it. It could have been anyone. Rogue Muslims of the same branch or a different branch . . . Not knowing who had attacked him made me realize that their hatred was *my* hatred. It didn't matter *who* held it. It was *wrong*."

"That was a pretty big thought for a teenager to grasp."

"It wasn't just a 'thought,' Jack. It was a *vision*—from Allah. What you Christians call an epiphany. I could not shake it.

"My mother had a breakdown and had to be hos-pitalized. My father was inconsolable, and within

the year I knew I had to get away from there." She
paused. "So I moved to London and vowed that I
would do whatever I could to keep another Kafir
from being lost to the world."

She was silent then. Jack could feel the emotion
draining away, her shoulders relaxing. He wanted to
respond, to find the perfect words to soothe her.

But before he could speak, they heard a loud,
steady beep coming from the living room.

Faisal's laptop.

They had to scramble to get dressed before the beeping woke Faisal. They just made it to the living room
when he stumbled in and plopped in front of his
laptop, punching a key to cut the notifier and examine the results.

It didn't look as though their lovemaking had
bothered him. Jack and Sara shared a secret smile.

That felt good, too.

"There's another level of encryption," Faisal said.
He was still half asleep and yawning, staring at the
computer screen with bleary eyes. "Whoever sent
these e-mails didn't want people like us getting nosy."

"So Alain was right," Sara said to Jack. "This
could be significant information."

There were five open e-mails stacked on the
screen, each sent to *tdl@alliedharborassoc.net,* and
each with a single line of text. The lines, however,
were a jumble of letters and numbers that made no
sense:

EFDH3054383
gjvaf
Nhthfg gjragl
Gjragl Uhaqerq UEF
uggc://ovg.yl/umfLZ3

Jack looked from the hash to Faisal. "I thought that program was supposed to translate all this stuff."

"That was the second level of encryption," Faisal said. "The difficult one. But not to worry, these all look like simple ROT-13 cyphers."

Jack was clueless. "What's that?"

"It's a rudimentary form of code based on the old Caesar cypher. A lot of gamers use it to hide cheat codes and spoilers on Internet forums. They're extremely easy to crack, which is why the sender used that second level of encryption."

"So how does it work?" Jack asked.

"You replace each letter by the one located thirteen letters after it in the alphabet. For example, an *A* becomes an *N*. I have the lookup table here."

He punched a key and a small window popped up, showing:

ABCDEFGHIJKLMNOPQRSTUVWXYZ
abcdefghijklmnopqrstuvwxyz
NOPQRSTUVWXYZABCDEFGHIJKLM
nopqrstuvwxyzabcdefghijklm

"Decryption is a fairly mindless task at this point," he went on. "The numbers will remain the same. All we need do is transpose the letters and we'll know what these messages say."

Faisal had already gone to work, using another computer application to quickly translate the lines. When it was done, he stacked the decryptions on the screen:

RSQU3054383
twins
August twenty
Twenty Hundred HRS
http://bit.ly/hzsYM3

Nobody spoke for a long moment. Jack felt his heart begin to race. "I think we've just hit pay dirt," he said to Sara. "You realize what this is, don't you?"

"I'm not sure what the first two lines are all about," Sara said, "but that last one's an Internet address. So I'm guessing these are the date, time, and target of an attack."

Jack nodded. "The first one looks like a serial number of some kind. Or maybe the ISO number for a shipping container."

"Could be a shipment from Chilikov, if Haddad was successful."

"That's what I was thinking," Jack said. "But what about this 'twins' line? You think it's a reference to the twin towers? A reminder of their last big hit?"

"The infidels will soon see destruction that will make 9/11 seem like child's play."

"It could be that," Sara said. "It could also be two

prongs of an attack, two cells, matching automobiles being used for smuggling—anything. But whatever it means, August twentieth is only three days from now. Saturday night."

Jack gestured to Faisal. "Can you paste that URL into a browser? I want to see what they have in mind." He added as an afterthought, "Please?"

Faisal did as he was asked. When he clicked the address, Google Maps came to life on screen, showing a satellite image of San Francisco. Flagged in the middle of it by a big letter *A*, was one of the city's best-known landmarks.

The California Palace of the Legion of Honor.

Jack's mind suddenly flashed on that afternoon at Pagliaci's, when Danny Pescatori gave Tony a VIP invitation to the museum gala. He'd forgotten about it until now.

And it was scheduled for this Saturday night.

"My God," he said, his heart kicking up a notch as the realization sank in like a depth charge to the brain. "They're going after the President."

PART THREE

Countdown

30

San Francisco, California

Talia "Tally" Griffin was convinced that *this* time she'd struck gold.

After years of dating all the wrong guys, winding up in relationships that went absolutely nowhere, she was certain that she had finally found her Prince Charming.

His name was Victor Massri.

Tall. Handsome. With deep, dark eyes, smooth brown skin, and that exotic, wispy little black goatee.

Tally didn't normally go for men with beards, but Victor was the exception to the rule, and from the right angle he reminded her of Johnny Depp.

He was Egyptian, he'd told her, born and raised in London, and ever since they'd started corresponding online—through the SF Singles Hotline dating service—she knew she'd found someone very special.

Until this moment, the only contact they'd had were e-mails and text messages, a few photos they'd exchanged, and several prolonged phone calls, but seeing him walk out of that airline terminal flashing those beautiful white teeth was everything she'd hoped for, and more.

He greeted her with a platonic hug. She wanted more but she also didn't want to scare him. The man was not one of her local jerks, he was *foreign*. She didn't know what his customs were.

"Just the one suitcase?" she asked.

"I always travel light," he told her, tossing the bag into the backseat.

They stood there awkwardly for a moment until Tally said, "I can't believe you're finally here."

"Nor can I," he told her.

It wasn't just Victor's dark good looks, however, that got Tally's engine running hot. The two had clicked the moment she answered his request for an online meet. He told her that he'd seen her photo and thought she was "lovely," and was doubly pleased when he read her profile and discovered she was an urban explorer. Her exact words to him were, "I love all old buildings, especially ones that have all the original furniture and fixtures."

Victor told her he was an architect who had a great love for history, and had done quite a bit of exploring himself. He said he'd been to many abandoned sites around the world, from the eerie, fortresslike apart-

ments of Battleship Island, Japan, to the decrepit unused underground railway stations right in his own
hometown.

"You're even more lovely in person," he told her,
and Tally knew she had to get this guy alone, real
soon. Whatever cultural reserve he might have, she
was determined to bridge it.

They climbed into her Toyota and she took him
straight to her apartment.

This was going to be a night to remember.

Hassan Haddad had never forgotten just how dis-
turbingly aggressive American women could be. But
if he were to judge by this one, he'd say they'd gotten
even worse over the last decade.

The moment he set foot in her apartment and
dropped his suitcase, this althletic blond, blue-cyed
ex-hippie with the ridiculous name and the wild curly
hair was already pulling his jacket away and, when
he didn't object—indeed, he forced himself to smile
with encouragement—starting on the buttons on his
shirt.

Before she had even finished that task, Tally was
kissing his chest and somehow unbuckling his pants
at the same time as the trail of her kisses moved down
toward his abdomen. Then she was on her knees and
had him in her mouth and, aggressive or not, Haddad found himself unable to resist.

He was suddenly swept back to those nights at
Berkeley, when his two dorm mates would tend to
him as if they were his personal sex slaves, their

enthusiasm matched by their skills—which were considerable. He had a hard time now remembering their names. Sabrina . . . and Jennifer?

Yes, that was it.

They were wild women, almost as wild as this one, and they had been more than willing to share themselves with Haddad. While he preferred women who obeyed men and acted in the way Allah had intended, he found himself unable to resist the charms of Sabrina and Jennifer.

Most of the students and professors he encountered in those days were far to the left of the average American, and he had difficulty hiding his contempt for them. In fact, he despised everything about them but pretended to share their views in order to get to know them and understand their thinking. Most of these radical leftists were Jews, which reconfirmed his inherent beliefs about all Jews: they were "chosen" by God to spread disorder across the globe.

On occasion, however, he would notice the ultrareligious Lubavitch Chasidic Jews as they walked to prayer with their children on Saturdays. He couldn't help but admire their family solidarity, their piety, but most significantly their dignity.

He hated to admit, even to himself, that they reminded him of his own people, especially the most pious. He could not afford to feel charity toward a people who were oppressing so many Muslims. He rejected the argument that the Jews were just protecting their homeland. All they had to do was return to the Diaspora that God had intended and all would be well—

He remembered the Friday night when his life's work crystallized. Sabrina (or was it Jennifer?) took him to the Chabad house near the campus. She kept telling him how much he was going to love the people there because they reminded her of him.

How stupid could these American girls be, comparing him, a son of Allah, with these pathetic children of Yahweh? But he needed to play his role so he went. As he entered the room he was enveloped within the loud singing. He noticed the women were on one side of the room and on the other there was a large circle of men dancing, with one hand on the shoulder of the man in front. Some had their small children with their legs around their necks, riding their shoulders.

Haddad was stunned when a very tall man with red hair and a full red beard reached from the circle and pulled him in. He recalled the man's piercing blue eyes as he was drawn into the whirl of dancing men. He was momentarily swept up in the intoxicating mixture of the loud voices singing in unison in the cousin-language of Hebrew, the feel of the old wooden floors swaying beneath his feet.

For a fleeting instant he felt he was back in Pakistan, among his own kind.

And then he remembered who he was, and who *they* were. He felt revulsion by their proximity, by their smiles, by their revelry. He wanted to transform it all to still, bloody sorrow. He endured their presence so he could study their weaknesses. So he could protect those Muslims in Pakistan and elsewhere whom these "Chosen People" had chosen to persecute.

Haddad felt that same hatred now. For the Jews, for their American allies, for the sluts like Tally who corrupted all of womanhood.

She wanted to be used? Haddad would oblige. When the time was right he would show this aggressive bitch what few American men would ever dare. She would be tamed and dominated. She would understand what true aggression was.

But he had no time for such things right now. He needed her to be fully on his side until he got from her the information he needed, so he let her have her way with him, right there on her living room floor.

It wasn't, he supposed, the worst compromise he could make.

"You read all the newspaper columns I wrote," Tally said, "but they really only touch on the surface of San Francisco's underground."

"I am eager to hear more," Haddad told her truthfully.

"I'm so glad!" she enthused. "So few people know about it, even those who live here. But there's an entire secret history beneath the city that's largely ignored or forgotten."

It was the next day, and they were driving in

Tally's Toyota. Her aggressiveness behind the wheel matched her sexual aggressiveness.

"Educate me," he said, as he watched the road. It would be absurd for him to die in a car crash after all the effort it had taken to get to this point.

"Well, first there's Chinatown," she told him. "During the gold rush, hundreds of thousands of Chinese immigrants came to the city and were forced to live in slums. By the late eighteen hundreds that area was a network of underground sewer tunnels and passageways topped by crowded tenement buildings. It was one of the most dangerous places in San Francisco."

Haddad laughed inside. He had seen his share of slums in his time, and knew quite well how dangerous they could be.

"Most of the immigrants were destitute, and many of them were sold as slaves to work in kitchens and laundries. Young girls would be forced into prostitution, and those who tried to protect them used the underground tunnels to hide them away."

Heathen behavior, Haddad thought, but typical of a country run by infidels whose greed and base interests knew no bounds.

She babbled on. But it wasn't that part of the city's underground that he was interested in. He had done enough research on his own to know that there was something far more useful to him than a Chinese history lesson. Bloggers had announced the general area of the entrance; she had saved him having to search for it. Fault line maps created by the U.S. Geological Survey—charts showing dip, azimuth, depth, and other data used by San Andreas Geophysical Operations for threat assessment—had unwittingly delineated the tunnels themselves. The route for the assault was planned. Haddad merely had to see the tunnels for himself, make sure they were clear.

Finally, trying not to show his impatience, he directed her towards his needs.

"What about the bunker you referred to in one of your articles?"

"Ah," she said. "Even fewer people know about that, maybe some old-timers and a handful of urban explorers like me."

"When were they built?"

"During the Second World War," she said. "San Francisco was considered a very vulnerable target if the war were ever to come to our shores, so the military built a massive underground bunker in preparation for an attack."

"How could people not know about this?"

"Because it was a military secret to begin with. After the war ended the place was completely sealed up so that nobody would find it."

"That seems a waste. Surely they've utilized it—say, for storage?"

She shook her head. "Some cities did things like that. New York, for instance. Stocked them with canned goods in case of a nuclear attack. It scared people so they stopped. It was easier just to pretend the bunkers didn't exist."

"And you've managed to find a way inside the bunker?"

She smiled. "Yep."

"And it truly leads to this place you told me about?"

She gave him a sly smile.

Haddad felt a sudden flash of anger and wanted to slap the smile from her face. Why couldn't she just answer the question? He did not have time for games.

"When can we go there?" he asked. "This—this is too exciting."

The smile widened. "That's where we're headed right now. Normally, I'd have to blindfold you."

"Are you serious?"

"Sort of," she admitted. "Only a few people know about this spot and we don't want it to become common knowledge. But I can trust you, right?"

"Of course," Haddad said. "With your life."

They took a gently winding road along the bay.

Haddad looked out at its clear blue waters, marveling at its beauty as he watched the distant sailboats bob along its surface. He had always loved this view, with the Cliff House Restaurant, the Marin coastline beyond, and the tattered sea-swept ruins of the Sutro Baths on the shore below—which had once been the world's largest indoor swimming establishment until it burned down before Haddad was even born.

And yet, it was soon to be so different.

By his hand.

There were times when he wished that he could simply go back to his college days, when life was less complicated. When he could hate without having to rein that in, so he could carefully engineer an expression of that loathing. And to be honest, though he had been here to learn and to study the ways of the infidels, there were times he envied them their blissful obliviousness to the world and its dangers. He wondered what life would be like without a larger goal than making money and raising infidel children. He wondered if, in his lifetime, he would ever know the peace and contentment of a Sharia world.

They drove around a bend along Point Lobos Avenue, until they came to a large car park on their left, near the Sutro Baths. Tally pulled in and found a spot, then shut off the engine and turned to Haddad.

"Okay," she said. "Almost there. We're in a national park so we have to be aware of other visitors and watchful eyes."

"I'll trust you to guide me without incident," Haddad told her.

She smiled again. "You are just so damn cute, you know that?"

She parked, then leaned over and kissed him, making it very clear that she enjoyed his company. He managed to keep from recoiling and actually returned her smile.

"Shall we?" she said, as she popped open her door.

"Indeed."

They found their way to Lands End Trail, which was far from rustic and perfectly maintained, surrounded by lush green foliage. They followed a winding path, feeling the wind in their faces, enjoying the quiet—which seemed so unusual considering that they were still in the city.

As they passed the USS *San Francisco* memorial— little more than a flagpole and plaque surrounded by a few large gunmetal-gray pieces of an old warship that, to Haddad, looked like giant Dumpsters—Tally glanced about, then grabbed his arm and steered him toward the edge of the cliff.

"This way," she said.

The cliff looked quite steep, but they were both wearing clothes for climbing—jeans, flannel shirts, rugged shoes—so Haddad followed her down through the rocks and trees, until they were very close to the water. He could feel the ocean spray on his face as she led him around a small outcropping, then upward again until they found a secluded patch of land just below the cliffside, full of dirt and rock and grass and surrounded by thick green trees.

Glancing around again for prying eyes, Tally moved up to a large grouping of stones gathered near the base of one of the trees. Taking hold of the largest stone, she said, "Help me with this."

Haddad grabbed on and they huffed and struggled a few moments until they rolled it aside to reveal a crevice just wide enough to squeeze through. The crevice was formed in a slab of cement, rather than earth, and Haddad could see that it was an exposed portion of a larger structure that had somehow been dislodged, possibly in an earthquake.

"This is it?" Haddad asked. "This is the entrance?"

"Only the brave know for sure," she said, casting

a look around to make sure they had not been observed. "You want me to go first?"

Not one to back down from a challenge, especially coming from a ridiculous female, Haddad waved her away, then studied the crevice, looking for the best way to proceed. Deciding to go feet first, he sat down and stuck his feet into the opening, then lay on his back and slowly wormed his way downward, shimmying into the hole.

As his feet penetrated the darkness, he felt the ground suddenly give way beneath them, nothing but open air below.

Catching hold of the edge of the slab, he said, "How far is the drop?"

"Not far," she told him. "Just let yourself go and be mindful how you land."

Haddad steeled himself and let go of the slab, working his way downward until his legs were dangling in open air. Then, turning his head to the side, he squeezed through and let himself drop.

He landed hard, but on his feet, the sound of the impact echoing against cement walls. Pulling a small flashlight out of his shirt pocket, he flicked it on and found himself inside a narrow concrete shaft. To his left was another shaft with a built-in rusted rebar ladder that led deeper into the earth.

"Watch out," Tally said, "here I come."

He shifted his flashlight beam upward as she shimmied through the hole, having a much easier time of it thanks to her smaller size. As he stepped back she dropped down beside him, faltering only slightly as she landed.

Pulling her own flashlight out, she flicked it on and gestured to the second shaft. "What are you waiting for, slowpoke? Let's do this."

She stepped onto the rebar ladder and started down.

Haddad followed her, perturbed by her familiar manner. In a way, that was more annoying than her purely biological need for sex. This behavior was learned.

When he got to the bottom of the ladder he saw only her flashlight shining into the darkness. What he saw was a marvel. A long, wide tunnel—big enough to fit a truck through—made of reinforced concrete. There was occasional graffiti spray-painted on the walls, names of other explorers and when they'd been here. Most of it dated several decades ago, which Haddad assumed meant that the place was only rarely frequented these days. Rusted remnants of a rail system with narrow-gauge tracks ran along the ceiling and he could clearly tell that this had indeed been a military bunker. He had seen this kind of setup before, in Egyptian coal mines in the north Sinai. It maximized space by allowing workers to walk under the cars.

The tunnel seemed to go on forever into the darkness.

"Pretty amazing, isn't it?" Tally asked.

"More than I imagined," Haddad said, thinking

that if this tunnel led where he believed it did, the final piece of Allah's plan was indeed in place. "How far does it go?"

"It branches in different directions," Tally told him. "Some of the old-timers say there are at least eighty-seven thousand square feet down here." She gestured. "But if you follow this tunnel right here without deviating from the path, it'll take you straight to the Golden Gate Bridge."

"Amazing," Haddad said. "And it also leads to the place we spoke about?"

She nodded. "Come on, I'll show you."

She took the lead, working her way through the tunnel with the confidence of a regular visitor. They walked through the dark tunnel for quite some time. As they turned to their right, moving into another tunnel, Haddad saw that it opened out into a space that could have been a bunkhouse or a storage supply. They continued past it, took another turn, and the floor began to rise, getting steeper with every step. They crested the rise and made another turn into a tunnel on their right, where it opened into a single rectangular room. There was another narrow shaft at the far side, a rebar ladder leading upward into darkness.

"This is it," Tally said, stopping.

"You're absolutely certain?"

"Oh, I'm sure. It's right over your beautiful Egyptian head."

Haddad's lips parted in a smile and Tally came toward him with a seductive look on her face. "Happy?"

"Better than you will ever know," Haddad told her as he grabbed her by the throat and shoved her into the cement wall, her eyes going wide as she slammed against it.

He ripped at her flannel shirt, breaking away the buttons, then gripped her exposed left breast and squeezed as hard as he could, enjoying the look of pain and terror in her eyes.

This was how all infidel whores should be treated, Haddad thought as the woman squirmed under his grip, her features contorted. They needed to be taught their place in the world.

When he was done here, there would be one less pig inhabiting the earth.

Thanks to her, countless others would soon follow.

31

Jack and Sara flew from London on a private char-
ter, a Gulfstream G550 courtesy of Senator Harold
Wickham.

Although Jack had been reluctant to get the senator involved before, he knew he had no choice now
but to bring him into this mess.

Harold Wickham was a Texas oilman, a hard-line
hawk who always put country first and politics last.
Jack had met him several years before, when he and
two fellow senators were visiting Iraq's green zone
while the search for WMDs was still ongoing. Jack
had interviewed Wickham for GNT. Wickham had
assured him that the weapons were out there somewhere and it was only a matter of time before they
were found.

Off the record, however, Wickham confessed to
Jack over a beer that he wasn't all that confident that

they ever would find the weapons. He had become convinced that the U.S. was either victim to sloppy intelligence or—more likely—that the WMDs had been quietly smuggled into Iran.

Neither scenario made the senator happy.

Over the years, Jack had interviewed Wickham many times, and during the days of *Truth Tellers*, the Texan became a regular panelist who always had insightful observations about the news and politics of the day. The senator leaned heavily right, but had an independent streak that sometimes rankled his fellow Republicans when he refused to vote the party line.

It was a trait that Jack had always admired. But what had sealed the deal was Wickham's unwavering support after the public relations fiasco that had destroyed Jack's career. Wickham had even made the rounds on the news show circuit, trying to rehabilitate Jack's reputation, but the tone had already been set and the senator was drowned out by the braying of the crowd.

So when Jack saw the message in those encrypted e-mails he immediately got on the phone to Wickham and laid it all out for him, from beginning to end. If either phone was tapped and someone was listening, they were welcome to the information. It was too late to be overly cautious.

Wickham had never been prone to alarm, but Jack heard a slight rise in his voice. "Goddamn it, Jack, are you sure about this?"

"As sure as I can be, Senator."

"You're talking about the British government, for God's sake! How far up the chain do you think this thing goes?"

"It's hard to say. Possibly all the way to the top. The group I told you about, the one that Copeland was involved with, has been shut down, and all of their databases are fried."

"So you've got no evidence."

"Just the USB key. But if I'm interpreting those messages correctly, there's gonna be big trouble at the Legion of Honor on Saturday night."

"With the President smack in the middle," Wickham muttered.

"I know it all sounds crazy, Senator, but I think we have a major crisis on our hands. The first thing you need to do is to find out who these e-mails went to. The initials are TDL, which doesn't help much. It could be a throwaway account. But it's someone at Allied, which leads me to believe they've got a shipment coming in."

Wickham sighed heavily. "I'm bowled over, Jack. Completely bowled over. If this thing is as pervasive as you seem to think it is, I'll have to go into stealth mode and tread very lightly."

"But *quickly*," Jack urged. "From what I've learned, the Hand of Allah isn't an organization you want to underestimate. I'm pretty sure their top soldier is already in San Francisco, doing God knows what. A guy named Hassan Haddad. Somebody has to find him and stop him."

Wickham was silent a moment, then said, "All

right, Jack. I'm gonna trust you on this one. Never had any reason not to."

"Thank you, Senator. Even if I'm wrong, it's like my father always told me: better to look inside the watch than wait till it stops ticking."

"Damn straight," Wickham said. "Now, what I need *you* to do is get on a jet and get back to the U.S. as fast as possible. I'll arrange to have a friend's plane fly you out here to San Francisco."

"San Francisco? What are you doing *there*?"

"The Legion of Honor dinner."

"You, too?"

"The President's in a nonpartisan mood and invited me to the gala on Saturday night. I decided I'd throw him a bone and make an appearance. So I've got personal reasons to hope you're wrong." He paused. "Now get on that jet and bring the woman with you. We're gonna want to hear what she has to say, too."

The knot of anxiety that had been plaguing Jack ever since he saw those messages was finally starting to dissipate. Wickham wouldn't let him down.

Jack asked him if he could have some clothes brought aboard. Nothing fancy, just clean. The senator said he'd do what he could.

An hour later, Jack and Sara boarded their flight. It was a Gulfstream 550 that Jack and Sara had all to themselves, attended by a lone flight attendant. The young attendant explained that they had a choice of four separate living areas, each with its own climate control. There was a wireless broadband network and satellite communications should they require it. Abundant sunlight streamed through the fourteen oval windows, illuminating the deep leather seats, each with its own DVD player. With brawny Rolls-Royce turbofan engines, this flying carpet had a range of 6,750 nautical miles and flew at 51,000 feet.

Jack and Sara just wanted to shower and change. There were a stack of boxes from Harrods onboard. Jack slipped into slacks, a button-down shirt, and a black blazer. Sara snuggled into a pantsuit. Jack was pleased that he'd guessed right when he gave the senator her size. She looked like a runway model, only more radiant.

Two of the boxes contained formal wear: a tuxedo for Jack and a gown for Sara. Obviously, the senator intended for them to go to the dinner.

Unlike commercial aircraft, the air was one hundred percent fresh, the sound levels were extremely low, and no sooner had they sat opposite one another on the sofas in the rear cabin than they were asleep. They slept for more than half the flight then enjoyed a leisurely meal from one of London's best restaurants. The ultralong-range jet took them directly to a private terminal adjacent to San Francisco International. They arrived in the late afternoon and found a limousine waiting for them at the bottom of the steps, a chauffeur standing with the rear passenger door open.

"Welcome back, Mr. Hatfield. Senator Wickham is looking forward to seeing you."

Jack looked at Sara then glanced into the rear of the limo. "He's not here?"

"He had another engagement," the driver said. "You'll be meeting him there."

"Where?"

The driver smiled. "At the dog show."

Jack had been to the Cow Palace many times in his life. Built on sixty acres of land in 1941 as a livestock pavilion, it was a San Francisco institution—although the only piece of it that actually stood on city land was a corner of the parking lot. The bulk of the property was in Daly City.

A large, indoor arena, the palace had been host over the years to the San Francisco Warriors, the San Jose Sharks, numerous rock concerts, wrestling events, two Republican national conventions, and a number of livestock exhibitions, including the Horse & Stock Show and the Grand National Rodeo.

Jack vividly remembered one trip here as a boy, when the palace was hosting an antiques exhibition. His father had known that a number of watch and clock collectors would be participating, and had brought Jack to show him some of their priceless wonders. They saw glass cases lined with watches from Rolex, Tudor, Lord Elgin, and Girard-Perrigaux, exhibit booths displaying grandfather clocks, Victorians, porcelains, cuckoo clocks, steeple clocks, and a variety of others, the rhythm of their ticking giving great comfort to young Jack.

It was a day he'd never forget.

The Cow Palace was an unimposing gray building from the outside, but once you set foot through the doors and moved past the concourse into the main arena, you were amazed by its size. A large oval, surrounded by high walls with satin curtains and gold and yellow seats, it boasted a capacity of up to sixteen thousand patrons, and often filled every single chair. Lights shone down from a maze of metal rafters overhead, reminding Jack of an alien craft hovering above the earth.

When they entered, Jack and Sara were guided by an usher toward a section near the arena floor. On the floor itself, men in blazers and women in conservative suits led dogs on leashes around a cordoned-off area, as the judges carefully eyeballed them, and the audience applauded. This was an all-breed conformation show, and there were a variety of purebreds in competition, including poodles, Irish wolfhounds, Boykin spaniels, German wirehaired pointers, Great Danes, mastiffs, Rottweilers—from large to small, fluffy to nearly hairless, all magnificent in their own way, the best of the best on display. An Irish wolfhound caught Jack's attention—a breed he had always admired for its beauty and fearlessness. They were known to hunt wolves in packs. There were also Turkish sheepdogs, their gigantic, spiked iron anti-wolf collars displayed beside them as they got to their feet. These Anatolian shepherd dogs hid among the sheep, giving an attacking wolf a huge surprise when they bit into their iron collars.

Jack had long been a dog lover, and seeing a gray poodle parade proudly across the floor made him instantly miss Eddie. But he knew the little guy was in good hands with Tony, and he'd be home soon enough to greet him.

He hoped, he prayed, it wasn't to say good-bye. That was the thought that had haunted him from the moment they landed—that this city he loved, his *home,* would be harmed, possibly destroyed, by some lunatic with no regard for anything but his own, sick zealotry.

The usher led them to a pair of seats that were just a few yards from the arena floor. As they approached, Senator Harold Wickham rose from his chair and held out a hand. The men shook warmly. From the corner of his eye, Jack saw Wickham's bodyguard—an athletic, powerfully built guy in a dark suit—watching them closely.

"Good to see you, Jack," Wickham said. "Even if it's under such pressing circumstances."

Jack was immediately comfortable in his presence. "Good to see you, too, Senator."

Wickham was trim and well built, with thinning silvery hair that framed an angular, green-eyed face. He wore an expensive charcoal-gray suit, and carried himself with what could only be called Republican charm—warm, fatherly, with a quiet twinkle in his eyes. The gentle Texas accent completed the picture.

Wickham's gaze shifted to Sara in the way that most men seemed to look at her when she entered a room—with sudden great interest.

"I take it you're Ms. Ghadah?"

Sara shook his hand and smiled. "Sara."

"Well, Sara, it's a great, great pleasure to meet you. I'm sorry you've found yourself caught up in this mess."

"Completely by choice," she said. She added quietly, "I want to stop these madmen as badly as you do."

Wickham smiled. "That's good to hear." He gestured. "Have a seat. Both of you."

Jack glanced at Wickham's bodyguard, who didn't seem to approve of either of them. In a way it was fitting. Jack just found out what it was like to be a Muslim under suspicion. Jack noted, curiously, that the bodyguard had what looked like a laser pointer clipped to the breast pocket of his jacket and wondered what it was for. Did he use it as some kind of defensive weapon? Jack certainly couldn't imagine the guy giving PowerPoint presentations.

All of this vacated Jack's mind as he and Sara sank into the two chairs next to Wickham. The senator was quiet for a moment, staring out at the show in progress, applauding as others applauded.

Then he said, "Such noble creatures, don't you think?"

Jack nodded. "Definitely."

"Look at that Newfoundland, for example. That thick black coat. The way he sits so straight and tall, waiting for his master's command."

"He's beautiful," Sara said.

"Did you know that a Newfoundland once saved

Napoleon Bonaparte from drowning when he fell off a ship? Napoleon didn't know how to swim, but Newfoundlands are notorious for their affinity with water. After the rescue, Napoleon himself is supposed to have said, 'Here, gentlemen, a dog teaches us a lesson in humanity.'" Wickham chuckled. "Indeed.

"Loyalty," Wickham went on, "that's what it's all about. You know the story about Greyfriars Bobby, don't you, Jack?"

Jack nodded, but the senator pointed to a waiting group of Skye terriers and continued. "Greyfriars became famous in nineteenth-century Edinburgh after reportedly spending fourteen years guarding over the grave of his owner, John Gray. A year after this loyal little dog died himself, in 1873, a statue and fountain were built in the Scottish capital to remember him."

"I know the story well," Jack said with a nod. "From the 1961 Disney film about that angel with fur called *Greyfriars Bobby*."

Wickham smiled warmly. "Saw it as a boy. Made me what I am today. I don't just mean the dog lover. I mean the concept of loyalty, dedication, no matter the inconvenience or cost. Without it, you're nothing."

Jack was enjoying the conversation, but had more pressing matters on his mind. "Senator, we need to talk about the Hand of Allah."

Wickham quickly glanced around as if hoping no one had heard, a tiny bit of paranoia that seemed out of character. Then he leaned toward them, keeping his voice low. "Not to worry, son. Thanks to you and Ms. Ghadah here, we've got it all under control."

"You found the guy from Allied?"

"We did indeed. It took some careful maneuvering with people I knew I could trust, but right now he's in the middle of a sit-down with a contact of mine from Homeland Security."

"Who is he?"

"A young Saudi kid who went to work for Allied about a year ago. We're still checking whether or not he's legal, but I'm guessing he isn't. Which means our illustrious friend Mr. Soren may be in a bit of trouble—although I doubt he'd see much more than a fine. It isn't likely he knew what was going on under his nose. Not many would."

"What about the shipping container? Did you find it?"

Wickham nodded. "We did. But it was clean. So either the device has already been taken or it never existed at all."

The "already been taken" part caused Jack some distress. "Has the President been apprised?"

"Yes, but he's playing it cautiously. He doesn't want to jump until we have concrete evidence. That USB key will help. Do you have it on you?"

Sara took it from her pocket and handed it across to him.

Wickham turned it in his fingers. "Amazing how much the world has changed, isn't it? In my day it would have been a simple slip of paper left at a des-

ignated drop zone. Now we can transfer all the
world's secrets with the touch of a key. Something
that WikiLeaks bastard learned to our great detri-
ment."

"What about Hassan Haddad?" Jack asked. "Have
you located him?"

"We have evidence he came into the city a couple
days ago on a diplomatic visa, but we haven't been
able to find him so far."

That was a second bit of bad news.

"Senator," Jack said, "with Haddad on the loose
and an empty container, shouldn't they be thinking
of canceling the gala tomorrow night?"

Wickham scoffed. "Not a chance."

"But—"

"I know what you're gonna say, Jack, but I don't
think you understand the magnitude of the situation.
The Legion of Honor is having a black-tie gala to
celebrate the art of Islam."

"How touching," Jack said.

"You see the problem," Wickham said. "It's open
only to high-end museum patrons and the whole
damn point of the exercise is to demonstrate solidarity and acceptance among people of all cultures, to
put all this anti-Muslim sentiment behind us. If we
jump the gun and accuse the Hand of Allah of a terrorist plot that doesn't exist, we'll have more PR
damage than we'll know what to do with."

"And if it does exist, we may have more real damage than we know what to do with, including a dead
President."

"Not gonna happen," Wickham said. "That place will be sealed up tight. No way anyone who even smells of trouble will make it through those doors without being fully scanned. Even the big museum patrons and politicians."

Jack still didn't like it. His gut told him they were thinking too small, too locally. And there was still the unexplained reference to the "twins." "What about the British government? Any progress on that front?"

Wickham balked. "Come on, Jack, this is a very delicate matter. We have to move slowly and with deliberation before we can determine who's friend or foe over there. Trust me, we'll be looking into this Zuabi character and any ties he might have to MI6 or the Home Office. It'll all come out in the wash."

"I hope you're right."

"I think our first concern," Wickham said, "is finding Hassan Haddad. Even if the legion is secure, I'm not particularly comfortable with him running around in the wild."

"I agree with that. So what's the plan?"

"My man in Homeland Security is trying to get something out of Allied about this character, but he's playing by the rules so who knows how much luck he's having? In the meantime, I've put together a small team to look at this thing. People who can be trusted. We've taken over the bed-and-breakfast at a little island lighthouse station for the night to work out a strategy. Sent the caretakers on a short vacation so we can talk freely." He looked at Jack and Sara. "I'd like you two to join us. I'm sure the others would love your input. Especially you, Sara, since you seem to know the most about who and what we're up against."

Jack and Sara exchanged a glance, then Sara said, "Absolutely. Count us in."

Senator Wickham smiled that charming Texas smile of his, then took a fond, parting look at the arena and got to his feet. "Glad to hear it," he said. "Why don't we head on out there now?"

32

The East Brother light station was practically unknown outside of the Richmond–San Rafael area.
Established in 1874, it was located just off Point San
Pablo in the northern part of the bay, perched atop
one of the tiny islands called the Brothers. Ships
making their way to Sacramento, through the strait
between the San Francisco and San Pablo bays, had
to negotiate numerous small islands and indented
coastline that were treacherous at night or in fog.
The lighthouse was the solution. East Brother Island
was dominated by a large two-story beige Victorian-
style bed-and-breakfast, fronted by the rectangular
tower of the lighthouse itself. Despite being only a
quarter mile from the shore, the island was isolated
and quiet, except for the occasional bray of a foghorn.

It was the perfect place to get work done without interruption.

When Jack spent time in his apartment off the Embarcadero, he often looked toward the Richmond Bridge from his bay window, thinking about the night he'd spent at the light station with Rachel. He had fallen in love with the place back then—at least *that* love was real—but all these years later he had yet to repeat the experience.

Wickham's driver took them down a desolate, rutted access road that threatened to destroy the limousine's suspension. After about twenty thumping minutes they reached an old, dilapidated pier.

The light station stood just across the water, the windows of the house lit up, the lighthouse beacon shining like a large star in the night sky. It was a foggy night, but the light broke through the fog in dispersed rays.

There was a twenty-eight-foot open Chris-Craft waiting for them, its pilot nodding to them politely as Jack, Sara, Wickham, and his bodyguard stepped aboard. The sun was down and the air had grown chilly, the sea breeze whipping at their clothes and hair as they found seats and sat down.

Wickham and his bodyguard sat in back, and the senator took a cigar from his pocket, lighting it under a cupped hand as the pilot started the engine. Then, as they pulled from the dock, he contentedly tilted his head back and blew smoke into the air.

"Gorgeous foggy night," he said over the whine of

the motor. "Nights like this make it hard for me to go back to Texas. Or worse yet, D.C."

"There's no place else on earth like the bay," Jack said.

Sara's jacket apparently wasn't doing its job, because she sidled up next to Jack, trying to use his body to buffer the cold wind. As the boat rumbled, skimming the surface of the water, he put an arm around her and pulled her close, thinking about their brief encounter back in Faisal's apartment. As corny as it might sound, he felt as if he'd finally found his soul mate, the one woman in this world he would ever want or need.

A Muslim woman, if that didn't beat all.

She nestled her head against his shoulder and murmured softly. "Who are these people we're meeting?"

"Friends of the senator. Probably upper-echelon law enforcement and government types. People he thinks he can trust."

"Why out here? The isolation?"

Jack nodded. "Barely a smudge on the map. They want to stay as far off the radar grid as possible. Just like—"

He stopped himself but it was too late.

"Brendan and Alain and the others?" she said.

"Sorry," he said. "I really am."

"No need," she said. "It *is* like our headquarters in Paris. That is a tribute to my fallen comrades."

She pulled him closer and kissed his cheek and for a moment he managed to forget what they'd been through, and tried to think about what was to come.

The key was stopping Hassan Haddad, wherever he might be. If he was out there in the wild with some kind of explosive, they all needed to be very worried.

Jack thought again about nearly bumping into the man outside that pub near al-Fida's flat.

If only he had known.

If only.

After several minutes they pulled up to a long dock and boathouse that extended from the side of the island. There were already two boats moored side by side there, a thirty-eight-foot Downeast cruiser with an open cockpit and an older, smaller Luhrs. Two rubber dinghies with outboard motors bumped up against the dock on the opposite side. Beyond them was a fast Novurania rigid inflatable. Jack guessed it was used by a caretaker to speed over to the shore for provisions. He probably came and went in a larger vessel, better equipped to handle bigger loads from the mainland.

The pilot maneuvered their small boat into an empty space next to a ladder, then tied the boat down and gestured for everyone to disembark. They all climbed up and stepped onto the dock, then moved up a short ramp that led under an umbrella of trees onto the island itself. They continued along a small cement concourse past the old wooden fog signal building— which was little more than a large wooden shed with two pneumatic foghorns mounted on its roof—and moved toward the Victorian bed-and-breakfast on the far side of the island.

West Brother Island was visible just beyond this, a dry, elongated chunk of earth that was crowded with cormorants, gulls, and other bay birds sharing the bare, steep rock. Nesting pelicans had taken over the entire grassy area of the island. Just as with humans, the strongest birds had the best real estate. Off to their left, about one mile across the bay, was the Richmond–San Rafael Bridge, its iron cross-work frame obscured by the fog.

"It's beautiful here," Sara said.

"Tell that to my ex-wife."

She looked at him. "What?"

He shook his head. "Actually, forget I said that. It's not worth talking about."

Poking up from the center of the concourse was the large rounded surface of a cistern. Jack knew that there were no water lines out here and the island had been specially designed to collect rain. Water was so scarce, in fact, that the night he and Rachel visited, they hadn't been allowed to shower before bed. Such a privilege was granted only to visitors on extended stays.

They moved past the cistern toward the main house, and the closer they got, the more reticent Jack began to feel. He couldn't quite put his finger on it but he suddenly felt as if something were off, his fight-or-flight instinct quietly kicking into gear.

He glanced at Wickham's bodyguard, Mr. Laser Pointer, who was standing just to his right, then turned to Wickham himself as they approached the house.

"Senator, who exactly are we meeting with?" Jack asked.

"I already told you," Wickham said. "People we can trust. Probably the *only* people we can trust."

Then they passed under a set of white stairs that led to the second floor and moved onto the small porch fronting the first-floor entrance.

The interior of the house matched its exterior—old, quaint, with a Victorian-style flavor, all the way down to the furniture. The foyer walls were lined with framed black-and-white photos of the light station in years gone by, along with old photos of Richmond and San Francisco and the bay.

As they stepped inside, Jack could hear voices.

"It's just past dinnertime," Wickham said, "so they're probably all in the dining room to your left. Let's go in and make introductions."

It sounded more like a command than a request, but Jack and Sara turned to their left, moving through a doorway into a narrow room dominated by a long white-clothed dining table.

Everyone stopped talking when they entered.

Seven men sat at the table, dirty dishes and drinks and ashtrays in front of them, cigars in hand, the sickly-sweet smell of their smoke hanging in the air. Jack recognized a few of the men immediately, all of them old-timers like Wickham—Senator Mitch Tomlinson, a Democrat from Maine; William Arland, a high-powered financial consultant and former

chairman of the Federal Reserve; James Feather-
stone, an undersecretary at the British Home Office;
and Clyde Parkinson, former assistant director of the
FBI. The others were undoubtedly movers and shakers of the same caliber, but their faces weren't familiar to Jack.

Except one.

At the far end of the table sat a man who always got
his blood pumping. A man he had hated with such
ferocity for the last two years that he felt like leaping
across the table and strangling him. It was the man
responsible for the smear campaign that had destroyed
his career.

He spoke directly to Jack with a distinct Austrian
accent. "Have a seat, why don't you, Mr. Hatfield."

It was billionaire Lawrence Soren.

33

"What the hell *is* this?" Jack said, turning to Wickham. "What's going on?"

"I think you should do as he says. Sit."

It was like a command to one of his dogs.

Sara looked completely deflated. Jack grabbed her arm and started to back from the table, but Wickham's bodyguard got up behind them in the doorway and Jack felt the muzzle of a gun against his lower back.

This wasn't good.

"You and your girlfriend are looking as shy as mail-order brides," Wickham said with a smile. "Nothing to be afraid of here. We're the good guys."

"Is that why I've got a gun at my back?"

Now Lawrence Soren smiled. He was about seventy-six years old, with thin blond hair, a pasty-white complexion, and large bulbous blue eyes. Jack had always thought he looked like a former SS officer.

"We have to be cautious," Soren said. "You're an unpredictable sort. You've certainly proven that over the last several days—if not your entire career. So *do* be seated. Or, contrary to what the senator says, there *will* be something to fear."

Another man stepped in through a doorway behind Soren. He was carrying a Glock 9mm.

Jack and Sara exchanged glances, but what choice did they have? They pulled out chairs and sat, Jack feeling his chest grow tight with tension.

"You need to relax," Soren said, correctly reading his expression. "All this hatred you hold for me is not healthy. Perhaps if we took the time to discuss the world, we might find we have more in common than you think."

"I doubt it," Jack said.

"Oh?" Soren's thick white brows went up. "Look around you. Here you have a room full of men from all ends of the political spectrum, yet we've managed to put aside our differences and come together for a common cause."

"And what cause is that?"

"Restoring sanity to the world. Surely you can appreciate such a sentiment."

"Depends on your definition of sanity. Yours no doubt has something to do with preserving the sanctity of your fascist agenda, along with your all-important pocketbook."

Soren nodded in acquiescence. "There are always

concerns about money, of course. We here are men of privilege who have no interest in losing what we've earned. Which is why we've learned, over the years, to back the winning horses."

"Meaning what?"

Soren leaned back in his chair. "I think anyone who looks at the world today can clearly see that the Zionists are the cause for all the unrest in the Middle East."

"*That* big lie? You gotta be kidding me."

"The policies of Israel and the United States are strangling Israel's neighbors. And it's obvious to anyone with any intelligence that the Jews rule the world by proxy. Right now, as we speak, preparations are being made to ship plutonium to the Jewish state, out of our very own ports. Here we are, helping the Israelis build their nuclear arsenal while we treat the countries around them, Muslim countries"—he made a point of glancing at Sara—"with complete disrespect, telling their leaders that they're too unruly and immature to have such weapons of their own."

"Israel is a democracy and our only ally—"

"And *you* talk of big lies?" Soren interrupted with a dismissive laugh. "But that discussion is for another time, assuming you have another time. What I've just told you is why we, a consortium of concerned citizens, have decided to back the underdog in this race. We've begun channeling money and resources into the Hand of Allah in the hope of putting an end to this Zionist stranglehold."

Jack rose from his chair. "What is *wrong* with you

people?" He turned to Wickham. "Hal, tell me you're not falling for this racist crap?"

"You're one to talk about racism," Soren remarked.

Jack wanted to punch him. Again. He ignored the SOB, continued to stare at Wickham.

The senator shrugged and took a puff off his cigar. "I'm a businessman first, Jack, you know that. These people have control of resources I need. I figure it's better to make friends with them than to kick 'em in the ass and try to steal it."

"And commit treason in the process?"

Wickham frowned. "One man's treason is another man's revolution."

"So you lied to me," Jack said. "You didn't do a thing with that information we gave you. Haddad and his crew are still out there planning their assault on the Legion of Honor as we speak."

Wickham said nothing and the gun touched Jack's back again as a hand on his shoulder forced him down into the chair.

"True regime change is rarely peaceful," Soren said with affected regret. "We may manage it here in America every four years or so without bloodshed, but all we get for our trouble are the same Zionist puppets with the same policies that are destroying this country and the world. As you know, I had high hopes for our current President, but he's turned out to be quite a disappointment to all of us on many different levels. So if we're to succeed in bringing our own vision to fruition, we need to shake things up a bit. The Hand of Allah will help us do that. It's 1933 all over again. You end the Depression in Germany by firing up the masses, having them reclaim *their* wealth from the Jews. You end the threat to America's homeland by scaring the masses, assuring them they will be safe from future attacks if they restore Arab land taken by the Jews."

"Helluva role model you've chosen," Jack remarked.

"You're missing the point."

"No, I've got it. Scapegoating works. I experienced that firsthand."

"This is not scapegoating," Soren said. "It's about forging a strategic alliance with someone who can control hundreds of millions of people and billions of dollars in resources. If you took just a moment to listen to him, you'd realize that Faakhir Zuabi is a great visionary and a great leader. And I think our partnership with him will be of benefit to all of us. Including you."

Jack balked. "What the hell are you talking about?"

"You're a wonderful communicator, Jack. You have a friendly, trustworthy manner about you, but you can be a bulldog when you need to and people respond to it."

"That's all in the past, thanks to you."

"Something that can be easily remedied. What if, in the face of devastation, you were to become the spokesperson for America? *Our* spokesperson."

"Wait—you want me to *join* you?"

Soren shrugged. "It's either that or die."

Sara stood now, her eyes blazing. "You wanks are certifiably insane."

Hearing that expression come from Sara's mouth shocked Jack nearly as much as anything else he'd heard here.

Soren offered her a patient smile as the bodyguard nudged her back into the chair. "We're merely pragmatists, my dear. You cannot blame anyone for that." He looked at Jack again. "So what do you say, my friend. Are you with us or no?"

Jack stared at him, the urge to leap across the table still burning in his gut. "Up yours."

Soren sighed. "I expected as much. But I had to try." He rose from his chair and gestured. "Gentlemen, shall we adjourn to the parlor upstairs? I believe Mr. Hatfield and his lovely friend here have an appointment."

Chairs scraped back around the table, the men all glancing at Jack and Sara as they filed out past the thug with the Glock and disappeared from sight.

Soren, however, stopped just shy of the doorway and turned. "It's a shame, Jack. You and I have been at odds for so long. Imagine what we could do if we were to come together for a common cause."

Jack reiterated his earlier words by raising a fist and showing Soren his middle finger.

Soren stood there for a moment, smiling almost sadly, then stepped out of sight.

Now Jack turned his head toward the bodyguard

behind him. "Real nice people you associate with. So what now?"

"I believe I can answer that," a familiar voice said from across the room.

Jack jerked his head around as Adam Swain stepped in through the opposite doorway, accompanied by two more of his men, including the ape with his magic wand, who grinned at Jack as he walked into the room.

Wonderful.

Jack reached under the table and gently squeezed Sara's hand. It was a signal for her to wait for his move. He had no idea if she'd gotten the message, but she squeezed back firmly and that was good enough.

She hadn't even flinched when Swain entered.

Good girl, he thought.

Swain said, "It looks as if we'll be playing another round of touch my pole, old boy. You understand. As a precaution?" He smiled. "But not to worry, we'll be gentle this time."

"Now why do I doubt that?" Jack said.

"True enough, but perhaps you'll be more forthcoming this time. Shall we adjourn to the fog signal building? We'll have more privacy there."

Jack and Sara didn't move.

Swain frowned now, then took his own Glock from under his jacket and waved it at them. "I'm not very good at begging."

The two slowly got to their feet. Jack had no way of signaling Sara again, so he hoped she was ready for what he was about to do.

The senator's bodyguard was still behind him and shoved the gun into his back again.

"Move."

Jack did as he was asked. As soon as he was clear of the chair he kicked back and down, a low Krav Maga blow to the bodyguard's kneecap. The man grunted but did not go down; Jack hadn't wanted him to. As the foot came down he was literally standing beside the bodyguard. That brought him right beside the gun—another Glock 9mm. Helped by the momentum of his backward step, Jack ripped it from the bodyguard's hand by twisting his hand outward, a painful pronating wristlock.

At the same moment, Sara took hold of the edge of the dining table and, with a loud grunt and a heave, flipped it sideways, sending dishes and whiskey glasses and ashtrays flying.

Swain and his men ducked the debris as Swain fired a shot in Sara's direction. But the bullet went wild and she dove to the floor, behind the table. Meanwhile, Jack had continued turning the man's wrist until he was on the floor, on his back. Jack stomped on his face and ripped the laser pointer from the bodyguard's breast pocket.

Another shot flew past Sara, who snatched one of the ashtrays from the floor. She stood and hurled it hard at the gunman's head. It hit his mouth hard and he fell back against the wall, spitting blood.

Flicking the laser pointer on, Jack shone its penetrating red beam directly into Swain's eyes, blinding him, then squeezed off two quick shots as he grabbed

hold of Sara's forearm and spun her toward the door.
"Go! Let's go!"

They moved together into the foyer and burst
through the main doorway onto the concourse and
into the cold night air.

"The boats," Jack said. "We have to get to the
boats."

They took off running, but the dock was on the
other side of the concourse and they had several yards
of cement to traverse before they'd reach it.

Halfway across they heard a shot, a bullet scorch-
ing the cement behind them. Jack jerked Sara sideways and glanced over his shoulder. The shot seemed
to have come from on high, and as he looked up toward the lighthouse, he saw shadowy movement; one
of Swain's thugs was stationed up there.

The thug squeezed off shot after shot but the fog
made it difficult for him to see. Jack and Sara dropped
behind the cistern in the center of the concourse, using it for cover. They kept their heads low as bullets
pinged around them mercilessly.

"You all right?" Jack asked.

She nodded.

The foghorn building stood several feet behind
them. "I'm gonna give you cover," Jack said. "Get
into that shack as quickly as you can. I think there's a
door on the other side that'll lead down to the dock.
Get to the white Novurania next to the dinghies, and
get it started."

"What about you?"

"If I'm not along in about thirty seconds or so,

get the hell back to shore and contact a friend of mine at the Shoreside Marina. Tony Antiniori. Can you remember that?"

"Yes, yes. Who is he?"

"The only one I can trust at this point."

Another shot echoed through the fog. They ducked as the front door of the Victorian flew open and Swain and two of his men strode purposefully onto the concourse.

"There's nowhere to go, Jack! You spend five minutes in that water and we'll be carving an ice sculpture out of you just for the fun of it. You might as well give it up."

"On the count of three," Jack whispered to Sara. "One, two, *three*—"

Jack and Sara jumped to their feet simultaneously, Sara zigzagging for the shack behind them, Jack flashing the laser pointer again and opening fire, taking down one of the thugs as Swain and another gunman dove for low ground.

The guy in the lighthouse tower started firing again, and Jack returned several shots before ducking back behind the cistern.

Sara slammed through the door behind him.

Jack checked his magazine, saw that he had just a few more rounds, then mentally counted to three again and jumped to his feet. He headed for the foghorn building, firing indiscriminately as he ran. Just as he reached the door, a bullet clipped his shoulder and he stumbled forward.

Shots splintered wood above him as Jack gripped

the door frame and yanked himself inside, pulling the door shut behind him as he grasped his shoulder and collapsed onto one knee.

"Could've been worse," he said, feeling the edges of the wound through his torn shirt.

The room was full of machinery, pneumatic pumps that once powered the foghorns. Now that the system was electronic, they were no longer needed.

Still clutching his shoulder Jack called out. "Sara?"

No answer. But the door on the opposite side of the shack was hanging open and that was a good sign. She was probably down to the dock by now, and that was where Jack needed to be.

Wincing against the pain, he grabbed a piece of machinery and pushed himself to his feet, the room swaying slightly as he stood. He knew that Swain and his goons would be bursting through that door any second now, so he steeled himself and worked his way around the maze of machinery to the rear, moving as quickly as his body would carry him.

He heard the rip of an outboard motor and knew that Sara had made it to the RIB.

He was picking up speed as Sara's scream ripped the air. He crashed through the doorway, running toward the white picket railing that overlooked the dock.

By the time he reached it, one of Swain's thugs had dragged Sara to the dock and was pulling her toward the Luhrs, the ugly black barrel of a gun pressed against her head.

34

Jack forgot about his shoulder and ran, heading straight for the ramp, raising the Glock as he approached them.

"Let her go!" he commanded.

But now Swain and his other men were emerging from the foghorn building and moving in his direction.

"Give it up, Hatfield," Swain called back. "You gave us a good fight but now it's over." He snickered. "Think of the environment, Jack. All this gunfire can't be good for the gulls and seals."

Jack froze and looked at Sara and her gaze locked on his.

Even through the mist he could see that her eyes had gone cold, all vulnerability gone. He knew this was her game face. She wasn't Sara the victim but Sara the hardened ex-Interpol agent.

"Leave me, Jack!" she said. "If they take us both, it's over."

It was a ridiculous notion. "No way."

"You *have* to! *I* would if the situation were—"

"Shut up," the thug spat, rapping the gun barrel hard against her head.

"As much as I'm enjoying this, get her the hell out of here," Swain snarled.

The gunman backed Sara closer to the Luhrs.

Jack momentarily forgot the mission. There was only Sara—Sara, who was a captive and needed his help.

He shone the laser pointer in the thug's eyes. "Let her *go,* you son of a bitch!"

The thug squinted.

Swain turned to Sara. "Turn that off or I'll kill her right now! *Do it!*"

Jack didn't hesitate. He lowered the light.

Sara said, "Go, Jack."

Jack looked at her, his heart breaking, not wanting to do as she asked. There had to be a way out for both of them.

But even as he thought that, he knew he had no choice. Time seemed to suspend for a moment. The watch repairman's son needed a *tick tick tick* to spur him to action.

Swain gave it to him by drawing closer, raising his gun as he approached. There would be no more talk. Jack guessed that the only reason Swain held his fire was proximity: he wanted to see Jack's face clearly, through the fog, as he took everything from him. Not just his life but his love.

Jack gave Sara one last mournful glance then swung around, once again shining the beam of the laser pointer into Swain's eyes. As Swain recoiled, Jack jumped from the ramp, ignoring the pain in his shoulder as he hit the Novurania.

While Swain and his men struggled to get a bead on him in the thick darkness, Jack threw off the line, shots gouging the dock above him. The forty-horse power Yamaha outboard roared defiantly and Jack took off, more shots punching the water behind him, Swain's shouts in his wake.

"Go! After him!"

But Jack was already out of reach. The acceleration of the Novurania was flawless. There was no hesitation in the slightly choppy waters as the boat responded easily to the throttle control.

The shore was only a quarter mile away but there was nothing there save for desolation, no sign of civilization. Jack knew they would catch him on the two-mile run to the nearest roadway, especially with him losing blood. He had a better idea. Maxing out the engine, he steered toward the Richmond–San Rafael Bridge, trying to squeeze as much speed from the RIB as he could.

Jack heard a motor fire up behind him and turned to see that two of Swain's thugs had commandeered one of the boats from the other side of the dock and were already headed in his direction.

Good luck, he thought gravely. The boats were

bigger but they were also slower. They didn't have a chance in hell of catching him.

That didn't keep them from shooting, however. The muffled sounds of gunfire punched through the night, bullets whizzing past Jack's head. They probably sounded closer than they were, though Jack couldn't take that chance. He ducked and returned fire until his ammo was spent.

He kept goosing the throttle, heading for one of the towers of the bridge. He could see the lights of the bridge through the fog—dim, beautiful beacons on top of the main towers used to warn away low-flying aircraft. Having boated by the area hundreds of times, he remembered the built-in maintenance ladders that led toward the roadway above. He could hear the bridge as he saw it, the bounce of his own engine coming back at him as it struck the stanchion.

Covered by the fog, Jack tied a rope to the Novurania's engine and climbed out. He had sent the boat toward Tiburon, some four miles to the west, then he clambered onto the landing where the workers' ladders began.

More shots were fired—at the boat, not him—as he grabbed hold of the ladder and worked his way upward, slowly, painfully, rung by rung. Jack was halfway up when he heard his pursuer's boat roar by, headed in the direction of the RIB.

As he reached the top of the bridge, Jack paused to slip off his belt and use it as a tourniquet. Then he threw a hand up trying to flag someone down, but all he got were squealing tires and angry horn blasts in return. The bright red blood staining his shirt wasn't exactly a stoplight and the gun in his hand didn't help much, either.

There wasn't time to walk. A carjacking? Bring the damn thing full circle?

Then he remembered something else. He recalled seeing workers on bicycles up here. Maintenance personnel used them to move around on the roadway. He needed to find where they kept them.

He took off down the bridge roadway, looking left, right, and ahead as he shambled along. He found the bikes chained to a rail near the end of the bridge. The chain was held in place by a padlock—an old Wilson Bohannan, brass case, brass shackle. He'd finally caught a break.

Jack knelt beside the bikes, not caring whether anyone saw him or not. Let someone call the cops; at least Jack would get a phone call and he could let Tony know what was going on.

Holding the laser pointer in his mouth, Jack focused it on the Glock. The slide stop lever was set in a ridge in the trigger pin. He pushed on the trigger pin as he wiggled the slide stop lever. That enabled him to push the trigger pin and the upper pin free. Using the gun parts as a lock pick, he went to work. In less than a minute the chain was off. Sliding the pieces of the Glock into his pants pocket, he sat on an old two-wheeler that was badly rusted by the sea breeze. It worked fine, if noisily, and he churned down the road to the Richmond side, to the railroad yards he remembered there. Up ahead he saw several long rows of sleek train cars silhouetted in the darkness, idle for the night.

That would be his second stop. First, there was something he needed to find.

Jack got off the bike and reassembled the Glock as he walked. He didn't need it to work, only look like it would. He moved quickly through the solemn darkness of the yards, a graveyard for the relics of a passing era. The cars afforded some relief from the cold, blocking the wind and releasing some of the baking heat they'd stored during the day. One of the trains—the only one that appeared to have any activity—smelled of livestock. Jack was looking for a light, any light, that would suggest a night watchman, a security shack . . . a phone.

He didn't find one. What he *did* find—bless its antique self—was a pay phone. It was housed inside a green booth with a door that folded in the middle. Jack staggered toward it, legs aching from the bike ride. The light bulb was long dead but Jack didn't need it. He lifted the receiver, holding his breath, and caught his second break of the night as he heard a dial tone. He exhaled, thanking God for technology that wasn't designed to be so disposable.

He dialed—actually *dialed*—the *O* and placed a collect call. The operator actually sounded surprised as she put it through.

Jack waited, still running the night's play through his head, wishing to Christ he hadn't left Sara behind.

But what else could he have done?

She had *wanted* him to go because she knew he was their only chance of stopping this thing, and she was willing to sacrifice herself for the greater good. Still, he couldn't help feeling as if leaving her had been a mistake, and he knew he had to divorce himself from his feelings—just as Sara had. He needed to forget that he'd fallen in love with her and concentrate on doing what had to be done.

What had to be done was that Jack needed to build a small army. Fast. And there was only one person who could do that.

A moment later a familiar voice came across the line.

"Hello?"

Tony Antiniori.

Jack struggled to speak, then finally got the words out. "I need you to gather the troops and come get me."

"Jack—where the hell are you?"

"I'm at the rail yards in Richmond, but I can't stay here—meet me at the north end of the Oakland yards in about two hours," he said.

"Okay—"

"And get some manpower. We've got a war to wage."

"What kind of manpower?"

"MARSOC," Jack said. "Bare-bones assault."

Jack had asked for a Marine Special Operations Command. Tony would understand he wanted three or four good men. If he had other questions—and Jack was sure he did—Tony didn't bother to ask them.

Jack hung up and hurried back to the train where he'd smelled livestock. The door was partly ajar for ventilation and he confirmed what his nose had suspected: the car was loaded with goats bound for the slaughterhouse. From there, no doubt, many of the carcasses would be sent to the halal market.

"Hope you don't mind if I ride with you," Jack said as he painfully pulled himself in, his arm aching and his legs wobbly from the unaccustomed bike ride. He nestled himself in a corner, beside a water tank that fed a plastic hose into the pen. "I promise that at least one of us is going to give those guys indigestion before lunchtime."

35

By the time Jack and his team hit the island, everyone was gone.

They came at it hard, at three in the morning,
Tony Antiniori commandeering the *Sea Wrighter* as
three of their friends—all ex-military, faces painted,
weapons in hand—jumped onto the now empty dock
and charged up the ramp toward the concourse.

Despite Jack's loss of blood, Tony had used his
skills as a medic to do a quick patch job and get him
back on his feet. But as he headed out after the others, Tony held him back.

"I don't think so, buddy. Leave this to us."

"Try and stop me," Jack said.

Tony sighed and backed off.

Then Jack was off the boat and pounding up the
ramp, a borrowed Colt AR-15 assault rifle in hand,
moving with the others like commandos on a village

raid. Even though Jack knew the exercise was probably futile he had to try, had to see if by some miracle
Sara was still here, maybe tied up in a room somewhere, maybe in the foghorn building.

They covered the entire compound in less than
ten minutes, crashing through doors, moving from
room to room in the old Victorian, finding nothing
but the mess left behind by Soren and his band of
madmen, and the remnants of the fight in the dining
room.

Jack took the winding stairs up to the lighthouse
and scanned the concourse below, then the bay itself,
looking for any signs of a body on the surface. His
wound opened again but he didn't care. His heart was
stuck in his throat as his light played across the water.
He was relieved when he saw nothing but the black
water lit by the sinking moon.

Tony clambered up the stairs behind him. He
stared out as well.

"They probably took her to use as a hostage,"
Tony said. "You've proved pretty resilient—and they
know you got away."

"Yeah," Jack said.

He hoped that Tony was right.

"Come on," Tony said, urging him back down the
stairs.

Jack followed docilely.

Jack thought about that last look she'd given him,
that cold, unflinching gaze, the one that said she was
prepared to deal with whatever came next, that she
could take care of herself. But try as he might, he

could not quite forgive himself for doing as she'd asked.

A mix of dread and anger sluiced through his body as he walked back past the lighthouse tower, clutching the AR-15. The woman he loved, the city he cherished, both at risk thanks to a man he loathed. It was an emotional cocktail that sharpened his focus to a razor edge.

As they exited the lighthouse they encountered a wiry former Navy SEAL who came jogging toward them.

"It's all clear," said Jonah Goldman. "Nobody on-site."

Tony nodded. Jack was looking out at the bay.

"She's not out there," he said. "You've got to believe that."

Jack sucked down a long, slow, tremulous breath.

"Now it's time to go," Tony said.

They hustled back to the boat, Jack lagging, Tony running watchfully at his side. The long night and loss of blood were conspiring against him.

The world turned and he dropped straight down as they reached the dock.

When Jack woke the sun was shining through a port-hole. He was lying in his cabin, Eddie snuggled next to him.

Jack was instantly alert—and angry. He had passed out and they'd let him *stay* passed out. He swiveled his head and found Maxine sitting in a chair across from the bed. He was surprised to see her.

"How long have I been out?" he asked.

"Couple of hours," she said. "They kept you sedated so they could deal with this."

She held up a small bottle containing a nugget of metal—the bullet Tony had dug out of Jack's shoulder sometime in the middle of the night. "No permanent damage, but it seems you've gotten yourself in pretty deep."

"You don't know the half of it." Jack sighed.

"So tell me."

He did as he tried to overcome the lingering effects of whatever they'd pumped into his veins. He told her about the trip to Tel Aviv, the tense moment at Ben Gurion International, the near-miss with Hassan Haddad, breaking into Abdal al-Fida's apartment, the encounter with Swain and his magic wand, the deaths of Brendan and the others, the e-mails Alain had discovered, Lawrence Soren and the firefight on the island. But mostly he talked about Sara, because it was his only way of hanging on to her right now.

"I shouldn't have left her on that island," he said.

"What choice did you have?"

"The one I didn't take."

"The one where you wind up dead?"

"Might be better than this," he said bitterly.

"Uh-huh," Max said. "And if this Swain guy is using her for leverage, then it seems to me you may have saved *both* of your lives by getting away." She paused. "But more importantly, we are facing very organized, very powerful, very well connected megalomaniacs who are planning something bad. Stopping them is more important than anything else."

"What are you saying?"

She leaned toward him now, her expression intense. "I want to help you, Jack. We all want to help you find Sara. But even more, we want to help our country. That gala starts in a little less than six hours and we need to do everything in our power to keep those bastards from blowing the place up."

"And how are we supposed to do that?"

"Teamwork," Max said. "Teamwork and a whole hell of a lot of luck."

They had turned the salon and pilothouse of the *Sea Wrighter* into a makeshift command center, reminding Jack of the apartment house in Paris. The *Sea Wrighter* itself was anchored in the middle of the bay, away from prying eyes and ears, and who knew what else. If they were going to make some kind of move, it had to be done with the greatest of stealth.

Three of Tony's buddies were here, the same three who had helped them assault the island. Jack had met them over the months in various bars that he and Tony frequented around town, old hardened war vets who still remembered what it meant to fight for your country. Back in the days when the bad guys were easier to spot and you knew who your friends were by the uniform they wore.

Now those uniforms had been replaced by street clothes, and you never knew who might be hiding behind a simple T-shirt and a pair of jeans. And thanks to fascists like Lawrence Soren and the people he bankrolled, there was no way to know when a look of concern or surprise was genuine, or merely a façade designed to manipulate and deceive.

But like Tony himself, his buddies were old-school, the kind of guys you could rely on in a pinch.

There was Mike Abernathy, a steel-eyed sixty-five-year-old former army combat commando badass, who looked as limber as a kid out of high school. Mike had done four tours in Vietnam, earned a chest full of medals, and at one time was even on the short list for a Medal of Honor.

Then there was Jonah Goldman, a fifty-year-old former Navy SEAL whose search-and-rescue missions around the globe were legendary, a guy who looked like a young Arnold Schwarzenegger.

And finally, Doc Matson, former medic and paratrooper who had trained Tony himself. Grizzled, white haired, Doc was the oldest of the bunch, and possibly the toughest, and the others sometimes kidded that he'd fought alongside Ulysses S. Grant.

It was a motley crew, all right, but these men were as tough as they came and had the mental and physical prowess to best any twenty-year-old coming out of the box.

But the biggest surprise here was Dave Karras, Max's old flame and computer hacker extraordinaire. After that night in his apartment Jack figured he'd never see the guy again, especially in the same zip code as Max herself. Yet here he was, with a shave and a haircut, commandeering three laptop computers that projected their images onto Jack's sixty-inch television screen.

Jack shot Max a quizzical look and she just shrugged and said, "What can I tell you? I'm a sucker for men who grovel."

Jack still couldn't picture them as a couple, but he'd given up on trying to figure out the ways of the heart a long time ago.

"Okay, guys," Karras said. "I found it."

He punched a button on one of the laptops and the television screen came to life with a building blueprint.

The California Palace of the Legion of Honor.

The Legion of Honor was a revered part of San Francisco's history, a common destination for tourists and locals alike. Built in 1924, it was a smaller, multicolumned replica of France's Palais de la Légion d'Honneur, which sits on the west bank of the River Seine.

San Francisco's palace stood on a small hill in Lincoln Park, surrounded by a golf course and beautiful ocean vista, looking out toward the Golden Gate Bridge. Jack had always thought its architecture was reminiscent of the buildings in Washington, D.C., and Thomas Jefferson himself had used the original French palace as inspiration for Monticello, his estate in Virginia.

The Legion of Honor had served as a museum since its doors first opened, and had one of the finest collections of ancient and European art in the world.

Jack had been there many times, but looking at it in the form of a blueprint was a new experience for him.

"All right, folks," Tony said, stepping over to the TV screen. "If Jack's intelligence is correct, we're looking at a possible terrorist assault on the museum at twenty-one hundred hours." He looked at Max and Karras and winked. "That's nine o'clock for the civilians in the crowd."

Max raised an eyebrow. "Thanks for clearing that up."

"Happy to oblige," Tony said, then turned to the rest of them. "We have to assume they're not going to call off the operation. Jack's escape leaves them potentially exposed. They have nothing to lose by finishing what they've started, though I guarantee the thin black line is going to be even more vigilant now."

"Thin black line?" Max asked.

"An enemy police action, blended into the shadows by using homegrown operatives," Tony explained. "The question is *how* they're going to pull this off. With the President's appearance there, security will be locked so tight the chances of bringing in some kind of explosive device are remote, if not impossible."

"What about the X factor?" Jack asked. "Harold Wickham."

"Do you think he'll show?" Tony asked. "I mean, if they're going to blow the place up—"

"He may put in a token appearance and leave," Jack said. "But he has clout. He'll have full access."

"What about the Secret Service?" Max said.

"They got to MI6, didn't they?" Jack said. "Who knows how far this reaches."

"Inside man or not," Mike Abernathy said, "anyone who enters that place will have to go through a security scanner, a pat down, and a dog sniff, so a simple walk-on isn't likely."

"Right," Tony said. His voice and his expression flattened. "That's the problem. Me and Mike and Jonah here spent the morning trying to come up with potential alternative scenarios that might make the impossible possible, but we came up blank. Especially with Haddad as a wild card."

"So we're wasting our time," Karras said.

"No," Jack told him. "This function *is* the target, even if it's not ground zero. They made no bones about letting me and Sara know that."

"Then how the hell are they gonna hit it?" Max asked.

"That's where Doc here comes in," Tony said. He gestured to Doc, who was sprawled on Jack's sofa, picking at his teeth with the corner of a matchbook. "He was downstairs grabbing a nap when the discussion started, but once he decided to get his ass outta the sack he already knew the answer to your question. Which is why I always have to remind myself he's older than God."

"You kiddin' me?" Doc said. "Who do you think raised the Almighty?"

"So what's the answer?" Jack asked impatiently.

Doc stopped picking his teeth, dropped the match-book into his shirt pocket, and got to his feet.

"I started thinking about that little headquarters they appropriated in the bay," he said. "Wickham told you they picked it because it was isolated."

"Yeah. So?" Jack said.

"Plenty of places in the city are isolated, secure, *convenient*," he said. "That thing's a pain in the ass to get to, and there's always the chance a Coast Guard patrol will stop you, especially with the President coming to town—"

"Cold son of a bitch, too," Goldman observed.

"No," Doc went on. "There had to be another reason they picked it."

"*What* reason?" Max asked.

Doc replied, "Location, location, location." He waited a moment to let that sink in. "I called a buddy at the National Reconnaissance Office. They've got a MATS—Maritime Anomalous Traffic Satellite— that flags divergence from normal patterns in the nation's major waterways. Sort of like NORAD for shipping. All that stuff we're supposedly *not* doing to protect our ports? We are."

"Draw your enemy out by pretending not to be watching," Jack said.

"Exactly," Doc told him. "I had him look at the images from that region. He said there's been very limited nighttime activity along the mainland coast near the island. The infrared images did not raise any alarms at the NRO because it failed to fit any standard danger profiles: it wasn't adjacent to a populated center, only small vessels came and went, and it stopped."

"Someone knew what they could get away with," Jack suggested.

"Obviously," Doc said. "But it got me poking around that region. And I remembered something. After the Japs struck Pearl Harbor, California was considered a prime target. Not only that, our armed forces relied heavily on munitions and other cargo being shipped out of the bay, so a lot of the existing bunkers along our coastline were fortified and several new facilities were built. Some of those newer bunkers were located under park land."

"Lincoln Park?" Max asked.

Doc nodded. "Officially, nobody knows the exact locations. This was all very top secret. But years after the war was over, several of these installations were discovered and explored by thrill seekers, until the government went to considerable expense and trouble in the seventies to seal them all off once and for all."

"I'm a San Francisco native," Karras said. "So why don't I know about this?"

"Because you aren't supposed to. Nobody is. The military has been operating on the theory that they never know when these bunkers might be of use again, so they've kept a lid on their existence. After the tunnels were sealed off and the decades went by they became an urban legend."

"Only this one turns out to be true," Tony said.

Doc nodded. "A few years back, a small group of urban explorers discovered a way into the Lincoln Park bunker, purely by accident. Nature has a way of shifting the earth and one of them found a hole in the ground and got curious."

"And they might not be the only ones who know about it," Max said.

"You know how things travel on the Internet these days," Tony said. "If some enterprising terrorist wanted to explore the situation, he might—for love or money—find someone willing to show him one of our city's biggest secrets."

"Hassan Haddad," Jack said.

"And you're sure there's one of these underground bunkers in Lincoln Park?" Karras asked.

"Absolutely," Doc told him. "And a section of it that leads straight to the Legion of Honor."

"How do you know all this?" Max asked.

Doc grinned. "Because, my dear, I've seen it first-hand. I used to work in those tunnels."

"You're kidding me."

"It was my first deployment, straight out of boot camp, about a year before they closed the whole operation down. That's why I stayed here—fell in love with the city. I must've traveled the length of those bunkers a thousand times. And I can tell you, they aren't just limited to Lincoln Park and the Legion of Honor."

"What do you mean?" Jack asked.

"They run all the way to the Golden Gate Bridge. It's like an express highway system down there, but without the traffic."

"Okay, so we know of a possible way into the building," Jack said.

"Not possible," Doc told him. "Probable. The Legion of Honor was built back in nineteen twenty-four." He gestured to Karass and pointed to the blueprint on-screen. "Show me the subbasement on that thing."

Karass did as he was told and the blueprint came up on the screen. Doc pointed to it. "Back in my day, there was a way into the tunnels by an elevator located in this subbasement right about here. They sealed that off after the tunnels were closed but there was a special hatch built close by, in case the elevator wasn't working." He shifted his finger to point out the location of the hatch. "It's a few years since I've been down in that basement, but the last time I saw that hatch it was secured by a simple chain and padlock."

"Wouldn't the Secret Service know about this?" Tony asked.

"No doubt they would and they'd have a man guarding it," Doc said. "But if these savages have a friend on the inside, who's to say he couldn't neutralize the agent and open the hatch?"

"Jesus," Max said. "Can't we just call in a bomb scare?"

"With what proof?" Jack said. "They get a hundred of those a day, and they undoubtedly do routine sweeps."

"So what's the solution?" Karras asked.

Tony said, "A two-pronged attack. Doc has a friend he thinks can give him a pretty good idea where the exterior entry point to the bunkers is. I say we wait for cover of darkness then go and see what we find."

"And what's the second prong?" Jack asked.

"You and me," Tony said, then reached into his pocket and took out the VIP invitation to the gala that Danny Pescatori had snagged for him. "Better break out your tuxedo, brother. We're gonna be rubbing shoulders with the President tonight."

36

Hassan Haddad sat at a corner table in the Bilal café, savoring some of the best meat and potato curry he'd had in months, when the man he was waiting for finally arrived.

It was well past the hour of their appointment, and Haddad had considered a number of times simply getting up and walking away. But as he waited, quietly sipping hot tea, the spicy smell of the curry kept wafting in from the kitchen and he knew he couldn't leave this place until he'd at least sampled it.

He wasn't disappointed.

This meeting had not been Haddad's idea. He had been going about his business these last two days, making preparations as needed, procuring Chilikov's device from the shipping yards, and selecting seven men out of a field of twenty who he thought would best serve Allah.

Many of Allah's soldiers showed great confidence when a mission was proposed, but the moment it became a reality some found their confidence start to wane, and Haddad had to know who he could and could not rely on to carry out his orders. The last thing he needed was another Abdal al-Fida on his hands.

Haddad had interviewed each of the twenty, looking for any signs of regret or weakness or fear, and had relied on his instincts to choose the men he needed. All of his preparations had been made and his men were now in position, and everything was going as planned—until he received an unexpected phone call that morning on his pay-as-you-go cell phone.

Only one person knew its number.

"*Assalamu alaikum,* my friend," the familiar old voice said.

Imam Zuabi.

Haddad expressed surprise at the sound of his voice. Had something gone wrong? Was this a call to tell him to abort? Such a thought sickened Haddad after all he had gone through to make this moment a reality.

But his imam gave him assurances that all was well.

"I am merely calling to wish you the blessings of the Prophet, my friend. Allah is smiling on you every moment of every day. He knows that what you do to avenge us is not without sacrifice, and He thanks you for your efforts. As do I."

"There is no need to thank me," Haddad said. "I am His servant. I do as He asks without question."

"Excellent, my friend. Excellent. Because there is someone I would like you to meet. Someone who has been helping us carry out Allah's plan."

Haddad frowned. "I do not understand. I have all the men I need. They are ready and committed to the cause."

"Yet you have asked many times about our benefactors, no? The people who have helped us these last years, procuring for us the things we need. Helping us smooth the way."

"Yes, of course," Haddad said. "I've been curious, but—"

"Today that curiosity will be sated," Zuabi informed him.

Haddad didn't understand. "What are you asking of me, Faakhir?"

"That you go to the Bilal restaurant at one P.M. today and order tea. A man will be there shortly and present himself to you. He is your final key to gaining entry to the place you seek. It is important that you meet him so that you may form a bond of trust."

Haddad knew it would be unwise to refuse this request, so he agreed—as Zuabi knew he would.

Haddad sat in the restaurant just long enough to get hungry as he waited for this man to arrive—a man he had known nothing about until the imam's phone call. He was deeply disturbed by this turn of events.

He did not like surprises.

Twenty minutes into the hour, the bell over the door jangled and a tall, muscular-looking man with a crew cut and sunglasses entered the restaurant and walked without hesitation to Haddad's table.

He gestured to the chair opposite Haddad. "May I?"

"By all means," Haddad told him, recognizing a British accent, not unlike his own. The man looked very dangerous and Haddad did not know what to make of him. Was he not Muslim? And if not, how could he possibly have a role in what they were about to do?

But even more disturbing was the thought that Imam Zuabi would associate with someone like this. If this man worked for one of their benefactors, what did these benefactors want for the money they'd given to Zuabi? Whose agenda was Haddad being asked to carry out? That of Allah or some unseen entity?

The man pulled out a chair, sat, and removed his sunglasses. The eyes behind them were like ice. "Good afternoon, Mr. Haddad. I've heard many great things about you."

"I wish I could say the same of you," Haddad answered. "Shall I order you tea, Mr . . . ?"

"Swain," the man said. "Adam Swain." He showed Haddad a set of credentials. "I'm with MI6."

Haddad's eyes widened but the man held up a hand to reassure him. "Take it easy, mate. We're on the same side."

It wasn't for that reason Haddad was aghast. He knew that Imam Zuabi had been working with certain people within the British government to help—which is why Haddad had traveled here on a diplomatic visa—but he had no idea how deeply Zuabi's network went.

Did the Hand of Allah truly have MI6 in their control? Or was it the other way around?

"I assume you have everything in order," Swain said. "Your men will all be in place at the proper time?"

"Yes," Haddad said, still trying to recover. "Yes, of course."

"All right," Swain told him. "The big man's speech is scheduled to begin at twenty-one hundred hours and they're usually pretty punctual about these things. Someone on the inside will slip away well before then, and the door to the kingdom will be open and waiting for you."

Haddad considered this and nodded.

"I assume you know your way around those tunnels?" Swain asked.

"I have been through them personally," Haddad said. "There will be no mistakes."

"Good. That's what we like to hear."

We? Haddad thought. Was he speaking of Zuabi or someone else entirely?

Haddad was becoming uneasy.

A waitress came over, asking Swain if he wanted something to eat, but he waved her away. Rather rudely, Haddad thought, as if she were somehow beneath him.

Not a promising sign, and not a good way to stay unnoticed.

"There's just one last thing," he said to Haddad. "A slight change in plans."

Haddad's discomfort grew. "Oh?"

"We're going to need your full commitment on this mission."

"Of course," Haddad said. "As always."

Swain shook his head. "I don't think you understand. Your *full* commitment."

It took Haddad a moment to realize what he was saying. The request was surprising to him, considering what a valuable soldier he had been over the years, but if this was Allah's will, then he would give himself without question.

He did, however, have to wonder.

Why now?

Was it because of what happened in Sofia? Or what he'd done to Abdal al-Fida in London? Had the imam deduced that the fool's death wasn't a suicide and felt he had to punish Haddad for going against orders?

Haddad did not think Zuabi could be so small-minded, but the imam had been showing signs of weakness lately. His willingness to consort with infidel outsiders like Swain was ample proof of this.

But Haddad knew that whatever happened truly

was Allah's will. And if he was to die tonight to help bring about the fall of the infidel, then so be it. He would sacrifice himself a thousand times if he could.

He looked at Swain. "I give whatever Allah requires of me."

"Good," Swain said, then checked his watch. "Now, if you don't mind, I'm in a bit of a hurry. I have a plane to catch. But I've brought a gift for you."

One of Haddad's eyebrows went up. "What sort of gift?"

"You'll find out soon enough."

Getting the message, Haddad pushed his plate aside then dropped some bills on the table and stood.

"Show me," he said.

Swain grinned then got to his feet and gestured for Haddad to follow. A moment later they were outside and walking down the street. They turned together into a narrow alley where a van was parked.

Haddad wondered if he had been too quick to accept this man as an ally, yet he sensed no threat in Swain's demeanor. He did not think this man was capable of subtlety. If he meant you harm, it would be telegraphed.

Moving around to the back of the van, Swain took out a key and unlocked the doors. He gestured for Haddad to open it.

"Another new martyr for the cause," he said. "We want her with you when you pull the trigger."

Haddad studied him quizzically then reached forward and pulled the van doors open.

Inside was a woman, bound and gagged, her large

eyes staring up at them—a woman Haddad recognized immediately.

It was al-Fida's girlfriend.

Sara Ghadah.

37

Legion of Honor, San Francisco

"Invitation, please?"

The woman at the reception dais was young, beautiful, and not the least bit impressed by two old guys in their finest evening attire.

Jack hated tuxedos with a passion, especially the way this one tugged at his still tender shoulder—and Tony didn't seem all that enamored with them either as he dug around in his inner jacket pocket and produced the oversized invitation Danny Pescatori had scored for him. It had taken them nearly twenty minutes to get to the front of the line, which started just outside the Roman triumphal arch entrance to the Legion of Honor and ran all the way down the long stone ramp toward the shimmering blue pool of the circular fountain that fronted the palace. It was dark out, and the ramp was lit on either side by small glowing globes placed low to the ground.

Whenever Jack visited the palace he felt as if he'd stepped into another part of history, back to a grander time, when our nation was still young and buildings like this were symbols of our greatness. A massive, magnificent neoclassical structure, it had been an Armistice Day gift from Alma de Bretteville Spreckels, who wanted to honor California's fallen soldiers of World War I with a world-class museum. If it weren't for the moon-dappled bay beyond, with views of the Marin headlands and the brightly lit Golden Gate Bridge, you might mistake it for one of the many ancient buildings of Rome or Athens.

The woman took the invitation from Tony. "Your names?"

"Anthony Antiniori and Jack Hatfield," he said.

She passed the information along to an assistant who carefully ran a ruler down a reservations list and checked them off.

Now she was all smiles. "Welcome to the Legion of Honor, gentlemen. Enjoy your evening."

Tony doffed an imaginary cap, then the two men moved into yet another line, queuing up for the body scanners just inside the entrance.

Jack knew that the Secret Service would have done a background check when Tony RSVPed, but it would have been a cursory one. Jack was banned from the U.K. but that wouldn't show up on a level-one scan, designed to make sure that domestic felons and watch-list terrorists weren't trying to get in.

Given the many events a President attended, it was the quickest filter available to his security team. The thinking was that no one would have an invitation that the White House did not want here.

A large banner spanning the archway read CELEBRATE THE ART OF ISLAM!, which Jack still thought a bit ironic, considering the circumstances. He didn't think tonight's celebration would be exactly what the museum curator had in mind. Another irony, thought Jack, was the French motto sculpted above the stone entrance, *"Honneur et Patrie."* " 'Honor and Nation,' " sneered Jack, "yeah, right."

The security line, like the line to the dais, was full of San Francisco dignitaries, all dressed as if they were going to the Oscars. The capacity of the museum was fifteen hundred people, and there had to be close to that many tuxedos and black evening gowns in evidence, movers and shakers from all over California, from movie stars to politicians. This was one of the biggest tickets of the year. Of course, the room was also packed with the poseurs, those Pacific Heights inheritance cases whose inheritances had long been diminished or had disappeared entirely. Like most provincials they strutted and displayed their fake jewels most dramatically.

The mayor and his wife stood not three feet away, and Jack was pleased to see that even *he* hadn't been spared the security check. Just beyond the line, Jack saw the new governor talking with his predecessor, both of them laughing over some unheard joke.

The crowd was too dense to know for sure, but

Jack doubted that Senator Harold Wickham or Lawrence Soren or Swain or any of the other men he'd
met on that island were present. He'd have caught a
glimpse of one of them by now. He imagined they
were all far away by now, in transit or already relaxing in their homes, waiting to read about the success
of their treachery in tomorrow's newspapers. That
was further indication that whatever they were planning was still a go. Otherwise, those men would be
here.

Cowards, every single one of them. Leaving the
dirty work to the fanatics they'd snookered into believing it was the will of Allah.

As Tony and Jack waited their turn, a uniformed
officer moved along the security line with a bomb-
sniffing German shepherd on a leash.

Jack checked his watch, a spare Rolex he always
kept in the drawer by his bed. It would never replace
his father's Hamilton, but it was accurate, and that
was good enough for now.

The time was nearing half past eight.

The President wasn't due to make his remarks until nine P.M., and no sign of his motorcade had been
in evidence. As usual, he'd make a last-minute entrance, give his speech, then let the Secret Service
whisk him back to Air Force One for the flight back
to D.C.

Assuming he was still alive.

As they moved to the front of the security line,
Jack and Tony took their keys from their pockets and
deposited them into a tray provided by a uniformed

guard. Tony went through the scanner first and got through clean. But as Jack stepped through the beeper went wild and his heart kicked up a notch. The security guard stopped him, gesturing to the Rolex, and Jack quickly removed it, laying it in the tray. He went through the scanner again and managed not to set off any more alarms. He was glad, then, he was wearing a vest and jacket. His shirt was miserably damp with perspiration.

He moved with Tony to retrieve their belongings.

Hurdle one taken care of.

Just past the security station was the museum's Court of Honor, a large, rectangular courtyard surrounded on all sides by lighted Ionic marble columns. A gigantic bronze cast of Rodin's masterpiece *The Thinker* sat on a high pedestal near the front of the courtyard, and just beyond this, rising up from the floor, was a blue glass pyramidal skylight.

Placed in strategic viewing positions all about the courtyard were roped-off glass display cases, each featuring a work of Islamic art—a thirteenth-century Syrian glass beaker with an ornate design running through it, a piece of carved Egyptian ivory depicting men at war, a Kashan wall tile featuring a fire-breathing dragon, a Mughal dagger with a hilt made of gold, rubies, and emeralds. . . .

People were everywhere, browsing the displays, laughing, talking, drinking white wine and champagne and sampling hors d'oeuvres offered on trays by waiters in crisp white jackets. A string quartet of

lovely young women played a gentle classical tune—
Beethoven, String Quartet No. 1 in F major, Opus
18. He and Tony moved together, working their way
from display to display.

Exchanging glances, they each reached into their
pockets and worked at unscrewing the miniature
flashlights attached to their key chains. These were
really nothing more than hollowed-out tubes. Inside each tube was an earbud transmitter-receiver
that Mike Abernathy had scored through his black
market contacts. They connected wirelessly to plastic
microphones in their ties—the kinds that wouldn't
upset metal detectors—and were activated by a depression switch inside a cuff link. They were military grade and set to a seldom-used frequency that
the Secret Service wasn't likely to detect.

That was the theory anyway.

Each man glanced around for prying eyes, but the
other patrons were too rapt in their own small talk to
pay attention to them. Pretending to scratch his head,
each man nonchalantly popped the device into his
right ear. It was small enough that it sat snugly inside
the ear canal and was nearly invisible to the naked
eye.

When Jack had his in place he activated it and
said softly, "Can you hear me?"

Maxine Cole's voice immediately came alive in his
ear. "I hear you, Jack."

Max and Dave Karras were out in a far corner of
the museum parking lot, sitting in a small Chevy van

they'd rented for the occasion. Karras had brought along a laptop and was busy trying to hack into the museum's network.

"We're also reading you loud and clear," another voice said.

It was Doc Matson, who was exiting a battered Jeep Roadster, along with Mike Abernathy and Jonah Goldman. They were parked in the roadside parking lot of the Cliff House restaurant down the hill, which overlooked the ruins of the Sutro bathhouse.

Doc had paid a visit to one of his urban explorer friends, who drew him a map to the approximate location of the one known entrance to the Lincoln Park bunkers, which was located just beyond the cliffside. Their plan was to scope the area out to try to determine if anyone had made entry.

"Excellent," Jack said. "Tony, are you reading me?"

"I'm standing right next to you, genius."

Jack shot him a frown. "Is your com unit working or not?"

Tony smiled. "Loud and clear, brother."

Jack's heart was thumping like crazy and he was sweating like mad. And while he knew what they were about to attempt might prevent a major catastrophe, he couldn't stop thinking about Sara. Wondering what they had done to her.

Wondering what they *would* do to her if she were still alive.

You've got to stop thinking about her, he told himself. He needed to focus on the task at hand or untold millions would die. Sara would understand that. Hopefully, one day, so would he.

"Okay," he said to Tony. "Let's split up and do our best to blend in. I figure we've got about fifteen, twenty minutes before the show starts. Dave, have you hacked into their security cameras yet?"

"Still working on it."

"Come on, man, the clock is ticking."

"Take it easy, Jack. These custom jobs take a little extra time. I'll let you know as soon as I'm in."

"All right," Jack sighed, then turned to Tony. "Shall we join the party?"

Tony nodded, and they moved to the nearest waiter. Each grabbed a glass of plain soda water, to stay sharp, before heading in opposite directions.

As Jack walked, smiled, mingled, he let his mind work on something else that still bothered him, something he hadn't been able to figure out. Something from the encrypted e-mail.

The reference to "twins."

The men had spent the night in the tunnels, coming in under cover of darkness when the park was deserted and no eyes were watching. They had slept and prayed on coarse mats they kept rolled up in their satchels, and ate crackers and drank bottled water for sustenance.

They were all good soldiers of Allah, ready to give their lives in his honor, but only one of them would be chosen tonight and the hour was almost upon them. Their leader, Hassan Haddad, was one of the Hand of Allah's great soldiers and they were privileged to be serving under his command.

Haddad ordered them to stand at attention in a line against the wall, then slowly moved from man to man, carefully studying the eyes of each as he asked, "Are you ready to give your life for the eternal glory of Allah?"

"Yes," each man replied in turn.

When Haddad made his choice—a slender twenty-year-old named Rashid—he pulled the young man out of line and they all prayed together, asking Allah to watch over his mission and his immortal soul.

Then the others followed as he led Rashid through the tunnel and into the small rectangular room that stood directly beneath the basement of the palace. They took the vest they had prepared during the night and quietly slipped it over Rashid's head and arms and belted it around him.

It held enough explosives to level the museum.

The young man's breathing increased visibly, audibly. Haddad held his cheeks and looked into his eyes and smiled. After a moment, the young man relaxed. Haddad then set the timer and an LED readout rapidly began counting off the seconds. It was set to go off in exactly thirty-five minutes.

Right in the middle of the President's speech.

Haddad gestured toward the rebar ladder that led up through a narrow shaft in the corner of the room. "Your destiny awaits you up there, my son. When

the time is right, Allah will show you the way. Are
you ready?"

"Yes," Rashid said quietly.

Haddad looked at the other men. "And if Rashid
should suffer a failure of strength, or if others should
prevent him from achieving his goal, who among
you will step forward in his place?"

"I will!" the others said in unison.

Haddad smiled. His work here was done.

Bidding them all *assalamu alaikum*, he went back
into the tunnel and disappeared into the darkness.

"Okay, Jack, I'm finally in and I've got visuals," Dave
Karras said. "This place is massive."

No kidding, Jack thought. There was four thousand years' worth of art stored inside the Legion of
Honor and at least twenty-four huge rooms split between two floors dedicated to displaying it. A third
floor below was the archive basement, where works
that weren't currently on display were stored. That
left the subbasement, another elevator stop down.

After parting company, Jack and Tony had circu-
lated through the building, moving room to room,
each looking for a way to get down to the subbasement. But every stairwell that Jack encountered was
being guarded, and the public elevators had been
locked off to restrict travel to only the main two floors.
Tony reported that he'd discovered the same thing.

The good news was the Secret Service seemed to
be concentrating on the main courtyard, where the

President would be making his appearance, leaving the museum security staff to handle the rest. Not that these men and women weren't capable, but Jack felt more comfortable running up against a museum guard than he did a trained Secret Service agent.

That said, the place was still sewn up tight and the clock was counting down. The President would be arriving at any moment.

Jack needed to get down to that subbasement.

He was standing in the main foyer now, looking out toward the courtyard. "Tell me you've got something for me," he said to Karras.

"The main concern of the video network is protection of the artwork," Karras said. "Each exhibit room is equipped with a camera mounted high in the corner with a wide-angle lens. Unfortunately, it looks like nearly every corridor in the place has something on display, and even the stairwells themselves are equipped with video. You try to make a move, they'll be on you like piranha."

"Maybe you should just walk up to one of these guys and tell them there's a bomb in the building," Max suggested.

"You forget," Jack told her, "we don't know who we can and can't trust. And how exactly am I supposed to convince them I'm not just some kind of wack-job?" He paused and said, "What about the basement, Dave? Any cameras in there?"

"Not a one, as far as I can tell. And—hold on. I think I may have a way to get you down there."

"Tell me."

"You have a problem with small spaces?"

"I live on a boat, remember?"

"I'm talking laundry-chute small."

"Spit it out, Dave, or I'll have Maxine smack you around a little."

Karras paused, as if considering the benefits of hesitating, then said, "According to these blueprints, in the far right corner of the building on the terrace level there's a small room near the café with a laundry chute. It's probably where they dump all their soiled linen."

"I can confirm that," Tony piped in. "I saw one of the white coats pushing a cart in there just five minutes ago."

"Right," Karras said. "I've checked all the cameras and there's none in the corridor that leads to that room. It's a complete dead spot. Apparently wine-stained tablecloths aren't a security priority."

"So the laundry chute is our way in," Jack said.

"That's the long and short of it."

Outside in the courtyard the string quartet suddenly stopped playing, then launched into a rousing rendition of "Hail to the Chief," as a caravan of limousines pulled up to the palace entrance. The crowd of gawkers outside grew visibly excited and started migrating toward the cars as Secret Service men gestured them back.

"All right," Jack said, checking his watch. "We don't have much time. Tony, meet me in that corridor in three minutes."

"Will do," Tony acknowledged.

Jack turned to head back toward the rotunda. As he did, a voice sang out behind him.

"Well, well, if it isn't the illustrious Mr. Hatfield."

Jack turned to find Special Agent Carl Forsyth approaching him from the courtyard—the agent who had tried very hard to humiliate him at that FBI press conference several days ago.

Forsyth gestured to the courtyard behind him. "The President's this way, Jack. Aren't you headed in the wrong direction?"

Jack hesitated. "Bathroom break."

Forsyth smiled. "Come on now, hotshot, we both know that isn't true. You know what I think? I think you're here to stir up trouble."

Forsyth's smile faded as two more special agents stepped up behind him, reaching into their jackets.

They didn't look like they were there for the wine.

38

Even with the map it took Doc Matson a while to find the entry point.

Doc's friend had only been able to give them a vague location and a couple of signposts. He'd told Doc that the real expert on the bunker was a woman named Tally Griffin, but she'd been out with a new boyfriend the last couple days and no one had seen or heard from her.

That didn't sound good to Doc. A hunch told him the bad guys had found out about Tally, used her to get in, and didn't want anyone to know.

So Doc did his best, using what little information he had, to lead Abernathy and Goldman down the cliff toward the water, and around an outcropping of rocks. The full moon helped, but finding the precise tree with the precise grouping of stones had not been easy, and Doc cursed the thought that this entire half-baked enterprise might be derailed by a tree that some piss-sniffing dog could find.

Now that he had time to think, he was probably crazy doing this in the first place. They all were. But Doc and Tony Antiniori went back a long way, and if you couldn't count on your friends when your back was against the wall, who *could* you rely on? Besides, it had been a while since Doc had gotten an adrenaline shot like the last twenty-four hours, and a guy his age needed as much excitement as he could find.

They were a ragtag crew, the three of them, no question about it, and Doc kinda felt as if he were a refugee from some Sylvester Stallone movie. Only this was real life, and if they were right about what was going on in those tunnels they wouldn't be facing Hollywood special effects but real, honest-to-God Muslim fanatics, with real, honest-to-God firepower.

But Doc had lived a long, fruitful life and had fought many wars in the defense of his country. If today was the day he finally gave his life for that cause, so be it. His only real family was Tony and these two guys, so he couldn't think of better company to do it in.

After further exploration they found the tree with the three stones in front of it. The largest stone had already been moved, and there, under the beam of Doc's Mini Maglite, was a crevice in the ground that left no doubt that they'd found what they were looking for.

Time to get to it.

They had decided to travel light for easy maneu-

verability, so they each carried only handguns—
Abernathy with his SIG 9 mil, Goldman sporting a
Smith & Wesson .45, and Doc carrying his usual
Beretta 92FS Semi-Auto 9mm.

Doc shimmied in through the crevice first, taking
a short drop into the darkness and landing on a cement floor. He stood there for a moment, listening
for any sounds, but the place was as silent as a tomb.
Flashing his light toward the opening, he waited as
Abernathy and Goldman shimmied through and
dropped, then shone his beam toward the rebar ladder that led down a shaft to their right.

Goldman took the lead this time, hopping onto the
ladder and working his way down, and a moment
later they were all standing in one of the massive cor-
ridors that Doc had called home as a naïve, eager
eighteen-year-old, for the first six months of his military career. Except for a smattering of graffiti the
place hadn't changed much. He could remember the
personnel moving through here as carrier cars moved
along on the overhead rails carrying equipment
barged to the shore. All these years later he still knew
exactly where he was.

"This way," he said to the others.

Using their Mini Maglites sparingly, they worked
their way up the tunnel and turned right, moving
into another tunnel, which opened out into a space
on the left that Doc remembered had once been a
bunkhouse. It was one of several that had been inte-
grated into the place. His own assigned bunk had
been closer to the Golden Gate Bridge side of the

tunnel, which was where he spent most of his duty hours as well.

Doc was about to continue on when he caught a glimpse of something in his flashlight beam. Swinging it back into the bunkhouse again, he froze as dread chilled his spine.

"Holy crap," Abernathy murmured directly behind him.

They moved quickly to a figure lying prone on the cement floor, a blond, life-sized Raggedy Ann, a flannel shirt tossed carelessly over her naked body, looking as if she'd been discarded like a used tissue.

Her face was mottled with bruises. There were black-and-blue marks under her ears.

Doc felt for a pulse and got exactly what he was expecting—nothing. He also had a pretty good idea who this was. He told the others it was probably Tally Griffin, the bunker expert.

This thing was suddenly more real than it had ever been. He activated his ear com and said, "Tony, Jack, do you read me?"

All he got was static.

"Tony?"

More static.

"Damn," he said to the others. "Coms aren't working down here. The walls must be interfering with the frequency."

"Screw it," Abernathy said, his voice tight with anger. "Let's find the bastards who did this."

* * *

Tony Antiniori heard the last strains of "Hail to the Chief" being played as he worked his way down the corridor to the room where he'd seen the white-coated server with the laundry cart disappear earlier.

He'd waited several minutes for Jack. Obviously something was holding him up, and with the music signaling the arrival of the President, Tony didn't have time to wait anymore.

Just as he reached the room he heard voices and several of the white coats came around the corner. He held his hand to his ear, as if he had a cell phone, and pretended to talk into it. The men walked by chattering to one another, eyeing Tony indifferently as they passed. He waited until they were gone, then moved to the door and checked the knob.

Unlocked.

Taking one last glance around he slipped inside, closed the door behind him, and flicked on the light. It was a large square room with several canvas laundry carts inside, and shelves along one wall stacked with napkins, tablecloths, towels, and other linens. On the far wall, behind one of the laundry carts, was the chute Karras had told them about. It was nothing more than a square hole in the wall with plastic flaps in front of it.

He studied it warily and activated his com line. "Hey, Karras, I'm in the linen room. You sure I won't break my neck going down this thing?"

"No guarantees," Karras said. "Hell, my grandpa broke his neck stepping into the bathtub."

"You callin' me 'grandpa'?" The kid didn't know him well enough to be talking to him like this.

"No offense," Karras said, "but those older bones of yours might be fragile."

"Yeah?" Tony fumed. "Remind me to kick your fat behind next time I see you. Then we'll talk about bones."

That shut the kid up, but he thought he heard Max laughing under her breath.

Pushing back the flaps, he checked the chute more closely. The angle wasn't too severe, so he figured the speed of his trajectory would be manageable. Hell, he couldn't count the number of free falls he'd done at twenty-five thousand feet, so this should be a piece of cake—assuming there was something down there to buffer his landing.

Removing his tuxedo jacket and cummerbund, he tossed them into a nearby bin then grabbed the lip of the chute and climbed inside, positioning his legs in front of him.

He said a quiet prayer and let go.

The ride was short but exhilarating, a ten-second rush of adrenaline that ended with Tony flat on his back in an industrial-sized laundry bin that was already half full of dirty linen. Sitting up, he peeked over the top and scanned the area.

Typical commercial building subbasement, from what he could see, all cement, with ducts and pipes and fluorescent light fixtures, a couple of big industrial-sized sinks; quite a contrast to the beauty of the museum above. But this was only one room in a massive floor plan, with doors leading to other rooms, and Tony had no idea which way to go. Fortunately, the place seemed deserted, no white-coated servers or maintenance workers moving about.

Climbing from the bin, Tony grabbed a napkin and walked toward the sink.

"Okay, that was fun. And no broken bones, thank you very much. Where do I go from here?"

"You're actually pretty close," Karras told him. "Depending on how you're positioned, there should be a door to your left, followed by a long corridor that eventually opens out into an old boiler room. You'll find the sealed-off elevator to your right with the auxiliary hatch to the left of it. If anyone's coming up, that's where you'll find them."

"What's going on upstairs in the courtyard?" Tony asked as he ran the napkin under water.

"The Prez is shaking hands and making small talk, but he's making his way inside."

Minutes mattered now.

Seconds.

"Is that running water I hear?" Max asked.

"Yeah. I'm wetting a napkin so I can wring it real tight. Makes a helluva whip if you crack a guy across the eyes with it."

"Sweet," Karras said.

"Yeah, if I don't run across more than a rogue or two. Either of you heard from Jack?"

"Not a peep," Max told him.

"Wonderful."

What the hell is he up to?

Tony wrung out the napkin, twisted it tight, and looped it in his hand, ready to use if necessary. He located the door on his left and made his way to it. He turned the knob, opening it just a crack.

The corridor beyond was dimly lit, the ceiling and one wall lined with huge round plumbing pipes. As Tony moved into it, he wished they had figured some way to smuggle weapons into the place. He'd hate to run into a small army of terrorists while carrying nothing more than a wet napkin.

Quietly closing the door behind him, he worked his way down the corridor, following it as it curved slightly to the left. As he approached the mouth of the corridor, which opened onto the old boiler room, he heard the faint sound of a radio playing. An easy-listening station.

Someone was down here.

Edging to his right, Tony took cover behind a large plumbing duct and peered into the dimly lit room.

What he saw froze his heart.

A uniformed museum guard lay on the floor next to an old cage-style elevator. The doors to the cage were shut and secured with a thick chain and padlock. And just to the left of this was a small hatch in the floor. It had also been secured by a chain and padlock, but they lay discarded next to it and the hatch was hanging open.

This was not good.

Scanning the room and seeing no sign of a threat, Tony stepped from behind the duct and quickly moved to the guard. Crouching down, he grabbed the young man's wrist and felt a faint throbbing.

Still alive.

Activating his com line, Tony said, "Jack, if you're out there, we have a serious—"

Before he could finish, something solid hit him across the back of the head and he spiraled into darkness.

"We were warned you might show up here," Forsyth said.

They had taken Jack through a hallway just off the museum foyer and sat him in a small square room with stiff-backed chairs and an interview table. One wall had a large window that looked into a room full of security monitors, two uniformed guards manning them. The two special agents hovered nearby, eyeballing Jack as Forsyth took a seat across the table from him.

"Warned by who?" Jack asked, although he had a pretty good idea.

"It was one of those trickle-down situations," Forsyth said. "When I heard your name, I got very interested.

"We saw you arrive, watched you work your way from room to room, but the funny thing is, you seem more interested in casing the place than admiring any of the artwork."

Jack didn't explain. Not yet. "What's the FBI doing here?" he asked.

"Everyone's a little touchy after what happened

downtown, Jack. You understand. And since the President refused to cancel this trip, the Secret Service asked us to lend a hand. So here we are." He paused. "But the real question is, why are *you* here?"

Jack studied him carefully. He hadn't liked Forsyth from the minute he met him at the bomb site nearly two weeks ago. He was an arrogant SOB, and after that press conference Jack knew the guy had participated in a cover-up. The question was, how deep did his involvement go?

Jack glanced at one of the security monitors and saw the President shaking hands with guests in the courtyard.

Time was running out.

"Nothing to tell me?" Forsyth asked.

"Not yet," Jack said. He was still trying to decide if he could trust this man and, if so, what he should tell him. Tony and the others were still out there and he didn't want to compromise what they were doing.

Forsyth shook his head. "I keep racking my brain, trying to figure you out. Considering your affection for Muslims, it makes some kind of crazy sense that you're here to disrupt the evening's proceedings. But I can't imagine exactly what you were hoping to accomplish."

"What do you think?"

"I honestly don't know, Jack."

Jack had been studying him closely. The man truly did seem confused. Jack decided to test him.

"You know why I'm here," he said. "You know what's going on. Hell, you're *part* of it."

inside as he

None of the three men sp
working together telepathic
quick weapons check in the
Tension crept into Doc's
couple neck rolls to try to
voices, the three of them we
had was surprise.

They'd have to do this kamikaze style and hope for the best.

Bracing himself, he turned slightly and whispered, "On three," then quietly counted off.

They made the turn into the room running, not waiting for a reaction before they opened fire.

The room erupted in shouts and cries. There were at least seven of the bastards, all young and very, very quick as they jumped for cover and came up again with weapons in hand, the room exploding in gunfire.

Doc hammered one between the eyes and he flew back against the wall, dead before he hit it. But then one of his buddies swung toward him with an automatic rifle and opened fire.

Doc dropped and rolled back toward the bend in the tunnel to regroup. He felt pain sting his right calf and then another shot hit his arm and his Beretta went spinning.

The shouts and ugly flashes of gunfire continued.

steady and deafenin
nathy and Goldr
of complete

The o
A qui
Se

Forsyth fro
am I a part o

"You're

others—"

The frow

Jack had one

"And you've got Sar

Now the frown turned in credulity. "Sara? Who the hell is S like a crazy man, Hatfield. *Are* you been your problem from the get-go?"

Jack was beginning to think that maybe Forsy was clean. Back at the press conference, he seemed to know—or at least, not *want* to know—that they were scapegoating the Constitutional Defense Brigade. He had to play along with that one, let the justice system work its magic.

But killing a President?

Jack glanced at the security monitors and saw that the President was moving toward a podium on a small stage as the guests applauded enthusiastically.

Returning his gaze to Forsyth, Jack studied him carefully, studied his eyes, then decided to take a leap of faith.

"All right," Jack said, "listen to me very carefully. The President and everyone in this place is in danger."

Forsyth's expression went cold as he leaned forward in his chair. "Meaning what, exactly?"

"A group called the Hand of Allah is smugglin a bomb into the building. It may already be h

...g. He had no idea where Aber-
...an were, but after several seconds
...haos, the tunnel suddenly went silent.
...ly sounds were muffled, ragged breaths.
...t moan.
...oc hugged the darkness, dread washing through
...m as he heard the Arab voices pick up again, sound-
...as stunned as he felt.

At least three of them were left.

Mustering his strength, he crawled back toward the room, peering into it from the darkness. He saw Goldman crumpled in a corner and Abernathy on his back, blood seeping from a wound in his neck.

He would mourn his brave friends later. There was still a mission to complete.

The three remaining Arabs hurriedly checked the others. They obviously hadn't seen how many men rushed them, didn't look to see if there were any more. They were young and inexperienced, but Doc guessed they were also on a timetable. This firefight had set them behind.

They chattered shakily as they quickly slipped into white coats—servant's coats. One of them was strapped with enough C4 to take out a city block. There was blood on his chest, just below the right shoulder, but Doc couldn't tell if he'd been hit or if it was someone else's. The little rat didn't seem to be affected by it. He was a slender man—a boy really— and when he buttoned the coat over the vest only a seasoned eye would know there was anything off about it.

...nning to set it ...
...peech."

...ith all the security."

...ity's been compromised. You ...
...m for that."

...ck as he considered what Jack had

... the agent said thoughtfully, "I was ...about you. You *are* crazy."

oc, Goldman, and Abernathy worked their way rough the dark tunnel with quiet deliberation, staying low to the ground, using their flashlight beams sparingly.

Doc continued on point and allowed his memory to guide them. It had killed him to leave that woman lying naked in the bunk room, but there was no helping her now. He had vowed to her that he would return, and he would. Right now, they had other business to take care of.

Moving close to the wall, Doc remembered a right turn up ahead. He flashed his Mini Maglite, indicating the turn, then led the team around the corner.

The floor began to slant upward, getting steeper with every step. As they crested the rise, they saw faint light spilling out from another bunk room up ahead, voices echoing faintly—

—Arab voices.

Doc motioned the others to stop, then listened arefully. No question about it.

The three men moved together to a narrow shaft in the corner of the room, glancing briefly at the carnage behind and using fingers to try and unclog their firefight-clouded ears before climbing the rebar ladder and disappearing into the darkness above.

Doc pulled himself upright, wincing against the pain in his arm and calf. He didn't have time to check on his friends, to see if they were dead or alive. Not now. Retrieving Abernathy's SIG 9 mil and his own Beretta, he tried activating his com unit again. All he got was static.

He didn't know how he'd manage it, but he knew he had to get up that ladder and send out a warning call before it was too late.

Jack glanced at the security monitors and saw that the President was being introduced by the museum curator.

"Look," he said, his desperation growing, "I'm telling you the truth. If we don't act now, we're gonna have one helluva disaster on our hands. Not that any of us will be alive to see it."

But Forsyth wasn't buying it.

"That's a nice story, Jack, but you want to tell me how anyone could get a bomb into this place? We're isolated. This museum has been sniffed fifty ways to Sunday. You'd be lucky to get nail clippers past that security—"

"Through the tunnels," Jack told him.

Forsyth studied him a moment and sighed. "The

tunnels? You're talking about the old Second World War bunkers?"

"They lead straight to the basement."

"We're aware of that. That's why we put a security man down there. But those things were locked down years ago, and even if someone managed to get inside, there's no possible way—"

Jack's earpiece suddenly came alive. "Jack? Max? Does anyone read me?"

It was Doc Matson.

Jack immediately responded. "Here, Doc. What's going on?"

Forsyth and his two companions all jerked back. They gave Jack a quizzical look.

"The hatch is open and Tony's down," Doc said. "They got through, three of them in white coats. All Arab. They're posing as servants and one of them is strapped to explode."

Jack felt the bottom drop from his stomach. "Is Tony alive?"

"Yeah, he's coming around."

Forsyth frowned. "Hatfield?"

"Doc, get him into that tunnel and get the hell away from here," Jack said. "Max, Karras? You two get out of here as—"

"Who the hell are you talking to?" Forsyth demanded.

One of the other agents saw the small device in Jack's ear. He pointed it out to Forsyth.

"Are you completely out of your mind?" Forsyth demanded.

Jack got to his feet. "I told you, we don't have time to argue about this! The bombers are *here*. They're posing as—"

"Sit *down,* goddamn it! This interview isn't over until I say it's—"

"We don't have time!" Jack shouted, then suddenly swung his arm straight out. He clotheslined one of the special agents as he ran forward, then flipped the other as he tried to grab Jack from behind. The agent went over his wounded shoulder, but that only pissed Jack off. He was out the door and running before Forsyth could reach his shoulder holster, headed through the foyer toward the courtyard. He came to a stop at the museum entrance and stared out at the crowd.

The place was packed. The glitterati had gathered around the podium and were still applauding as the President put his hands up to silence them. Jack scanned the courtyard desperately, looking for white jackets, but they seemed to be everywhere and there was no way of knowing who might be their guy.

Would it be Hassan Haddad?

As the applause died down, the President said, "I want to thank you all for coming here tonight to this important event. A gathering of people of all political persuasions, who have joined to celebrate the art of a religion and culture that has given the world so much, yet has come under great scrutiny these last several years, much of it negative."

"Given the world so much," Jack thought bitterly as he heard footsteps pounding behind him. He didn't

have to look back to know it was Forsyth and his
men racing down the hall. They would have radioed
other agents, the Secret Service. Operatives would be
peeling off, converging on this spot. He stepped into
the courtyard and started threading his way through
the crowd, searching it desperately, looking for Arab
faces to match the white jackets.

Looking for a man with a wispy goatee.

"Hatred takes many forms," the President continued, "and much of that hatred stems from our lack of
knowledge about those we hate. We form ideas about
others based on stereotypes, and those stereotypes,
while sometimes grounded in a sliver of reality, do
not tell us about the whole person. The whole culture."

As he continued to search, Jack noted movement
around him, agents with earpieces wending toward
him from all sides. He ignored them, shifting his gaze
from white jacket to white jacket.

"So tonight, thanks to the work of the California
Palace of the Legion of Honor, we have a chance to
see a side of the Islamic culture that we don't often
see. A glimpse into the artistry and passion that helps
to define a people."

Then Jack saw it. Not a face. Not the sign he expected, but there it was—a red stain spreading across
the shoulder of one of those white jackets, and he
sure as hell didn't think the guy had cut himself in
the kitchen.

Not in the chest he hadn't.

Jack shot forward, shoving people aside, moving

toward that red-stained jacket as it weaved in and out of the crowd, getting closer to the podium. Jack suddenly felt hands grabbing him, roughly pulling him aside—Forsyth and his two men, with two Secret Service agents getting into the act.

"Not *me, him*!" Jack told them, trying to point toward the jacket with the red stain.

A ripple went through the crowd, caused by the commotion in their midst. Several Secret Service agents assigned directly to the President sensed something wrong and started toward the podium, first at a fast walk and then at a trot.

Just ten yards from the podium, the man with the red-stained jacket realized this was as far as he'd get. He stopped and shouted, *"Allah Akbar!"* as he ripped open his jacket, spinning around to show the crowd a vest full of C4 with an LED timer attached—

—the timer ticking down from ten seconds.

Jack stared. It wasn't Hassan Haddad at all. It was a twentysomething-year-old kid.

"Allah Akbar!" the man cried again, his face turned toward the heavens, as the entire place descended into pandemonium.

Jack struggled with the men who had grabbed him, their grip loosening as they began to see that he wasn't the problem. Wrenching free, Jack jumped toward the Arab as the President was rushed from the venue and guests screamed in terror as they scrambled for the exit.

Jack was fighting against a human tide as he watched the timer tick down—

—eight, seven, six, five, four—

A shot cracked, tearing a bloody hole in the side of the bomber's head. Brain splattered on the guests as the force of the impact spun him around.

—three, two, one—

The kid dropped to the floor, lost in the panicked mob, and Jack knew it was too late, knew that nothing could be done to stop it as—

—nothing happened.

39

Everything seemed to be moving in slow motion.

Jack felt his heart thumping in his ears, as the crowd continued to rush for the doors, most of them unaware of what had just transpired. Jack himself wasn't quite sure as he joined Forsyth and his men and a handful of Secret Service agents as they pushed through the thinning crowd to the bomber.

Sirens blew in the distance and Jack knew that half the city's law enforcement and emergency services were already speeding in their direction.

One of the agents shouted, "Stay back! This thing could still blow."

The agent crouched over the dead man. He ran his fingers over the C4-laden vest with the confidence of a man who knew exactly what he was doing. Then an odd, almost comically quizzical look crossed his face.

"What the hell?" he said, then looked up at the others. "This thing is a fake. It's a goddamn fake."

Forsyth pushed toward him, Jack right behind him.

"What are you talking about?" Forsyth asked.

"These detonators aren't even wired. This thing was never meant to go off."

"Are you sure?" Jack asked.

"Positive," he said.

They all looked at one another, trying to comprehend this new information, when suddenly, without warning, the LED counter beeped loudly and the words *PRAISE ALLAH* scrolled across it in bright red letters.

They all fell back, waited for *something,* then looked at one another in complete surprise.

"What *is* this, Hatfield?" Forsyth demanded. "Some kind of sick goddamn joke?"

"What are you talking about? This isn't *me*. I didn't have anything to do with it!"

Jack was still trying to process the moment because it made absolutely no sense. No sense at all.

"*You* were the one screaming about a bomb, and now we've got a dead man wearing a goddamn joke. The way I see it, this is all on you."

Jack's head was spinning. The emergency sirens were drawing closer, their shrill whine swirling through his brain like an invading army.

"Don't be an idiot," Jack said. "Do you think I'd set a man up to be killed to make a *joke*?"

Forsyth didn't answer. His boss was on the radio

and the agent was trying to talk to him as the Secret Service moved in to take charge of the dead man.

Jack backed away slowly, sinking in confusion. Why would Soren and Zuabi and Swain and Hassan Haddad go to all this trouble, all this planning, just to have it end like this? Jack thought about everything he'd been through, the threats, the torture, the deaths—Copeland in that Dumpster, al-Fida dead in that bathtub, Sara being dragged away by an MI6 thug—all because of some sick joke whose symbolism escaped him?

No.

Soren and his extremist friends wouldn't have avoided the bash if they knew how this was going to play out. Besides, the way they were talking they were after something else, a major statement. One that would chill the world, send it scurrying in terror, so that they could seize power from men whom they considered weak and rule by fear and intimidation. No matter how you parsed it, what had happened here simply made no sense.

Unless—

The sirens continued to wail as a tidal wave of thoughts rolled through Jack's mind, things remembered from the last few days—

Al-Fida's promise to Sara: *"The infidels will soon see destruction that will make 9/11 seem like child's play—"*

Copeland babbling on the phone: *"Gotta get out of here . . . Gotta look after the twins. . . ."*

The word *twins* in one of those e-mails. Still bothering him, its meaning still undeciphered.

Lawrence Soren smugly telling Jack about regime change and puppets and power.

Why? Soren didn't care about this President. He had no need to assassinate the man. One resident of the White House was the same as the next as far as he was concerned, merely there to be controlled and manipulated by whoever managed to grab power.

And then Jack remembered the papers Copeland had left in that package on his boat. The Department of Defense papers that spoke of a clandestine transport of a tanker full of experimental solid rocket fuel.

Operation Roadshow?

As the sirens continued to grow closer, it suddenly struck Jack that this wasn't just some sick joke. It was far, far more than that.

Forsyth had finished with his call, the room had pretty much emptied, and a fresh set of suits grabbed hold of him.

"Listen to me, Forsyth," Jack said as they tried to walk him out. "You've *got* to listen to me carefully."

"We've heard enough from you. Get him out—"

"*Think,* goddamn it. If I had anything to do with this, why would I have warned you there was a bomb in the building?"

"How the hell should I know? You miss the attention? You're out of your friggin' mind."

"No," Jack said. "No. This is just a footnote to what's really going on."

"Get him out of my sight."

Forsyth's men started to drag him away but Jack struggled against them. "You hear those sirens?" he said. "That's half the city's emergency personnel headed in our direction because they think the President's in danger. But don't you get it? This is a goddamn decoy."

"For what?" Forsyth called after him.

"I've spent the last week trying to track these people down—been to Europe and back trying to figure out what the hell they're up to. This all goes back to the bombing downtown. Agent Forsyth, do you *seriously* think that was the work of a bunch of disgruntled yahoos?"

Jack saw a shift in Forsyth's eyes. The same shift he'd seen when he'd confronted him at that press conference. Forsyth *knew* that was all a cover story. He *knew* the whole setup wasn't kosher.

"Come on," Jack said. "If you know anything about me at all, you know I'm a goddamn patriot. I'd never do anything to harm this country. I'm telling you the *truth*."

Forsyth mulled that over for a moment and Jack thought he saw another subtle shift in his expression. He gestured for the men to release Jack. They stepped away but stayed close.

"Okay, let's pretend for a minute I believe you," Forsyth said. "What do you think the real target is?"

"I figure they're looking to make a major statement here. I think they're going after San Francisco's twin towers."

"What?"

"I've been too damn busy following the trail they laid out, thinking they'd converge. But they *don't*. This was designed to keep us distracted."

"A decoy?"

"Yeah. There's a top soldier for the Hand of Allah named Hassan Haddad who's been running point on this whole operation. Smart son of a bitch. I'm guessing he was also in those tunnels tonight, and if you follow them to their farthest point, where do you think they lead?"

Forsyth thought about this for a long moment. And all at once he seemed to get it.

"Christ," he said. "The twin towers. The Golden Gate Bridge."

They took off in a caravan, Jack riding shotgun with Forsyth, his two agents in back—the ones Jack had hurt, and who didn't look like they forgave him. A police cruiser and a Secret Service car followed, their sirens screaming. Forsyth was on the radio shouting for support—fire department, bomb squad, SFPD, sky patrol—as he wound along Lincoln Boulevard, crossing the double yellow line to bypass cars, moving at speeds that sometimes threatened to send them off the road, down the steep cliff to the dark waters below. They raced through the old Presidio army base, past Pershing and Stillwell roads. Named for military commanders who knew how to defeat the enemy, not placate the media and foreign lobbyists.

"If you're wrong, Hatfield, I've just kissed my career good-bye."

"I've never been more sure of anything in my life," Jack told him. "Isn't this what we both signed on for? Uncovering truth and upholding liberty?"

Forsyth clearly wasn't comfortable being in the same vehicle as Jack, let alone in the same philosophical arena. But he didn't argue the point.

A trip that would normally take ten minutes was cut down to five, and soon they were looping under the roadway and then around onto the bridge itself, more police cruisers joining in behind them.

The Golden Gate Bridge is one of the longest suspension bridges in the world, boasting two five-hundred-foot-high suspension towers, the first of which—the south tower—now loomed in front of them, its orange-red majesty lit up against the night sky.

Behind them the cruisers began to slow, moving in a serpentine formation to keep more civilian cars from rolling onto the bridge. Then Forsyth cut his siren and brought the SUV to a halt, the other vehicles in the caravan pulling up next to them. They all jumped out, Forsyth pointing a pair of Bushnell Night Vision field glasses toward the top beam of the south tower, which spanned the width of the bridge. He squinted against the magnified brilliance of the lights on top of the bridge.

"Holy shit," he said. "There are two people up there and one of them is a woman."

"What?" Jack reached for the field glasses.

Forsyth handed them over. His heart slamming hard, Jack aimed them toward the top beam.

It was Sara.

He was torn with emotion. She was up there and she was alive, standing 746 feet above the bay, against the protective railing. Hassan Haddad was holding her by the bare upper arms. They were both standing spread-eagled against the wind gusts, their position precarious at best.

Jack knew that this was Swain's last little "up yours," and it had nothing to do with holding Sara hostage or waiting for Jack to arrive before hurling her to her death. In fact, Jack no longer had any doubts about the game plan. He was convinced that what he saw strapped to Sara's back was the device Haddad had procured from Chilikov in Bulgaria.

It was a backpack nuke.

40

It was quite possibly the most beautiful sight Haddad had ever seen.

The only sound he could hear was the wind, and he felt as if he were only a step away from *Janna*—from Paradise—where he would soon have a home. Where he would feel no pain, suffer no sickness, experience no sadness. Where Allah would look after him and he would find true peace in his arms.

The peace he couldn't find in this life.

Here he stood at the very top of the infidel world, on a narrow catwalk, pressed against the rail, looking down at the bowing suspension cables of the bridge, following their lines all the way down through the darkness to the road where the cars looked no bigger than beetles, moving silently between the white dotted lines.

He saw the ineffectual police cars with their flashing lights, but they were far too late to stop him now.

The wind was strong but he did not feel cold. Allah was insulating him from its sting. And in a few moments he would feel nothing but the embrace of death followed by his feet on the pathway to the Garden.

The woman was trembling, however. As he gripped her arm, her flesh felt icy.

She was disavowing the inevitable. She could not accept the fact that she was about to die.

When he had first seen her in the back of Swain's van, her hands tied, her mouth gagged, he was surprised. He had long suspected that she was exploiting al-Fida, but he had not known the depth of her betrayal to her faith and to her people. He had not known that she was in league with the Turk and the Gypsy whore, and many others who fought to destroy the Hand of Allah.

Swain had told him many things about this woman, and Haddad at first felt anger. He wanted to use his hands on her as he had on the whorish blonde when she was no longer of any use to him.

But soon his anger gave way to pity. Pity that one of their own had lost her way, had forsaken her faith in Allah and his word.

So he had agreed to do as Swain had asked. To martyr her in the Lord's name, just as he was about to martyr himself.

"You don't have to do this," she said suddenly.

She was yelling so he could hear her above the sound of the wind.

He tore his gaze from the view and looked at her. He remembered thinking that she was beautiful, but the ugliness in her soul clouded that beauty now.

"I do as Allah commands," he said.

"Allah would *never* command such a thing. You are about to take the lives of innocent people. Women. Children. Countless Muslims."

"These people are not innocent. They live their lives in ignorance of their god. They elect leaders who kill our Muslim brothers and sisters."

"And how are they any different from the men who control you?"

He scowled at her. "I answer only to Allah."

"And Imam Zuabi."

"Zuabi is a great leader. The Lord sometimes speaks through him. He has counseled me since I was a child."

"And what about Swain? Does the Lord speak through him as well? He and the people he works for are no different than those you wish to—"

"Be silent!" Haddad snapped.

Haddad no longer wished to listen to this woman. She had been subverted by Western ways and she was trying to trick him, to keep him from doing what he had come to do here at the top of the world.

He turned from her, returning his gaze to the road below, using a pair of field glasses to look toward the north side of the bridge now, waiting for his signal that the time was near. That the moment was upon them.

And then he saw it, little more than a crawling bug in the distance.

The tanker truck was rolling onto the bridge.

Jack's gut was on fire.

He needed to get to Sara. If they were all going to die, he wanted to die *with* her.

Emergency personnel were swarming onto the bridge behind them—a lot of sound and fury but not much else at this point. What *could* they do?

Jack turned to Forsyth. "We've gotta get up there."

"And do what? We go rushing up there, he'll pull the trigger and you can kiss this bridge and everything on it good-bye."

"He's gonna pull that trigger anyway," Jack told him. "And if that tanker truck I told you about is anywhere in the vicinity, it'll be a lot more than this bridge that goes up. If it ignites, the smoke and ash will carry lethal doses of radiation across Northern California."

"The bridge authority is moving to close it down as we speak. As soon as the southbound traffic has cleared, it'll be deserted."

"Great. That's a terrific plan. We've still got a madman up there with a nuke."

"We don't *know* that it's a PTND," Forsyth said.

Jack shook his head ruefully. A Portable Tactical Nuclear Device. The FBI made everything seem so sterile—manageable because it had a classification.

"Look, I'm sorry about before," Forsyth said, "and I understand you're upset about the girl. But we've got to wait for the negotiating team. If we can try to reason with the guy—"

"*Reason* with him!" Jack shouted. "Do you know who this man is? The only way to reason with him is to put a bullet in his head."

"If it comes to that we will. We've got a chopper headed this way with a sniper on board."

They're doing it by the book, Jack thought. *That's all these people know—and one day it would be their downfall.*

Probably today, in fact.

But Jack wasn't part of their team and he'd make his own rules, as he'd done since this damn thing started.

What was it the Reb always said about Israeli negotiating tactics? *"Every Jew a twenty-two—"*

Jack gestured to Forsyth. "Give me your gun."

"What?"

Jack moved toward him. *"Give me your damn gun!"*

"Back off, Hatfield, that's not gonna—"

Jack lunged, thrusting his hand inside Forsyth's jacket and ripping the Glock from his holster. Forsyth grabbed him but Jack wrenched free with a furious tug and ran, heading across three lanes of highway toward the pedestrian walkway.

"Stop him!" Forsyth shouted as he took off after him, several of the others joining in the chase.

"Shoot?" someone called back.

"Negative!" Forsyth said with something that sounded like regret. "Just freakin' *stop* him!" He started running, joined by four other agents.

Jack leaped over the rail and hit the sidewalk, running for all he was worth, heading for the right flank of the tower. He heard shouts behind him but ignored them as he covered the last several yards to the base of the spire. Few people knew that there was a door built into the design, but Jack was one of those few and he reached for the handle, finding it locked.

His pursuers were closing in fast.

Stepping back, he raised the Glock and fired, shattering the latch and nearly clipping himself with the ricochet. He wrenched the door open and went inside.

The interior of the tower reminded Jack of an old World War II submarine. A short, narrow corridor led to a small, rickety elevator with steel-mesh sides, looking like something you'd find in a mine shaft.

Voices and footsteps were closing in from behind. Jack quickly shut himself inside the elevator as Forsyth reached the doorway. Jack looked back, saw a face full of desperation and fury.

"Hatfield! You're gonna *blow* this!"

Maybe—but he hadn't so far.

He jammed the elevator into motion and the car began to rise, rattling its way toward the top of the tower.

No, Jack and his team had carried the ball farther than he could have hoped, could ever have imagined. God—his God, a just God—wouldn't let him fail. Not now.

Jack refused to think about it. All he *could* think about was getting to Sara.

The elevator came to a stop at the lower part of the tower beam. Jack threw the door open and stepped into a small vestibule, then over to a worn steel ladder that led up through a narrow hatch.

Tucking the Glock in his waistband, he grabbed hold of a rung and started up, not quite sure what he'd do once he reached the top. He had no plan here. Was running purely on blind instinct, but if he didn't do *something,* he knew that this bridge—and Sara—were doomed.

He stopped as he reached the hatch door. Sucking in a breath, he pushed a hand against it and lifted it only a crack, peering out at the catwalk that stretched across the bridge.

It was several feet long and slightly over three feet wide, guarded by a rail on either side. Sara and Haddad stood at the far end, against a rail, Sara's hands bound in front of her. Haddad had her by the arm and was looking down toward the road with a pair of field glasses, probably waiting for the tanker to arrive. And if it was already on the bridge, Jack knew he had only minutes to spare before Haddad set off the bomb that was strapped to Sara's back.

Except for the wind, it was so quiet up here it felt surreal.

Jack knew he might be able to use the Glock and take Haddad down from this distance but decided against it. He was no sharpshooter, like the guy who took the kid down near the podium. Besides, the bastard had Sara as a shield. And if he happened to hit the backpack, God knows what would happen to the bomb.

He couldn't take those risks, any of them.

He had to assume that Haddad's mind would be in a thousand different places right now, concentrating on the tanker, thinking about his fate. So Jack made a choice. The tower was lit but, hoping there was enough darkness for cover, he carefully raised the hatch door and pulled himself through.

He tried not to look at the view below, at the moonlit waters of the bay, the lights of the city—they were a haunting, dizzying distraction. Instead, he took the Glock from his waistband and concentrated on his target, slowly inching down a short set of stairs. He stepped onto the catwalk and moved toward Haddad and Sara.

Haddad was looking toward the north, through his field glasses, and it was Sara who saw him first. Her eyes widened slightly as she realized who it was. She seemed to be warning him off with her gaze but he shook his head once, slowly, and kept creeping forward, trying to close the gap between them.

Then suddenly Haddad lowered the binoculars and turned, following Sara's gaze and looking at Jack without surprise.

"Please stop where you are," he said with the calmness of a man who had accepted his fate. Dropping the field glasses against his chest, he reached into his pocket and held up a small cell phone, his thumb hovering over the keypad.

A remote detonator.

"Another step and I'll hit speed dial. I'm sure you can imagine what will happen then."

Eerily, the winds died just then. Jack stopped where he was and looked past Haddad.

"Are you all right, Sara?"

"My hands are tied and I have a nuke strapped to my back. Other than that—"

"I should never have left you on that island," he said mournfully.

Smart girl, letting him know she was tied up. The way she was standing, he couldn't be sure.

Haddad frowned, studying Jack carefully. "You must be the man Swain told me about. The Jew. It's very resourceful of you to show up here. I was expecting the FBI."

"They're waiting on the negotiators. They have this crazy idea that they can reason with you."

Haddad smiled, gesturing to the Glock. "I see you don't share that belief."

"Not for a minute," Jack said.

"Still, I'd advise you to put the weapon down or I'll be forced to make my call prematurely."

"Or I could just shoot you."

Haddad's smile widened. "You'd have to be a very precise shot to keep me from pressing this key."

"Worth a try," Jack said, starting to raise it.

Haddad's smile vanished and he raised his arm menacingly.

"Moments are like a lifetime as death nears. You still have a little time to spend with each other as long as you put the weapon down and kick it to me."

Jack hesitated, looked at that long, cruel thumb poised over the keypad, then slowly crouched. He laid the Glock on the catwalk floor and kicked it toward Haddad.

"Thank you," Haddad said.

At least he was a polite lunatic.

Jack shot a glance at Sara and noticed at once that she had her game face on. She obviously had a plan of some kind, something that had occurred to her while he and Haddad were talking.

That meant, keep Haddad talking.

"So what's the plan?" Jack asked. "You do realize they're closing the bridge. So if you're waiting on that tanker—"

"It's already here, and right on schedule," Haddad said. "They won't turn any cars *back*. They'll have to wait until they've cleared the bridge before they can seal it off."

"Oh?" Jack said, looking over the rail toward the road below. "Because it looks to me like they're already escorting the tanker back the way it came."

Haddad frowned and swiveled his head, looking at the road. It took him a moment to realize his mistake, but by then it was too late. Sara made her move, swinging her bound hands at his face, knocking him sideways.

He fumbled the cell phone and it landed at his feet. But Jack was already in motion, leaping across the catwalk, grabbing for it. He felt it brush his fingers as his momentum knocked it spinning toward the rail.

Haddad lunged for it, but Sara threw her hands over his head and, with a grunt, yanked him toward her using her bonds as a garrote. His expression ferocious, Haddad snapped his head back, butting her face. Sara stumbled back, dazed, and he slipped from her grasp. He reached for the cell phone again but Jack was on his feet. He kicked it, sent it spinning to the opposite side of the catwalk. Haddad raced forward as it clattered against the steps.

Roaring, Haddad set out after it. Jack looked frantically for the Glock, couldn't see it in the dark, and lunged after Haddad. He hit shoulder first. Jack had forgotten about his wound; the impact was a forceful reminder as his nerve endings exploded, sending pain down his arm and torso.

Jack couldn't let that stop him. He dug in and continued to press the man forward, slamming Haddad into the rail. But Haddad was not an amateur. He turned as he went back, facing Jack, and brought a knee into his groin. Jack stumbled backward toward the opposite rail. The tower was slick with mist and he lost his footing. Sara screamed as Jack fell against the rail, hitting his head. Her cry kept him from losing consciousness.

Sara needed him.

But his body had had enough. It didn't want to move.

Now Haddad was on his feet and moving toward

him with feral eyes. Before he could reach Jack, Sara blindsided him, shoving him to the floor. The backpack and her bonds made it difficult for her to move and Haddad threw her off effortlessly. Then he was on his feet again, kicking her mercilessly in the head and stomach.

"Jack . . ."

Sara needs me.

Marshaling every scrap of his strength, Jack used the rail to pull himself up and he ran at Haddad.

Blinded by fury, by pain, Jack hit the man like a linebacker. They both went down. Climbing to his knees, Jack punched down, blow after blow, driving the man's head against the metal of the bridge. Haddad's hands came up defensively but Jack yelled and swatted them aside, continuing to slam his fists at that evil face, fueled by hatred for everything the man had done, everything he stood for. Ignoring the pain in his shoulder, Jack thought only about Sara and Copeland and Drabinsky and Jamal, thought about the havoc people like this brought to the world, used his fists to turn thought into action.

And then Haddad stopped struggling, his breath coming in bloody gurgles, his face raw and torn. But if he somehow expected Jack to be merciful, he'd picked the wrong night. Without a second thought, Jack grabbed hold of the man's shirt and dragged him back against the rail, flopped him against it, stared at the pulped flesh and bloody wisp of a beard.

"Enjoy the virgins, asshole."

Jack slammed his open hands hard against Haddad's chest, the terrorist's battered eyelids going wide with horror as he sailed over the side of the tower to the pavement five hundred feet below, his terrified screams rising into the night sky.

The fall took just three seconds. It ended with ugly abruptness.

A moment later, the wind kicked up again.

Once more, the city could breathe.

Jack staggered, dropping to one knee, and grabbed the rail for support. He heard Sara moan, and crawled over to her. Using what little energy he had left, he ripped the bonds from her wrists and unstrapped the backpack, laid it aside. He noted the location of the cell phone.

He'd get it later. Or someone would.

Right now, all he wanted to do was pull Sara into his arms and hold her as if he'd never let her go.

41

In the months that followed, the world did not miraculously change.

The good guys had won, but that didn't necessarily mean the bad guys would be punished. Not in the way that Jack would have liked, with handcuffs and trials and lifetime-without-parole.

Instead, the rich and powerful managed to prevail, as they often do.

Despite Jack's statements to the FBI and Homeland Security and the twenty other law enforcement agencies that seemed to be involved in the investigation, there was no hard proof to put Lawrence Soren and his cronies behind bars. And no real proof that MI6 or the British Home Office had ever been involved.

The island in the bay had been scrubbed, sanitized. The boats the men had used were MIA. Abdal al-Fida was a suicide, Bob Copeland was listed as an "accidental death," and Jamal Thomas was an OD. There were no e-mails, no enhanced photos, there was nothing even remotely incriminating on the computers of Dave Karras or Faisal al-Jubeir. Someone had gotten to the machines and washed them, too. Bribes had been paid to the right officials.

There was only the word of Jack and Sara.

And that, unfortunately, was not enough.

The only good news was that the San Francisco District Attorney dropped the charges against the Constitutional Defense Brigade, citing "lack of evidence." In time—enough time for the FBI to save face—the car bomb was added to the charges against the small band of Muslim extremists, led by Hassan Haddad, who had tried and failed to blow up the Golden Gate Bridge.

There was no mention of the tanker and the hydrazine-based rocket fuel that would have been used as an accelerant. Jack hadn't told Forsyth the worst of it. The destruction of the bridge was a visual symbol to show the world, to encourage other terrorists to strike. On the ground, though—that was where the real disaster would have occurred. He and Tony had done some rough calculations: given the speed and direction of the wind, the heat from that fire would have risen high enough to blanket all of the San Francisco and Oakland regions with lethal levels of radiation from the exploded nuke. There would have been thousands of deaths within days, tens of thousands within weeks, over a million within a month—many of those among people who would have been needed to keep the infrastructure from collapsing. Doctors, police, workers at power plants and sewage centers. The environment would have become so toxic that rescue workers couldn't have gotten into the area, and poisoned food and water would have added exponentially to the death toll. Airdrops of fresh supplies would have led to riots, more death. Silicon Valley would have been ravaged, all but destroying the U.S. computer industry.

Fortunately, Tony, Doc, and the other members of the team survived their wounds. After calling Jack, Doc had phoned in a 911 then gone back to the bunker to minister to the others. He stopped the bleeding as best he could and propped them in such a way as to limit the flow of blood toward the wounds. Given everything else that was going on, it was morning before help arrived; Doc had gone back out the tunnel to wait for them.

They were all tough old birds, and Jack had figured it would take more than a firefight with a gang of fanatic Muslim murderers to put them down.

Maxine went back to doing what she did best, and found herself inundated with work when her own role in the counterespionage activities hit the press—courtesy of Jack, who tipped off a few colleagues. Max and Karras even managed to maintain something that resembled a relationship.

At least there was also *some* justice in the world.

Two months after the attempt, Senator Harold Wickham was caught in a compromising situation with one of his office staff members and was forced to resign his seat. He insisted that he had been set up, that he didn't even know any hookers from Bulgaria, but video doesn't lie.

Especially when the person at the other end of the fiberoptic cable is Maxine Cole.

Several of the other men in that bed-and-breakfast dining room also left their jobs, suddenly and surprisingly, citing the need to spend time with their families.

Lawrence Soren himself was caught in a financial scandal that threatened to destroy a good portion of his media empire, when some enterprising reporters at GNT rival Flux News found out about the profit he'd earned from his hedge fund that had made millions shorting Tokyo Electric the same day as the massive earthquake and tsunami hit Fukushima. Even the most rapacious investors don't want so-called BBFs—Body Bag Funds—as a line item in their annual reports. Still, Jack did not doubt that Soren and the others would be back. These were not the type of men who give up easily.

The press called Jack and Sara heroes, and while he found the hypocrisy mildly offensive—these were some of the same reporters who had called him a traitor to American ideals—Jack was gratified to find himself fielding phone calls regarding job offers from all the major networks, including his old friends at GNT.

He let most of those calls pile up on voice mail.

As he and Sara recovered emotionally as well as

physically, they spent many of their days at sea, lounging on the *Sea Wrighter,* letting the sun and the salty ocean air work their natural healing effects. Their nights were spent in the harbor, drinking wine with Tony, with Eddie curled up at their feet.

Despite his disappointments, despite the lumps he took to get here, Jack couldn't imagine a better life.

He was in the city he cherished, close to people he cared for and who cared for him, with all the material things he needed—and what, after all, could matter more than that?

Well, there was one thing. And he vowed to do something about that.

Six months after the showdown on the bridge, on a cold Friday night in London, the body of Adam Swain was found by a girlfriend in his apartment near Westminster. He had been strapped to a chair by an unknown assailant, his body covered with burns that were determined to have been made by the application of an electric baton.

For several hours, according to the Office of the Chief Medical Examiner.

Coincidentally, on that same night, the imam of a local mosque, Faakhir Zuabi, was found dead in his office, a .22 caliber bullet hole in his forehead.

Neither of the murders was ever solved.

The following day, two men boarded a plane at Heathrow and flew into Ben Gurion International with a group of their fellow Chabad-Lubavitcher Chasids.

Their names were Rabbi Mel Neershum and Jacob Samuel Heshowitz.

They spent the next few days visiting with the Reb's cousin Ohad before returning to San Francisco. But before they left, Jack and Sara and Reb, each at the same time, went to his own church or mosque or temple and prayed.

All of them prayed to God.

To the same God.

Acknowledgments

I want to thank Jeff Rovin for his brilliant suggestions in shaping aspects of this story. To my editors at St. Martin's Press, Charles Spicer and Yaniv Soha, thank you for your eagle eyes. And my agent, Ian Kleinert, deserves a bucket of stardust for bringing it all together.

Read on for an excerpt from
Michael Savage's next book

Betrayal of Trust

Coming soon in hardcover from St. Martin's Press

Prologue

Tangi Valley, Afghanistan

Chief Petty Officer James Grand sat on the rattling, red canvas seat among thirty-eight of his fellow SEALs as the Chinook 47-D slashed across the dusty valley. He didn't really see the men sitting across from him, wasn't aware of the white sunlight coming through the big windows, washing color from the cabin—save for the bright red, white, and blue of the flag stretched across the roof three feet above him. Some genetic part of him was always aware of Old Glory wherever he was, wherever it was, however small or large, whether it was a grocer's lapel pin or high on a staff.

But right now, ferrying the quick-reaction team to a firefight, James Grand wasn't thinking of the present. He did what he always did when the uncertainty of the war closed in, when nothing was guaranteed but the present, this moment. He went back to his one pure and perfect time—the 13th of May, 2010.

Spring was new and their life together was younger still. James Grand and Genie Bundy stood in her parents' backyard under a sharp blue Arizona sky, two dozen friends and relatives watching them marry. It was the last thing Chief Petty Officer Grand would do before shipping off to Naval Amphibious Base, Little Creek, in Virginia Beach, Virginia.

Joining the SEALs was a tradition begun by his grandfather in 1963, a year after the Navy's special operation force was founded. Taking a bride was part of that "big, holy deal," as his own father had once described it. You wed, you wore your country's uniform, and you served God by doing both. That was the proud Grand way, dating to the French and Indian War and Major Richard Grand of the Virginia Militia. An only child of an only child, Jim felt a particular pride in being the standard-bearer for a generation.

The shrill, clipping sound of the Chinook's wings edged into his mind. CPO Grand willfully held on to the image of Genie in her simple white gown, like a little ray of sun given form and breath and a loving, trusting expression. As he spoke the vows and looked into her innocent eyes, life seemed full and complete, the future given form and clarity, the world made comprehensible. He smiled at the memory.

The smile lasted as long as a heartbeat. A moment later the Chinook make a sickening drop that kicked

Grand's entire body up against the padded roof of the cabin. There were shouts, but they were just words: "Power . . ." "Down . . ." "Christ . . ." His body, along with those of the other men, didn't come down until the helicopter did, smacking the barren ground like a monstrous flyswatter, the fore and aft rotors springing earthward and then up before settling into ugly, still-twisting shapes as the cabin collapsed beneath them. Sand billowed from the impact zone, followed by a fanning array of sparks. Then they were swallowed by a massive red-orange fireball that punched from the olive green chopper to both sides of the valley before the wreckage had even settled. The flames rolled back, seeking something to burn, as black smoke churned upward, driven by the dying turns of the rotors.

A Grand tradition perished in an instant, along with thirty-eight lives and countless futures.

Sammo Yang, the man nearest the explosion—the only man in this remote section of the valley—smiled.

He was behind a large rock, dead brushwood and gnarled juniper branches piled high on either side for camouflage. The Chinese national was still crouched on the balls of his feet, ready to retreat in case the helicopter was not traveling alone. It was difficult to be sure with the deafening echo generated by the twin Chinook rotors and visibility limited by winds that whipped up swirling dust devils the size of a mango tree. These windstorms were made visible by the dead foliage and sand they swept up.

The ideal intruder betrayed by its environment, the young man thought. What is the point of being invisible if you disrupt your surroundings?

There is no control if you've only mastered one part of an objective. He had learned that when he was eight years old.

The rolling heat of the explosion hit the boulder like a silent scream, blazing around him. When he felt the initial punch roll past him, the man pulled a billowing sleeve over the device strapped to his forearm. He looked over the rock, did not see another helicopter.

A solo flight, as most of these missions were. Tandems typically came if there was a firefight and reinforcements were required. He wondered briefly about the Navy SEALs, their mission, the mind that had conceived of their mission and put them in an older model of helicopter, not in the best repair. But such thoughts were smoke.

The man pushed the dried foliage away, his forehead facing down so he could see over the fabric drawn across his nose. He eased out on cramped legs and scooped up sun-dried strips from the boar he had shot and dressed earlier. Flies scattered from the meat and settled on the bloody carcass nearby. He had been living off the fresh kill for two days. The jerky still smelled of blood and death. It would require days more in the sun before that odor left. By then, he would be home.

The thin slabs were laced through with a thick

leather thong, which he slung over his left shoulder beside one half-full canteen and one empty one. He couldn't leave it behind as evidence; he had even cut the bullets from the dead boar.

The young man picked up the Y56 assault rifle that had been hidden beneath the branches and slipped it over his right shoulder. Then he stepped sure-footedly along the rocky foothill, away from the blast. After four hours since his last break, it felt good to stand, to move. He picked his way across a field of rocks the size of fists.

The short man was dressed in the *shalwar kameez* of the region, a loose-fitting, long-sleeved black tunic over drawstring trousers. He wore a beard cut in the short style of Tangi Valley tribesmen and his head was covered with a black-and-white-checked *Keffiyeh*. The sweltering Arab headdress was not requisite—a *topi* or *kufi* pillbox cap would have sufficed—but he did not want anyone to see his features or skin color. Though his superiors had selected a region that was rarely traveled on the ground, there were still roving Taliban and unaffiliated bandits. If seen, he would rather not attract their attention. The Taliban would execute you if you weren't groomed and dressed in accordance with Islamic law, and a *Keffiyeh* was indicative of respect for tradition over comfort; the other would kill you if they thought you were an outsider carrying goods that could be sold on the black market. That included tribal messages about alliances with Americans, Pakistanis, Iranians, or local warlords, as well as American troop locations, temporary special forces outposts, and drone patterns. In war, information was as valuable as currency.

He had none of that. What he carried was far more valuable.

The young man rounded the edge of a bare, thousand-foot outcropping that stood jagged against the bright, late morning sky. A rugged slope spread before him. It was ten kilometers to the base: that was where he would meet his ride from Pakistan, an Aérospatiale SA 330 Puma. He didn't have to check the GPS device tucked in an inside pocket. He knew, from photographs, the precise geologic location of latitude 34 degrees, 41 minutes, 25.08 seconds, longitude 68 degrees, 23 minutes, 54.96 seconds—the outside limit of the helicopter's fuel capacity.

At least the trek home was downward, though he had to cross it before sunset. Satellite reconnaissance showed that the slopes—a popular route for drug-runners and Taliban fighters—were rarely traveled during the daytime when the temperature was headed to a noontime high of 120 degrees. Even scorpions and marauders waited until dusk before stirring.

He ignored the perspiration that slipped past the folds of his headdress. He hooked a finger around the fabric and pulled it from his mouth so he could breathe the hot air. He ran the finger from side to side to expose some of his cheek to the hot wind. It let body heat out, helped to keep him from overheating. He moved quickly, wanting to put as much distance between himself and the crash site as possible. It wouldn't be long before the Americans came to see what had happened to their chopper and to check for any survivors among the SEALs.

The young man moved across the rocks, their radiant heat rising up his pant legs. He left trails of sweat where he walked, but it evaporated quickly. He kept his eyes on the horizon, felt for footholds rather than looked for them, since the shadows and perspiration-blurred vision could be misleading.

He had trained for this mission in secret, in hostile environments, so he would be ready. The first part had gone exactly as planned. But it was just the beginning of a process that would end with an enemy broken forever and, more importantly, humbled. Economies can be restored, armies repopulated, and cities rebuilt. But "face," a nation's honor, was something not even the centuries could repair.

In less than a month, there would be only one world power.